*How t*



# COLES NOTES

## Ke y Point

*Basic concepts in point form.*

## Close Up

*Additional hints, notes, tips or background information.*

## Watch Out!

*Areas where problems frequently occur.*

## Quick Tip

*Concise ideas to help you learn what you need to know.*

## Remember This!

*Essential material for mastery of the topic.*

COLES NOTES

Getting Along in...

# Greek

For travellers and students

Useful phrases with pronunciations

Travel & culture tips

## ABOUT COLES NOTES

COLES NOTES have been an indispensable aid to students on five continents since 1948.

COLES NOTES now offer titles on a wide range of general interest topics as well as traditional academic subject areas and individual literary works. All COLES NOTES are written by experts in their fields and reviewed for accuracy by independent authorities and the Coles Editorial Board.

COLES NOTES provide clear, concise explanations of their subject areas. Proper use of COLES NOTES will result in a broader understanding of the topic being studied. For academic subjects, COLES NOTES are an invaluable aid for study, review and exam preparation. For literary works, COLES NOTES provide interesting interpretations and evaluations which supplement the text but are not intended as a substitute for reading the text itself. Use of the NOTES will serve not only to clarify the material being studied, but should enhance the reader's enjoyment of the topic.


**COLES PUBLISHING. A division of Prospero Books.**
Toronto - Canada
Printed in Canada

**Cataloguing in Publication Data**
Coronetopoulos, Eugenie, 1964-
Getting along in — Greek : for travellers and students,
useful phrases with pronunciations, travel & culture tips

(Coles notes)
Written by Eugenie Coronetopoulos.
ISBN 0-7740-0626-9

1. Greek language, Modern - Conversation and phrase books - English.
I. Title. II. Series.

PA1059.C67 1999 489'.383421 C99-932458-6

Publisher: Nigel Berrisford
Editor: Paul Kropp Communications
Writer: Eugenie Coronetopoulos
Book design: Karen Petherick
Layout: Richard Hunt

Printed and bound in Canada by Webcom Limited
Cover finish: Webcom's Exclusive DURACOAT

# Contents

# Getting Along in Greek

*Getting Along in Greek* is a handy phrase book and guide designed to equip travellers to Greece with essential communication and travel tips.

The pronunciation and grammar guides give some highlights of the Greek language and tips on pronunciation that will give the English speaker an easy way to pronounce the words.

The basics section provides the traveller with key words and expressions that will be useful both for the novice and seasoned traveller.

The rest of the guide is organized in sections that cover most of the possible situations that the traveller might encounter (accommodations, hotels, etc.).

Greece is a friendly country with a long history in tourism, and has many things to enjoy. Keep in mind that Greece has traditionally been popular for tourists, so line-ups and delays are part of the experience. Be patient and maintain a sense of humor. There is plenty to see even while waiting. Greece has its own pace, hectic in some areas but quite leisurely in others. The best advice is to go with the flow and enjoy the often spectacular views and weather.

Greek people are generally outgoi'ng and quite hospitable. They are seasoned hosts of tourists and are appreciative of those who are attempting to communicate in their language. They know that Greek is a difficult language to master, and they are delighted when others try to learn it.

Smile, enjoy the beautiful Mediterranean sun and make the most of every glorious minute.

## Greek in a nutshell

Here's a list of the most basic expressions in Greek – well worth memorizing before your arrival.

| | | |
|---|---|---|
| Hello/Goodbye (formal/informal) | Γεια σου/ σας | yia soo/sas |
| Good morning | Καλημερα | kalee**mera** |
| Good evening | Καλησπερα | kalee**spera** |
| Good night | Καληνυχτα | kalee**nee**hta |
| Yes/no | Ναι/οχι | ne/**o**hee |
| Okay | Ενταξει | en**da**xee |
| Please | Παρακαλω | paraka**lo** |
| Thank you | Ευχαριστω | efharee**sto** |
| You're welcome | Παρακαλω | paraka**lo** |
| Excuse me | Συγγνωμη | seeg**no**mee |
| I'm from Canada | Ειμαι απ'τον Καναδα | **ee**me ap'**ton** kana**tha** |
| Do you speak English? | Μιλατε Αγγλικα; | mee**la**te anglee**ka** |
| I don't speak Greek | Δεν μιλω Ελληνικα | then mi**lo** eleenee**ka** |
| I don't understand | Δεν καταλαβαινω | then katala**ve**no |
| What is this in Greek? | Τι ειναι στα Ελληνικα; | tee **ee**ne sta eleenee**ka** |
| My name is… | Το ονομα μου ειναι… | to **onoma** moo **ee**ne… |
| Where is (the)…? | Που ειναι (ο/η/το)…; | poo **ee**ne (o/ee/to) |

CHAPTER ONE

# Pronunciation

The Greek language is quite complicated, but you don't have to master all the grammatical rules to get by on a vacation. Here are some concepts you might need to know so that you can communicate more effectively.

Verbs are conjugated, and nouns and adjectives are declined. There are masculine, feminine and neutral forms of nouns and adjectives.

***NOUNS***

The most common **masculine noun endings** are:
-os, -ηs, (-ees) and -as,

| | | | | |
|---|---|---|---|---|
| for example: | γιατρ*os*, (yia**tros**) doctor | > | plural: | γιατρ*οι* (yia**tree**) |
| | ναυτ*ηs*, (**naf**tees) sailor | | | ναυτ*ες* (**naf**tes) |
| | πατερ*αs*, (pa**te**ras) father | | | πατερ*ες* (pa**te**res) |

All masculine nouns use the article -ο, –οι (ee) for plural

**Feminine nouns** usually end in -a, ρια (ria) or -η (ee).

| | | | | |
|---|---|---|---|---|
| for example: | μητερ*α* (mee**te**ra) mother | > | plural: | μητερ*ες* (mee**te**res) |
| | φοιτητ*ρια* (fee**tee**treea) student | | | φοιτητ*ριες* (fe**tee**reees) |
| | φιλ*η* (**fee**lee) friend | | | φιλ*ες* (**fee**les) |

Feminine nouns use the article -η, -οι for plural (ee)

Neutral nouns usually end in -i (ee), there are -o, -ωs and -as

| for example: | παιδι, (pe**thee**) child | > | plural: | παιδια (pe**thia**) |
|---|---|---|---|---|
| | βουνο (voo**no**) mountain | | | βουνα (voo**na**) |
| | φως, (fos) light | | | φωτα (**fo**ta) |
| | κρεας (**kre**as) meat | | | κρεατα (**kre**ata) |

All neutral nouns use the article -το (to as in Tom), τα for pural (ta as in tax).

Some nouns, specifically the ones that indicate professions, have the same ending for both masculine and feminine:

| | | |
|---|---|---|
| o/η γιατρος | (yia**tros**) | doctor |
| o/η ηθοποιος | (eethopee**os**) | actor |
| o/η ζωγραφος | (zo**gra**fos) | artist |
| o/η μηχανικος | (meehanee**kos**) | engineer |

**ADJECTIVES** have masculine, feminine and neutral forms as well.

**good**

-os, -η, -o

| | |
|---|---|
| for example | καλος (ka**los**), καλη (ka**lee**), καλο (ka**lo**) |
| plural | καλοι (ka**lee**), καλες (ka**les**), καλα (ka**la**) |

**beautiful**

-os, -a, -o

| | |
|---|---|
| for example | ωραιος (o**re**os), ωραια (o**re**a), ωραιο (o**re**o) |
| plural | ωραιοι (o**re**ee) , ωραιες (o**re**es), ωραια (o**re**a) |

**deep**

-υs, -ια, -υ

| | |
|---|---|
| ex. | βαθυs (va**thees**), βαθια (va**thia**), βαθυ (va**thee**) |
| plural | βαθιοι (va**thiee**), βαθιες (va**thies**), βαθια (va**thia**) |

**VERB** conjugations are too complicated to cover here, but what you need to know is that the second person *plural* is identical to the **formal** usage of the verb. The second person *singular* is **informal**:

for example: εισαι (**ee**se) you are is second person singular
and εισαστε(**ee**saste) you are is the second person plural

The former is informal and the latter is used in a formal situation. Most first person verbs end in -ω. Here is a typical conjugation:

TO DANCE

| | | | | | |
|---|---|---|---|---|---|
| 1st singular: | χορευω | (ho**re**vo) | plural: | χορευουμε | (ho**re**vome) |
| 2nd | χορευεις | (ho**re**vees) | | χορευετε | (ho**re**vete) |
| 3rd | χορευει | (ho**re**vee) | | χορευουν | (ho**re**voon) |

The Greek language has many irregular verbs, but the one you'll probably find yourself using most often is the verb TO BE.

| singular | | plural | |
|---|---|---|---|
| ειμαι | (**ee**me) | ειμαστε | (**ee**maste) |
| εισαι | (**ee**se) | εισαστε | (**ee**saste) |
| ειναι | (**ee**ne) | ειναι | (**ee**ne) |
| ειναι | (**ee**ne) | ειναι | (**ee**ne) |
| ειναι | (**ee**ne) | ειναι | (**ee**ne) |

The verbs in this book are given mostly in formal usage unless they are for more informal social situations.

Unlike many other languages, including English, personal pronouns are **not** required in Greek. The verb **ending** indicates who's speaking.

## *THE ALPHABET AND PRONOUNCING LETTERS.*

| *letter* | *closest English sound* | *shown by* | *example* | *pronounced* |
|---|---|---|---|---|
| Α,α | bad | a | ματι | **ma**tee |
| Β,β | vase | v | βημα | **vee**ma |
| Γ,γ | yeast | yee/yia | γιατρος | yia**tros** |
| | γυρο | **yee**ro | | |
| or | greet | g | γραφω | **gra**fo |
| | (a soft gr, say it as if you're gargling) | | | |
| Δ,δ | breathe | th(ee) | δικη | **thee**kee |
| Ε,ε | met | e | ενα | **e**na |
| Ζ,ζ | zone | z | ζωνη | **zo**nee |
| Η,η | meet | ee | κορη | **ko**ree |
| Θ,θ | thin | th | θεση | **the**see |
| Ι,ι | seed | ee | παιδι | pe**thee** |
| Κ,κ | key | k | και | ke |
| Λ,λ | land | l | λαδι | **la**thee |
| Μ,μ | make | m | μενω | **me**no |
| Ν,ν | nail | n | νυχτα | **nee**hta |
| Ξ,ξ | tax | x | ξενο | **xe**no |
| Ο,ο | cot | o | οχι | **o**hee |
| Π,π | pie | p | πετα | pe**ta** |
| Ρ,ρ | ride | r | ροδα | **ro**tha |
| Σ, σ, s | sun | s | σημα | **see**ma |
| or | | | ροδες | **ro**thes |
| Τ,τ | top | t | τιμη | tee**mee** |
| Υ,υ | greet | ee | υπνος | **ee**pnos |
| Φ,φ | food | f | φωτια | fo**tia** |
| Χ,χ | heat | h | χορο | ho**ro** |
| Ψ,ψ | lapse | ps | ψαρι | psa**ree** |
| Ω,ω | lot | o | ωρα | **o**ra |

### *COMBINATION LETTERS*

| *letter* | *closest English sound* | *shown by* | *example* | *pronounced* |
|---|---|---|---|---|
| ει | **mee**t | ee | ειδοs | **ee**thos |
| ευ | **lef**t | ef | ευκολο | **ef**kolo |
| or | **lev**ee | ev | Ευγενια | **ev**yeneea |
| οι | **mee**t | ee | πολλοι | pol**ee** |
| ου | **foo**d | oo | που | poo |
| αι | **m**e**t** | e | παιδι | pe**thee** |
| αυ | **af**ter | af | αυτο | af**to** |
| or | **lav**atory | av | αυριο | **av**rio |
| ια | **yi**kes | ia | παιδια | pe**thia** |
| μπ | **b**eer | b | μπυρα | **bee**ra |
| or | **am**b**er** | mb | καμπος | **kamb**os |
| or | **amp**le | mp | συμπαν | **seemp**an |
| ντ | **d**oor | d | ντοματα | do**ma**ta |
| or | be**nd** | nd | πεντε | pe**nde** |
| γκ,γγ | **g**ood | g | γκαζι | **ga**zee |
| or | **ang**le | ng | Αγγλια | **anglee**a |
| τζ | **j**azz | j | τζαζ | jaz |

Greek **syllables** consist of at least one vowel or combination of vowels with or without consonants. The stressed letter is always highlighted.

> **Why no accent marks?**
>
> For this Coles Note, we've left the accent marks off the Greek expressions. It's tough enough for you to wrestle with a new language and a new alphabet without having to deal with accent marks as well.
>
> Ancient Greek had many different accents; modern formal Greek keeps some of these accents.
>
> In the last twenty years, however, popular Greek has eliminated all but the οξεια (like the French accent grave) diacritical mark – and often that is no longer printed since Greeks already know where to put the emphasis in a word. The **bold** type in our pronunciation gives you the same information.

CHAPTER TWO

# The basics

The following expressions have been grouped together for quick reference. You will use these over and over again in polite conversation and in many situations in your travels.

### *GREETINGS*

| | | |
|---|---|---|
| Hello/goodbye.* (informal) | Γεια σου. | **yia** soo |
| Hello/goodbye.* (formal) | Γεια σας. | **yia** sas |
| Good morning. | Καλημερα. | **kalee mera** |
| Good evening. | Καλησπερα. | **kalee spera** |
| Good night. | Καληνυχτα. | **kalee nee**hta |
| Let's go! | Παμε!/Φυγαμε! | **Pa**me |

*The same expression works both ways with no difference in pronunciation.

### *INTRODUCTIONS*

| | | |
|---|---|---|
| My name is... | Με λενε/<br>Ονομαζομαι | me **le**ne/<br>ono**ma**zome |
| What's your name? | Πως σε λενε; | pos se **le**ne |
| How do you do? (informal) | Τι κανεις; | tee **ka**nees |
| How do you do? (formal) | Τι κανετε; | tee **ka**nete |
| Very well, thank you. | Καλα, ευχαριστω. | ka**la**,efharee**sto** |
| And you? | Εσυ, Εσεις; | **esee**, **esees** |

| | | |
|---|---|---|
| Pleased to meet you. | Χαιρω πολυ. | **he**ro pol**ee** |
| I'm from Canada. | Ειμαι απ' τον Καναδα. | **ee**me ap'**ton** kana**tha** |
| Do you speak English? | Μιλας Αγγλικα; | mee**las** anglee**ka** |
| | Μιλατε Αγγλικα; | mee**la**te anglee**ka** |
| I don't speak Greek. | Δε μιλω Ελληνικα. | the mee**lo** eleenee**ka** |
| I speak a little Greek. | Μιλω λιγα Ελληνικα. | mee**lo** **lee**ga eleenee**ka** |
| I don't understand. | Δε καταλαβαινω. | the katala**ve**no |
| What did you say? (informal) | Τι ειπες; | tee **ee**pes |
| What did you say? (formal) | Τι ειπατε; | tee **ee**pate |
| A bit slower, please. | Πιο σιγα, παρακαλω. | pi**o** see**ga** parak**alo** |
| Please repeat it. (informal) | Μπορεις να το επαναλαβανεis; | bo**rees** na to epanala**mva**nees |
| Please repeat it. (formal) | Μπορειτε να το επαναλαβανετε; | bo**ree**te na to epanalam**va**nete |
| Write it, please. | Μπορεις να το γραψεις; | bo**rees** na to **grap**sees |
| Write it, please. | Μπορειτε να το γραψετε; | bo**ree**te na to **grap**sete |
| I have a question. | Εχω μια ερωτηση. | **e**ho **mee**a **ero**teesee |
| How do you say it in Greek? | Πως λεγεται στα Ελληνικα; | pos **le**yete sta Eleenee**ka**? |

## *COURTESIES*

| | | |
|---|---|---|
| Okay/Sure. | Ενταξει. | en**da**xee |
| Of course. | Οπωσδηποτε. | opos**thee**pote |
| Perhaps. | Ισως. | **ee**sos |
| Please. | Σε παρακαλω. | se paraka**lo** |
| Thank you (very much). | Ευχαριστω (πολυ). | efharee**sto** **polee** |
| You're welcome | Παρακαλω. | parakal**o** |
| Excuse me./ I'm sorry. | Ενταξει. | see**gno**mee |
| No, thank you. | Οχι, ευχαριστω. | **o**hee, efharee**sto** |
| Just a second. | Ενα λεπτο. | **e**na le**pto** |
| That's all right/okay. | Ενταξει. | en**da**xee |
| It doesn't matter. | Δε πειραζει. | the pee**ra**zee |
| It's not a problem. | Καθολου. | ka**tho**lou |

## *DIRECTIONS*

| | | |
|---|---|---|
| Could you please help me? | Μηορειτε να με βοηθησετε; | bo**ree**te na me voee**thee**sete? |
| I'm lost. | Εχω χαθει. | **e**ho ha**thee** |
| Which way to go…? | Πως μηορω να παω στο…; | pos bo**ro** na **pa**o…? |
| left | αριστερα | aristе**ra** |
| right | δεξια | the**xia** |
| straight ahead | ισια απ' εδω | **ee**sia **apo** **etho** |
| go back | γυρισε πισω | **gee**reese **pi**so |
| Where is the washroom? | Που ειναι η τουαλετα; | poo **ee**ne ee tooa**le**ta? |
| Where is the Canadian Embassy? | Που ειναι η Καναδικη Πρεσβεια; | poo **ee**ne ee Kanathee**kee** pres**vee**a? |

***MONEY***

The currency in Greece is the Δραχμη (drachma) both coin and paper money:

| | | |
|---|---|---|
| Δεκα δραχμες | (10 drachmas) | **the**ka thrah**mes** |
| Πενηντα δραχμες | (50 drachmas) | pe**nee**nda thrah**mes** |
| Εκατο δραχμες | (100 drachmas) | eka**to** thrah**mes** |
| Χιλιες δραχμες | (1000 drachmas) | **hee**lies thrah**mes** |
| Πεντε χιλιαδες | (5000 drachmas) | **pen**de heelia**thes** |
| Δεκα χιλιαδες | (10000 drachmas) | **the**ka heelia**thes** |

CHAPTER THREE

# Dates and times

In Greece, the 24-hour clock is used for trains and buses, but most people use the same 12-hour clock that we do. The Greeks, generally, are a little less precise in dealing with times for appointments than people in other countries. A little flexibility will take you a long way.

| | | |
|---|---|---|
| What time is it? | Τι ωρα ειναι; | tee **ora** **ee**ne |
| *It is…* | *Ειναι…* | ***eene*** |
| noon | μεσημερι | meseemeree (**me** bold) |
| midnight | μεσανυχτα | me**sa**neehta |
| early/late | νωρις / αργα | no**rees**/**ar**ga |
| *It is…* | *Ειναι* | ***eene*** |
| 1:00 | μια η ωρα | **mee**a ee **o**ra |
| 2:00 | δυο η ωρα | **thee**o ee **o**ra |
| 3:15 | τρεις και τεταρτο | trees ke **te**tarto |
| 4:05 | τεσσερις και πεντε | **te**serees ke **pen**de |
| 5:30 | πεντε και μιση | **pen**de ke mee**see** |
| 20 to 7 | εφτα παρα εικοσι | ef**ta** **pa**ra **ee**kosee |
| morning | το πρωι | to pro**ee** |
| afternoon | το απογευμα | to a**po**yevma |
| night/evening | το βραδυ | to **vra**thee |

### *DAYS OF THE WEEK*

| | | |
|---|---|---|
| *Today is…* | *Σημερα ειναι…* | ***seemera eene…*** |
| Monday | Δευτερα | the**fte**ra |
| Tuesday | Τριτη | **tree**tee |
| Wednesday | Τεταρτη | te**tar**tee |
| Thursday | Πεμπτη | **pem**ptee |
| Friday | Παρασκευη | paraske**vee** |
| Saturday | Σαββατο | **sa**vato |
| Sunday | Κυριακη | keeria**kee** |

### *MONTHS*

| | | |
|---|---|---|
| *This month is…* | *Αυτος ο μηνας ειναι…* | *af**tos** o **mee**nas **eene*** |
| January | Ιανουαριος | eeanoo**a**reeos |
| February | Φεβρουαριος | fevroo**a**reeos |
| March | Μαρτιος | **mar**teeos |
| April | Απριλιος | **apree**leeos |
| May | Μαιος | **ma**eeos |
| June | Ιουνιος | ee**oo**neeos |
| July | Ιουλιος | ee**oo**leeos |
| August | Αυγουστος | **a**vgoostos |
| September | Σεπτεμβριος | sep**tem**vreeos |
| October | Οκτωβριος | o**kto**vreeos |
| November | Νοεμβριος | no**em**vreeos |
| December | Δεκεμβριος | the**kem**vreeos |

### *APPOINTMENTS*

| | | |
|---|---|---|
| When are we meeting? | Ποτε θα συναντηθουμε; | **po**te tha seenatee**thou**me |
| today | σημερα | **see**mera |
| tomorrow | αυριο | **a**vreeo |
| the day after tomorrow | μεθαυριο | me**tha**vreeo |

| | | |
|---|---|---|
| yesterday | χτες | htes |
| in the morning | το πρωι | to pro**ee** |
| in the afternoon | το απογευμα | to **apo**yevma |
| tonight | αποψε | a**po**pse |
| next week | την αλλη εβδομαδα | teen **a**lee evtho**ma**tha |

## *HOLIDAYS*

| | | |
|---|---|---|
| New Year's Day | Πρωτοχρονια | protohro**nia** |
| January 7 | Τα Φωτα | ta **fo**ta |
| Mardi Gras | Αποκριες | apokree**es** |
| March 25 | Εικοστη–πεμπτη Μαρτιου | **ee**kosee**pem**ptee mar**tee**oo |
| Easter | Πασχα | **pa**sha |
| August 15 | Της Παναγιας | tees panay**ee**as |
| October 28 | Εικοστη–ογδοη Οκτωβριου | **ee**ko**stee** og**tho**ee oktov**ree**ou |
| December 24 | Παραμονη Χριστουγεννων | paramo**nee** hreestoo**ye**non |
| December 25 | Χριστουγεννα | hree**stoo**gena |

## *GREETINGS AND WISHES*

| | | |
|---|---|---|
| Hello | Γεια σου | yee**a** soo |
| Good-bye | Γεια | yee**a** |
| Happy holidays | Καλες Γιορτες | ka**les** yeeor**tes** |
| Merry Christmas | Καλα Χριστουγεννα | ka**la** hree**stoo**yena |
| Happy New Year | Καλη Χρονια | ka**lee** hro**nia** |
| Congratulations | Συγχαρητηρια | seenharee**tee**reea |
| Good luck | Καλη επιτυχια | ka**lee** epeetee**hee**a |
| Have a good trip | Καλο ταξιδι | ka**lo** tax**ee**thee |
| Have a good meal | Καλη ορεξη | ka**lee** **o**rexee |
| Happy Easter | Καλο Πασχα | ka**lo** **pa**sha |
| Happy Birthday | Χρονια Πολλα | **hro**nia **po**la |

***NUMBERS***

| | | |
|---|---|---|
| 1 | ενα | **ena** |
| 2 | δυο | **thee**o |
| 3 | τρια | **tree**a |
| 4 | τεσσερα | **te**sera |
| 5 | πεντε | **pen**de |
| 6 | εξη | **exee** |
| 7 | εφτα | ef**ta** |
| 8 | οχτω | o**hto** |
| 9 | εννια | e**nia** |
| 10 | δεκα | **the**ka |
| 11 | ενδεκα | **en**theka |
| 12 | δωδεκα | **tho**theka |
| 13 | δεκατρια | theka**tree**a |
| 14 | δεκατεσσερα | theka**te**sera |
| 15, etc. | δεκαπεντε, κτλ. | theka**pende** |
| 20 | εικοσι | **ee**kosee |
| 21 | εικοσι ενα | **ee**kosse **e**na |
| 22 | εικοσι δυο | **ee**kosee **thee**o |
| 23, etc. | εικοσι τρια, κτλ. | **ee**kosee **tree**a |
| 30 | τριαντα | tree**an**da |
| 40 | σαραντα | sa**ran**da |
| 50 | πενηντα | pe**neen**da |
| 60 | εξηντα | ex**een**da |
| 70 | εβδομηντα | evtho**meen**da |
| 80 | ογδοντα | og**thon**da |
| 90 | εννενηντα | ene**neen**da |
| 100 | εκατο | eka**to** |
| 101 | εκατο–ενα | eka**to**-ena |
| 140, etc. | εκατο–σαραντα | eka**to**-sa**ran**da |
| 200 | διακοσια | theea**ko**sia |
| 300 | τριακοσια | treeo**ko**sia |
| 400 | τετρακοσια | tetra**ko**sia |

| | | |
|---|---|---|
| 500 | πεντακοσια | penda**ko**sia |
| 600 | εξακοσια | exa**ko**sia |
| 700 | εφτακοσια | efta**ko**sia |
| 800 | οχτακοσια | ohta**ko**sia |
| 900 | εννιακοσια | enia**ko**sia |
| 1,000 | χιλια | **hee**lia |
| 1,500 | χιλια–πεντακοσια | **hee**lia-penda**ko**sia |
| 2,000 | δυο χιλιαδες | **thee**o hee**lia**thes |
| 3,000 | τρεις χιλιαδες | trees hee**lia**thes |
| 4,000 | τεσσερις χιλιαδες | **te**seres hee**lia**thes |
| 100,000, etc. | εκατο χιλιαδες | eka**to** hee**lia**thes |
| 1,000,000 | ενα εκατομμυριο | **e**na ekato**mee**reeo |
| 1,000,000,000 | ενα δισεκατομμυριο | **e**na theesekto**mee**reeo |
| 1,000,000,000,000 | ενα τρισεκατομμυριο | **e**na treesekato**mee**reeo |

## *ORDINAL NUMBERS*

| | | |
|---|---|---|
| 1st | πρωτο | **pro**to |
| 2nd | δευτερο | **the**ftero |
| 3rd | τριτο | **tree**to |
| 4th | τεταρτο | **te**tarto |
| 5th | πεμπτο | **pem**pto |
| 6th | εκτο | **eh**to |
| 7th | εβδομο | **ev**thomo |
| 8th | ογδοο | **og**thoo |
| 9th | εννατο | **e**nato |
| 10th | δεκατο | **the**kato |
| 11th | ενδεκατο | en**the**kato |
| 12th | δωδεκατο | tho**the**kato |
| 13th | δεκατοτριτο | thekato**tree**to |
| 14th etc | δεκατοτεταρτο κτλ | thekato**te**tarto |
| 100th | εκατοστο | ekato**sto** |
| 1000th | χιλιοστο | heelio**sto** |

CHAPTER FOUR

# Upon your arrival

ΚΑΛΩΣΟΡΙΣΑΤΕ ΣΤΗΝ ΩΡΑΙΑ ΕΛΛΑΔΑ!
WELCOME TO BEAUTIFUL GREECE!

There are many travellers coming to Greece and the airport is usually packed, so be patient and enjoy the view through the windows.

Get a porter (αχθοφορο - ahtho**foro**). He'll help you through several formalitites and make things easier.

At customs (τελωνειο - teloneeo) they will ask you: Do you have anything to declare? Εχετε τιποτα να δηλωσετε; (**e**hete **tee**pota na thee**lo**sete)

There are buses and taxis readily available, but you might have to wait. The cheapest way into town is the bus and often the major hotels provide shuttle service from the airport to the hotel and back.

## SIGNS

| | | |
|---|---|---|
| Airport terminal | Αεροδρομιο/ Αερολιμηνας | aero**thro**meeo/ aerolee**mee**nas |
| Arrivals | Αφιξεis | **a**fee**x**ees |
| Baggage claim | Αποσκευες | aposke**ves** |
| Connections | Ανταποκρισεις | andapo**kree**sees |
| Domestic flights | Εσωτερικες πτησεις | esoteree**kes ptee**sees |
| International flights | Εξωτερικες πτησεις | exoteree**kes ptee**sees |
| Departures | Αναχωρησεις | anaho**ree**sees |
| Boarding gate | Εισοδος επιβιβασεως | **ee**sothos epee**va**seon |
| Exit | Εξοδος | **e**xothos |
| No Exit | Απογορευεται η εξοδος | apago**re**vete ee **e**xothos |
| No smoking | Απογορευεται το καπνισμα | apago**re**vete to **ka**pneesma |

### *CUSTOMS*

### What you may hear

| | | |
|---|---|---|
| Your passport, please. | Το διαβατηριο σας, παρακαλω | to thiava**tee**reeo sas, paraka**lo** |
| Do you have anything to declare? | Εχετε τιποτα να δηλωσετε; | **e**hete **tee**pota na thee**lo**sete |
| Please, open your suitcase. | Παρακαλω, ανοιξτε τις βαλιτσες σας | paraka**lo**, a**nee**xte tees va**lee**tses sas |
| You'll have to pay duty on this. | Θα πρεπει να πληρωσετε φορο σ'αυτο. | tha **pre**pee na plee**ro**sete **fo**ro s'af**to** |
| Proceed. | Προχωρειστε. | proho**ree**ste |

## Things you might say

| | | |
|---|---|---|
| *Where is...?* | *Που ειναι...;* | *poo* ***eene****...* |
| customs | το τελωνειο | to telo**nee**o |
| baggage claim | οι αποσκευες | ee apos**keves** |
| *Here is...* | *Να...* | *na...* |
| my passport | το διαβατηριο μου | to thiava**tee**reeo moo |
| my identity card | η ταυτοτητα μου | ee taf**toteeta** moo |
| my driver's license | η αδεια οδηγησης | ee **a**theea othee**gee**sees |
| my luggage | οι αποσκευες μου | ee apos**keves** moo |
| I have nothing to declare | Δεν εχω τιποτα να δηλωσω. | then **e**ho **tee**pota na thee**lo**so |
| I'm here on holidays | Ειμαι εδω για διακοπες | **ee**me e**tho** yia thiako**pes** |
| ...on business. | ...για δουλεια | ...yia thoo**lies** |
| *I'll be staying...* | *Θα μεινω...* | *tha* ***mee****no* |
| a week | μια εβδομαδα | **mee**a evtho**ma**tha |
| 10 days | δεκα μερες | **the**ka **meres** |
| 2 weeks | δυο εβδομαδες | theeo evtho**ma**thes |
| a month | ενα μηνα | **e**na **mee**na |
| I'm passing through. (Greece) | Ειμαι περαστικ–os (–η) | **ee**me perastee**k-os** **(-ee)** |

### *BAGGAGE CLAIM*

| | | |
|---|---|---|
| Where is tourist information? | Που ειναι οι πληροφοριες για τουριστες; | poo **ee**ne ee pleerofo**r**ies yia too**ree**stes |
| This is mine. | Ειναι δικο μου. | **ee**ne thee**ko** moo |
| Are there any luggage carts? | Που ειναι τα καροτσια για τις αποσκευες; | poo **ee**ne ta ka**ro**tsia yia tees apos**ke**ves |
| I need a porter. | Χρειαζομαι αχθοφορο. | hree**a**zome ahtho**fo**ro |
| How much do I owe you? | Ποσο σου χρωστω; | **po**so soo hro**sto** |

| | | |
|---|---|---|
| I have lost my luggage. | Εχασα τις αποσκευες μου. | **e**hasa tees aposke**ves** moo |
| Where do I report it? | Που πρεπει να το αναφερω; | poo **pre**pee na to ana**fe**ro |

## *EXCHANGING MONEY*

| | | |
|---|---|---|
| Where is the exchange desk? | Που ειναι το γραφειο συναλλαγματος; | poo **ee**ne to gra**fee**o seena**la**gmatos |
| *I want to change…* | *Θελω να αλλαξω…* | ***the**lo na a**la**xo…* |
| $100 | εκατο δολλαρια | eka**to** tho**la**reea |
| traveller's cheques | ταξιδιωτικες επιταγες | taxithiotee**kes** epeeta**yes** |
| What are bank hours? | Ποιο ειναι το ωραριο της τραπεζας; | Pi**o** **ee**ne to o**ra**reeo tees **tra**pezas |
| What's the exchange rate? | Ποια ειναι η τιμη συναλλαγματος; | Pi**a** **ee**ne ee tee**mee** seena**la**gmatos |
| What is your commission? | Τι ειναι η προμηθεια σας; | tee **ee**ne to see**na**lagma pro**mee**theea sas |
| *I'd like money in…* | *θελω τα χρηματα σε…* | ***the**lo ta **hree**mata se* |
| big bills | μεγαλα χαρτονομισματα | me**ga**la hartono**mee**smata |
| small bills | μικρα χαρτονομισματα | mee**kra** hartono**mee**smata |
| small change | ψιλα | psee**la** |
| Do you accept credit cards? | Δεχεστε πιστωτικες καρτες; | **The**heste peestotee**kes** **kar**tes |
| Which ones? | Ποιες; | pee**es** |

| | | |
|---|---|---|
| What bus should I take to go to…? | Ποιο λεωφορειο πρεπει να παρω να πaω στο/στη… | pio leofo**ree**o **pre**pee na **pa**ro na **pa**o sto/stee |
| How much is the fare? | Ποσο ειναι το εισιτηριο; | **po**so **ee**ne to eesee**tee**reeo |
| Where is the bus stop? | Που ειναι ο σταθμος λεωφορειου; | poo **ee**ne o stath**mos** leofo**ree**oo |
| …the train station | …τραινου; | …**tre**noo |
| Where can I get a taxi? | Που μπορω να βρω ταξι; | poo bo**ro** na vro tax**ee** |
| I would like to go to… | Θελω να παω στο… | **the**lo na **pa**o sto… |
| How much? | Ποσο; | **po**so |
| Are you free? | Εισαι ελευθερ(–os /–η); | **ee**se **el**efther-(os/-ee) |
| I do not want others in the taxi. | Δε θελω αλλους στο ταξι. | the **the**lo **a**loos sto tax**ee** |
| The address is… | Η διευθυνση ειναι… | ee the**ef**theensee **ee**ne |
| Thank you. Goodbye. | Ευχαριστω. Γεια σας. | efharee**sto**. yia sas |

## What you may hear

| | | |
|---|---|---|
| Yes. I'm free. | Ναι. Ειμαι ελευθερ(–os/η) | ne. **ee**me **el**efther(-os/-ee) |
| Where do you want to go? | Που θελετε να πατε; | poo **the**lete na **pa**te |
| You owe… | Χρωστατε/χρωστας… | hro**sta**te/hos**tas**… |

## Handy taxi phrases

| | | |
|---|---|---|
| Do you know where…is? | Ξερετε που ειναι.. | **x**erete poo **ee**ne |
| Is there an extra charge? | Χρεωνετε τιποτα παραπανω | hre**o**nete **tee**pota para**pa**no |
| I'll pay only what's on the meter. | Θα πληρωσω μονο οτι ειναι στο χρονομετρο | tha plee**ro**so **mo**no **o**tee **ee**ne sto hro**no**metro |
| I'm in a hurry. | Βιαζομαι. | **via**zome |
| Please, hurry. | Γρηγορα, παρακαλω. | **gree**gora, paraka**lo** |
| Please, slow down. | Πιο σιγα, παρακαλω. | pio see**ga**, paraka**lo** |
| Stop… | Σταματηστε… | stama**tee**ste… |
| here | εδω | **etho** |
| at the corner | στη γωνια | stee go**nee**a |
| at the next street | στο επομενο δρομο | sto e**po**meno **thro**mo |
| at the lights | στα φωτα | sta **fo**ta |
| Please, wait for me. | Παρακαλω, περιμενετε. | paraka**lo**, peree**me**nete |
| Wait a minute. | Περιμενετε ενα λεπτο. | peree**me**nete **e**na le**pto** |
| I don't have change. | Δεν εχω ψιλα. | then **e**ho psee**la** |

CHAPTER FIVE

# Accommodations

The major cities in Greece are world class, and so are the prices of their hotels. Expect to pay a premium - and book in advance - for a good hotel in Athens (Αθηνα - a**thee**na) and Thessaloniki (Θεσσαλονικη - thesalo**nee**kee). The hotels go by a five-star system, five being the highest.

The Greek islands (νπσια) are very popular in summer, so booking ahead is important. Besides hotels, you'll find that rooming houses make for good accommodation even though you'll have to share a bathroom.

Camping is a popular option for young travellers in Greece. There are designated camping grounds throughout the country and on some beaches. You can't, however, throw your sleeping bag on any beach - it's against the law. Remember, too, that some beaches and campgrounds are for nudists, so be prepared to ask.

If you're in less-expensive accommodation, it's usually best to keep your documents and valuables with you since the owners do not guarantee their safety.

## Levels of accommodation

| | | |
|---|---|---|
| Hotel | Ξενοδοχειο | xenotho**hee**o |
| Hostel | Ξενωνας νεοτητος | xe**no**nas ve**o**teetos |
| Rooming house | Ενοικια ζομενα δωματια | eneekia**zo**mena tho**ma**teea |
| Camping grounds | Τοπος κατασκηνωσεως | **to**pos kataskee**no**seos |
| Nudist | Γυμνιστων | yeemnee**ston** |

## Avoid the summer rush!

The best times to visit Greece and enjoy good weather - as well as more reasonable rates - are April, late August, September and October.

### *REGISTRATION*

| | | |
|---|---|---|
| I have reserved a room. | Εχω κλεισει δωματιο. | eho **klee**see tho**ma**teeo |
| My name is… | Το ονομα μου ειναι… | to **o**noma moo **ee**ne |
| My surname is… | Το επωνυμο μου ειναι… | to e**po**neemo moo **ee**ne |
| *Does this room have…?* | *Εχει το δωματιο….* | **e**hee to tho**ma**teeo… |
| air conditioning | κλιματισμο | kleematee**smo** |
| a double bed | διπλο κρεβατι | thee**plo** kre**va**tee |
| two beds | δυο κρεβατια | **thee**o kreva**tia** |
| a private bath | ατομικο μπανιο | atomee**ko** **ba**nio |
| hot water | ζεστο νερο | ze**sto** ne**ro** |
| a shower | ντους | doos |
| a phone | τηλεφωνο | tee**le**fono |
| a television | τηλεορασηη | teele**o**rasee |
| a refrigerator | ψυγειο | psee**yee**o |
| What floor is it on? | Σε ποιο οροφο ειναι το δωματιο; | se pio **o**rofo **ee**ne to tho**ma**teeo |
| May I see the room? | Μπορω να δω το δωματιο; | bo**ro** na tho to tho**ma**teeo |
| *I would like a…* | *Θα ηθελα…* | *tha **ee**thela* |
| bigger room | μεγαλυτερο δωματιο | mega**lee**tero tho**ma**teeo |
| smaller room | μικροτερο δωματιο | mee**kro**tero tho**ma**teeo |
| better room | καλυτερο δωματιο | ka**lee**tero tho**ma**teeo |
| cheaper room | πιο φτηνο δωματιο | pio ftee**no** tho**ma**teeo |
| quieter room | πιο ησυχο δωματιο | pio **ee**seeho tho**ma**teeo |

| | | |
|---|---|---|
| What time is check-out? | Τι ωρα πρεπει να αδειασω το δωματιο; | tee **o**ra **pre**pee na **a**thia**so** to tho**ma**teeo |
| I don't have a reservation. | Δεν εχω κλεισει δωματιο. | then **e**ho **klee**see tho**ma**teeo |
| *I would like a room…* | *Θα ηθελα ενα δωματιο…* | *tha **ee**thela ena tho**ma**teeo* |
| for tonight | για αποψε | yia a**po**pse |
| for a few days | για μερικες μερες | yia meree**kes** **me**res |
| *I need a room…* | *Χρειαζομαι δωματιο…* | *hree**a**zome tho**ma**teeo* |
| with a private bath | ατομικο μπανιο | me atomee**ko** **ba**nio |
| with a shower | με ντους | me doos |
| for non-smokers | για μη καπνιστες | yia mee kapnee**stes** |
| with a blacony | με μπαλκονι | me bal**ko**nee |
| with a nice view | με ωραια θεα | me o**rea** **the**a |
| with Internet access | με συνλεοη για ιντερνετ | me **seen**thesee yia internet |
| How much does this room cost? | Ποσο στοιχιζει αυτο το δωματιο. | **po**so stee**hee**zee af**to** to tho**ma**teeo |
| I don't like this room. | Δεν μΠαρεσει το δωματιο. | the m'**a**resee to tho**ma**teeo |
| I'd like another room. | Θα ηθελα αλλο δωματιο. | tha **ee**thela **a**lo tho**ma**teeo |
| *I'll take this room for…* | *Θελω το δωματιο για…* | ***the**lo to tho**ma**teeo yia…* |
| one night | ενα βραδυ | **e**na **vra**thee |
| a few nights | μερικα βραδια | meree**ka** **vra**thia |
| one week | μια εβδομαδα | mia evtho**ma**tha |
| *How much…?* | *Ποσο στοιχιζει…;* | ***po**so stee**hee**zee…* |
| with breakfast | με πρωινο | me proee**no** |
| without meals | χωρις γευματα | ho**rees** **yev**mata |
| for the children | για τα παιδια | yia ta pe**thia** |
| Is everything included? | Συμπεριλαμβανονται ολα; | seempereelam**va**nonte **o**la |

## *AT THE FRONT DESK*

| | | |
|---|---|---|
| The key to room # please. | Το κλειδι για το δωματιο παρακαλω. | to klee**thee** yia # to tho**ma**teeo paraka**lo** |
| *Are there any… for me?* | *Εχετε… για μενα;* | ***e**hete… yia **me**na* |
| messages | μηνυματα | mee**nee**mata |
| letters | γραμματα | **gra**mata |
| Did anyone call for me? | Εχω μηνυματα; | **e**ho tmee**nee**mata |
| My passport, please. | Το διαβατηριο μου, παρακαλω. | to thiava**tee**ree**o** moo, paraka**lo** |
| I'd like to speak to the manager. | Θελω να μιλησω στην διευθυνση. | **the**lo na mee**lee**so steen thi**ef**theensee |
| It's very important. | Ειναι πολυ σπμαντικο. | **ee**ne po**lee** seemantee**ko** |
| Please call me at… | Παρακαλω, τηλεφωνειστε μου στις… | paraka**lo**, teelefo**nee**ste moo stees… |
| *Where is…* | *Που ειναι…* | *Poo **ee**ne…* |
| the bank | η τραπεζα | ee **tra**peza |
| the currency exchange | το κεντρο συναλλαγματος | to **ken**dro seena**la**gmatos |
| the post office | το ταχυδρομειο | to taheethro**mee**o |
| a fax machine | το τηλεαντιγραφικο | to teeleandeegrafee**ko** |
| I'd like to rent a car. | Θελω να νοικιασω αυτοκινητο. | **the**lo na nee**kia**so afto**kee**neeto |
| Where can I rent…? | Που νοικιαζουν…; | poo neeki**a**zoon… |
| Can you call me a taxi? | Μου φωναζετε ενα ταξι; | moo fo**na**zete ta**xee** |
| Where can I get a bus to…? | Που σταματα το λεωφορειο για… | poo stama**ta** to leofo**ree**o yia… |
| How can I get to…? | Πως μπορω να παω στο… | pos bo**ro** na **pa**o sto… |
| Where can I get a tour ? | Που μπορω να βρω περιηγηση; | poo bo**ro** na vro peri**ee**yeesee |

| | | |
|---|---|---|
| *I'm (we're) leaving...* | *Θα φυγω (φυγουμε)...* | *tha **feego** (**fee**gome)..* |
| this afternoon | το απογευμα | to a**po**yevma |
| tomorrow morning | αυριο το πρωι | **a**vrio to pro**ee** |
| tonight | αποψε | a**po**pse |
| Please, have my bill ready. | Παρακαλω, θελω το λογαριασμο | Paraka**lo**, **the**lo to logaria**smo** |
| Can you explain my bill? | Μου εξηγειτε τον λογαριασμο | moo exeeyeete ton logaria**smo** |
| I'll need help with my luggage. | Χρειαζομαι βοηθεια με τις βαλιτσες | hree**a**zome vo**ee**theea me tees va**lee**tses |

If you go in September, check out the wine festival (Γιορτη Κρασιου - yiort**ee** krasi**oo**) at Δαφνι (tha**fnee**). You buy a mug and sample all you want and and you can dance among the trees and stars to various live bands.

### *SERVICE/REQUESTS*

| | | |
|---|---|---|
| *Please bring me...* | *Παρακαλω, μου φερνετε...* | *paraka**lo**, moo **fer**nete...* |
| an ashtray | ενα τασακι | **e**na ta**sa**kee |
| breakfast | πρωινο | proee**no** |
| dinner | βραδυνο | vrathee**no** |
| a drink list | καταλογο ποτων | ka**ta**logo po**ton** |
| a glass | ενα ποτηρι | **e**na po**tee**ree |
| some hangers | μερικες κρεμαστρες | meree**kes** pet**se**tes |
| lunch | μεσημεριανο | meseemeria**no** |
| a menu | καταλογο φαγητου | ka**ta**logo fayee**too** |
| a pillow | ενα μαξιλαρι | **e**na maxee**la**ree |
| some shampoo | σαμπουαν | sampoo**an** |
| some soap | σαπουνι | sa**poo**nee |
| some toilet paper | χαρτι τουαλετας | har**tee** toua**le**tas |

| | | |
|---|---|---|
| a towel | πετσετα | pet**se**ta |
| some water | λιγο νερο | **lee**go **ne**ro |
| some writing paper | χαρτι αλληλογραφιας | har**tee** aleelogra**fee**as |
| The room needs to be cleaned. | Το δωματιο χρειαζεται καθαρισμα. | to tho**ma**teeo hree**a**zete ka**tha**reesma |
| What time is…? | Τι ωρα ειναι το…; | to **o**ra **ee**ne to… |
| *We'll have… in the room.* | *Θελω… στο δωματιο.* | ***the**lo… sto tho**ma**teeo* |
| breakfast | πρωινο | proee**no** |
| lunch | μεσημεριανο | meseemeria**no** |
| dinner | βραδυνο | vrathee**no** |
| Please wake me at… | Παρακαλω, ξυπυπστε με στις… | paraka**lo**, xee**pnee**ste me stees… |
| *This needs to be…* | *Χρειαζεται… παρακαλω.* | *hree**a**zome…paraka**lo*** |
| dry-cleaned | καθαριστηριο | kathareesteereeo |
| pressed only | Σιδερωμα μονο | see**the** roma |
| repaired | επιδιορθωση | epeetheeorthosee |
| washed | πλυσιμο | **plee**seemo |
| When will it be ready? | Ποτε θα ειναι ετοιμο; | **po**te tha **ee**ne **e**teemo |
| *I need it…* | *Το χρειαζομαι..* | *to hree**a**zome…* |
| as soon as possible | το γρηγοροτερο | to yreego**ro**tero |
| today | σημερα | **see**mera |
| tomorrow | αυριο | **av**reeo |
| This needs care. | Χρειαζεται προσοχη. | hree**a**zete proso**hee** |
| Is it ready? | Ειναι ετοιμο; | **ee**ne **e**teemo |

### *PROBLEMS?*

| *The… is not working.* | *Δεν δουλευει…* | *then thoulevee* |
|---|---|---|
| air conditioning | ο κλιματισμος | o kleematee**smos** |
| cold water | το κρυο νερο | to **kree**o ne**ro** |
| electric socket | η ηλεκτρικη πριζα | ee eelectree**kee breez**a |
| electricity | το ρευμα | to **rev**ma |
| elevator | το ασανσερ | to asan**sere** |
| fan | ο ανεμιστηρας | o anemee**stee**ras |
| faucet | η βρυση | ee **vree**see |
| heating | η θερμανση | ee **ther**mansee |
| hot water | το ζεστο νερο | to ze**sto** ne**ro** |
| light switch | ο διακοπτης | o thia**ko**ptees |
| light | το φως | to fos |
| radio | το ραδιοφωνο | to ra**thio**fono |
| television | η τηλεοραση | ee teele**o**rasee |
| telephone | το τηλεφωνο. | to tee**le**fono |

| *…is clogged* | *…ειναι φραγμενο. (os)* | *…**eene fragmeno*** |
|---|---|---|
| The wash basin | Ο νεροχυτης | o nero**hee**tees |
| The shower | Το ντους | to doos |
| The toilet | Η τουαλετα | ee tooa**le**ta |
| The window/door is jammed. | Το παραθυρο/ η πορτα ειναι σφηνωμενη. | to pa**ra**theero/ ee **porta** **ee**ne sfeeno**me**nee |

### *AT THE DOOR*

| | | |
|---|---|---|
| Who is it? | Ποιος ειναι; | pios **ee**ne |
| Just a minute. | Ενα λεπτο. | ena le**pto** |
| Come in. | Ελατε μεσα. | elate **me**sa |
| Put it on the table, please. | Βαλτε το στο τραπεζι, παρακαλω. | **val**te to sto tra**pe**zee, paraka**lo** |
| Thank you. | Ευχαριστω. | efharee**sto** |

CHAPTER SIX

# Travel

***Cars:*** If you can avoid driving in Greece, especially in the urban centers, do so. There is much traffic and drivers tend to drive aggressively.

> If you're planning on driving make sure that you have your international driver's license before you leave on your trip. Getting it in Greece can be complicated and time consuming.
>
> In Athens at least, cars with odd or even license plates are alternately allowed to drive in the city. So make sure you know which day is which, if you decide to drive!

***Taxis:*** Keep in mind that taxi drivers might want to take more than one customer at a time, so don't be shy to voice your objection. Taxi drivers are often willing and able to serve as tour guides, but make sure you settle on a flat rate before you agree to anything.

***Public transportation:*** You need to buy pre-paid tickets for buses or trolleys and you can find them at most newstands (περιπτερα - pe**ree**ptera). A booklet of tickets (δεσμιδα εισιτηριων - thes**mee**tha eeseeteer**ee**on) (ten tickets) is the most economical purchase. If you're planning on using a lot of public transportation within the city, it might be a good idea to purchase a card (καρτα - **kar**ta), which in Athens can be bought at a περιπτερο εκδοσηs εισιτηριων (pe**ree**ptero ekothosees leofo**ree**on), located downtown at Πανεπιστημιου και Σινα (panepeestee**mee**oo ke see**na**). You'll need to bring your own photograph which can be taken anywhere, just say it's for... καρτα απεριοριστων διαδρομων (**kar**ta aperioreestons thia**thro**mon). This card allows you to get on any bus or trolley within the city at any time during its one month valid period.

Neither the tickets nor the card can be used on the electric rail (ηλεκτρικο - eelektree**ko**). You have to buy special tickets for that at the station.

When you get on the bus or trolley, there is an electric scanner that you have to place your ticket into and take it out from. This is proof of payment. Keep it, because there might be a surprise inspection. If you don't have your scanned ticket, you will be fined!

***Boats:*** There are boats of various sizes and destinations that leave from the main harbor near Greece called Πειραια (peere**a**). Tickets can be bought at a travel agent or at the harbor ticket office (γραφειο εκδοσηs εισιτπριωυ - gra**fee**o thia**tho**sees leofo**ree**on). Many tour boats leave as early as 5:00 a.m., so check for times and routes (ωρεs αναχωρησεωυ / αφιξεωυ - orees anaho**ree**seon/ a**fee**xeon)

## *CAR RENTAL*

| | | |
|---|---|---|
| Where can I rent a car? | Που μπορω να νοικιασω αυτοκινητο; | poo bo**ro** na nee**kia**so afto**kee**neeto |
| *I'd like to rent...* | *Θελω να νοικιασω...* | *thelo na nee**kia**so...* |
| an automatic | αυτοματο | af**to**mato |
| an economy | οικονομικο | eekonomee**ko** |
| a large | μεγαλο | me**ga**lo |

| | | |
|---|---|---|
| a luxury | πολυτελης | poleete**lees** |
| a moped | μηχανακι | meeha**na**kee |
| motorcycle | μοτοσικλετα | motosee**kle**ta |
| a small | μικρο | mee**kro** |
| a truck | φορτηγο αυτοκινυτο | fortee**go** afto**kee**neeto |
| a van | σκευοφορο | skevo**fo**ro |
| *How much does it cost…?* | *Ποσο στοιχιζει…* | ***po**so stee**hee**zee…* |
| per day | την ημερα | teen ee**me**ra |
| per week | την εβδομαδα | teen evtho**ma**tha |
| for the weekend | για το Σαββατοκυριακο | yia to savato**kee**riako |
| per kilometre | το χιλιομετρο | to heli**o**metro |
| How much is insurance? | Ποσο ειναι η ασφαλεια; | **po**so **ee**ne ee as**fa**leea |
| Is there total coverage? | Εχετε πληρη καλυψη; | **e**hete **plee**ree **ka**leepsee |
| Here is my license. | Να η αδεια οδηγησης μου. | na ee **a**thia o**thee** yeesees mou |
| Is the gas tank full? | Ειναι το ντεποζιτο βενζινης γεματο; | **ee**ne to de**po**sito ye**ma**to ee ven**zee**nee |
| What kind of gasoline does it take? | Τι ειδος βενζινης παιρνει; | tee **ee**thos ben**zee**nees **per**nee |
| Do I need to fill the tank before I return it? | Πρεπει να το επιστρεψω με το ντεποζιτο γεματο; | **pre**pee na to epee**stre**pso me to de**po**sito ye**ma** to |
| When do I have to return it? | Ποτε πρεπει να το επιστρεψω; | **po**te **pre**pee na to epee**stre**pso |
| Can I drop off the car in another city? | Μπορω να το αφησω σε αλλη πολη; | bo**ro** na to a**fee**so se **a**lee **po**lee |
| Are there any other charges? | Υπαρχουν αλλες χρεωσεις; | ee**par**hoon **a**les hre**o**sees |
| May I get a road map? | Εχετε οδικο χαρτη; | **e**hete othee**ko** **har**tee |
| **DIRECTIONS** | ΚΑΤΕΥΘΥΝΣΕΙΣ | KA**TEF**THEENSEE |
| Is this the way to…? | Ετσι πανε στο/στη… | **et**see **pa**ne sto/stee |
| Can you show me where we are on the map? | Μου δειχνετε που ειμαστε στο χαρτη; | moo **thee**hnete poo **ee**maste sto **har**tee |

| | | |
|---|---|---|
| Excuse me, how do I get to…? | Συγνωμη, πως πανε στο… | see**gno**mee pos **pa**ne sto |
| In what direction is…? | Σε ποια κατευθυνση ειναι | se pia ka**tef**theensee **ee**ne |
| Right | Δεξια | the**xia** |
| Left | Αριστερα | areeste**ra** |
| Straight ahead | Ισια απ'εδω | **ee**sia ap'e**tho** |
| At the next lights | Στα επομενα φωτα. | sta e**po**mena **fo**ta |
| After the lights | Μετα τα φωτα | me**ta** ta **fo**ta |
| At the next corner | Στην επομενη γωνια | steen e**po**menee go**neea** |
| highway number… | νουμερο εθνικης οδου | **noo**mero ethnee**kees** othoo |
| At the next village | Στο επομενο χωριο | sto e**po**meno ho**rio** |
| How far is it from here? | Ποσο μακρυα ειναι απ'εδω; | **po**so makree**a** **ee**ne ap'**etho** |

### *GAS STATION*

| | | |
|---|---|---|
| Where is a gas station? | Που ειναι το πρατηριο βενζινης; | poo **ee**ne to pra**tee**reeo ven**zee**nees |
| Fill it up please. | Παρακαλω, γεμιστε το. | paraka**lo** ye**mee**ste to |
| *Please check….* | *Παρακαλω, κοιτατε…* | *paraka**lo** kee**ta**te…* |
| the battery | την μπαταρια | teen bata**reea** |
| the brakes | τα φρενα | ta **fre**na |
| the oil | το λαδι | to **la**thee |
| the tire pressure | την πιεση στα λαστιχα | teen **pee**esee sta **la**steeha |
| the washer fluid | το υγρο του υαλοκαθαριστη | to ee**gro** too yialokatharee**stee** |

| **PARKING** | ΣΤΑΘΜΕΥΣΗ | **STATH**MEFSEE |
|---|---|---|
| Where can I park? | Που μπορω να σταθμευσω; | poo bo**ro** na stath**me**fso |
| How long can I park here? | Για ποσο μπορω να σταθμευσω εδω; | yia **po**so bo**ro** na stath**mefso** e**tho** |

| | | |
|---|---|---|
| How much does it cost? | Ποσο στοιχιζει; | **po**so stee**hee**zee |
| per half hour | για μιση ωρα | yia mee**see o**ra |
| per hour | για μια ωρα | yia **mee**a **o**ra |
| per day | για την ημερα | yia teen ee**me**ra |
| Is it okay to park here? | Ειναι ενταξει να σταθμευσω εδω; | **ee**ne en**da**xee na stath**mef**so e**tho** |
| Is it safe here? | Ειναι ασφαλες εδω; | **ee**ne asfa**les** e**tho** |
| Is there an attendant? | Υπαρχει φυλακας εδω; | ee**par**hee **fee**lakas e**tho** |
| Is there parking? | Επιτρεπεται η σταθμευση | epee**tre**pete ee **stath**mefsee |

### *CAR PROBLEMS*

| | | |
|---|---|---|
| The car won't start. | Δεν ξεκινα το αυτοκινητο. | then xekee**na** to afto**kee**neeto |
| Can you check my car? | Ελεγχετε το αυτοκινητο; | e**len**hete to afto**kee**neeto |
| There's something wrong. | Κατι δεν παει καλα. | **ka**tee then **pa**ee ka**la**. |
| Can you tow this car? | Μπορειτε να ρυμουλ κησετε το αυτοκινητο. | bo**ree**te na reemool**kee**sete to afto**kee**neeto |
| Where is the nearest mechanic? | Που ειναι ο πιο κοντινος μηχανικος. | poo **ee**ne o pio kondee**nos** meehanee**kos** |
| I have run out of gas. | Εμεινα απο βενζινη. | **e**meena a**po** ben**zee**nee |
| I've locked the keys in the car. | Κλειδωσα τα κλειδια λαστιχο. | **klee**thosa ta klee**thia** **me**sa |
| I have a flat tire. | Εχω ξεφουσκωμενο λαστιχο. | **e**hcc xefooskom**e**no **la**steeho |
| How much will it cost? | Ποσο θα στοιχισει; | **po**so tha stee**hee**see |
| How long will it take? | Ποσο καιρο θα παρει; | **po**so ke**ro** tha **pa**ree |
| Can you give me an estimate? | Θα μου δωσετε εκτιμπση; | tha moo **tho**sete **e**kptosee |
| Does the insurance cover this? | Το καλυπτει η ασφαλεια; | to ka**lee**ptee ee as**fa**leea |

## What you may hear

| | | |
|---|---|---|
| *Θα ειναι ετοιμο…* | *tha **ee**ne **e**teemo…* | *It will be ready…* |
| αυριο | **av**reeo | tomorrow |
| μεθαυριο | me**thav**reeo | day after tomorrow |
| αποψε | a**po**pse | tonight |
| την αλλη εβδομαδα | teen **a**lee evtho**ma**tha | next week |
| το πρωι/βραδυ | to pro**ee**/**vra**thee | in the morning/night |
| Θα παρει πολυ καιρο/ωρα. | tha **pa**ree po**lee** ke**ro**/**o**ra | It will take a lot of time. |
| Δεν διορθωνεται. | then thior**tho**nete | It can't be fixed. |
| Δεν μπορουμε σημερα. | then bo**roo**me **see**mera | We can't do it today. |
| Δεν εχουμε το εξαρτημα/τα εξαρτηματα. | then **e**home to ex**ar**teema/ta exar**tee**mata | We don't have the part(s). |
| Θα στοιχισει… πολλα. | tha stee**hee**see po**la** | It will cost a lot. |

### *TAXI*

| | | |
|---|---|---|
| Where can I get a taxi? | Που μπορω να βρω ταξι; | poo bo**ro** na vro ta**xee** |
| What is the number for a taxi? | Τι ειναι το νουμερο για ταξι; | tee **ee**ne to **noo**mero yia ta**xee**. |
| Are you free? | Εισαι ελευθερος; | **ee**se e**lef**theros |
| *Can you take me to…?* | *Μπορειτε να με παρετε…* | *bor**ee**te na me **pa**rete* |
| the airport | στο αεροδρομιο | sto aero**thro**meeo |
| the bus station | στο σταθμο λεωφορειου | sto stath**mo** leofo**ree**oo |
| downtown | στην πολη | steen **po**lee |
| the harbor | στο λιμανι | sto lee**ma**nee |
| the hotel | στο ξενοδοχειο | sto xenotho**hee**o |

| | | |
|---|---|---|
| the main square | στην πλατεια | steen pla**tee**a |
| the road/street… | στην οδο… | steen o**tho…** |
| the train station | στο σταθμο τραινου | ston stath**mo** **tre**noo |
| How much to go to…? | Ποσο ειναι να παω στο… | **po**so **ee**ne na **pa**o sto… |
| I'm in a hurry. | Βιαζομαι. | viazome |
| Please, slow down. | Πιο σιγα, παρακαλω. | pio see**ga** paraka**lo** |
| I do not wish to share this taxi. | Δεν θελω αλλους στο ταξι. | then **the**lo **a**loos sto ta**xee** |
| Stop here please. | Σταματηστε εδω, παρακαλω. | stama**tee**ste e**tho**, paraka**lo** |
| at the next corner | στην γωνια | steen yo**nee**a |
| after the light | μετα τ α φωτα | me**ta** ta **fo**ta |
| Wait for me, please. | Περιμενετε εδω, παρακαλω | peree**me**nete e**tho** paraka**lo** |
| I'll be right back. | θα γυρισω αμεσως | tha yee**ree**so **a**mesos |
| I think you're going the wrong way. | Νομιζω πως πηρατε λαθος δρομο. | No**mee**zo pos **pee**rate **la**thos **thro**mo |
| How much do I owe you? | Ποσο σου χρωστω; | **po**so soo hro**sto** |
| Is the meter working correctly? | Δουλευει ο μετρητης σωστα; | thoo**le**vee o metree**tees** so**sta** |
| Keep the change. | Τα ρεστα δικα σου. | te **re**sta thee**ka** soo |
| I need change. | Χρειαζομαι ρεστα. | hree**a**zome **re**sta |
| I don't think this is the right change. | Νομιζω πως κανατε λαθος στα ρεστα. | no**mee**zo pos **ka**nete **la**thos sta **re**sta |
| This is for you. | Αυτο ειναι για σενα. | af**to** **ee**ne yia **se**na |
| Thank you. | Ευχαριστω. | afharee**sto** |

## What you may hear

| | | |
|---|---|---|
| Ναι/οχι. | ne/**o**hee | Yes/no. |
| Που θελεις (θελετε) να πατε; | poo **the**lees (**the**lete) na **pa**te | Where do you want to go? |
| Θα περιμενω. | tha peree**me**no | I'll wait. |

| | | |
|---|---|---|
| Δεν μπορω να περιμενω. | then **bo**ro na peree**me**no | I can't wait. |
| Θα γυρισω. | tha yee**ree**so | I'll return. |
| Δεν ξερω που ειναι. | then **xe**ro poo **ee**ne | I don't know where it is. |
| Εχει πολυ κινηση, μπορει ν'αργησομε. | **e**hee po**lee** **kee**neesee, bo**ree** n'ar**yee**soome | There's a lot of traffic, we might be late. |
| Χρωστας… | hro**stas** | You owe… |
| Δεν εχω ρεστα. | then **e**ho **re**sta | I don't have change. |

## *PUBLIC TRANSPORTATION*

| | | |
|---|---|---|
| *Where is the nearest… station/stop* | *Που ειναι ο πιο κοντινος… σταθμος/σταση* | *poo **ee**ne o pio kondee**nos** stath**mos**/**sta**see* |
| bus | του λεωφορειου | too leofo**ree**oo |
| tram | του τραμ | too tram |
| trolley | του τρολει | too **tro**lley |
| subway | υπογειου | eepo**yee**oo |

| | | |
|---|---|---|
| What is the fare? | Ποσο ειναι το εισιτηριο; | **po**so **ee**ne to eesee**tee**reeo |
| Where can I buy tickets? | Που πουλανε εισιτηρια; | poo poo**la**ne eesee**tee**reea |
| What…do I take to go to..? | Τι…να παρω να παω στο… | tee…na **pa**ro na **pao** sto… |
| Do you go to…? | Πατε στο…; | **pa**te sto… |
| How many stops to…? | Ποσες στασεις για…; | **po**ses **sta**sees yia… |
| Must I change routes? | Πρεπει ν'αλλαξω δρομολογιο; | **pre**pee n 'a**la**xo thromo**lo**yeeo |
| I want to get off at… | Θελω να κατεβω στο… | **the**lo na ka**te**vo sto… |
| Where do I get off? | Που πρεπει να κατεβω; | poo **pre**pee na ka**te**vo |

### *TRAIN*

| | | |
|---|---|---|
| Where is the train station? | Που ειναι ο σταθμος του τραινου; | poo **ee**ne o stath**mos** too **tre**noo |
| *I'd like a ticket…* | *θελω εισιτηριο…* | ***the**lo eeseetee**reeo*** |
| for first class | για πρωτη θεση | yia **pro**tee **the**see |
| for second class | για δευτερη θεση | yia **thef**teree **the**see |
| sleeping car | κλιναμαξα | kleen**a**maxa |
| return trip | με επιστροφη | me epeestro**fee** |
| one way | χωρις επιστροφη | ho**rees** epeestro**fee** |
| a non/smoking car | βαγονι για μη/καπνιστες | va**go**nee yia mee/kapnee**stes** |
| Is there a dining car? | Εχει βαγονι–εστιατοριο; | **e**hee va**go**nee-estia**to**reeo |
| Which train do I take to get to… | Ποιο τραινο να παρω να παω στο… | pio **tre**no na **pa**ro na **pa**o sto… |
| Do I have to change trains? | Πρεπει ν'αλλαξω τραινα; | **pre**pee n'**a**laxo **tre**na |
| From which platform does the train leave? | Απο ποια αποβαθρα φευγει το τραινο; | a**po** pia a**po**vathra **fev**yee to **tre**no |
| Does this train stop at…? | Σταματαει το τραινο στο… | stama**ta**ee to **tre**no sto… |
| When does the train for… depart? | Ποτε φευγει το τραινο για… | **po**te **fev**yee to **tre**no yia… |
| When does the train arrive at…? | Ποτε φτανει το τραινο στο… | **Po**te **fta**nee to **tre**no . yia.. |
| Is the train on time? | Ειναι το τραινο στην ωρα; | **ee**ne to **tre**no steen **o**ra |
| Where is the luggage check? | Που παραδινουν τις αποσκευες; | poo para**thee**noon tees aposke**ves** |
| I need a porter. | Χρειαζομαι αχθοφορο. | hree**a**zome ahtho**fo**ro |

CHAPTER SEVEN

# Getting acquainted and socializing

Greek people are very friendly and accommodating to tourists. They're famous for their freedom from formality, their love of life and joy in entertaining.

While in Greece, you'll find there are many social activities at all times of the day and night. Many tourists wonder how Greeks make it through the work day, but that's why there are long lunch hours and mid-day naps.

The usual workday goes from 7:00 to 1:00, although many private companies have 9:00 to 5:00 work days. At midday there's a two-hour break for a leisurely lunch and, sometimes, a nap. Dinner tends to be a lighter meal, served around 8:00. Nightlife ordinarily begins around 10:00 and goes past the wee hours of the morning.

### *GREETINGS AND REPLIES*

| | | |
|---|---|---|
| Good morning. | Καλημερα | kalee**me**ra |
| Good evening. | Καλησπερα | kalee**spe**ra |
| Good night. | Καληνυχτα | kalee**nee**hta |
| Hello/Goodbye. | Γεια σου (σας) | yee**a** soo (sas) |
| See you soon. | Καλη ανταμωση | ka**lee** an**da**mosee |
| See you tomorrow. | Μεχρι αυριο | **meh**ree **a**vrio |
| Let's go. | Παμε | **pa**me |
| Do you speak English? | Μιλατε Αγγλικα: | mee**la**te aglee**ka** |
| Yes/no. | Ναι/οχι | ne/**o**hee |
| I'm a tourist. | Ειμαι τουριστ–ας (ρια) | **ee**me tou**ree**stas |

| | | |
|---|---|---|
| I don't speak English. | Δεν μιλω Ελληνικα | then mee**lo** eleenee**ka** |
| I speak very little Greek. | Μιλω λιγα Ελληνικα | mee**lo** **lee**ga eleenee**ka** |
| Please, speak more slowly. | Παρακαλω, μιλατε πιο σιγα. | paraka**lo**, mee**la**te pio see**ga** |
| Repeat that, please | Επαναλαμβανετε, παρακαλω | epanalam**va**nete paraka**lo** |
| I have understood. | Καταλαβα | ka**ta**lava |
| I don't understand. | Δεν καταλαβαινω | then katala**ve**no |
| I didn't understand. | Δεν καταλαβα | then ka**ta**lava |

## *QUESTIONS*

| | | |
|---|---|---|
| Who | Ποιος | pios |
| What | Τι | tee |
| Why | Γιατι | yeea**tee** |
| When | Ποτε | **po**te |
| Where | Που | poo |
| How | Πως | pos |
| How much | Ποσο | **po**so |
| May I ask a question? | Μπορω να κανω μια ερωτηση; | bo**ro** na **ka**no mia e**ro**teesee |
| Could you please help me? | Μπορειτε να με βοηθησετε; | bo**ree**te na me voe**thee**sete |
| Okay/sure. | Ενταξει | en**da**xi |
| Of course. | Οπωσδηποτε | opos**thee**pote |
| What does that mean? | Τι θα πει; | tee tha pee |
| What do you call this in Greek? | Πως το λετε στα Ελληνικα; | pos to **le**te sta eleenee**ka** |
| Where is the washroom? | Που ειναι η τουαλετα; | poo **ee**ne ee toua**le**ta |

## *INTRODUCTIONS*

| | | |
|---|---|---|
| *I'd like to introduce you to…* | *Θελω να σας συστησω στον/(στην)…* | *thelo na sas seesteeso ston/steen* |
| Mr… | Κυριο… | **kee**reeo |
| Mrs… | Κυρια… | kee**reea** |
| Miss…. | Δεσποινις… | thespee**nees** |
| This is my… | Αυτος(η) ειναι ο /(η)…. | af**tos ee**ne o/ee |
| These are… | Αυτοι ειναι οι… | af**tee ee**ne ee |

## *FAMILY AND FRIENDS*

| | | |
|---|---|---|
| aunt | θεια | **thee**a |
| brother | αδελφος | athel**fos** |
| brother-in-law | γαμπρος | gam**bros** |
| colleague (male) | συναδελφος | seenathelfos |
| colleague (female) | συναδελφος | seena**the**lfos |
| cousin (male) | εξαδελφος | **exa**thelfos |
| cousin (female) | εξαδελφη | exa**the**lfee |
| daughter | κορη | **ko**ree |
| father-in-law | πεθερος | pethe**ros** |
| father | πατερας | **pa**teras |
| fiance (male) | αρραβωνιαστικος | aravoniastee**kos** |
| fiancee (female) | αρραβωνιαστικια | aravoniastee**kia** |
| friend (male) | φιλος | **fee**los |
| friend (female) | φιλη | **fee**lee |
| grandfather | παππους | pa**poos** |
| grandmother | γιαγια | yia**yia** |
| husband | ανδρας | **an**dras |
| mother | μητερα | mee**te**ra |
| mother-in-law | πεθερα | pethe**ra** |
| parents | γονεις | go**nees** |
| sister | αδελφη | athel**fee** |
| sister-in-law | νυφη | **nee**fee |

| | | |
|---|---|---|
| son | γιος | yee**os** |
| uncle | θειος | **thee**os |
| wife | γυναικα | yee**ne**ka |

### *REPLIES*

| | | |
|---|---|---|
| Pleased/very pleased to meet you. | Χαιρω πολυ. | **hero polee** |
| A pleasure. | Χαρηκα. | **ha**reeka |
| How are you? | Τι κανεις; (κανετε) | tee **ka**nees (**ka**nete) |
| Fine, thank you. | Καλα, ευχαριστω | ka**la** efhari**sto** |
| And, you? | Και, εσυ (εσεις ); | ke, e**see** (e**sees**) |
| How's it going? | Πως παει; | pos **pa**ee |
| You're welcome. | Παρακαλω. | paraka**lo** |

### *PERSONAL INFO*

| | | |
|---|---|---|
| Where do you live? | Που μενεις (μενετε); | poo **me**nees (**me**nete) |
| *I live in…* | *Κατοικω στο…* | *Katee**ko** sto…* |
| Canada | Καναδα | kana**tha** |
| Toronto | Τοροντο | to**ron**to |
| I'm staying at/with…. | Μενω στο/με τον /την/τους | **me**no sto/me ton/teen/toos |
| How old are you? | Ποσο χρονων εισαι/εισαστε | **po**so hro**non ee**se/ **ee**saste |
| I'm… | Ειμαι… | **ee**me… |
| How old is she/he? | Ποσο χρονων ειναι ο/η…? | **po**so hro**non ee**ne o/ee |
| She/he is… | Ειναι… | **ee**ne… |
| Are you married? | Εισαι παντρεμενος (η) | **ee**se panthre**me**nos (ee) |
| I'm married | Ειμαι παντρεμενος (η) | **ee**me panthre**me**nos (ee) |
| single | ελευθερος (η) | e**lef**theros (ee) |
| a widow/widower | χηρα/χηρος | **hee**ra/**hee**ros |
| Do you have any children | Εχεις (εχετε) παιδια; | **e**hees/**e**hete pe**thia** |

| | | |
|---|---|---|
| How many? | Ποσα; | **po**sa |
| One daughter/son | Μια κορη/ενα γιο | **mee**a **ko**ree/**e**na io |
| Two daughters/sons | Δυο κορες /γιους | **thee**o **ko**res/ioos |
| What is your occupation? | Τι δουλεια κανετε; | tee thou**lia** **ka**nete |
| I'm not working . | Δεν δουλευω | the thou**le**vo |
| I'm retired. | Ειμαι συνταξιουχος | **ee**me seentaxee**oo**hos |

***OCCUPATIONS***

| | | |
|---|---|---|
| *I am (a/an)…* | *Ειμαι…* | *eeme* |
| accountant | λογιστης | loyee**stees** |
| actor | ηθοποιος | eethopee**os** |
| architect | αρχιτεκτονας | arhi**tek**tonas |
| artist | ζωγραφος | zo**gra**fos |
| baker | φουρναρης | foor**na**rees |
| business person | επιχειρηματιας | epeeheereema**tee**as |
| butcher | χασαπης | ha**sa**pees |
| carpenter | μαραγκος | maran**gos** |
| clerk | μπαλληλος γραφειου | ee**pa**leelos gra**fee**oo |
| cook | μαγειρας | **ma**yeeras |
| dentist | οδοντιατρος | othond**ee**atros |
| doctor | γιατρος | yia**tros** |
| economist | οικονομολογος | eekonomo**lo**gos |
| editor | συντακτ–ης (ρια) | seen**dak**tees (reea) |
| electrician | ηλεκτρολογος | eelektro**lo**gos |
| engineer | μηχανικος | meehanee**kos** |
| farmer | αγροτης | **agro**tees |
| film director | σκηνοθετης (σκηνοθετρια) κινηματογραφου | skeeno**the**tees skeeno**the**treea - skeeneemato**gra**foo |
| hairdresser | κομμωτ–ης (κομμωτρια) | komo**tees** (komo**treea)** |
| journalist | δημοσιογραφος | theemoseeo**gra**fos |
| lawyer | δικηγορος | theekee**go**ros |
| manufacturer | βιομηχανος | veeo**mee**hanos |

| | | |
|---|---|---|
| mechanic | μηχανικοs | meehan**ee**kos |
| musician | μουσικοs | moosee**kos** |
| nurse (male)/(female) | νοσοκομ–οs /α | noso**ko**mos |
| painter | μπογιατζ–ηs | boy**adzees** |
| pilot | πιλοτοs | pee**lo**tos |
| professor | καθηγητηs (ρια) πανεπιστημιου | kathee-yee**tees** (**yee**treea) panepee **stee**meeoo |
| salesperson | πωλητ–ηs (ρια) | polee-**tees** (**lee**treea) |
| scientist | επιστημοναs | epee**stee**monas |
| sculptor | γλυπτ–ηs (ρια) | **glee**ptees (reea) |
| shopkeeper | καταστηματαρχ–ηs (ρια) | katasteegma**tar**hees (reea) |
| student (pre-university) | μαθητη–ηs (ρια) | ma-thee**tees** (**thee** treea) |
| student (university | φοιτητ–ηs (ρια) | fee-tee**tees** (**tee**treea) |
| teacher (primary) | δασκαλ–οs (α) | **tha**-skalos (**ska**la) |
| teacher (secondary) | καθηγητ–ηs (ρια) | kathee-yee**tees** (**yee**treea) |
| waiter/waitress | σερβιτοροs (α) | servee**to**ros |
| writer | συγγραφεαs | seengra**fe**as |

## Occupations

When the masculine ends in -ns and the feminine in -pia, the accent of the former is the last syllable and for the latter the second to last syllable,

| | | | |
|---|---|---|---|
| i.e. | καθηγητηs, | katheeyee**tees** | (masculine) |
| | καθηγητρια) | kathee**yee**tees | (feminine) |

### *SOCIALIZING*

| | | |
|---|---|---|
| *May I buy you…?* | *Μπορω να σαs κερασω…;* | ***Boro** na sas **keraso*** |
| a drink | ενα ποτο | ena po**to** |
| a coffee | ενα καφε | ena ka**fe** |

| | | |
|---|---|---|
| With pleasure. | Με ευχαριστηση. | me ef**haree**steesee |
| Gladly. | Ευχαριστως. | ef**haree**stos |
| Cheers. | Στην υγεια σας. | steen ee**yia** sas |
| Do you mind if I smoke? | Σας πειραζει αν καπνισω; | sas pee**ra**zee an kap**nee**so |
| No, not at all. | Οχι, καθολου | **o**hi, ka**tho**loo |
| Yes, it bothers me. | Ναι, με πειραζει | ne me pee**ra**zee |
| I'm not/<br>I'm married... | Δεν ειμαι/<br>Ειμαι παντρεμεν–ος (η) | then **ee**me/<br>eeme panthre**me**nos (ee) |
| I have a boy/girlfriend. | Εχω φιλο/φιλεναδα | **e**ho **fee**lo/feele**na**tha |
| That's okay. | Ενταξει | en**da**xi |
| Can I take you somewhere? | Μπορω να σας παω καπου | bo**ro** na sas **pao** **ka**poo |
| I'll take a taxi, thank you. | Θα παρω ταξι, ευχαριστω | tha **pa**ro tax**ee**, efharee**sto** |
| Can I see you again? | Μπορω να σας ξαναδω; | bo**ro** va sas xana**tho** |
| Thanks for everything. | Ευχαριστω για ολα | efharee**sto** yia **o**la |

## A note to women

Greek men are invariably charming and quite often attentive; however, there are some national habits that can be quite annoying to female tourists. Greek men sometimes comment on the beauty of passing women in ways that would be unacceptable in Canada, and some might actually try to touch you.

The way to deal with the comments is to ignore them, and if they are persistent say firmly: Ασε με ησυχη – **a**se me **ee**seehee (Leave me alone.). If they try to touch you, yell to draw attention to their actions and shout: Mη μ'αγγιζεις! – mee m'a**gee**zees (Don't touch me!). There are more phrases on page 48 and in the emergency chapter that will be useful in these situations.

### *Movies/theatre*

| | | |
|---|---|---|
| What kind of movies do you like? | Τι φιλμ σου αρεσουν; | tee feelm soo **ar**esoon |
| adventure | περιπετειωδη | pereepetee**o**thee |
| classics | κλασσικα | klasee**ka** |
| comedies | κωμωδιες | komo**thee**es |
| horror | φιλμ τρομου | feelm **tro**moo |
| dramas | δραμα | **thra**ma |
| musicals | μουσικα | moosee**ka** |
| mysteries | φιλμ μυστηριου | feelm meestee**ree**oo |
| romantic comedies | ρομαντικες κωμωδιες | romandee**kes** kom**thee**es |
| science fiction | επιστημονικης φαντασιας | epeesteemonee**kees** fanda**see**as |
| Who is your favorite actor? (female) | Ποιος (ποια) ηθοποιος σου αρεσει; | pios (pia) eethopee**os** soo **ar**esee |
| Would you like to go to a movie? | Θα ηθελες να παμε στον κινηματογραφο; | tha **ee**theles na **pa**me ston keeneemato**gra**fo |
| Have you seen…? | Εχεις δει…; | **e**hees thee… |
| What's on? | Τι παιζει; | tee **pe**zee |
| What do you feel like watching? | Τι θελεις να δουμε; | tee **the**lees na **thoo**me |
| Would you like to see a play? | Θελεις να παμε στο θεατρο; | **the**lees na **pa**me sto **the**atro |
| Which play do you feel like seeing? | Ποιο εργο θελεις να δουμε; | pio **er**go **the**lees na **thoo**me |

### *Music*

| | | |
|---|---|---|
| What kind of music do you like? | Τι ειδος μουσικη σου αρεσει; | tee **ee**thos moosee**kee** soo **ar**esee |
| *I like…* | *Μου αρεσει η… μουσικη.* | moo **ar**esee ee… moosee**kee** |
| classical | κλασσικη | klasee**kee** |
| dance/DJ | χορευτικη/ντι τζει | horeftee**kee**/dee jay |

| | | |
|---|---|---|
| folk | φολκ/λαικη/δημοτικη | folk/laee**kee**/ theemotee**kee** |
| jazz | τζαζ | jaz |
| rap | ραπ | rap |
| reggae | ρεγγε | regge |
| rock | ροκ | rok |
| What is your favorite band? | Ποιο ειναι το αγαππμενο σου συγκροτημα; | pio **ee**ne to ayapee**me**no soo see**kro**teema |
| Who is your favorite singer? (female) | Ποιο(ποια) τραγου–διστ(η/ρια) προτιμας; | pio (pia) trayoo-**thee**st (**ee**/reea) protee**mas** |
| *Would you like to go…?* | *Θελεις να παμε…;* | ***the**lees na **pa**me…* |
| to a concert | σε συναυλια | se seenav**lee**a |
| to a club | σε κλαμπ | se club |
| dancing | να χορεψουμε | na ho**re**psoome |

| | | |
|---|---|---|
| **SPORTS/ GAMES** | ΣΠΟΡ/ΠΑΙΧΝΙΔΙΑ | **SPOR/PEHNEETHEEA** |
| Would you like to (see a … game)? | Θελεις να παμε σε παιχνιδι… | **the**lees na **pa**me s peh**nee**thee… |
| Would you like to go…? | Θελεις να παμε για… | **the**lees na **pa**me yia… |
| Would you like to play…? | Θελεις να παιξομε… | **the**lees na **pe**xoome… |

## Mini dictionary: sports & leisure

| | | |
|---|---|---|
| backgammon | ταβλι | **ta**vlee |
| basketball | μπασκετ μπολ | basket ball |
| billiards | μπιλιαρδα | bi**liar**tha |
| cards | χαρτια | har**tia** |
| chess | σκακι | **ska**kee |
| cycling | ποδηλασια | potheela**see**a |
| fishing | ψαρεμα | **psa**rema |
| hiking | πεζοπορια | pezopo**ree**a |
| horseback riding | ιππασια | eepa**see**a |

| | | |
|---|---|---|
| sailing | ιστιοπλοια | eesteeoplo**eea** |
| skating | παγοδρομια (πατιναζ) | payothro**meea** pateenaz |
| (water) skiing | θαλασσιο σκι | tha**la**seeo skee |
| soccer (football) | ποδοσφαιρο | po**tho**sfero |
| swimming | κολυμπι | kol**eem**bee |
| tennis | τενις | **te**nis |
| video games | βιντεο παιχνιδια | **vee**deo peh**nee**thia |
| volleyball | βολειμπολ | **vo**ley bol |

## *I'D LIKE TO KNOW YOU*

| | | |
|---|---|---|
| I like you. | Μου αρεσεις. | moo **a**resees |
| I love you. | Σε αγαπω. | se aya**po** |
| Would you like to go out with me? | Θα ηθελες να βγεις μαζι μου; | tha **ee**theles na vyees ma**zee** moo |
| Here's my address. | Να η διευθυνση μου. | na ee thee**ef**theensee moo |
| Here's my phone number. | Να το τηλεφωνο μου. | na to tee**le**fono moo |
| I've had a nice time. | Περασα πολυ ωραια. | **pe**rasa po**lee** o**re**a |
| I'll call you. | Θα σου τηλεφωνησω. | tha soo teelefo**nee**so |
| Bye. | Γεια. | yia |

## *JUST IN CASE...*

| | | |
|---|---|---|
| I'm travelling with friends. | Ταξιδευω με φιλους. | taxee**the**vo me **fee**loos |
| We're leaving tomorrow. | Φευγομε αυριο. | **fev**gome **a**vrio |
| I'm not interested. | Δεν ενδειαφερομαι. | then enthia**fe**rome |
| Go away! | Φυγε. | **fee**ye |
| Leave me alone. | Ασε με ησυχο/η. | **a**se me **ee**seeho/ee |
| I'm going to call the police. | Θα φωναξω την αστυνομια! | tha fo**na**xo teen asteeno**mee**a |

CHAPTER EIGHT

# On the phone

Most public telephones can be found at newsstands called περιπτερα (per**ee**ptera), which are open long hours. Some of the downtown news stands are open 24 hours. There are also telephones booths (τηλεφωνικος θαλαμος - teelefonee**kos tha**lamos), which can be found downtown in the larger cities.

Local and long distance calls are tallied by units (μοναδες - monathes), that is, by the minute. It's a good idea to get the local and long distance rates before making the call. Most phones display the units, but if they don't, ask the newsstand vendor (περιπτερα - pereepte**ra**) to see the counter.

In Greece, when the line is ringing you'll hear two long **too-toos** together. When it's busy, you'll hear a fast series of **too-too-toos**.

For convenience, newsstands sell calling cards (καρτα τηλεφωνου - **kar**ta teele**fo**noo), which contain a varied and preset amount of units so you can keep track.

| | | |
|---|---|---|
| *Where is the…?* | *Που ειναι…?* | *poo* ***eene***… |
| telephone | το τηλεφωνο | to tee**le**fono |
| telephone book | ο τηλεφωνικος καταλογος | o teelefonee**kos** s ka**ta**logo |
| Where can I buy a card for the telephone? | Που μπορω να παρω καρτα για το τηλεφωνο; | poo bo**ro** na **pa**ro **kar**ta yia to tee**le**fono |
| Is a card needed for the phone? | Χρειαζεται καρτα για το τηλεφωνο; | hree**a**zete **kar**ta yia to tee**le**fono |
| How much for a local call? | Ποσο στοιχιζει το αστικο τηλεφωνημα; | **po**so stee**hee**zee to astee**ko** teele**fo**neema |
| What is the rate to call…? Canada. | Ποσο ειναι η μοναδα για…τον Καναδα; | **po**so **ee**ne ee mo**na**tha yia ton Kana**tha** |
| May I have extension #… | Θελω το εσωτερικο #… | **The**lo to esoteree**ko** # |

### *OPERATOR*

| | | |
|---|---|---|
| *May I have…?* | *Μπορω να εχω…;* | *bo**ro** na e**ho***… |
| the number for… | το νουμερο για.. | to **noo**mero yia… |
| information | πληροφοριες | pleerofo**ree**es |
| the international operator | την τηλεφωνητρια εξωτερικου | teen teelefo**nee**treea esoteree**koo** |
| Please connect me with… | Παρακαλω, συνδεστε με το… | paraka**lo**, seen**the**ste me to |
| Do you speak English? | Μιλατε Αγγλικα; | mee**la**te aglee**ka** |
| *I'd like to make…* | *Θα ηθελα να κανω…* | *ha **ee**thela na **ka**no*.. |
| a local call | τηλεφωνημα αστικο | teele**fo**neema astee**ko** |
| a long distance call | τηλεφωνπμα υπεραστικο | teele**fo**neema eeperastee**ko** |
| What is the area code for…? | Τι ειναι ο κωδικος για… | tee **ee**ne o **ko**theekos yia… |

| | | |
|---|---|---|
| I'd like to use my credit card. | Θα χρησιμοποιησω την πιστωτικη καρτα. | tha hreeseemopeeeeso teen peestotee**kee** **kar**ta |
| How much per minute? | Ποσο στοιχιζει το λεπτο; | **po**so stee**hee**zee to lep**to** |
| My number is… | Το νουμερο μου ειναι… | to **noo**mero moo **ee**ne… |
| How many points are on this card? | Ποσες μοναδες εχει η καρτα; | **po**ses mo**na**thes **e**hee ee **kar**ta |

## What you may hear

| | | |
|---|---|---|
| Εμπρος, ποιος ειναι; | em**bros** pios **ee**ne | Hello, who is it? |
| Ειναι ο (η)… | **ee**ne o (ee) | It's… |
| Δεν απαντα κανεις. | then apan**da** ka**nees** | No one is answering. |
| Δεν μπορω να σε ακουσω. | then bo**ro** na se a**koo**so | I can't hear you. |
| Εχετε λαθος νουμερο. | **e**hete **la**thos **noo**mero | You have the wrong number. |
| Ποιον καλειτε; | pion ka**lee**te | Who are you calling? |
| Περιμενετε, παρακαλω. | peree**me**nete, paraka**lo** | Wait, please. |
| Η γραμμη ειναι απασχολημενη. | ee gra**mee** **ee**ne apasholee**me**nee | The line is busy. |
| Εχει διακοπει η γραμμη. | **e**hee thiako**pee** ee gra**mee** | The line is disconnected. |
| ξανατηλεφωνηστε. | xanateelefo**nee**ste | Call again. |
| Ναι, σΠακουω. | ne, s'a**koo**o | Yes, I hear you. |
| Το τηλεφωνο δεν δουλευει. | to tee**le**fono then thou**le**vee | The phone doesn't work. |
| Να ξαναδοκιμασω; | **the**lete na xanathokee**ma**so | Should we try again? |
| Θελετε να αφησετε μυνυμα; | **the**lete na a**fee**sete **mee**neema | Would you like to leave a message. |

CHAPTER NINE

# Dining out

One thing you'll soon find out, Greeks love to eat! Make sure you sample many of the tradtional foods and take advantage of the abundant fresh fish, seafood, fruit and vegetables!

| | | |
|---|---|---|
| Καλη ορεξη! | ka**lee** **o**rexee | **Have a pleasant meal!** |

***PLACES TO EAT***

| | | |
|---|---|---|
| ψησταρια | pseest**aria** | great for barbeque and charbroiled meats |
| ψαροταβερνα | psarota**ver**na | specialize in fish and seafood |
| ταβερνα | ta**ver**na | pub with great munchies, beer and wines |
| καφενειο | kafe**nee**o | for great coffees and traditional desserts |
| ζαχαροπλαστειο | zaharopla**steeo** | great for desserts! |

## Some traditional Greek entrees

| | | |
|---|---|---|
| ντολμαδακια | dolma**tha**kia | vine leaves stuffed with rice and meat |
| παστιτσιο | pas**tee**tsio | Greek-style lasagna |
| μουσακα | moosa**ka** | vegetables and meat layered and baked,topped with bechamel (cream) |
| παπουτσακια | papoo**tsa**kia | baked eggplant stuffed with meat and topped with bechamel |

| | | |
|---|---|---|
| αυγολεμονο | avgo**le**mono | chicken broth with rice and a lemon-egg sauce |
| λεμονατο | lemo**na**to | usually lamb with artichokes in a lemon-egg sauce |
| γεμιστα | yemee**sta** | tomatoes, peppers, zucchini and other vegetables stuffed with rice or meat |

## *DINING OUT*

| | | |
|---|---|---|
| I'm hungry. | Πειναω. | pee**nao** |
| I'm thristy. | Διψω. | thee**pso** |
| Do you know a good restaurant? | Ξερετε ενα καλο εστιατοριο; | **xerete ena kalo** estia**to**reeo |
| Do you need a reservation? | Χρειαζεται να κλεισω τραπεζι; | hreeazete na **klee**so tra**pe**zee |
| Is it expensive? | Ειναι ακριβο; | **eene** akree**vo** |
| What's the restaurant called? | Ποιο ειναι το ονομα του εστιατοριου; | pio **eene** to **o**noma too estiato**ree**oo |
| Where is it located? | Που ειναι; | poo **eene** |
| Is it close/far? | Ειναι κοντα/μακρυα; | **eene** kon**da**/makree**a** |
| *I would like to make a reservation for…* | *Θελω να καθισω τραπεζι για…* | ***the**lo na **klee**so tra**pe**zee yia…* |
| tonight | αποψε | **apo**pse |
| tomorrow evening | αυριο βραδυ | **av**rio **vra**thee |
| for two (three) | για δυο (τρεις) | yia **theeo** (trees) |
| *I would like to sit…* | *Θελω να καθισω…* | ***the**lo na ka**thee**so…* |
| inside | μεσα | **me**sa |
| outside | εξω | **e**xo |
| by the window | κοντα στο παραθυρο | kon**da** sto para**the**ero |
| in smoking/non-smoking | στους καπνιστες /μη καπνιστες | stoos kapnee**stes**/ mee kapnee**stes** |
| I would like a table for… | Θελω τραπεζι για | …**the**lo tra**pe**zee yia… |

### *ORDERING*

| | | |
|---|---|---|
| Waiter! Waitress! | Σερβιτορε! Σερβιτορα! | servee**tore**/servee**tora** |
| The menu, please. | Τον καταλογο, παρακαλω | ton **ka**talogo, para**kalo** |
| The wine list, please | Τον καταλογο κρασιων, παρακαλω. | ton **ka**talogo kra**sion** para**kalo** |
| What would you recommend? | Τι συνιστατε; | tee seenee**state** |
| I'd(we'd) like to order now. | Θελω (θελουμε) να παραγγειλ (ω/ουμε) τωρα. | **the**lo(**the**lome) na para**geel**(o/ome) **tora** |
| *I (we) would like…* | *Θελ(ω/ομε)…* | ***thel**(o/ome)* |
| something light | κατι ε λαφρυ | **katee** ela**free** |
| only appetizers | μονο ορεκτικα | **mo**no orektee**ka** |
| a full meal | πληρες γευμα | **plee**res **yev**ma |
| What's the specialty? | Τι ειναι το σπεσιαλιτε σας; | tee **ee**ne to specialee**te** sas |
| How big are the portions? | Τι μεγεθος ειναι η μεριδα; | tee **me**yethos **ee**ne ee me**ree**tha |
| generous | γενναιοδωρη | yene**o**thoree |
| small | μικρη | mee**kree** |
| *To start with, we'd like…* | *Θα αρχισουμε με…* | *tha ar**bee**some me…* |
| a drink | ενα ποτο | ena po**to** |
| beer | μπυρα | **bee**ra |
| white/red wine | ασπρο/κοκκινο κρασι | **as**pro/**ko**keeno kra**see** |
| a glass of | ενα ποτηρι | ena po**tee**ree |
| a litre of | ενα λιτρο | ena **lee**tro |
| a half litre of | μισο λιτρο | mee**so** **lee**tro |
| some…water | λιγο … νερο | **lee**go…ne**ro** |
| mineral | μεταλλικο | metalee**ko** |
| carbonated | αεριουχο | ae**roo**ho |

| *Next we'd like…* | *Μετα θελουμε…* | ***meta thelome…*** |
|---|---|---|
| a plate of appetizers | ορεκτικα | oreektee**ka** |
| some soup | σουπα | **soo**pa |
| the main course | γευμα | **ye**vma |
| dessert | γλυκο | glee**ko** |
| coffee | καφε | ka**fe** |
| tea | τσαι | **tsa**ee |
| a dessert wine | γλυκο κρασι | glee**ko** kra**see** |
| fruit | φρουτο | **froo**to |
| Nothing else, thank you. | Τιποτα αλλο, ευχαριστω | **tee**pota alo, efharee**sto** |
| The bill, please. | Τον λογαριασμο, παρακαλω. | ton logaria**smo**, paraka**lo** |
| *Please bring us…* | *Παρακαλω, φερε μας…* | *paraka**lo**, **fe**re mas…* |
| an ashtray | ενα τασακι | ena ta**sa**ki |
| another plate | ακομα ενα πιατο | a**ko**ma ena **pia**to |
| cup | φλυτζανι | flee**dza**nee |
| fork | πιρουνι | pee**roo**nee |
| glass | ποτηρι | po**tee**ree |
| knife | μαχαιρι | ma**he**ree |
| napkin | πετσετα | pet**se**ta |
| saucer | πιατακι | pia**ta**kee |
| spoon | κουταλι | koo**ta**lee |
| teaspoon | κουταλακι | koota**la**kee |
| toothpick | οδοντογλυφιδα | othondoglee**fee**tha |
| some bread | λιγο ψωμι | **lee**go pso**mee** |
| butter | βουτυρο | **voo**teero |
| ketchup | κετσαπ | **ket**sap |
| lemon | λεμονι | le**mo**nee |
| margerine | μαργαρινη | marga**ree**nee |
| mayonnaise | μαγιονεζα | mayo**ne**za |
| mustard | μουσταρδα | moo**star**tha |

| | | |
|---|---|---|
| olive oil | ελαιολαδο | ele**o**latho |
| oil | λαδι | **la**thee |
| pepper | πιπερι | pee**pe**ree |
| hot pepper | καυτο πιπερι | kaft**o** pee**pe**ree |
| salt | αλατι | a**la**tee |
| sugar | ζαχαρη | **za**haree |
| syrup | σιροπι | see**ro**pee |
| vinegar | ξυδι | **xee**thee |
| That's enough, thank you. | Αρκετα, ευχαριστω. | arke**ta**, efharee**sto** |
| A little more, please. | Λιγο παραπανω, παρακαλω. | **lee**go para**pa**no, paraka**lo** |
| Another (more), please. | Κ'αλλο, παρακαλω. | k'alo, paraka**lo** |

### *Restrictions*

| | | |
|---|---|---|
| I am allergic to… | Ειμαι αλλεργικ(os/η) στο… | **ee**me alergeek(**os/ee**) sto |
| I can't eat anything with… | Δεν μπορω να φαω τιποτα με… | then bo**ro** na **fao** **tee**pota me |
| *I don't eat…* | *Δεν τρωγω…* | *then **trogo*** |
| dairy | γαλακτερα | galakte**ra** |
| eggs | αυγα | av**ga** |
| fat | λιπos | **lee**pos |
| fried food | τηγανιτα | teeganee**ta** |
| flour | αλευρι | a**le**vree |
| meat | κρεαs | **kre**as |
| nuts | ξηρουs καρπουs | xee**roos** kar**poos** |
| pork | χοιρινιο | heeree**no** |
| salt | αλατι | a**la**tee |
| seafood | θαλασσινα | thalasee**na** |
| sugar | ζαχαρη | **za**haree |

| | | |
|---|---|---|
| I don't drink alcohol. | Δεν πινω αλκοολ | then **pee**no alko**ol** |
| I'm diabetic. | Ειμαι διαβητικος. | **ee**me thiaveetee**kos** |
| I'd like a sweetener. | Θελω ζαχαρινη. | **the**lo zaha**ree**nee |
| Do you have vegetarian dishes? | Εχετε πιατα για χορτοφαγους; | **e**hete **pia**ta yia horto**fa**goos |

### *PROBLEMS*

| | | |
|---|---|---|
| I didn't order this. | Δεν το παρηγγειλα. | then pa**ree**geela |
| *This dish is too…* | *Ειναι πολυ…* | ***eene polee**…* |
| cold/hot | κρυο/ζεστο | **kree**o/ze**sto** |
| overcooked | παραψημενο | parpsee**me**no |
| rare | μισοψημενο | meesopsee**me**no |
| salty | αλμυρο | almee**ro** |
| spicy | πικαντικο | pee**kan**deeko |
| sweet | γλυκο | glee**ko** |
| tough | σκληρο | sklee**ro** |
| undercooked | αψητο | **a**pseeto |
| I don't like it. | Δεν μου αρεσει. | then moo a**re**see |
| This is not clean. | Δεν ειναι καθαρο. | then **ee**ne katha**ro** |
| This is not fresh. | Δεν ειναι φρεσκο. | then **ee**ne **fre**sko |
| I found a bug/a hair in the food. | Βρηκα εντομο/τριχα στο φαγητο μου. | **vree**ka entomo/**tree**ha sto fayee**to** moo |

### *PAYING THE BILL*

| | | |
|---|---|---|
| The cheque… | Τον λογαριασμο… | ton logaria**smo**… |
| Separate cheques… | Ξεχωριστο λογαριασμο… | xehoree**sto** logaria**smo** |
| Is the service included? | Συμπεριλαμβανεται το φιλοδωρημα; | seempereelam**va**nete to feelo**tho**reema |
| I don't think the bill is correct. | Υπαρχει καποιο λαθος στον λογαριασμο. | ee**par**hee **ka**pio **la**thos ton logaria**smo** |

| | | |
|---|---|---|
| What's this amount for? | Για τι ειναι αυτο το ποσο; | yia tee **eene** af**to** to po**so** |
| The service is very good. | Η εξυπηρετηση ηταν καλη. | ee exeepee**re**teesee **ee**tan ka**lee** |
| The meal was delicious. | Το γευμα ηταν νοστιμο. | to **ye**vma **ee**tan **no**steemo |
| This is for you. | Αυτο ειναι για σενα. | af**to** **ee**ne yia **se**na |

## What you may hear

| | | |
|---|---|---|
| Τι θα παραγγειλετε; | tee tha para**gee**laete | What will you order? |
| Συνιστω… | seenee**sto**… | I recommend… |
| Το σπεσιαλιτε ειναι.. | to spesialee**te** **ee**ne | The special is… |
| Τι θελετε να πιειτε; | tee **the**lete na **piee**te | What would you like to drink? |
| Με τι θελετε ν'αρχισετε: | me tee **the**lete n'ar**hee**sete | What will you start with? |
| Συγγνωμη, δεν εχουμε | see**gno**mee, then **e**home… | …I'm sorry, we don't have… |
| Καλη ορεξη! | ka**lee** **o**rexee | Good appetite. |
| Θα παρει λιγη ωρα. | tha **pa**ree **lee**gee **o**ra | It will take some time. |
| Θελετε τιποτα αλλο; | **the**leta **tee**pote **a**lo | Would you like anything else? |
| Θελετε να δειτε τον καταλογο κρασιων; | **the**lete na **thee**te ton ka**ta**logo kra**sion** | Would you like a wine? |
| Για ποσους; | yia **po**soos | For how many? |

## Food dictionary

| **FISH AND SEAFOOD** | ΘΑΛΑΣΣΙΝΑ | **THALASEENA** |
|---|---|---|
| anchovies | αντσουγιες | ant**soo**ges |
| clams | αχιβαδες | ahee**va**thes |
| crab | καβουρι | ka**voo**ree |
| lobster | αστακο | asta**ko** |
| mullet(red) | μπαρμπουνι | bar**boo**nee |
| mussels | μυδια | **mee**thia |
| octopus | οχταποδι | ohta**po**thee |
| oysters | στρειδια | **stree**thia |
| salt cod | μπακαλιαρο | baka**lia**ro |
| shrimp | γαριδες | ga**ree**thes |
| sole | γλωσσα | **glo**sa |
| squid | σουπια | soo**pia** |
| swordfish | ξιφιας | xeef**ee**as |

| **MEAT** | ΚΡΕΑΣ | **KRE**AS |
|---|---|---|
| bacon | μπεικον | **ba**kon |
| beef | βοδινο | votheen**o** |
| chop | μπριζολακι | breezo**la**kee |
| ham | χοιρομερι | heero**me**ree |
| lamb | αρνι | ar**nee** |
| liver | συκωτι | see**ko**tee |
| meat balls | κεφτεδες | kef**te**thes |
| pork | χοιρινο | heeree**no** |
| rib | παιδακι | paee**tha**kee |
| roast beef | κρεας ψητο | **kre**as psee**to** |
| salami | σαλαμι | sa**la**mee |
| sausage | λουκανικο | loo**ka**neeko |
| steak | μπριζολα | bree**zo**la |
| tongue | βοδινη γλωσσα | vothee**nee** **glo**sa |

| | | |
|---|---|---|
| tripe | πατσα | pa**tsa** |
| veal | μοσχαρι | mos**ha**ree |
| | | |
| **POULTRY** | ΠΟΥΛΕΡΙΚΑ | POOLEREE**KA** |
| chicken | κοτα | **ko**ta |
| pheasant | φασιανο | fasia**no** |
| rabbit | κουνελι | koo**ne**lee |
| turkey | γαλοπουλα | galo**poo**la |
| venison | κρεας ελαφιου | **kre**as ela**fioo** |
| | | |
| **VEGETABLES** | ΧΟΡΤΑΡΙΚΑ | HORTARI**KA** |
| artichokes | αγγιναρες | agee**na**res |
| beans (kidney) | φασολια | fa**so**lia |
| beans (string) | φασολια/ φασολακια | fa**so**lakia/faso**la**kia |
| beets | παντζαρια | pa**dza**ria |
| broccoli | μπροκολο | **bro**kolo |
| cabbage | λαχανο | **la**hano |
| cauliflower | κουνουπιδι | koonoo**pee**thee |
| cucumber | αγγουρι | an**goo**ree |
| eggplant | μελιτζανα | melee**dza**na |
| green onion | κρεμμυδακια | kremee**tha**kia |
| green peas | μπιζελια | bee**ze**lia |
| mixed salad | σαλατα | sa**la**ta |
| mushrooms | μανιταρια | manee**ta**ria |
| onion | κρεμμυδια | kre**mee**thia |
| pepper | πιπεριες | peepe**ries** |
| potatoes | πατατες | pa**ta**tes |
| radish | ρεπανακι | repa**na**kee |
| tomatoes | ντοματες | do**ma**tes |
| yams | γλυκοπατατες | gleekopa**ta**tes |
| zucchini/pumpkin | κολοκυθι/κολοκυθα | kolo**kee**thee/ kolo**kee**tha |

| **FRUIT** | ΦΡΟΥΤΑ | **FROOTA** |
|---|---|---|
| apple | μηλο | **mee**lo |
| apricot | βερικοκο | ve**ree**koko |
| cantaloupe | πεπονι | pe**po**nee |
| cherries | κερασια | ke**ra**sia |
| dates | χουρμαδες | hoor**ma**thes |
| figs | συκα | **see**ka |
| grapefruit | φραπα (γκρειπ–φρουτ) | **fra**pa (grapefruit) |
| grapes | σταφυλια | sta**fee**lia |
| lemon | λεμονια | le**mo**nia |
| orange | πορτοκαλι | porto**ka**le |
| peach | ροδακινο | ro**tha**keeno |
| pear | αχλαδι | **ahla**the |
| strawberries | φραουλες | **fra**ooles |
| watermelon | καρπουζι | kar**poo**zee |
| | | |
| **DAIRY** | ΓΑΛΑΚΤΕΡΑ | **GALAKTERA** |
| milk | γαλα | **ga**la |
| yoghurt | γιαουρτι | yia**oo**rtee |
| cheese | τυρι | tee**ree** |
| sweetened milk | γλυκο γαλα | glee**ko** **ga**la |
| cream | κρεμα | **kre**ma |
| ice cream | παγωτο | pago**to** |
| custard | ψημενη κρεμα | psee**me**nee **kre**ma |
| | | |
| **BEVERAGES** | ΠΙΟΤΑ | **PIOTA** |
| coffee (American) | καφε Αμερικανικο | **kafe** ameri**ka**neeko |
| coffee (Greek) | καφε Ελληνικο | **kafe** eleenee**ko** |
| coffee (frappe) | καφε φραπε | **kafe** fra**pe** |
| tea | τσαι | **tsa**ee |
| tea (mountain) | τσαι βουνου | **tsa**ee voo**noo** |
| carbonated water | αεριουχο νερο | ae**roo**ho ne**ro** |

| | | |
|---|---|---|
| tomato juice | χυμο ντοματας | hee**mo** do**ma**tas |
| orange juice | πορτοκαλαδα | portoka**la**tha |
| lemonade | λεμοναδα | lemo**na**tha |
| fruit juice | χυμο φρουτου | hee**mo** **froo**too |
| | | |
| **ALCOHOL** | ΠΟΤΑ | **POTA** |
| beer | μπυρα | **bee**ra |
| champagne | σαμπανια | sam**pania** |
| dry wine | ξηρο κρασι | xee**ro** kra**see** |
| red wine | κοκκινο κρασι | **ko**keeno kra**see** |
| sweet wine | γλυκο κρασι | glee**ko** kra**see** |
| white wine | ασπρο κρασι | **as**pro kra**see** |
| brandy | κονιακ | ko**niak** |

CHAPTER TEN

# Shopping

***STORES! STORES! AND MORE STORES!***

There's a section in Athens called Μοναστηρακι (monasteerakee) where, along with great restaurants, cafes and music bars, you'll find small stores and vendors who sell everything from gold to natural dried herbs. Check it out, and don't be afraid to haggle.

Most stores are open around 7:00 a.m. and close around 2:00 p.m. On a couple of days in the week, usually Wednesdays and Fridays, stores reopen in the evening around 6:00 and stay open until around 10:00. Ask to make sure.

Taxes are usually included in the price, so if there's a price tag, what you see is what you pay. Of particular shopping interest are handmade jewelry, clothing, and crafts produced by local artisans.

Usually on Wednesdays or Saturdays, there are moveable flea markets (Λαικη Αγορα - lae**kee** ago**ra**) in designated parts of the town or in several different locations in a large city. Merchants, farmers and craftspeople from many parts of Greece come to sell their produce and crafts. Flea markets start around 7:00 in the morning and usually run to around 1:30 pm. Take the opportunity to browse and stock up on food if you need to.

A good technique to bargain is to feign disinterest or gently suggest that the price is beyond your reach. If there's room for movement in the price, the vendor will take it from there. Don't aggressively start the process; let the vendor take the initiative. Remember, you don't want to insult anyone.

## *SHOPPING*

| **STORES** | ΜΑΓΑΖΙΑ | **MAGAZIA** |
|---|---|---|
| Bakery | Ζαχαροπλαστειο | zaharopla**stee**o |
| Bookstore | Βιβλιοπωλειο | veevleeopo**lee**o |
| Butcher | Κρεοπωλειο | kreopo**lee**o |
| Cosmetics | Καλλυντικα | kaleendee**ka** |
| Department store | Καταστημα | ka**ta**steema |
| Flea market | Λαικη αγορα | laee**kee** ago**ra** |
| Fish store | Ιχθυοπωλειο | eehtheepo**lee**o |
| Grocery store | Μπακαλικο | ba**ka**leeko |
| Jewelry store | Κοσμηματοπωλειο | kosmeematopo**lee**o |
| Liquor store | Καβα ποτων | **ka**va po**ton** |
| Market | Αγορα | ago**ra** |
| Music | Μουσικη | mousee**kee** |
| Newspaper stand | Περιπτερο | pe**ree**ptero |
| Pharmacy | Φαρμακειο | farma**kee**o |
| Shoe store | Παπουτσιδικο | papoo**tsa**theeko |
| Supemarket | Υπεραγορα | eeperago**ra** |
| Variety store | Ψιλικατζιδικο | pseeleeka**dzee**theeko |
| Wine store | Οινοπωλειο | eenopo**lee**o |

### *BEING SERVED*

| | | |
|---|---|---|
| Can you help me? | Μπορειτε να με βοηθησετε; | bo**ree**te na me voee**thee**sete |
| Where can I find…? | Που μπορω να βρω…; | poo bo**ro** na vro |
| Can you show me…? | Μπορειτε να μου δειξετε…; | bo**ree**te na moo **thee**xete |
| this | αυτο | af**to** |
| that | εκεινο | e**kee**no |
| the one in the window | αυτο στη βιτρινα | af**to** stee vee**tree**na |
| something better | κατι καλυτερο | **ka**tee ka**lee**tero |
| something less expensive | κατι λιγοτερο ακριβο | **ka**tee lee**go**tero akree**vo** |
| a different color | σε διαφορετικο χρωμα | se thiaforetee**ko** **hro**ma |
| a different style | σε διαφορετικο στυλ | se thaiforetee**ko** steel |
| *I would like something for my…* | *Θελω κατι για…* | ***the**lo **ka**tee yia…* |
| husband | τον ανδρα μου | ton **an**dra moo |
| wife | την γυναικα μου | teen yee**ne**ka moo |
| son | τον γιο μου | ton yee**o** moo |
| daughter | την κορη μου | teen **ko**ree moo |
| fiancee | τον αραββωνιαστικο (την αραββωναιστικια) μου | ton aravoniastee**ko** moo (teen aravoniastee**kia)** moo |
| father | τον πατερα μου | ton pa**te**ra moo |
| mother | την μητερα | teen mee**te**ra moo |
| sister | την αδελφη μου | teen athel**fee** moo |
| brother | τον αδελφο μου | ton athel**fo** moo |
| for a girl of three | για κοριτσι τριων χρονων | yia ko**ree**tsee tree**on** hro**non** |
| for a woman of thirty | για γυναικα τριαντα χρονων | yia yee**ne**ka tree**an**da hro**non** |
| for a boy of ten | για αγορι δεκα χρονων | yia a**go**ree **the**ka hro**non** |
| for a man of fifty | για ανδρα πενηντα χρονων | yia **an**dra pe**neen**da hro**non** |

| | | |
|---|---|---|
| Can I try it on? | Μπορω να το δοκιμασω; | bo**ro** na to thokee**ma**so |
| Do you have a mirror? | Εχετε καθρεφτη; | **e**hete ka**thref**tee |
| How much does this cost? | Ποσο στοιχιζει; | **po**so stee**hee**zee |
| *Can I pay...?* | *Μπορω να πληρωσω...;* | ***boro** na pleeroso* |
| in dollars | με δολλαρια | me tho**la**reea |
| with traveller's cheques | με ταξιδιωτικη επιταγη | me taxeethiotee**kee** epeeta**yee** |
| with a credit card | με πιστωτικη καρτα | me peestotee**kee kar**ta |
| Is there a tax? | Φορολογειται αυτο; | forolo**yee**te af**to** |
| Can you give me a discount? | Θα μου δωσετε εκπτωση; | tha moo **tho**sete e **ek**ptose |
| Can you wrap this? | Μπορειτε να μου το τυλιξετε; | bo**ree**te na moo to tee**lee**xete |
| Can I order it? | Μπορω να το παραγγειλω; | bo**ro** na to para**gee**lo |
| Can you deliver it to...? | Μπορειτε να το στειλετε στο...; | bo**ree**te na to **stee**lete sto |
| This is defective. | Ειναι ελαττωματικο. | eene elatomatee**ko** |
| Do you have another one? | Εχετε αλλο; | ehete **a**lo |
| It's very expensive. | Ειναι πολυ ακριβο. | **ee**ne po**lee** akree**vo** |
| I will (won't) take it. | (Δεν) Θα το παρω. | (then) tha to **pa**ro |
| I'm just looking. | Κοιταω μονο. | kee**tao mo**no |
| I'll think about it. | Θα το σκεφτω. | tha to skef**to** |
| I'm waiting for... | Περιμενω για... | peree**me**no yia |
| Can I exchange this? | Μπορω να το ανταλλαξω; | bo**ro** na to anda**la**xo |
| Here is the receipt. | Να η αποδειξη. | na ee a**po**theexee |
| I'd like my money back. | Θα ηθελα τα χρηματα μου πισω. | tha **ee**thela ta **hree**mata moo **pee**so |
| That will be all. | Τιποτα αλλο. | **tee**pota **a**lo |
| (No) thank you. | (Οχι) ευχαριστω. | (**o**hee) efharee**sto** |

## What you may hear

| | | |
|---|---|---|
| Καλημερα. | kalee**me**ra | Good morning. |
| Καλησπερα. | kalee**spe**ra | Good evening. |
| Περαστε. | pe**ra**ste | Come in. |
| Τι θελετε. | tee **the**lete | What would you like? |
| Μπορω να σας βοηθησω; | bo**ro** na sas vo**ee**theeso | May I help you? |
| Τι μεγεθος; | tee **me**yethos; | What size? |
| Τι χρωμα; | tee **hro**ma | What color? |
| Σας παει πολυ. | sas **pa**ee po**lee** | It suits you well. |
| Δεν εχουμε αλλο. | then **e**home **a**lo | We don't have any more. |
| Δεν εχουμε μεγαλυτερο (μικροτερο). | then **e**home megal**ee**tero (mee**kro**tero) | We don't have one (a smaller one). |

## Mini dictionary

| CLOTHING | ΡΟΥΧΑ | **ROO**HA |
|---|---|---|
| *I would like to buy...* | *θα ηθελα να αγορασω...* | *tha **ee**thela na ago**ra**so* |
| bathing suit | ενα μαγιο | ena ma**yio** |
| bathrobe | ενα μπουρνουζι | **mee**a boor**noo**zee |
| belt | μια ζωνη | **meea zo**nee |
| blouse | μια μπλουζα | **meea bloo**za |
| boots | μποτες | **bo**tes |
| bra | ενα σουτιεν | ena soo**tien** |
| briefs (men's) | σωβρακο | **so**vrako |
| coat | παλτο | pal**to** |
| dress | φουστανι | foo**sta**nee |
| evening dress | βραδυνο φορεμα/ τουαλετα | vrathee**no fo**rema/ tooa**le**ta |

| | | |
|---|---|---|
| fur coat | παλτο γουνινο | pal**to yoo**neeno |
| gloves | γαντια | **yan**dia |
| handbag | τσαντα | **tsan**da |
| hat | καπελο | ka**pe**llo |
| jacket | ζακετα | za**ke**ta |
| jeans | τζην | jeen |
| panties | κυλοττες | kee**lo**tes |
| pants | παντελονι | pande**lo**nee |
| pantyhose | καλτσον | kal**tson** |
| raincoat | αδιαβροχο | **athia**vroho |
| scarf | εσαρπα | **sar**pa |
| shirt | πουκαμισο | poo**ka**meeso |
| shoes | παπουτσια | pa**poo**tsia |
| shorts | σορτ | sort |
| skirt | φουστα | **foo**sta |
| socks | καλτσες | **kal**tses |
| sports jacket | ζακετα σπορ | za**ke**ta spor |
| suit | κουστουμι | koo**stoo**mee |
| sweater | πουλοβερ | poo**lo**ver |
| sweatshirt | αθλητικο πουκαμισο | athleetee**ko** poo**ka**meeso |
| T-shirt | φανελα | fa**ne**la |
| tie | γραβατα | gra**va**ta |
| umbrella | ομπρελα | om**bre**la |
| underwear | εσωρουχα | e**so**rooha |
| vest | γιλεκο | yee**le**ko |

## *MORE PHRASES...*

| | | |
|---|---|---|
| I don't know my size. | Δεν ξερω το μεγεθος μου. | then **xe**ro to **me**yethos moo |
| They're too narrow/wide. | Ειναι πολυ στενα/φαρδια. | eene po**lee** ste**na**/far**thia** |

| | | |
|---|---|---|
| They fit well. | Εφαρμοζουν καλα. | efar**mo**zoon ka**la** |
| Do you have a larger/ smaller size? | Εχετε μεγαλυτερο/ μικροτερο μεγεθος; | **e**hete mega**lee**tero/ mee**kro**tero **me**yethos |
| I'd like the same one in… | Θελω το ιδιο σε. | **the**lo to **ee**thio se… |
| I'll take them. | Θα τα παρω. | tha to **paro** |
| I don't know my size. | Δεν ξερω το μεγεθος μου. | then **xero** to **me**yeth**os** moo |
| Can I try it on? | Μπορω να το δοκιμασω; | bo**ro** na thokee**ma**so |
| Do you have a mirror? | Εχετε καθρεφτη; | **e**hete ka**thref**tee |
| It (doesn't) fit(s) well. | (Δεν) χωραει καλα. | (then) ho**ra**ee ka**la** |
| *It's too…* | *Ειναι πολυ…* | **ee**ne po**lee** |
| short | κοντο | kon**do** |
| long | μακρυ | ma**kree** |
| narrow/tight | στενο | ste**no** |
| wide/large | φαρδυ | far**thee** |
| Can you alter it? | Μπορειτε να το επιδιορθωσετε; | bo**ree**te na to epeethior**tho**sete |
| When will it be ready? | Ποτε θα ειναι ετοιμο; | **po**te tha **ee**ne **e**teemo |
| Do you accept returns? | Δεχεστε επιστροφες; | **the**heste epeestro**fes** |
| Do you give refunds? | Επιστρεφετε χρηματα; | epee**stre**fete **hree**mata |
| (We exchange only.) | (Ανταλλασσουμε μονο.) | anda**la**some **mo**no |

| **Color** | ΧΡΩΜΑ | **HRO**MA |
|---|---|---|
| *I would like something in…* | *Θα ηθελα κατι σε….* | *tha **ee**thela **ka**tee se…* |
| beige | μπεζ | bez |
| black | μαυρο | **ma**vro |
| blue | μπλε | ble |
| brown | καφε | ka**fe** |
| green | πρασινο | **pra**seeno |
| grey | γκριζο | **gree**zo |
| orange | πορτοκαλι | portoka**lee** |

| | | |
|---|---|---|
| pink | ροζ | roz |
| red | κοκκινο | **ko**keeno |
| purple | μοβ | mov |
| white | ασπρο | **as**pro |
| yellow | κιτρινο | **kee**treeno |
| lighter | πιο ανοιχτοχρωμο | pio anee**hto**hromo |
| darker | πιο σκουρο | pio **skoo**ro |
| in a solid color | σε μονοχρωμο | se mo**no**hromo |
| with stripes | με ριγες | me **ree**yes |
| with polka dots | με βουλες | me **voo**les |
| in plaid | καρρω υφασμα | ka**ro** **ee**fasma |
| checked | σε καρρω | se ka**ro** |

| | | |
|---|---|---|
| **Material** | ΥΦΑΣΜΑΤΑ | EE**FAS**MATA |
| *I'd prefer something in…* | *Προτιμω κατι σε…* | *prote**emo** **ka**tee se…* |
| corduroy | κοτλε | ko**tle** |
| cotton | βαμβακι | vam**va**kee |
| gabardine | γκαμπαρτινα | gabar**dee**na |
| jersey | φανελλα | fa**ne**la |
| lace | δαντελα | than**de**la |
| leather | δερμα | **ther**ma |
| linen | λινο | lee**no** |
| satin | σατεν | sa**ten** |
| silk | μεταξωτο | metaxo**to** |
| suede | καστορι | ka**sto**ree |
| synthetic | συνθετικο | seenthetee**ko** |
| velvet | βελουδινο | ve**loo**theeno |
| wool | μαλλινο | **ma**leeno |

| | | |
|---|---|---|
| ***HANDICRAFTS*** noun (adjectives) | *ΧΕΙΡΟΤΕΧΝΙΑ* | *HEEROTEH**NEE**A* |
| clay | πηλος (πηλινο) | pee**los** (**pee**leeno) |
| copper | χαλκος (χαλκινο) | hal**kos** (**hal**keeno) |

| | | |
|---|---|---|
| crystal | κρυσταλλο (κρυσταλλινο) | **kree**stalo (kree**sta**leeno) |
| glass | γυαλι (γυαλινο) | yia**lee** (**yia**leeno) |
| gold | χρυσο | hree**so** |
| jewelry | κοσμηματα | kos**mee**mata |
| lace | δαντελα (δαντελενιο) | than**de**la (thande**le**nio) |
| leather | δερμα (δερματινο) | **ther**ma (ther**ma**teeno) |
| pottery | κεραμεικο | kerame**eko** |
| straw | ψαθα (ψαθινα) | psa**thee** (**psa**theeno) |
| silver | ασημι (ασημενιο) | a**see**me (asee**me**nio) |
| (carved) wood | (σκαλιστο) ξυλο | (skalee**sto**) **xee**lo |
| wrought iron | κατεργασμενο σιδερο | katerga**sme**no **see**thero |
| bracelet | βραχιολι | vra**hio**li |
| candle | κερι (κερινο) | ke**ree** (**ke**reeno) |
| candle holder | κηροπηγιο | keero**pee**yeeo |
| cross | σταυρος | stav**ros** |
| earrings | σκουλαρικια | skoola**ree**kia |
| frame | κορνιζα | kor**nee**za |
| icon | εικονα | ee**ko**na |
| key chain | κρικο κλειδιων | **kree**ko klee**thion** |
| necklace | κολιε | kol**ye** |
| ring | δακτυλιδι | thaktee**lee**thee |
| sculpture | γλυπτο | glee**pto** |
| statue | αγαλμα | **a**galma |
| vase | βαζο | **va**zo |

| | | |
|---|---|---|
| ***NEWSSTAND*** | *ΠΕΡΙΠΤΕΡΟ* | *PE**REE**PTERO* |
| I'm looking for a newsstand. | Ψαχνω για περιπτερο. | **psa**hno yia pe**ree**ptero |

| | | |
|---|---|---|
| *I would like... please.* | *Θα ηθελα... παρακαλω* | *tha **ee**thela... paraka**lo*** |
| an English newspaper | Αγγλικη εφημεριδα | aglee**kee** efeeme**ree**tha |
| a map of the city | χαρτη της πολης | **har**tee tees **po**lees |

| | | |
|---|---|---|
| postcards | καρτ ποσταλ | kartpo**stal** |
| stamps | γραμματοσημα | grama**to**seema |
| an English magazine | Αγγλικο περιοδικο | aglee**ko** pereeotheeko |
| to make a phone call | να τηλεφωνησω | na teelefo**nee**so |
| gum | μαστιχα | **mastee**ha |
| candy | καραμελες | kara**me**les |
| cigarettes<br>(non) filtered | τσιγαρα<br>(χωρις) με φιλτρο | tseegara<br>(ho**rees**) me **feel**tro |
| light cigarettes | ελαφρα τσιγαρα | ela**fra** tsee**ga**ra |
| cigars | πουρα | **poo**ra |
| a lighter | ενα αναπτηρα | **e**na anap**tee**ra |
| matches | σπιρτα | **speer**ta |

| | | |
|---|---|---|
| **STATIONERY** | ΧΑΡΤΟΠΩΛΕΙΟ | HARTOPO**LEE**O |
| *I would like…* | *Θα ηθελα…* | *tha **ee**thela* |
| some envelopes | μερικους φακελους | meree**koos** fa**ke**loos |
| an eraser | μια γομα | **mee**a **go**ma |
| a notebook | σημειωματαριο | seemeoma**ta**reeo |
| a pen | ενα στυλο | **e**na stee**lo** |
| a pencil | ενα μολυβι | **e**na mo**lee**vee |
| a sharpener | μια ξυστρα | **mee**a **xee**stra |
| some stationery | χαρτι αλληλογραφιας | har**tee** aleelogra**fee**as |

| | | |
|---|---|---|
| **CAMERA SHOP** | ΦΩΤΟΓΡΑΦΕΙΟ | FOTOGRA**FEE**O |
| *I want…* | *Θελω…* | ***the**lo…* |
| a battery (some batteries) | μια μπαταρια<br>(μερικες μπαταριες) | **mee**a bata**ree**a<br>(meree**kes** bata**ree**es) |
| black and white/color film | ασπρομαυρο / εγχρωμο φιλμ | as**pro**mavro / **en**hromo film |
| a video tape | κασετα βιντεο | ka**se**ta **vee**deo |
| Hi 8 tape | κασετα για Hi 8 βιντεο | ka**se**ta yia Hi 8 **vee**deo |

| | | |
|---|---|---|
| May I have this developed? | Μπορειτε να το εμφανισετε; | bo**ree**te na to emfa**nee**sete |

| | | |
|---|---|---|
| How much does this cost? | Ποσο στοιχιζει; | **po**so stee**hee**zee |
| When will it be ready? | Ποτε θα ειναι ετοιμο; | **po**te tha **ee**ne **e**teemo |

| **TOILETRIES** | ΕΙΔΗ ΤΟΥΑΛΕΤΑΣ | **EE**THEE TOOA**LE**TAS |
|---|---|---|
| *I would like…* | *Θα ηθελα…* | *tha **ee**thela* |
| a brush | μια βουρτσα | **meea vroo**tsa |
| a cleanser | κρεμα προσωπου | **kre**ma pro**so**poo |
| a comb | μια χτενα | **meea hte**na |
| condoms | προφυλαχτικα | profeelahtee**ka** |
| deodorant | αποσμητικο | aposmeetee**ko** |
| diapers | πανες | **pa**nes |
| feminine napkins | σερβιετες | ser**vie**tes |
| headache medicine | παυσιπονο για τον πονοκεφαλο | paf**see**pono ia ton pono**ke**falo |
| razor blades | ξυριστικη λεπιδα | xeereestee**kee** le**pee**tha |
| a razor | ξυραφι | xee**ra**fee |
| shampoo | σαμπουαν | sampoo**an** |
| shaving cream | κρεμα ξυρισματος | **kre**ma xee**ree**smatos |
| soap | σαπουνι | sa**poo**nee |
| (lotion for) sunburn | κρεμα για εγκαυμα | **kre**ma yia **en**kavma |
| suntan lotion | κρεμα για ηλιοθεραπεια/ (αντιηλιακο) | **kre**ma yia eeliothera**pee**a (andeeeelia**ko** |
| tampons | ταμπον | tam**pon** |
| a toothbrush | οδοντοβουρτσα | othon**do**vrootsa |
| some toothpaste | οδοντοπαστα | othon**do**pasta |

| **BOOKSTORE** | ΒΙΒΛΙΟΠΩΛΕΙΟ | VEEVLEEOPO**LEE**O |
|---|---|---|
| *I need…* | *Χρειαζομεαι…* | *hree**a**zome…* |
| a city map | χαρτη της πολης | har**tee** tees **po**lees |
| an English-Greek dictionary | Αγγλο–Ελληνικο λεξικο | agloeleenee**ko** lexee**ko** |
| an English guide book | Αγγλικο οδηγο | αγλεεκο οτηεεγο |

| | | |
|---|---|---|
| an English magazine | Αγγλικο περιοδικο | agleeko pereeotheeko |
| an English novel | Αγγλικο μυθιστορημα | agleeko meetheestoreema |
| a road map | οδικο χαρτη | otheeko hartee |

| **MUSIC** | ΜΟΥΣΙΚΗ | MOOSEEKEE |
|---|---|---|
| *I'd like to buy...* | *Θα ηθελα να αγορασω...* | *tha eethela na agoraso* |
| a cassette | μια κασετα | meea kaseta |
| a CD | ενα CD | ena CD |
| *Where is the... section?* | *Που ειναι το τμημα. για..* | *poo eene to tmeema yia* |
| classical music | κλασσικη μουσικη | klaseekee mooseekee |
| folk Greek music | λαικη Ελληνικη μουσικη | laeekee eleeneekee mooseekee |
| the latest hits | μοντερνα μουσικη | moderna mooseekee |
| jazz music | τζαζ | jazz |
| modern Greek music | μοντερνα Ελληνικη μουσικη | moderna eleeneekee mooseekee |

CHAPTER ELEVEN

# Sightseeing

Greece is a treasure trove for sightseers. From ancient amphitheaters, some of which are still in use like Επιδαυρος (e**pee**thavros), to old churches carved into caves, and medieval castles (καστρο - kastro) still in tact, there are hundreds of historical sites to visit!

Natural spectacles such as huge caves with awesome stalactites and stalagmites, or the butterfly gardens in Rhodes (Ροδος - **Ro**thos) can be found.

Take a bus tour that leaves from major centers and visit the many fascinating sites, or take a boat cruise to the islands and maybe go island hopping! There is never a lack of something to pique the mind and the imagination. And if you just want to relax (and in some places literally let it all hang out), there are many, many beaches, each with its own character.

| | | |
|---|---|---|
| Where is…? | Που ειναι…; | poo **ee**ne |
| How do you get to…? | Πως πανε στον (στη/στο)…; | poo **pa**ne ston (steen/sto) |
| I'm lost. | Εχω χαθει. | **e**ho ha**thee** |
| Can you point out… for me? | Μπορειτε να μου δειξετε το..; | bor**ee**te na moo **thee**xete to |
| Where is the tourist information office? | Που ειναι το τουριστικο γραφειο; | poo **ee**ne to tooreestee**ko** graf**ee**o |
| Are there tours of the city? | Εχετε περιηγηση της πολης; | **e**hete peree-**ee**yeesee tees **po**lees |
| I need an English speaking guide. | Χρειαζομαι Αγγλοφωνο ξεναγο. | hree**a**zome a**glo**fono xena**go** |

| | | |
|---|---|---|
| *How much...?* | *Ποσο...;* | ***poso**...* |
| per hour | την ωρα | teen **o**ra |
| for the day | για την ημερα | yia teen ee**me**ra |
| We would like to see the city. | Θελουμε να δουμε την πολη. | **the**lome na **thoo**me teen **po**lee |
| Is there a tour to...? | Εχετε ξεναγηση για...; | **e**hete xe**na**yeesee yia... |
| When does the tour leave? | Τι ωρα αναχωρει το προγραμμα ξεναγησηs; | tee ora anaho**ree** to **pro**grama xe**na**yeesees |
| How long is the tour? | Ποσο διαρκει η ξεναγηση; | **po**so thiar**kee** ee xe**na**yeesee |
| There are four of us. | Ειμαστε τεσσεριs. | **ee**maste **te**serees |
| Where does the tour start? | Ποτε αρχιζει η ξεναγηση; | **po**te ar**hee**zee ee xe**na**yeesee |
| What's included in the tour? | Τι συμπεριλαμβανετε στη ξεναγηση | tee seempereelam**va**nete steen xe**na**yeesee |
| When do we return? | Ποτε γυριζουμε; | **po**te yee**ree**zome |

## *REPLIES*

| | | |
|---|---|---|
| *Παρε...* | ***pa**re...* | *Take...* |
| το νουμερο... (λεωφορειο) | to **noo**mero... (leofo**ree**o) | number... (bus) |
| τον υπογειο | ton ee**po**yeeo | the subway |
| το τραινο | to **tre**no | the train |
| το καραβι που παει στο... | to ka**ra**vee poo **pa**ee sto... | the boat that goes to... |
| Δε πατε στην σωστη κατευθυνση. | then **pa**te steen so**stee** ka**tef**theensee | You're not going in the right direction. |
| (Δεν) Μπορειτε να περπατησετε απ'εδω. | (then) bo**ree**te na perpa**tee**sete ap'e**tho** | You (can't) can walk from here. |
| Δεν εχει λεωφορειο που παει εκεί. | then **e**hee leofo**ree**o poo **pa**ee e**kee** | There is no bus that goes there. |
| Δεν ξερω. | then **xe**ro | I don't know. |
| Θα σας δειξω. | tha sas **thee**xo | I'll show you. |

| *Ειναι…* | ***eene…*** | *It's…* |
|---|---|---|
| αριστερα | areeste**ra** | left |
| δεξια | the**xia** | right |
| διπλα στο | **thee**pla sto | next to |
| απεναντι απο | a**pe**nadee a**po** | across from |
| στο δρομο | sto **thro**mo | on the street |
| στην γωνια | steen go**neea** | on the corner |
| στην διασταυρωση | steen thia**sta**vrosee | at the intersection |
| μπροστα στο… | bro**sta** sto… | in front of |
| πισω απο το | **pee**so a**po** to | behind |
| στον επομενο δρομο | ston e**po**meno **thro**mo | on the next street |
| μετα τα φωτα | me**ta** ta **fo**ta | after the lights |
| περιπου πεντε λεπτα… | pe**ree**poo **pen**de le**pta** | about five minute |
| περπατωντας | perpa**ton**das | walk |
| με το αυτοκινητο | me to afto**kee**neeto | by car |
| κοντα | kon**da** | near |
| μακρυα | makree**a** | far |
| ισια απ'εδω | **ee**sia ap'e**tho** | straight ahead |

## Mini dictionary

| | | |
|---|---|---|
| abbey | μονη | mo**nee** |
| amphitheater | αμφιθεατρο | amfee**the**atro |
| art gallery | πινακοθηκη | peenako**thee**kee |
| botanical gardens | βοτανικους κηπους | votanee**koos** **kee**poos |
| castle | καστρο | **ka**stro |
| catacomb | κατακομβες | kata**kom**ves |
| caverns | σπηλιες | spee**lies** |
| church | εκκλησια | eklee**seea** |
| convent | μονη γυναικων | mo**nee** yeene**kon** |
| downtown area | στο κεντρο της πολης | sto **ken**dro tees **po**lees |
| fortress | φρουριο | **froo**reeo |

| | | |
|---|---|---|
| fountains | συντριβανι | seendree**va**nee |
| harbor | λιμανι | lee**ma**nee |
| historic sites | ιστορικους τοπους | eestoree**koos to**poos |
| library | βιβλιοθηκη | veevleeo**thee**kee |
| monastery | μοναστηρι | mona**stee**ree |
| monument | μνημειο | mnee**mee**o |
| museum... | μουσειο... | moo**see**o... |
| archeological | αρχαιολογικο | arheoloyee**ko** |
| of art | καλων τεχνων | **ka**l**on** teh**non** |
| of folk art | λαικης τεχνης | laee**kees teh**nees |
| palace | παλατι | pa**la**tee |
| ruins | ερειπια | e**ree**peea |
| square | πλατεια | pla**tee**a |
| statue | αγαλμα | **a**galma |
| temple | ναο | na**o** |
| tomb | ταφο | **ta**fo |
| university | πανεπιστημιο | panepee**stee**meeo |
| zoo | ζωολογικος κηπος | zooloyee**kos kee**pos |

### *ADMISSION*

| | | |
|---|---|---|
| May we enter? | Μπορουμε να μπουμε. | bo**roo**me na **boo**me |
| Is it open/closed? | Ειναι ανοιχτο/κλειστο; | **ee**ne anee**hto**/klee**sto** |
| Is there an admission fee? | Εχετε εισιτηριο εισοδου; | ehete **ee**sothoo eesee**tee**reeo |
| How much is the admission fee? | Ποσο ειναι το εισητηριο; | **po**so **ee**ne to eesee**tee**ree |
| *Is there a discount for...?* | *Εχετε εκπτωση για...;* | ***e**hete **ek**ptosee yia...* |
| students (in university) | μαθητες (φοιτητες) | mathee**tes** (feetee**tes**) |
| children | παιδια (ανηλικους) | pe**thia** (a**nee**leekoos) |
| seniors | ηλικιωμενους | eeleekio**me**noos |
| Are there any pamphlets? | Εχετε φυλλαδια; | **e**hete fee**la**theea |
| Do you have any souvenirs? | Πουλατε ενθυμια; | poo**la**te en**thee**meea |

### *PHOTOGRAPHY*

| | | |
|---|---|---|
| Can we take pictures? | Μπορουμε να παρουμε φωτογραφιες; | bo**roo**me na **pa**rome fotogra**fies** |
| I won't use flash. | Δεν θα χρησιμοποιησω φλαs. | bo**ro** na hreeseemo-peee**e**so flash. |
| Can you take our picture? | Μπορειτε να μαs βγαλετε μια φωτογραφια; | Bo**ree**te na mas **uga**lete **mee**a fotogra**fee**a |
| One more shot please. | Ακομα μια παρακαλω. | a**ko**ma **mee**a paraka**lo** |
| Can I use a video camera? | Μπορω να χρησημο–ποιησω την βιντε οκαμερα; | bo**ro** na hreeseemopee-**ee**so teen veedeo**ka**mera |

CHAPTER TWELVE

# Emergencies

| | | |
|---|---|---|
| **DIAL 100!** | ΕΚΑΤΟ | **ΕΚΑΤΟ** |
| Help. | Βοηθεια. | vo**ee**theea |
| I need help. | Χρειαζομαι βοηθεια. | hree**a**zome vo**ee**theea |
| This is an emergency. | Ειναι επειγον. | **ee**ne e**pee**gon |
| There has been an accident. | Εχει γινει ατυχημα. | **e**hee **yee**nee a**tee**heema |
| He needs a doctor. | Χρειαζεται γιατρο. | hree**a**zete yia**tro** |
| She needs a dentist. | Χρειαζεται οδοντιατρο. | hree**a**zete othon**dee**atro |
| We are hurt. | Ειμαστε τραυματισμενοι. | **ee**maste travmatees**me**nee |
| Do you speak English? | Μιλατε Αγγλικα; | mee**la**te aglee**ka** |
| Where is the nearest hospital? | Που ειναι το πιο κοντινο νοσοκομειο; | poo **ee**ne to pio konde**eno** nosoko**meeo** |
| Where is the doctor's office? | Που ειναι το ιατρειο; | poo **ee**ne to eea**treeo** |
| Where is the dentist's office? | Που ειναι το ιατρειο του οδοντιατρου; | poo **ee**ne to yia**tree**o too othondoeea**troo** |
| I (don't) have medical insurance. | (Δεν) εχω ιατρικη περιθαλψη. | (then) **e**ho eeatree**kee** per**ee**thalpsee |
| My insurance number is... | Το νουμερο ασφαλειας μου ειναι... | to **noo**mero as**fa**leeas moo **ee**ne... |
| My name is... | Το ονομα μου ειναι... | to **o**noma moo **ee**ne... |
| I'm staying at... | Μενω στο... | **me**no sto... |

| | | |
|---|---|---|
| The phone number is… | Ο αριθμος τηλεφωνου μου ειναι… | o areeth**mos** teele**fo**noo moo **ee**ne… |
| My date of birth is… | Η ημερομηνια γεννησεως μου ειναι… | ee eemeromee**nee**a ye**nee**seos moo **ee**ne… |

## Mini dictionary

| *My… hurts.* | *…μου ποναει.* | *…moo po**na**ee* |
|---|---|---|
| ankle | ο αστραγαλος | o **a**s**tra**galos |
| arm | το μπρατσο | to **bra**tso |
| back | η πλατη | ee **pla**tee |
| bone(s) | το κοκαλο (τα κοκαλα) | to **ko**kalo (ta **ko**kala) |
| breast | ο μαστος | o mas**tos** |
| chest | το στηθος | to **stee**thos |
| ear | το αυτι | to af**tee** |
| elbow | ο αγκωνας | o **an**gonas |
| eye(s) | το ματι (τα ματια) | to **ma**tee |
| face | το προσωπο | to **pro**sopo |
| finger | το δακτυλο | to **thak**teelo |
| foot | το ποδι | to **po**thee |
| gums | τα ουλα | ta **oo**la |
| hand | το χερι | to **he**ree |
| head | το κεφαλι | to kefa**lee** |
| kidneys | τα νεφρα | ta ne**fra** |
| knee | το γονατο | to **go**nato |
| leg | το ποδι | to **po**thee |
| lungs | τα πνευμονια | ta pnev**mo**nia |
| mouth | το στομα | to **sto**ma |
| muscles | οι μυς | ee mees |
| neck | ο λαιμος | o le**mos** |
| nose | η μυτη | ee **mee**tee |
| penis | το πεος | to **pe**os |

| | | |
|---|---|---|
| ribs | τα πλευρα | ta plev**ra** |
| skin | το δερμα | to **ther**ma |
| shoulder | ο ωμος | o **o**mos |
| spine | η σπονδυλικη στηλη | ee spontheelee**kee** **stee**lee |
| stomach | το στομαχι | to sto**ma**hee |
| testicles | οι ορχιδες | ee ar**hee**thes |
| throat | ο λαιμος | o le**mos** |
| toe | το δακτυλο του ποδιου | to **thak**teelo too po**thioo** |
| tongue | η γλωσσα | ee **glo**sa |
| tooth | το δοντι | to **thon**dee |
| vagina | ο κολπος | o **kol**pos |
| wrist | ο καρπος | o kar**pos** |

## *WHAT'S WRONG?*

| *I have…* | *Εχω…* | ***e**ho…* |
|---|---|---|
| a blister | μια φουσκαλα | **mee**a foo**ska**la |
| a bump | κτυπημα | **ktee**peema |
| a cut | κοπει | ko**pee** |
| chills | κρυαδες | kree**a**thes |
| a cold | κρυολογημα | kreeo**lo**yeema |
| a (bronchile) cough | βρογχικο βηχα | vronhee**ko** **vee**ha |
| diarrhea | διαρροια | thia**ree**a |
| a fever | πυρετο | peere**to** |
| the flu | γριππη | **gree**pee |
| hayfever | αλλεργικο συναχι | aleryee**ko** see**na**hee |
| a headache | πονοκεφαλο | pono**ke**falo |
| heartburn | καουρα | ka**oo**ra |
| an itch | φαγουρα | fa**yoo**ra |
| a lump | ενα εξογκωμα | **e**na **ex**ongoma |
| nausea | αναγουλα | ana**yoo**la |

| | | |
|---|---|---|
| a rash | εξανθημα | **exan**theema |
| a swelling | πρηξιμο | **pree**xeemo |
| a sunburn | εγκαυμα ηλιομ | **en**kavma ee**leeo** |
| sunstroke | ηλιαση | ee**lee**asee |
| a wound | τραυμα | **tra**vma |
| I'm having trouble breathing. | Δυσκολευομαι να αναπνευσω. | theesko**le**vome na ana**pnef**so |
| I think I'm having a heart attack. | Νομιζω πως επαθα καρδιακη προσβολη. | no**mee**zo pos **e**patha karthia**kee** prosvo**lee** |
| He's lost a lot of blood. | Εχασε πολυ αιμα. | **e**hase po**lee** **e**ma |
| I'm very tired. | Ειμαι πολυ κουρασμεν(os/η). | **ee**me po**lee** kooras**men**(os/ee) |
| I'm pregnant. | Ειμαι εγκυοs. | **ee**me **en**geeos |
| I feel dizzy. | Αισθανομαι ζαλαδεs. | es**tha**nome za**la**thes |
| I feel very ill. | Αισθανομαι πολυ ασχημα. | es**tha**nome po**lee** **as**heema |
| I broke a tooth. | Εσπασα δοντι. | **e**spasa **thon**dee |
| I lost a filling. | Εχασα ενα σφραγισμα. | **e**hase **e**na **sfra**yeesma |
| *I've had this problem for…* | *Εχω αυτο το προβλημα…* | *eho **af**to to **pro**vleema…* |
| a day | μια μερα | **meea** **me**ra |
| three days | τρειs μερεs | trees **me**res |
| a few days | μερικεs μερεs | meree**kes** **me**res |
| I'm diabetic | Ειμαι διαβητικ(os/η) | **ee**me thiaveeteek**(os/ee)** |
| *I'm allergic to…* | *Ειμαι αλλεργικ(os/η)…* | *eeme alleryeek**(os/ee)*** |
| antibiotics | στα αντιβιοτικα | sta anteeveeotee**ka** |
| penicillin | στην πενικιλινη | steen peneekee**lee**nee |

## What you may hear

| | | |
|---|---|---|
| Ποσο χρονων εισαι; | **po**so hro**non** **ee**se | How old are you? |
| Που πονάει; | poo po**naee** | Where does it hurt? |
| Τι ειναι το προβλημα; | tee **ee**ne to **pro**vleema | What is the problem? |
| Γδυθειτε, παρακαλω. | gthee**thee**te paraka**lo** | Undress, please. |
| Παιρνετε φαρμακα; | **per**nete **far**maka | Are you on medication? |
| Ποια; | pia | Which ones? |
| Εχετε αλλεργιες; | **e**hete aler**yee**es | Do you have allergies? |
| Σε τι; | se tee | To what? |
| Αναπνευστε βαθια. | ana**pnef**ste va**thia** | Breathe deeply. |
| Βηξε. | **vee**xe | Cough. |
| (Δεν) Ειναι σπασμενο. | (then) **ee**ne spa**sme**no | It (isn't) is broken. |
| Ειναι ραγισμενο. | **ee**ne rayee**sme**no | It's fractured. |
| Ειναι στραμπουλιγμενο. | **ee**ne strambooleeg**me**no | It's sprained. |
| Δεν ειναι σοβαρο. | then **ee**ne sova**ro** | It's not serious. |
| Θα σου δωσω ενεση. | tha soo **tho**so **e**nesee | I'll give a needle. |
| Θα κανω αναλυση… | tha **ka**no ana**lee**see… | I'll run a…analysis. |
| αιματος | **e**matos | blood |
| ουρων | **oo**ron | urine |
| Θα παρω ακτινογραφια. | tha **pa**ro akteenogra**fee**a | I'll take an X-ray. |
| Θα το δεσω. | tha to **the**so | I'll bind it. |
| Θα το σφραγισω. | tha to sfra**yee**so | I'll fill it. |
| Θα σου δωσω συνταγη. | tha soo **tho**so seeta**yee** | I'll give you a prescription. |
| Καθειστε στο κρεβατι για… | ka**thee**ste sto kreva**tee** yia | Stay in bed for… |
| δυο μερες | **theeo** **me**res | two days |
| μια εβδομαδα | **mee**a evtho**ma**tha | a week |

| *Γυριστε…* | *yee**ree**ste* | *Return…* |
|---|---|---|
| αυριο | **a**vreeo | tomorrow |
| σε δυο μερες | se **thee**o **me**res | in two days |
| την αλλη εβδομαδα | teen **a**lee evtho**ma**tha | next week |

| ***AT THE PHARMACY*** | *ΣΤΟ ΦΑΡΜΑΚΕΙΟ* | *sto farma**kee**o* |
|---|---|---|
| *I would like something for…* | *Θελω κατι για…* | ***the**lo **ka**tee yia…* |
| a burn | καψιμο | **kap**seemo |
| a cold | κρυολογημα | kreeo**lo**yeema |
| constipation | δυσκοιλιοτητα | theeskee**lio**teeta |
| corns | καλους | **ka**loos |
| cough | βηχα | **vee**ha |
| diarrhea | διαρροια | thi**a**reea |
| fever | πυρετο | peere**to** |
| hayfever | αλλεργικο συναχι | aleryee**ko** **vee**ha |
| headache | πονοκεφαλο | pono**ke**falo |
| indigestion | δυσπεψια | theespe**psee**a |
| sea(motion)sickness | ναυτια | naf**tee**a |
| stomach ache | πονοκοιλο | po**no**keelo |
| a sore throat | ερεθισμενο λαιμο | eretheesm**e**no le**mo** |
| sunburn | ηλιοκαμα | ee**lio**kama |
| a tooth ache | πονοδοντο | po**no**thondo |

## Mini dictionary

| *I'd like…* | *Θελω…* | ***the**lo…* |
|---|---|---|
| an antacid | κατι για ξινιλες | **ka**tee yia xee**nee**les |
| some antiseptic | αντισηπτικο | anteeseeptee**ko** |
| some aspirin | ασπιρινη | aspee**ree**nee |
| some band-aids* | μερικα μπαντ–ειντ* | meree**ka** band-aid |
| a bandage | μερικους επιδεσμους | meree**koos** epee**thes**moos |

* There is no generic term for band-aids in Greek. The Greeks usually refer to a specific brand name.

| | | |
|---|---|---|
| contact lens solution | υγρο για φακους επαφης | ee**gro** yia fa**koos** epa**fees** |
| some cough syrup | σιροπι του βηχα | see**ro**pee too **vee**ha |
| ear drops | σταγονες για το αυτι | sta**go**nes yia to af**tee** |
| eye drops | σταγονες για το ματι | sta**go**nes yia to **ma**tee |
| eye glasses | γυαλια | yia**lia** |
| iodine | ιωδιο | ee**o**theeo |
| a laxative | καθαρσιο | **ka**thar**see**o |
| some ointment | αλοιφη | alee**fee** |

## *POLICE*

| | | |
|---|---|---|
| Help! | Βοηθεια! | vo**ee**theea |
| Fire! | Φωτια! | fo**tia** |
| Stop him (her)! | Σταματα τον (την)! | sta**ma**ta ton(teen) |
| Call the police! | Φωναξτε την αστυνομια! | fo**na**xte teen asteeno**mee**a |
| Call the ambulance! | Φωναξτε ασθενοφορο! | fo**na**xte astheno**fo**ro |

| | | |
|---|---|---|
| *I've lost my...* | *Εχασα..* | ***e**hasa...* |
| *My... was stolen.* | *...μου εχει (εχουν) κλαπει.* | ...moo **e**hee(**e**hoon) **e** kla**pe** |
| camera | η φωτογραφικη μηχανη | ee fotografee**kee** meeha**nee** |
| car keys | τα κλειδια αυτοκινητου | ta klee**thia** aftokee**nee**too |
| credit card | η(οι) πιστωτικη(ες) καρτα(ες) | ee peestotee**kee(es)** **kar**ta(es) |
| handbag | η τσαντα | ee **tsan**da |
| identification | η ταυτοτητα | ee taf**to**teeta |
| jewelry | τα κοσμηματα | ta kos**mee**mata |
| money | τα χρηματα | ta **hree**mata |

| | | |
|---|---|---|
| passport | το διαβατηριο | ta thiavat**ee**reeo |
| suitcase | η βαλιτσα | ee val**ee**dza |
| traveller's cheques | οι ταξιδιωτικες επιταγες | ee taxeethiotee**kes** epeeta**yes** |
| wallet | το πορτοφολι | to porto**fo**lee |
| watch | το ρολοι | to ro**lo**ee |
| *Someone broke into…* | *Καποιος διαρρηξε…* | ***ka**pios thia**ree**xe…* |
| my room | το δωματιο | to tho**ma**teeo |
| my car | το αυτοκινητο | to afto**kee**neeto |
| I've been attacked | Μου εχουν επιτεθει | moo **e**hoon epeete**thee** |
| I've been robbed | Εχω ληστευτει | **e**ho leestef**tee** |
| Leave me alone! | Αφησε με ησυχ(ο/η). | **a**feese me **ee**seeh (o/ee) |
| Don't touch me! | Μη μΠαγγιζεις. | mee m'a**gee**zees |
| He's (she's) following me. | Με παρακολουθει. | me parakoloo**thee** |
| Get your hands off me! | Κατω το ξερα σου! | **ka**to ta xe**ra** soo |
| I'll call the police! | Θα φωναξω την αστυνομια | tha fo**na**xo teen asteeno**mee**a |

# Emergency Card

A crisis can reduce us to babbling unintelligibly even in our first language. Dealing with serious problems in a language we are just "trying on" is even more stressful. Complete this emergency card and keep a copy in your wallet with your ID.

Name: ______________________________

surname/ first name (επωνυμο/ονομα)

Address ______________________________

number/ street (νουμερο/οδος)

______________________________

(city/postal code/province (πολης/ταχυδρομικος κωδικας/επαρχια)

Telephone number: ______________ Blood type (ομαδα αιματος): ______

(νουμερο τωλεφωνου)

Health card number (νουμερο καρτας υγειας) ______________

Medical insurance company and policy number: ______________

(Εταιρια ιατρικης περιθαλψης και ασφαλιστικο νουμερο):

______________________________

Traveller's insurance company and policy number : ______________

(Ταξιδιωτικη ασφαλεια υγειας και ασφαλιστικο νουμερο)

______________________________

Allergies (αλλεργιες): ______________

Other medical conditions: ______________

(αλλες ασθενειες)

Medications (φαρμακα): ______________

**Person to contact in case of emergency/** (Προσωπο να ειδοποιηθει σε περιπτωση αναγκης)

Name: ______________________________

surname/ first name (επωνυμο/ονομα)

Address ______________________________

number/ street (νουμερο/οδος)

______________________________

(city/postal code/province (πολης/ταχυδρομικος κωδικας/ επαρχια)

Telephone number (νουμερο τηλεφωνου): ______________

# STONE COLD MORTAL

## A Tennessee England Novel: Book One

DISA DAWN

Yesternight Press, LLC
*Washington*

Cover Design by J Caleb @ jcalebdesign.com

Headshot Photo by Marie Pham @ mariephamphotography.com



For information, address:

Yesternight Press, LLC PO Box 831 Woodland, WA 98674

Or visit: disadawn.com

Ebook ISBN: 978-1-947411-02-9

Print ISBN: 978-1-947411-03-6

For Big Vic, the original Godzilla
Rest in Peace, bro

# 1.

# Side Hustle

Tennessee skidded the family hearse into its beachfront slot, shifting the rusted, dented, neglected thing into park before coming to a complete stop. She stomped the emergency brake then slid out of Riggy Morty, juggling her breakfast, backpack, and cell phone. She was already late, and her favorite barista was MIA, which meant wasted time explaining her usual to the new girl who couldn't work the register much less make a decent mindbender: six shots espresso drenched in steamed coconut cream, layered with salted caramel, cocoa, and amaretto, topped with whip and a drizzle of pure vanilla. What the hell was difficult about *that*?!

Tennessee gulped the sad attempt. She might have cussed had she been brought up differently; instead, she turned toward the Pacific, inhaling the salted midwinter air, crisp with potential. Knowing that all this was hers almost made up for the crappy mindbender. And it *was* hers. The parking lot, the mortuary, the sand and sea, even the damn seagull shit.

Tennessee tossed her keys lightly in her hand until the right one shook loose. She got the deadbolt unlocked as her cell phone clanked out "Bitch" by Meredith Brooks. The song put a snarl on Tennessee's face. She shoved her way into the mortuary, threw her backpack and keys onto the couch before slogging over to the

mini refreshment bar set out for buyers and mourners. She let the call go to voicemail, brewed a pot of coffee, popped the lid off her mindbender, found the sugar, and poured.

When "Bitch" started up again, she put the phone on speaker and smiled so her voice would sound less...well, bitchy.

"Good morning, Lillie." Tennessee dunked a finger into her coffee then plunged it in her mouth. Not even close. She grabbed a spoon, stirred, poured in more sugar.

A terse tone screeched through the speaker, as if she'd had this particular conversation one too many times.

"Deliver Santa to my house by six tonight or else, Tennessee!"

"Or else what, Lillie? Someone dies?" Tennessee chuckled, then paused to sip her coffee. Better, but not great. "Death is good for business, Lillie. I just got a new shipment of boxes, real beauties...etched mahogany, all the bells and whistles. Literally, there's a bell, you know, in case it's a mistaken burial...oh, how I miss them good ol' days."

"I'm not in the mood, Tennessee! Santa! Six! Tonight!"

It was too damn early to deal with Lillie. "I've got poor Mrs. Honeycomb to box, another body on ice, and two tissue-fests this week, Lillie, so dump your champagne problems on someone else!"

Lillie was accustomed to Tennessee's abrasiveness; most upbringings were *beneath* Lillie's, and such boorish behavior was to be expected. But Lillie Saint James wasn't just spoiled, she was smart.

"I read the obits too, Tennessee. You need *my* money to pay *your* rent. I'll settle this month and next *if* you deliver Santa."

Tennessee reached for the tiny silver cross dangling from her silver necklace. She rubbed the charm between her thumb and forefinger, forcing a pleasant smile, which usually helped her produce a pleasing tone essential for thwarting bitches. "Santa, you say?"

"That's right. The twins have been exceptional this week. Oh, and...you're welcome, Tennessee."

If Lillie paid attention to such things, she would have heard Tennessee's teeth clank shut as she held in a curse she knew would only come back to haunt her. Tennessee inhaled deeply before resetting her smile and responding in her most sincere tone, which years of practice had scrubbed clean of lingering sarcasm.

"Thank you, Lillie. See you at six."

Even the click of Lillie ending the call sounded smug.

Tennessee walked out the front door.

Screamed.

Walked back in.

~

Tracking down a Santa Claus in the dead of February who *hasn't* shaved his mustache and beard takes the kind of street savvy most party planners sorely lack, but Tennessee England knew a guy for most things legal, and all things not.

Pacing her family's spacious mortuary, she swiped her cell phone, considering each contact as if studying the backstories of congressional candidates. She was conscientious like that, even took her voting rights seriously, almost as seriously as hiring staff. She didn't do lazy, reckless, ruthless, or renegade. Follow her rules or get the hell out. And if you broke those rules and happened to die, well, you wouldn't be welcomed at Englands' Mortuary; that was Tennessee's one nonnegotiable. She'd stay in Saint James, help her parents, *only* if they refused whomever she had refused in life. It was a little grudge-holding, but mostly it was spiritual. Preparing a body for death was an intimate exchange of empathy, vulnerability, and respect; if Tennessee couldn't muster that for the living, she sure as hell couldn't muster it for the dead. Condemning anyone to that many hours of her unpleasantness just wasn't nice.

The name *England* was well-respected throughout the death industry, in country and abroad. There were once three Englands in the town of Saint James: Mister, Missus, and Tennessee. For as long as there were three, the family operated the lone mortuary

and crematorium on this tight-knit, blue-collar stretch of the Pacific Coast; smashed somewhere between Oregon and Washington, or was it California? Saint James wasn't on any map; the town paid extra for that. It was a slippery sort of town; took a stumble and two wrong turns to find.

The Englands made a living caring for the dead, not much above that. Everything about the Englands was modest: their dress, their speech, even the cars they drove, all rust buckets like Riggy, except for one pristine black hearse parked in the only covered slot located across the street, right next to Lin Min's House of Beauty.

Lin didn't mind. Tennessee was her best customer, and only she could calm Tennessee's frizz of a mane.

"You ethnic?" Lin had asked before names were exchanged.

"You betcha."

"Black?"

"Mixed Pacific Islander."

"Yeah, yeah, black. I do your hair like black woman. You have black woman hair."

Tennessee just laughed, and the two were best friends ever since.

Swiping over another set of deadbeats on her phone, Tennessee stepped outside to have a smoke before Lillie got there. The bitch always followed up a verbal contract with a personal visit. Ah, the life of a socialite. She was glad she wore her oldest pair of ripped jeans and her faded heather grey t-shirt with a peeling iron-on image of Strawberry Shortcake; the original, totally rad version with a red dress and green-and-white-striped tights.

Lillie would *hate* it.

From across the street, Lin paced the sidewalk, screaming into her cell phone; a sweet mix of her native tongue and urban ghetto. The *piff-paff* of her tiny wedged heels filled the silence when she was listening, not arguing, and her sky-blue dress fluttered under her tangerine, ruffled apron.

When the lady was done using very unladylike words, she

waved to Tennessee and hollered, "You suck cancer stick, you die!"

Tennessee motioned toward the building behind her. "You cross street, you die! Mrs. Honeycomb is this week's proof."

Tennessee was right. For the town's size, there was a disturbing amount of pedestrian deaths. Lin cursed in several languages before leaving Tennessee's bad habits for future lectures. "You come in at lunch hour...your hair ugly today!"

"Tomorrow. I gotta sip champagne and cosplay Mrs. Claus tonight, so ugly is perfect."

Lin grabbed the hand-tied straw broom her mother insisted would bring luck, but the thing was so short that even tiny Lin had to stoop over just to use it. "I do perma then weave...fit you in afta!" she ordered, sweeping bad juju from the concrete sidewalk.

"Lin, I like my ugly."

"No good for me, Tennessee! People see you *here* think I give ugly. I no give ugly!"

Tennessee cracked up, and Lin couldn't help but do the same.

"Layin' it on thick this morning." Tennessee flicked her cig before taking another long drag.

Lin smiled, a perfect crescent of pale pink lips on a tiny face of porcelain dipped in dayshine. Then with curious eyes that held their secrets close she declared in the crystalized tone of a woman educated at Stanford, "An unnecessarily lengthy conversation with Mother last night. I honor her today with my very best *every*-Asian impersonation."

"Ah, I thought maybe another social experiment."

"The empirical evidence holds up, Ness. A deeply pronounced accent is directly correlated to an increase in gratuity. And I could use the tips!"

Tennessee smiled, a less perfect crescent of dark brown lips. Her skin held a caramelized tan of summer year-round that paired well with her chestnut eyes *before* she smudged coal-black eyeliner all around them. She wasn't tall, only so-so fit, and bore the strong, soft traits of a woman made for womanhood.

"We still on for dinner tomorrow?"

Lin stopped sweeping, taking time to un-crick her back before standing upright. "If you like duckbill soup over rice noodle."

"Oh god, is your father coming, too? And so soon after you spat on your ancestors by denying the most eligible Mr. Won your hand in holy hell?"

You'd think such a tiny thing would have a tiny laugh, but Lin's joyous outbursts were like mini volcanic eruptions dancing with thunder. "Just Mother. Father say, 'Girl with no sense worth nothing.' So, Ness, I am to come to my senses, and that's about as likely as you quitting the cancer stick."

"You never know," Tennessee lifted her foot, killed the cig on the sole of her boot, then inspected the snuffed-out butt, "the habit's getting too elite for me."

A sedan carrying Lin's next cut and color pulled into the parking lot.

"Save your money, Ness. Let me fix your hair tomorrow then come to dinner. I can't be alone with Mother." Lin hurried inside, waving her tiny broom overhead.

Tennessee waved back as a brigade of goose bumps scaled her forearms; there wasn't even a breeze. She glanced left, right, caught a glimpse of a man walking toward the back of the mortuary. Sometimes locals took a shortcut to the beach that way, but he vibed odd and he wasn't carrying a surfboard.

"Hey, private property, dude!" she called out, then muttered about the rise in townie tweakers, leisurely turning her attention back to the mortuary sidewalk. It was a sandy, slippery mess. She looked around for a broom, but found only beach grass, rocks, weeds, and more sand. Maybe she'd ask Mamma Min for one of those midget broomsticks. Until then, mourners beware.

Lin complained about her family, but Mamma Min's meddlesome ways always made Tennessee ache for her own parents. She gazed back out to sea, surveying the natural barrier of rock and beach grass that protected the businesses along Old Town from storm-brewed waves. Beyond that, she counted five

surfers braving the freezing winter waters as the sun struggled to rise, armed with wetsuits and a sea-lust she totally understood.

With a hard sigh, Tennessee eyed her parents' property, pondering how the hell she ended up there alone. The mortuary itself sat on the business-side of a long stretch of white sand buttoned up with cozy coves ideal for lovebirds and sprinkled with stately bluffs perfect for spotting bald eagles hunting small game in the protected sand dunes. Those with enough patience might spot ospreys plucking fish from the cool coastal waters.

The enviable location, protected yet still with a sea view and set slightly away from the bustle, made it a tantalizing target for investors and gaudy tourist outfits lured in by the building's crumbling exterior that screamed *cheap* next to its spiffy cedar-shingled neighbors. It was old, but that's not why it stayed as-is.

Tennessee ran her hand over the wind-battered stone. Mister was the superstitious sort; he had a certain attachment to each hand-placed cathedral stone and would have bitten off any hand that tried to change it. But such declarations had a way of being tested, so when a pudgy, toddler-sized Tennessee fell ill and medical bills piled up, Mister rescinded. He'd give both his hands, *anything* and *everything*, to save his daughter.

But the town did not rally behind Mister selling the property, or his plight to save his daughter. Before the deal went to ink, the Founders voted to proclaim Englands' Mortuary a historical site, and as such protected from development. The town was small enough to get away with such lies, but big enough to need them.

Tennessee would have been in a bad spot if not for a rash of bizarre deaths that summer. Those deaths prevented Tennessee's death, but the doctors got to her aneurysm a little later than they would have liked. She kicked that *Historic Site* sign now, as if *it* was responsible for her slight slur that appeared when she was overtired or overworked, and only if you were looking for it.

For decades, that sign did its job, guarding the town against outsiders. It seemed so unnecessary now, not only because it was marred and barely readable, but because no one inquired again.

Now, the sign stood as a beacon for strays; their morning piss adding the acidic aroma of life to the perfumed scent of death.

Tennessee lit another cig, took a long drag of the filter-free smoke just as the roar of a little red Corvette drove seagulls squawking to flight.

"Rats," Tennessee grumbled. She killed her cig and hurried inside, where she was greeted, like all dispirited patrons, by a sense of hope draped in gloom. The aroma of fresh brewed coffee, the hope. Everything else, the gloom.

In its day, the mortuary was an ode to her mother's travels, a 2,000-square foot mini-trip around the world. Missus was once the gem of Saint James; the local soothsayer of the forgotten fishing town; a master of distraction, or, as some said, manipulation. She could up-sell ten stone-sober hobos on the Winter Solstice. But after the townspeople, many her lifelong friends, fought the sale that might save her daughter, Missus didn't feel right easing anyone else's pain. So, the once-gorgeous mortuary dusted over with greyish discontent.

The refreshment counter now served strong coffee, weak tea, and week-old pre-packaged sweets, if anything at all. The comfy chairs fit for the Queen herself lost their pomp and pouf. And the elegant writing desks provided for patrons to tackle the depressing forms required to bury the dead teetered and creaked, splashing lukewarm chamomile tea on fresh ink.

Tennessee didn't fuss with the décor; she saved all her talents for preparing the dead for an afterlife of delayed ruination.

The body prep room, crematory, and office were to the left. A short stroll to the right took patrons to the casket showroom camouflaged among bits of Africa, Asia, and old mother Russia; mostly indigenous art, replicated artifacts, and cold-war era posters. Despite the oddity of traversing the world to bury a loved one, the atmosphere was warm and welcoming in a *life is short* sort of way. Missus understood the delicacy of laying one to rest. She was also a sensible lady. A dignified burial takes time, which Missus fully accounted for in ample seating throughout her tour.

Never let it be said that the faint, depressed, or bored were left standing in Englands' Mortuary.

The Fiji room alone had fourteen comfortable seats, none of which were occupied when Tennessee walked in, once again swiping through her contacts. She was alone, unless you counted the partially dolled-up corpse in an open casket, when the front door jingled and high heels *clink-clanked* on the hardwood floors.

Tennessee stopped in front of dear old Mrs. Honeycomb.

"My apologies in advance, Betty."

Tennessee turned in time to see a twiggy, wannabe blueblood fast approaching.

"*Santa*, Tennessee! Did you get my *Santa*?" A fine woman, fortyish, prettier than her makeup permitted, screeched right over poor dead Honeycomb.

"Shh, Lillie." Tennessee didn't bother forcing a smile as she hit *call* and waited. Her gaze shifted to Lillie scrutinizing the pale corpse who still needed a bit more rouge to fool the living. Tennessee closed the lid protectively; a woman needs her lipstick, especially a dead woman. "I've got his voicemail..." A loud beep and Tennessee continued in a much friendlier tone, "Godzilla! It's Ness! Hey, I've got a gig for you tonight. Starts at six. It's solid for thirty minutes so holler back or it's vapor."

Lillie waited for Tennessee to finish, relaxing into an accomplished bitch face, then she blasted, "Why would you say *that*, Tennessee? The party's not until tomorrow!"

"Lillie," Tennessee fumed, "you said, '*Santa! Six! Tonight!*'" She nailed Lillie's tone, all bitch and snoot.

Lillie clicked through her cell phone. "Oh, that's right," she allowed.

A censorious expression reduced Tennessee's eyes to mere slits, accentuating her heritage. "I don't tell you how to waste money so don't tell *me* how to hire Santa!"

"Millie and Billie are *expecting* Santa!"

"The naughty ones usually do," Tennessee muttered as Lillie continued her mother-of-the-year rampage.

Tennessee liked kids. She'd penciled them in her ten-year plan, but Millie and Billie Saint James were the two reasons she didn't use ink. The twins were her bane from the moment of their lavishly celebrated births. After enduring seven *long* years of kid torture, a good part of her felt she'd repaid, with interest, all debts she owed to society. She'd emceed endless rounds of musical chairs, rigged scavenger hunts and sack races, stuffed piñatas galore, wrangled clowns; hell, she'd even shoveled pony shit; from *seven* ponies, in the heat of summer *and* downpours of fall. Tennessee organized all the major milestones from conception—Arabian Nights-themed invitro session—to age seven, and it pretty much scratched raw any itch she had to do it again.

Missus always said: *after seven, they're grown.*

No clowns, no confetti, and absolutely no Christmas in February!

Sadly, Tennessee had bills, and these absurd events paid them with enough overage to actually consider grad school, something managing her parents' mortuary didn't. Unfortunately, it'd take a natural disaster or scourge of one plague or another to produce enough dead people to make all of Tennessee's dreams come true. She had pretty dreams of pretty places that didn't smell of formaldehyde and chrysanthemums and the oppressive musk of loss.

"No Santa, no check, Tennessee."

"I only work in cash, Lillie." Tennessee sneered up at the woman. Dammit! Why had she worn the flat boots instead of the heeled ones sitting right beside her front door? She was all flabby gnome in these. Lillie had the height, porcelain bone structure, and the pedigree, but Tennessee had grit, an air of the exotic. Besides all that, she had enough scrap to wipe the floor with all five-ten of Lillie's privileged ass. The callous thought made her feel way less flabby.

It was a fluke, really, that she came to work for the extravagant Lillie Saint James and her philanthropic husband, William. It was

right after graduating with a B.S. in Psychology, her cap and gown thrown on the passenger seat of her rusted-out Cadillac hearse, that Tennessee showed up for her shift at the mortuary only to find a note from her parents:

*Congratulations on your college, Ness! We stayed to see you get the paper. Your prima is dying. We are catching the first flight home. You know how it is, for the money you pay, we will be gone a long time. You will make a good mortician if you practice the makeup. People die all the time so plenty practice. Move into the room upstairs to save money. We're staying with primo John. Love, Nana and Tata.*

As Tennessee was folding the note, Lillie walked in, a little lost rich girl sopped in tears. She went straight to the showroom and picked out the prettiest, tiniest casket. And without words, without men, the women buried a casket of bloody sheets under a willow tree on the Saint James Estate way up on Scraggle Bluff.

After that, Lillie hired Tennessee for everything; from her fortieth birthday to her wedding to her bribes for the twins she thought she'd never have. And by doing so, Tennessee became a well-sought-after party planner in addition to being the town's sole mortician.

Too busy bantering back and forth about Santa, Tennessee hadn't heard the jingle of the front door or the fine, patent leather shoes padding into the room until they stopped directly beside Lillie.

"We're running late, dear." William placed a strong hand on Lillie's shoulder and a gentle expression on his face.

"Then tell Tennessee to stop wasting our time!"

There he stood, gazing at the boxed Mrs. Honeycomb, looking like he would change places with the old bag in a heartbeat. One glance at the ill-matched pair and it was clear that William had all the sense, and Lillie, all the cash. William tamed Lillie for about six months. A decade later, Tennessee had yet to get the *true* story of how such a benevolent man got rolled into marrying such a splashy woman. Today, Tennessee was too busy to care; she had a Santa to book and a shitload of snotty first graders to

bribe to show up because even *they* couldn't stand the *Illies*, as they were known twenty towns over.

Only Lillie loved the moniker, which she considered an actual *title*; the woman couldn't see past the renown to feel disparaged. She even tried to get William to legally change his name to Willie after the wedding. It wasn't so farfetched; he *did* take *her* last name. But he seemed rather attached to *William*, because that was the only time Tennessee heard the gentleman utter a foul word at his wife, and he didn't stop at *one*. Lillie let the legal part go, but called him Willie from that day forward. Their fairy tale aside, the couple was, once again, standing before Tennessee; one tapping all ten French manicured fingers on Honeycomb's casket, and the other crossing the room to peruse the same old art.

Before Lillie could get another screech out, Tennessee's cell phone chimed out Kenny Roger's "The Gambler."

"Godzilla!" Tennessee hollered in Lillie's pretty, little face. "Cuttin' it short, don't ya think...full suit, dude, unless you wanna do a dime for flashing a bunch of first graders...nah, no elves this time...nah, just the typical bribe action..."

"Pardon me!" Lillie squawked.

"Shh." Tennessee turned her back, crossing toward the window to talk numbers.

"It's a reward, Tennessee!" Lillie squealed on. "If you had children..."

Tennessee turned, eyes hot, but William handled it with a quick hand on Lillie's wrist. He escorted his mouthy wife out of Fiji to a shadier side of London for tepid refreshment and stale croissants.

After closing the deal with Godzilla, Tennessee joined the couple in the reception area. William had settled Lillie with a cup of gut-rot coffee. Upon seeing Tennessee, he handed her the mindbender she'd left beside the sugar.

"How's the new barista?" William inquired.

"Horrible." Tennessee took a long sip.

"That explains why you're nearly out of sugar," he chuckled,

and Tennessee saw the apology behind his cerulean-blue eyes. Yeah, William was definitely *not* a Willie. He had height, better-than-decent bulk, a touch of native in his black hair, and a touch of cowboy in his cleft chin.

He wasn't quite like a brother to her, more like a distant cousin; distant enough to think he was cute, but that's it.

Tennessee gazed up at him. "Santa's coming to town, William. I hope you've been a good boy." She heard the flirt and laughed at it, and the expression on Lillie's face. Before Lillie's look turned audible, Tennessee added, "Millie and Billie will have their *reward* as planned. Now, if you'll excuse me, I've got one body to box and another waiting at the body shop, so..."

Lillie cringed, partially because it was too much reality for her, and because she knew Tennessee was talking about Johnny Cain, the high school quarterback who drove his truck into a wall. William spoke before his wife said something that'd make *him* cringe,

"Good kid, poor choices. I don't imagine it'll be open casket." Only William could blend genuine respect with a fascination for the job.

"He kept his good side...even so, he's a clean burn, but the family wants a smallish viewing before cremation. His father requested I blast Meat Loaf's 'Bat Out of Hell' while I work."

"Hmm," William contemplated a grin, "shouldn't be difficult. That album is third on your top ten best albums ever."

"Video rocks! Who doesn't like boneyards and motorcycles?"

"'Two Out of Three Ain't Bad' is better." William raised a discerning brow.

Tennessee balked. "Ballads are totally separate categories! But that's a classic...almost a tie with 'I'll Do Anything for Love.'"

"I'll accept that, but where does 'I'd Lie for You' place?"

"Boring!" Lillie clanked her cup on the refreshment counter. "I don't even like to *eat* meatloaf!"

She must have expected a different reaction because when the

two burst into laughter, Lillie grabbed William's hand and dragged him out the door.

"Always a pleasure, Tennessee," William sang before Lillie's demands for a perfect Santa smothered his sentiment.

Tennessee waved to William, ignored Lillie.

Tennessee's phone vibrated in her back pocket. Five messages, all from home. She unthinkingly sat where Lillie had, listening to each message before deleting them, awash in Lillie's expensive perfume. It smelled *really* good. Sinful, like an edible deluge of excess. Damn that woman.

Tennessee returned her mother's calls, leaving one mundane message for every one Missus left, then she walked back to Fiji feeling rooted and ready. She opened the casket she had closed earlier, and delicately set a picture of Mrs. Honeycomb, smiling in Paris, on the dead woman's chest.

"Ah, Betty, I see you rocked black eyeliner. All the hot ones do."

Smiling, Tennessee retrieved her makeup kit. Then she opened a music app and clicked on Madeleine Peyroux. Honeycomb wouldn't appreciate Meat Loaf; and while Tennessee didn't always respect the living, she downright honored the dead. When "J'ai Deux Amours" started playing, she tucked her phone into her back pocket, slid into a slick, black apron, and got to work.

~

Mrs. Honeycomb found peace in Rome. The Englands' Mother Mary Chapel was their most baroque viewing room designed for Catholics and the random goth who revered crucifixes and demon-slaying archangels, not for their religious affiliations but for their macabre panache.

After swooshing shut the grand royal purple drapes, Tennessee washed up in the bathroom, the russet walls of New Mexico warming the otherwise chilly mortuary. It was noon and Tennessee was hungry, but she had a caterer to bribe and Christmas decorations to pull from her storage unit. Lillie wanted

*new*, but what that woman didn't know put cash in Tennessee's pocket—win-win.

It should have been a grab and go, but Hill was having another damn storage auction, and that meant a mass of out-of-towners clogging the lot with trucks and trailers. Hill's auctions were ridiculously attended, having gained notoriety after she fearlessly auctioned off an infamous mobster's unit following his untimely death. From that sale alone, Hill could live in luxury; instead, she lived onsite in a singlewide trailer and rode a motor scooter to save on gas.

Bodies squashed in places they shouldn't squash waiting for the old auction queen to open her royal gates. Tennessee barely slid Riggy into a slot before a busted-up RV skidded in beside her, shelling her in grit and fumes, and honking for no good reason.

Tennessee got out, eyeing the dark tint obscuring the driver's side window as the door flung open.

A man, more hulk and monster than mortal, stepped gracefully from the RV; he towered above Tennessee, a bulky, brown beast with black eyes, fuzzy black 'stache to match a fuzzier black beard, and a frizzed 'fro on top. He would have been intimidating if he wasn't dressed like Santa.

"You're a wannabe thug, Godzilla." Tennessee shook her head, but smiled at her friend all the same.

Godzilla displayed a row of perfect white teeth. "You like thugs." His tone didn't let down; it was as rich and resonating as a man that big ought to possess. And when he wasn't getting Tennessee out of a bind, he sang karaoke to pay rent; for extras, he fixed whatever broke at Lin's and anywhere else, drove coaches for Tennessee, and routinely dressed as Santa to give Christmas as a bribe to the nastiest twins in town.

"Why are you already dressed? I said *six*. You'll get the suit dirty *again*!"

The huge man put his huge hands on his huge belly. "Relax, Ness. I already ate. Just here to make a bid. Plus, it's cold out; I might have worn it even if you hadn't begged me to." When

Godzilla laughed, his big belly jiggled just like Santa's belly should.

Tennessee noticed how tiny his gigantic hands looked against that belly, and then she was laughing too. "Well since you're here, you can help me load up the Christmas bins."

"Yeah, ma'am."

As Godzilla cleared a path to the gated entrance Tennessee relaxed. Tucking in behind an all-American lineman meant a sweet stroll through the crowd as men scattered like ants avoiding a giant foot.

"Open up, Hill!" Godzilla boomed, hands shaking the bolted chain link. "Ness has business for Madam Illie!"

Pockets of eager bidders swarmed in behind Tennessee, far enough to not crowd her but near enough to cause Godzilla to turn and roar. He liked to do that. Just roar. It was a good roar, gutturally primal in a big-man-tantrum sort of way.

The crowd dispersed, and all but two guys, roid-raging meatheads by their unreal puffiness, stood firm, challenging this roaring Santabeast.

Tennessee knew that look. Godzilla was a gentle giant but every meathead he encountered wanted a shot at him; a juvenile pissing contest among wannabe alphas. She saw it all the time with her Tibetan mastiff, Polar. It was old two decades ago; now it was just boring.

Boys.

Meathead One tagged in first, charging Santa with terrible form that would totally get his neck snapped on the field. Tennessee knew Godzilla was ready, but he just looked annoyed. He didn't bother blocking his attacker, he just stood there, and upon impact, Meathead One bounced off Santa's belly, effectively slicing his lip on Santa's belt.

As Meathead Two hyped up to avenge his teammate, a squatty woman, closer to death than most, appeared behind the locked chain link gates, blasting a deafening air horn right in Tennessee's face. Tennessee jumped back, covering her ears too late to make

a difference, but that still didn't stop her from noticing the new splotch on Santa's suit.

"Dang it, Godzilla, you got blood on the suit!"

"Chill, Ness." Godzilla dug a handkerchief from his pocket to wipe his belly. "It's red. Just like the ketchup stain you didn't notice."

Tennessee made a primal noise of her own before turning her attention on the elderly woman manning the locked gate. She already had a headache from the ineffective mindbender and skipping lunch; now she had trauma-induced tinnitus.

As the old lady, crooked cane in hand, hobbled over, the rabblerousing meatheads skulked off, hiding their shame in the growing mass of bidders.

"Good morning, Hill," Tennessee rubbed her ears, "mind pointing that *away* from me next time?"

Hill's weathered face lifted in momentary shock as she shoved the air horn inside her orange vest. "That you, Nessie? Why, I didn't recognize you. You've done somethin' frightful *there*." Hill pointed her rickety cane to Tennessee's hair. "Lin don't like that kind of advertisement."

"Been busy, Hill. May we come in? *Please*."

Hill repositioned her thick, retro, round glasses, inspecting Tennessee once again, and then Godzilla's attire. A motherly smirk crinkled the old woman's wrinkles. "Nothin' but rot, those twins. You two ain't doin' them no good. You keep this up and ain't no tellin' what calamity awaits."

"Yes, Hill," Tennessee sighed, "they be demons, but demon-minding pays the rent these days. And I *really* don't want to live at the shop."

Hill coughed out a smoker's croaky laugh. "I'll be dead soon enough, Nessie, then you two can put demon-mindin' in the past."

"Yes, Hill," Godzilla and Tennessee muttered with the same frowns they gave her when they were children.

Hobbling the last of the way to the heavy-duty padlock, Hill

unlocked the gates, allowing Tennessee and Godzilla through. The horde knew better than to rush in. Hill's beatings of too-eager bidders were as renowned as her famous mobster friend. You didn't get to be as old as Hill without a shady past, maybe even a bit of demon-minding of her own. She held the town's secrets close; was downright royalty among tightlipped spinsters.

Hill struck a match on her crooked cane, put the flame to her pipe, and puffed until a whiff of black cherry tobacco caught Tennessee's attention.

"I thought you quit."

Hill bit the pipe wedged at the corner of her mouth. "Don't play me stupid, Nessie. The deal was, *I* quit when *you* quit."

"Who says I didn't quit?"

"You reek." Godzilla barely nudged Tennessee's shoulder but she stumbled forward. He bared his teeth in a meek apology.

Tennessee headed to her storage unit, which was tucked way in the back of the lot. "Look, I was down to one smoke a day. Then that woman calls and I'm at half a pack by noon, another two cigs on the way here."

Godzilla frowned ruefully while Hill kept a keen eye on Tennessee.

"That's the putrefaction I'm sensing, Nessie. If it ain't the Illies it'll be somethin' else. You gotta manage that stress. You need a trip home...a dose of your island folk."

"Hill's right, Ness."

"Goes without sayin'." Hill puffed sweet cherry in Godzilla's face.

He coughed, then recovered with a sanction of his own. "Hill, you mainlanders freak out over everything and Ness learned every freak-out there is."

The old woman contemplated that, took two puffs, then shared a rare story. "When Nessie was ten, I told Mister and Missus they stayed too long...ought to take the girl home before this place uproots her. But Nessie got sick and money was tight. Sure

enough, she's better with the dead, a nervous live wire with the living...addicted to things she don't even like."

Tennessee was busy digging keys from her pocket. "Hey," she flashed a saucy smile before rounding the last corner, "I like my addictions."

Godzilla and Hill lagged behind, exchanging the town gossip on whose units were up for auction and why. So, as Tennessee walked the asphalt path to unit 336, no one witnessed what happened next.

# 2.

# Mindbender

At first glance Tennessee thought the man leaning against unit 336 was her ex, Phillip, but the figure was too tall, too formidable, to be Phillip. Besides being on the safer side, Phillip worked graves at the hospital, which meant he'd likely be sleeping or pulling a second shift; *and* he would never wear a hoodie, let alone with the hood *up*.

Phillip was an umbrella sort of man.

Still eyeing the stranger, Tennessee tossed her tangled keyring in her hand until the storage key shook loose. The man angled toward her, his gaze still shrouded in cheap cotton.

"Hey man, that unit's not for sale! Next one over!" Tennessee shouted, readily defiant. Already, she didn't like this man; he was a little too ordinary to be anything good.

He faced her now, but somehow, she still couldn't see his face.

When the man stepped forward, she reflexively stepped back. What the hell was taking Godzilla so long to round a goddamn corner? Maybe it was best to keep talking, but before she could actually *ask* who he was, the man's voice boomed inside her head. Her skull vibrated so violently, something snapped at the base of her neck. And there, at the precise spot where her skull splintered and cracked, the man's serrated tone pierced her awareness; gouging words on her mind's eye.

*"I belong to you."*

With barely a whoosh, the man stood directly in front of Tennessee. Then his palm cupped the base of her neck.

It was only painful until his next words came; then the agony took on weight, crushing her mind in a punishing burst of white light. A bleached burn spilled over her sight and the man's voice rumbled.

"*You must choose correctly, Tennessee,*" he warned, and she felt his hot breath on her face, a pause, then his fresh, almost relieved, exhales eased her fear. "*Our fate depends upon yours.*"

This wasn't the voice of a man set on hurting her, and yet her body quivered and shook and broke a little. He must have been holding her up, because she was certain she was falling.

That voice again, soft and somehow confiding, "*Ten, you must choose.*"

And that hot breath, an intoxicating mix of chocolate and salt, triggered a memory so primal her scorched mind cooled, leaving a seductive hint of *him* lingering fresh on her tongue.

"You," she exhaled serenely, right before passing out.

~

All Tennessee heard was Godzilla's grumpy curses as she pried her eyes open, her head pillowed on Santa's oddly firm, yet far from jolly, belly.

Hill was already on her cell. "Phillip! It's Nessie..."

"I'm fine!" Tennessee scrambled to get up, only to have a swoon force her to accept Godzilla's assistance. Godzilla was anything but subtle, except when it came to Tennessee. He maneuvered her in such a way any untrained onlooker would think *she* was helping *him*. They learned this delicate dance in childhood, when Tennessee was often too weak to play, and Godzilla, too big among a sea of little.

"Hang up, Hill!" Tennessee insisted, "I slipped! Someone's beater leaked oil or something. Should throw some kitty litter on it. I have some in my unit."

Hill sucked on her pipe, puffed three times before turning her back on her lying little friend. She muttered something to Phillip.

Tennessee heard the gist; they saw her falling for no apparent reason and Godzilla threw himself under her. That would be why she hadn't cracked her skull.

She'd splurge on a ribeye. Nothing says *thank you* like grilled meat. She was even considering making red rice and potato salad until he caught her eye and sadness stole his jolly; *that* was definitely off limits. Pity was unacceptable. She despised it.

"I slipped!" Tennessee hollered as Godzilla set her upright. She hoped they didn't hear the question buried in her assertion. If there had been a man, even a running-away man, Godzilla would have seen him; would have crushed the bastard.

But there *had* been a man!

She was as certain of that as she was of Godzilla's bear-like hands squaring her shoulders.

Hill held the phone out for Tennessee. "Phillip wants a word."

"Goodbye!" Tennessee blasted, clutching Godzilla's arm as she heaved him toward her unit.

Standing in front of the metal accordion door, exactly where the man had stood, Tennessee took one second too long to unlock the unit, prompting Godzilla to relay in quiet defiance, "Away from here, you're tellin' me everything, Ness."

Tennessee studied that burly face, shallow with worry, and promised. But what could she tell him? That an invisible man knocked her out? The last time she told someone that, she ended up on a cold operating slab with her skull sliced open. She'd have to think up something better than the truth. But right now, she had less than five hours to swing a Christmas miracle. Hallucinations be damned!

With a quick bend of his wrist, Godzilla had the roll-up storage door shrieking skyward in a cranky fit. Tennessee squeezed her eyes shut to prevent another swoon, thankful that Godzilla was too busy with Hill to notice.

"Could use some tending, Hill." Godzilla stood back, inspecting the aged pulleys and rusted tracks.

"Could do." Hill wrenched her pipe into the far-left corner of her thin, chapped lips.

Tennessee laughed a little as Godzilla effortlessly scored himself another odd job; even on bad days, he banked more than her. Everyone loved Godzilla, and he could do just about anything with almost nothing. The MacGyver of his generation. Hell, he could probably diffuse a bomb with a toothpick and a smile. That wacky ingenuity was why Tennessee still crushed on Richard Dean Anderson, the original MacGyver; when she wasn't crushing on private eye Simon; Cowboy Rick, not Suit A.J.!

If only it was 1985. Missus had a *thing* for the decade, a soft spot Tennessee inherited. If she managed a nowhere-to-be next morning, Tennessee made like it was the 80s, bingeing on classics and over-buttered popcorn, snuggled in old flannel PJs and pink bunny slippers.

Sadly, it was *now*. And neat, towering stacks of color-coded storage bins only reminded her that a worthy binge was long off, and the 80s even longer off. She strolled into the unit, passing the red-for-Valentine's-Day bins, pink-for-Easter bins, gold-for-St. Paddy's-Day bins, finally stopping directly in front of the largest stack: the green-for-Christmas bins.

Tennessee inherited the gift of thrift from her parents. They were from the islands, where little was had in the first place, so far less was wasted. Tennessee turned her natural inclination into cold, hard cash. Phillip called it scamming, but Tennessee was certain it was simply resourcefulness. If Phillip had to find red, heart-shaped paper doilies in the dead of winter, he might have nicer things to say about her methods. The war against Lillie's insanity would be won on the front lines with this treasure box of balloons, confetti, and tiki torches galore.

Tennessee got on her tiptoes to pull down a bin. Godzilla rushed over before she got a firm grip on the lid.

"Not fragile," she scoffed.

"Better safe than sorry." Godzilla grabbed a second bin with one hand.

"I was talking about *me.*" She reached for the third bin while Godzilla was full-up.

He cleared his throat. "So was I."

Hill's cherry smoke singed right through the cobwebbed air, offering a welcomed reprieve from the aroma of old and dust. The miserable muskiness skulked in from the unit adjacent to Tennessee's. Unit 335 was up for auction, but Hill wasn't expecting anyone to bid on it. The way Hill heard it, and repeated it, the owner was into dark stuff. Tennessee figured that meant the local mob; yes, even quaint beach towns have a *mob*, or at least a group of thugs who gorge on too many mafia flicks and own too many pinstriped suits to match their big, bad Tommy guns.

Another reason Tennessee hated Suits.

Hill gossiped as Godzilla pulled bins, offering his humble support in grunts and nods. Tennessee popped open one lid at a time; a quick look and bins were either kicked toward the door or back toward Godzilla for restacking.

He towered the bins, all but one.

"Our agreement was...no Missy Santy Claus, *no* Santy Claus." He kicked the bin clearly marked *Mrs. Claus* Tennessee's way. It slid across the floor, but rather than stop it, she kicked the bin toward the door; it somersaulted to a messy halt.

They both watched a reprimand gather steam in Hill's gaze as the old woman nudged the bin upright with her crooked cane.

"I'll let you youngins get on with it," Hill grumbled. "I've got an auction to git done...beasts are restless."

She was right, nothing but *boos* and hollers were flowing from the packed parking lot.

"Thanks again, Hill." Tennessee eyed the ancient woman, but stopped short of hugging her. Hill disliked that sort of thing. Tennessee offered up a sharp nod instead.

Hill winked at the girl, tapped her cane twice on the asphalt

before muttering something so low Tennessee wasn't sure she heard the old lady correctly.

After Hill walked off, Godzilla pushed a hand truck loaded with bins beside Tennessee,

"She say what I think she said?" His growly tone twisted grim. "*Call Phillip?*"

"She knows better. I wouldn't call Phillip even if I *was* dying." Tennessee kicked the last bin out of the unit.

"You know, Ness, we could bid on this unit here. Another Illie shindig and you're out of bin space."

That wasn't a bad idea. In fact, it was genius. She'd get more space, *and* bleach away that gross odor spoiling her monthly treasure hunts. Plus, if life went to hell, which it usually did, she'd always have a place to crash.

Tennessee dug in her back pocket. "Make it happen." She handed Godzilla cash, and while he straightened out the wad, she stole his hand truck, stomped on the kick bar, and jogged off toward the front gate.

It wasn't the cleanest getaway, but she just needed a minute alone. Inexplicably, the farther she got from her unit, the more she felt like herself. And by the time she was reunited with Riggy, she was free from any worries other than Lillie and her blasphemous Christmas miracle. The migraine that was threatening to ruin her week dissipated, as did the memory of the man who seemed to cause the headache in the first place. All that remained was a slight notion of salt on her tongue, which the windy seaside accounted for nicely.

Godzilla swooped toward her with bins in his arms and a demanding look. Tennessee tried to keep her promise, but she'd forgotten what she'd meant to say.

"Don't worry, big guy, I really did just slip." Now when she said it, she believed it. She raised one shoulder toward her ear, face scrunched in awkwardness. Godzilla wasn't buying it. Didn't matter, by the time she hopped in Riggy even the lingering tang

of salt on her tongue had faded to a murky memory of something long forgotten.

~

A double quarter pounder and large fry should be savored, not scarfed one-handed while whipping a hearse round a mountain with a drop-off that guaranteed the Englands a fruitful harvest season. But Tennessee had another stop to make before transforming the Illie Estate into a mini winter wonderland. What's Christmas without a goddamn Christmas tree?

She crammed a handful of fries into her mouth, eyeing her cell phone on the dash. Three closed caskets last summer reinforced her disdain for texting while driving, but it went deeper. With her parents retired back home, she was the only mortician left she could trust to properly box a body; even *her* body. No parent should box their own child.

Tennessee laughed out loud, knowing full well *hers* would.

No matter the season, day or night, the drive to the summit of Mount Orion had a way of wringing her out. It wasn't a slow, gentle sort of cleanse. It was swift, like a zap of energy vaporizing all the nonsense. After the "slip" at Hill's, she needed a little restoring.

Tennessee made a sharp left, wedging Riggy between two cedars. After unrolling her window, she cut the engine and reached for her smokes, shaking out the last cig.

"I'm either *lucky* or *unlucky*." She tucked the cig behind her left ear along with a shaggy wedge of coiled curls.

A ghost of gnats swarmed Riggy's windshield, gyrating like a mini flash mob before folding into the foggy ribbons obscuring evergreens, birch, even the deadly holly; their red-hot berries breaking through the mist. Tennessee inhaled an unexpected breath of crushed rock and burnt ash. Forest fires took half the mountain not that many years ago. This acreage still held old growth, but every so often sea winds churned up more than salt and foam.

Tennessee coughed out the slaggy bits of graveled air trapped

at the back of her throat then grabbed her backpack and walking staff. She didn't want another *slip*, and the staff made a decent weapon in a pinch; might be enough to scare a regular bear, not a mamma bear. Godzilla taught her a little self-defense. The dirty kind. Enough to make a run for it. Thankfully, she'd never been tested.

Mount Orion was her temple, and she roamed as if nothing could penetrate her bubble, not even a mosquito. By the time Tennessee trudged up the steep slope, still slick from remnants of last month's snowfall, the birds had gone and the bustlings of a busy forest stilled. The approaching scent of dew-soaked brush and damp dirt loosened her shoulders and when swift footfalls padded out of the fog, she smiled.

"Hey, Rocky, how you been?" Tennessee nuzzled the rusty red hair on the Doberman pinscher's head. He was a magnificent creature: lean, powerful, swift, show-ready, and proud. He *knew* he was beautiful; that's what made him so deadly. His charm got him close, making the strike too easy. This skill came in handy because his master had more enemies than friends.

Rocky closed his eyes, fully disarming as he leaned into Tennessee's touch. He loved Tennessee from the moment he saw what a good job she did making his dead master look alive. From that moment on, she was pack.

Tennessee continued with the loving pats as a stern reprimand plowed up the slope behind her.

"Your phone's dead again, huh?"

Despite knowing that voice, Tennessee spun so rapidly the blood in her head swooshed; she wobbled while all the fluid in her body jostled for balance. "Hello, Addy."

"If you can't keep your phone charged, at least tell me you're packin' that .22 I gave you."

Tennessee scrunched a look, crooked and guilty.

"Stupid girl." Adrienne lowered her rifle to meet Tennessee's eye before striding forward.

She always had a rifle, always locked sights first. Tennessee

figured it was something war did to people. She respected those who fought; the only enemy she ever faced was her health. She often thought she had it easy. Sure, she flatlined on the operating slab, but even *that* was easy.

The armed woman carried herself well. Her people were from hardy stock, somewhere cold, maybe Nordic, but she would never say. Long red hair, freckly, saved her smiles for friends.

Rocky bounded over to Adrienne, standing watch beside his master. They were both rescues, loyal to the bone.

"Your phone?"

"Why do you ask?" Tennessee checked her cell; fifty percent charged, nine missed calls. She reduced her eyes to slits. *All* Phillip.

That man used her cell phone as a virtual stalker; a tight leash around her neck. She rebelled by sending Phillip's calls to voicemail even when they were dating and even though she knew he considered voicemail an f-bomb in his face.

Mired on a misty bridge of past and present, an icy patch scorched the nape of her neck. She put her hand on it, willing it to warm; beginning the same ol' speech,

"Lillie wants..."

"Ah shit, don't tell me that bitch wants another tree!"

"Triple the rate? *And* a dozen trees planted in its place!"

Adrienne smiled now and might have sealed the deal if Rocky hadn't started repressing a growl directed at Tennessee.

He never did that; in fact, Tennessee was his second favorite person in all the world, the only other human he'd consider taking on as master.

"What's the matter, boy?" Adrienne cupped Rocky's muzzle, lifting his gaze to hers.

Tennessee scanned the woods behind her. Just fog. And too much quiet. They weren't alone. But when she stepped toward Adrienne, Rocky's frenzied barking put intruder thoughts right out of her mind.

Apparently, *she* was the problem.

"Go on, Ness." Adrienne set her rifle on the ground to better nuzzle Rocky. "Get what you need, but I'll take a nickel for the noble. Bitch always wants a noble."

"*Five hundred?*" Tennessee balked. Five bills for a six-foot tree would be a harder sell than a Santa who was more brown bear than jolly toymaker, but hey, miracles weren't cheap *or* perfect. Lillie, of all people, learned that long ago.

"Deal?"

"Deal."

With one last look of concern, Tennessee reluctantly left Rocky to Adrienne, and trekked off into the woods.

~

Adrienne wasn't from old money like Lillie. Adrienne was retired military, clocked enough tours to buy 100 acres near the summit of Mount Orion. She let family, and Tennessee, hunt her land. Locals knew better; Adrienne was a better shot than the GIs she dated. In four years, Rocky had yet to approve of one. Adrienne didn't mind; he was her loyal Doberman, after all. He knew best.

Tennessee strolled up to Adrienne's log cabin. It was tiny, barely enough room to swing a cat; that's what Tennessee's grandmother used to say—*swing a cat*. She was a Tennessee, too. Ever since meeting Lin, and hearing her go on and on about family honor and lineage, Tennessee resurrected her grandmother's sayings every now and again. It was something to do.

As for Adrienne's tiny cabin, it was built to leave minimal impact on the environment, but it also had to withstand winter storms, bear attacks, and Armageddon. The walls were reinforced with steel; even her rifle-ready windows were camouflaged with steel plates like a deer hunter's blind. She collected rainwater, dug her own compostable toilet, and hauled out trash every Sunday.

She worshipped this land. This was church.

After a romp, Tennessee found a noble fir worthy of Christmas. She unzipped her backpack and retrieved a collapsible handsaw

ideal for felling stubby trees. Not that a six-foot tree was *stubby*, especially given that Tennessee was considerably stubbier than that. She was from strong stock, too, only squattier and rounder; her line had heft.

She kneeled at the base of the tree, rubbing her tiny cross pendant as she said a little prayer. This was consecrated ground, after all.

Just as she brought her hands, folded in prayer, together at her chest, movement broke her meditation. She lifted her eyes and there in the middle of a shaded clearing, unremarkable in every way, manifested a misty figure; sinewy and somehow dewy.

"I'm imagining you." She stayed kneeling; it was a decent height to fall from. Since this was a hallucination and those usually ended badly—bruises, busted bones, she even chipped a tooth once—she kept her gaze on the figure as it gradually came into focus; hoodie and all.

Whatever happened next, happened fast. All she remembered was that same voice resounding in her head, only she couldn't make out the words over the frenetic barking and growling. And slobber?

Tennessee's hand flung to her face, to be immediately accosted by the second fattest, slipperiest, wettest dog tongue she'd ever encountered; no dog could outmatch her beloved Polar's tongue.

Then Adrienne's face was right there beside Rocky's.

"You were talking to someone," she interrogated as Rocky tried to shrink to fit on Tennessee's lap.

"Nah, just myself." Tennessee nuzzled Rocky for a bit before picking up the saw she had dropped. She hunched under Lillie's tree and killed it.

"We go back, Ness." Adrienne took a quick walk around the perimeter as the noble fell. "You're seeing him again, aren't you?"

They both knew what she was asking, and they both knew Tennessee would lie.

"I'll take care of the seedlings this weekend, okay?" Tennessee stood up and stretched. "Hey, let's barbeque!"

Adrienne's sneer softened, and the friends laughed. The last time they had a barbeque, the charcoal looked tastier than the ribs. It wasn't for lack of skill; it was gossip and booze.

"I'll bring *one* bottle of wine," Tennessee promised with a sly look that said *three*.

"Deal." Adrienne slung her rifle over her shoulder, leading her troop down her mountain.

~

It was just past 2:00 p.m. when Tennessee finally made her way to the Illie Estate.

She had Santa meeting her there, a fine-looking noble, her go-to caterer whipping up dinner and sweets, and enough lights to cause a mini blackout. What she didn't have was the patience to watch Lillie's security guard exit the mansion only to meander, sloth-like, across the sprawling, impeccably manicured meadow to open the goddamn gate.

Tennessee climbed on Riggy's hood to wait it out. She sat cross-legged, her gaze tracing the intricate designs on the new wrought iron gates. They were more handcrafted sculptures than daunting deterrent to keep out the riffraff. The work was clean and familiar. Archangels or fairies, magnificent winged creatures of fabled lore; not Lillie-chic at all. And Phillip hadn't lived at his family's estate in years; the siblings never agreed on a single upgrade, so it couldn't have been commissioned on his recommendation. No, it must be William's sole touch on the place. She'd ask him about the artist tonight, *if* she got a chance to speak with the adults. It was usually Tennessee at the kiddy table, playing the hired clown and cleaning puke.

Dammit, she needed a smoke.

She stretched out her legs, resting her head and back against Riggy's windshield. Maybe she'd catch a quick tan now that the afternoon sun cleared out the morning fog. She never burned, just got more caramelly. It wasn't hot, but even the moderate warming from a midwinter sun had Tennessee's hair growing; she

reached up to tame her frizz and knocked loose the cig locked in a curl tucked behind her ear.

"My lucky day," she sang, dangling the cig from her lips as she dug in her back pocket for her lighter.

"I'd have to agree." A man's smooth voice, coolly eloquent, preceded the metallic grind of iron splitting.

Tennessee cinched the cig back behind her ear before lifting her head to confirm her bad luck.

*Phillip.*

"Let me guess," she grumbled, "Hill ratted me out."

A sophisticated man ending his thirties stood dead center while the estate's massive gates separated, as if by his presence alone. Slipping the gate remote control into his jacket pocket, he strode out, pressed, pinstriped, and pointing at her like a principal or warden. Yeah, that was a warden's finger all right: rigid and bitter, far superior.

Six months ago, she had seen him at the Founders' Farmer's Market; made damn sure he didn't see her.

Now she was trapped.

Tennessee emptied her lungs in a hard huff, letting her head *thunk* back on Riggy's windshield.

"Careful, Tenny," Phillip rushed over, "you've hit your head enough for one day."

"As usual, you got it all wrong." She squinted, sinking into their embittered past.

Why did he still care what her head hit? They didn't fit, never had. Not really.

He was a Suit.

She preferred Cowboys.

She circled this mantra round her head until his warm hand pressed against her forehead.

"You're certain you didn't hit your head?"

Forced to engage with him, she opened her eyes; put a little glower in there. Okay, a *big* glower. "Godzilla caught me." She slapped his hand away.

"Well then, remind me to buy that man a steak," Phillip offered with a smile, the corners of his eyes crinkling the way they did when he stopped being a complete stiff. He took up her wrist, counting beats while staring into her eyes.

Tennessee didn't put any weight in Phillip's hard gazes, she already knew that Phillip rarely got steamy; holding hands was as *public* a display he would dare, and even *that* was reserved for occasions of commemoration or commiseration. Phillip's long gazes only meant he was checking for signs of stroke, concussion, or other head trauma. Tennessee had learned this early on in their short-lived romance. She once found him combing over her medical records when he claimed to be binge-watching *The West Wing*. Funny how he never played doctor when she *wanted* him to.

"I'm not your patient anymore, Phillip." Tennessee pushed herself to sitting, preparing a spectacular *screw you* dismount.

"Your eyes are clear. Pulse is slightly elevated," he declared dryly before stepping aside. He held his arm out to be of use. She shot him a disgusted look as a pukey spasm churned her gut, but Phillip wasn't put off. He stood his ground, all gentleman-like, and doctorly, and dismal as hell.

Tennessee noticed, but mentioning it wouldn't do any good. It never did.

"Maybe next time you'll humor me and swing by the hospital?" Phillip asked winsomely.

She leapt from the hood, avoiding all contact as she slid behind the wheel. "Sure thing, doc." She revved the engine before the door was even shut.

Phillip made a face; an expression Tennessee had seen only twice before. Once when he lost his mother; and the other, when they called it quits a year back. It wasn't a good face, but what could she do about *that* now? She had lights to string, a tree to trim, a hallucination to kill, and a scratchy Mrs. Claus outfit to squeeze her ample ass into.

"You look well, Tenny," Phillip managed to murmur as Riggy roared through the iron gates.

Tennessee caught Phillip's eye in the rearview mirror.
She stuck her hand out the window.
Flipped him the bird.

# 3.

# Sentinels and Suits

Lillie's mansion was exactly what you'd expect from a wealthy socialite drunk on notions of Grace Kelly. Any such elegance or effortless sophistication Lillie sought was instantly obliterated by her heavy-handedness. Lillie perched her narcissistic ode on the perilous tip of Scraggle Bluff. The twenty-room mansion was more glass than brick, balancing teeter-totter-like over the Pacific Ocean. Townsfolk contemptuously named the horror *The Mirror* due to its destructive pastime of harnessing the sun's rays to blind and burn at will.

The expansive parcel of land had been tied to the Saint James family for generations, following the mass slaughter of natives who were prone to *squat* on the prettiest of lands. Of course, that's not the way Old Man Saint James told it. According to tale, he won the exquisite parcel overlooking the majestic sea, fair and square, in a game of dice.

Simple.

The best lies are.

Each generation left their mark on the land, carefully preserving the Saint James legacy. They were an *add-to* family, revering all that came before. Everyone except Lillie. She skewed new, modern. Barely a month after she got her turn overseeing the estate, she leveled the lot and began erecting a colossal

monstrosity fashioned of steel and glass. Her Mirror had all the best views, all the best antiques and accents and furnishings.

All the best.

There were lots of problems with Lillie's mark, but one really oozed out—snoot. *Everything* was covered in Lillie's snooty, pompous privilege. Tennessee was raised stateside, but she was an Island girl, born with sandy toes and a sun-worshipped complexion that couldn't be faked. No amount of stateside living could extract or dilute the saltwater from her veins. She carried that unmistakable humility Islanders exude; an almost abashed nature that, if taken too far, got you stomped flat, especially if misinterpreted as weakness by elitist bitches.

Enter Lillie Saint James.

"Seriously, Tennessee?!" Lillie screeched as her butler opened the door to a waiting noble fir. "I called the morgue. It's only Johnny in there! You should have been here hours ago!"

Tennessee peeked around the tree, sharing a low laugh with Buster the butler. His real name was Castro Perez, a Dominican welterweight who busted more noses than any other boxer of his time, of *any* weight class.

"What up, Buster B!" Tennessee fist-bumped the balding, elderly man, dragging her noble offering into Lillie's extravagance.

"I *know* I was clear last time!" Lillie blocked Tennessee from entering the great hall. "Look up, Tennessee! What do you see?"

Buster looked up. Tennessee didn't.

"Vaulted ceilings, Tennessee! *Vaulted*!" Lillie huffed and puffed.

Tennessee wondered if Lillie knew how much she resembled the big bad wolf. Only that meant Tennessee was a little pig.

Crap.

Lillie puffed, "Any tree under *twelve feet* looks cheap and small!"

"Not next to the twins. *They're* small!"

"Midgets are small, Tennessee! My girls are *petite*," Lillie spewed. "And you, you're just *short*."

Tennessee's menacing look pushed Lillie back. Today, she

refused to be Lillie's pork chop. She released the noble, letting it plunk to a pile on Lillie's polished, imported tile. This wasn't the ladies' usual dance. Sure, Lillie barked orders and Tennessee barked back, but Tennessee *always* yielded.

Today, Tennessee's cold stare was an unexpected, highly unwelcome freestyle.

Buster stepped in to referee or save the noble from collateral damage. It wouldn't have been the first time a tree was launched into the sea from the Mirror.

"Madame Lillie, Master Willie requested *The Christmas* be conducted in the children's wing."

It was enough to untangle the women and leave Tennessee with a burning headache. She'd have to get that checked, by *anyone* other than Phillip. Lillie went on garbling orders, at least, that's how Tennessee heard them. In fact, even the greeting Buster was now giving Phillip was garbled, as if someone shoved Tennessee's head in an aquarium of piranhas, all of whom decided to gnaw on her spinal cord.

"Good afternoon, Master Phillip."

"It's *Mister*!" Lillie hollered from the hall, "My *dearest* brother relinquished all rights to that title when he turned his back on our family!"

Phillip graciously shook hands with the genteel butler, correcting his sister in delicate tones of authentic breeding. "My dearest sister, I wouldn't dream of denying you the pleasure of spending *both* our fortunes. Two shares are better than one, as our mother so sensibly counselled."

That was enough to set Lillie off; she turned back to deal with her horrible brother.

"*Money*," Tennessee grumbled to herself, lugging the noble into the children's wing, "hurts when you have it, hurts when you don't."

~

Erecting a six-foot Christmas tree alone was difficult. No matter how many times Tennessee did it, she never managed to get it

quite straight. She used the reflection cast in the wall of windows to get it good enough. Brushing pine needles from her arms and clothes, she lamented hauling in the green-for-Christmas bins crammed in Riggy's dead end. Did her life really amount to hauling those suckers in for the billionth time?

"Something's got to change," Tennessee mumbled just as Godzilla strolled in with a green-for-Christmas bin under one arm, pushing a hand truck stacked full of the very bins Tennessee was dreading retrieving.

He'd gone through the service entrance, the one reserved for the help; the stylists and lifestylists, florists and fashionistas. He'd done fixes around the estate for years, so his comings and goings went unquestioned; even when he stalked through the place as Santabeast.

"'Bout time you got here," Tennessee scolded, ignoring the gold-encrusted grandfather clock facing them that clearly proved Godzilla was early.

Santa shrugged off Tennessee's typical Illie-event crankiness. "How's Adrienne? Still with that Marine?" Godzilla thought his love for Adrienne was his secret, but the whole town knew it, including Adrienne. It'd never work between the two. Godzilla was as tough as they come, *tougher*, but he never served. Total deal-breaker for the badass survivalist.

Tennessee dug into the bins. "Nah, that fizzled." She glanced up to watch jolly spread across Santa's face.

He said nothing more; it was a secret, after all.

They talked of food, cremations, lawn maintenance, and what shows they were currently bingeing as they decked out the indoor playland with red stockings, wintergreen wreaths, sparkly garland, coconut-sized pinecones, and enough fake snow to smother a rainforest. When they were done, Godzilla snuck out the way he'd come in, and Tennessee was about to do the same when Phillip strolled in.

"Another miracle, I see." He smirked.

She hated that smirk; it made his eyes gleam, and when his

eyes gleamed, the black ring framing his sea-green irises blurred a stunning emerald. Phillip was by no means ugly. But that smirk made him handsome. *Really* handsome. "Spray this, will ya!" Tennessee chucked Phillip an aerosol can pumped full of pine scent before slipping out the servants' entrance without another word, or, god forbid, another glance from those emerald eyes.

She pulled the cig from behind her ear, lit up, and got the hell off Scraggle Bluff.

~

Tennessee had a few hours to kill before she had to cosplay Mrs. Claus. Polar wouldn't be too happy with her if she didn't take him for a quick run and feed him dinner. He ate a ton, more than he should, but she couldn't work out why a dog, who couldn't open a bag of dog food himself, should be limited to a few cups of food a day. When she left in the morning, she filled his bowl with more food than he needed, and when she got home in the evening, fed him more than he needed.

That's true love.

Polar was still a pup, a *big* pup even for his large breed. Standing just over three feet tall and weighing in at 170 pounds, he was already outgrowing their rental. They'd need a bigger place, maybe even a place of their own. It was a dream. Something to save for, another reason to take Lillie's shit.

Not everyone had an inheritance to take, or *not* take.

Her rental was in a good location, near town, but a long drive off the highway so you didn't catch a lot of traffic noise through the forest of burgundy-barked manzanitas, towering oaks, and dreamy laurels. She drove past her landlords' manor: a gorgeous nod to old Hollywood embroidered in rustic Spanish flair. The Jims lived there. Both retired from Union Pacific; one, a railroad conductor; the other, an engineer. They were good people. Expected rent on the first of the month, let Tennessee pick what she wanted from their award-winning vegetable garden and orchard, but otherwise left her alone.

Early into their retirement the Jims built a steel silo, artistically

sided with salvaged barn wood; Jim the Engineer had a desire to enter the grain game, Jim the Conductor went along with it, knowing full well it'd tank in six months. It did. In *four*. The nimble Jims renovated the circular space into a pretty nifty bungalow; a stunning modern-pioneer design that made a snazzy spread in a national paper. Still, it was a hard sell. They kept the original ladder system, which meant climbing a vertical wall to reach the second floor, and more wall to reach the breathtaking balcony perched roof-side. One slip on those narrow stairs bought you a one-way trip to the Englands'.

These peculiarities drew Tennessee in. She was tired of boxes; she boxed people all day. Circles were different; circles were good.

The second floor sealed Tennessee's love for the little silo. Windows cut into the silo's pitched roof allowed for the creation of dramatic designs as sunlight and moonlight swirled galaxies into the bedroom, adding a mystical vibe to the serene escape. Some days, when a depression set in for one reason or another, Tennessee would lay in bed all day, watching these light shows. She awoke to brilliantly broken rainbows and fell asleep to birthing constellations.

The Jims attached a swanky porch out front and furnished that space with a wicker rocking chair, antique steel table, and potted blooming perennials in aged cedar wine barrels. The grounds *must* always be presentable, so they tended these plants in addition to their acre of manicured grounds. The inside, they left to Tennessee.

She angled Riggy, so she could tear out easily if she was running late. She checked the time. She'd be running late.

Tennessee tossed her keyring in her hand, shaking loose the silo key. She opened the arched door fit for a church to a mass of white. There, blocking, guarding, otherwise restricting entrance, stood an enormous, shaggy-haired, lion-maned, albino Tibetan mastiff.

"Polar," Tennessee groaned, her sinisterly shallow tone and squared stance inviting a challenge.

The mighty lion obstinately fixed all four furry paws on the creaky floorboards, reinforcing his beastliness with a frightening growl, a guttural thunder that lifted his lips up over his threateningly pointy fangs.

He was still a puppy, but there was nothing puppy about those fangs.

Tennessee returned the growl, scrunching her lips upward to showcase her tiny overbite and crooked snaggletooth.

Polar eyed that tooth, and pounced.

Tennessee wailed into laughter as Polar knocked her to the ground; the pair rolled on the floor, exchanging rough hugs and nuzzles. Polar nosed Tennessee onto her back, slobbering her with wet kisses.

"Okay, okay!" She blocked his juicy licks with strategic swats. "I'll take you with me tomorrow. But don't you complain about the smells! The *end* always stinks."

Polar yapped his approval right in Tennessee's face. Next came an onslaught of pouring-wet licks. Polar loved wet kisses. His previous owner left a note duct-taped to Polar's kennel saying as much, then she left the kennel and Polar outside the England's Mortuary. Well, it might have been a *he*, but Tennessee couldn't imagine a man writing a note detailing dog kisses. She recalled that note every time Polar laid one on her. Who could give up all those kisses?

Tennessee wiggled free from her mighty protector. "You should've said something sooner, boy!" She roughed up Polar's furry face. There was a lot of lonely in his eyes. The poor dog thought he was a lion, and what good was a lion without a pride to protect? Polar couldn't help it, the guardian instinct raged in his blood; he was a mountain of a dog who needed a mountain to roam and a family to watch over. Tennessee understood that look, more than she ought at her age.

She kneeled in front of him, waiting for those eyes to brighten.

Unlike Rocky with Adrienne, Polar never had to vie for Tennessee's attention. He was her cool cat, after all, her gentle old

lion. Polar rested his face on his forepaws before rolling onto his back with a *humph* that sounded all too human.

Tennessee rubbed Polar's stomach before sprawling out on the hardwood floors right beside him. Finally, the lonely left Polar's eyes; and, soon, Tennessee's.

It was the break she'd been craving all damn day; gone was the terrible mindbender; long forgotten, that weird slip at Hill's; Lillie's bitch, silenced; and Phillip's smirk, expunged.

What a miraculous thing.

Dogs.

~

A quick run with Polar around the Jims' labyrinth of a vineyard was strangely refreshing. Runs usually weren't Tennessee's thing, but since adopting Polar, *fast walks* were a must-do, and, shockingly, one of the most enjoyable parts of her day. Phillip handled the runs at first, when Polar was a teensy-weensy 75-pound pup. He might be shocked to learn that she took the mid-day runs over. He probably thought the Jims did it.

"Why are men so dumb?" Tennessee coughed out, wheezing a little from the last sprint home.

Polar turned back, sprinting to her side, barking his annoyance.

"You and Rocky...and Godzilla excluded, of course. Okay, fine! You know *who* I mean! Man, you hold me to *everything*."

Polar barked again, nudging Tennessee toward the silo. He was right, she'd be really, really late if she didn't hurry. Only one *really* would do for an Illie event.

Tennessee stripped down to grab a quick shower when her cell phone rang. It was the old-fashioned ring, the one she set for unknown callers.

*Bbrrriiiinnnngggg*

*Bbrrriiiinnnngggg*

She usually didn't answer that ring, but she had a few new clients and wasn't current on her contacts. Standing stark naked in her bedroom, she answered the call.

"England."

"Miss England," said the sweetest voice in all the world. "Mrs. Willie Saint James instructed I summon *you* to retrieve Millie and Billie Saint James from Summerhold Academy."

But for the string of cusswords Tennessee muttered in her head, she was wordless.

"Hello? Miss England," continued the sweetest voice in all the world. "Mrs. Willie Saint James intimated, quite succinctly, that her nanny, one Miss Grimmie, was relieved of her duties today. As you may or may not be aware, students were released from their academics five minutes ago."

Tennessee swiped the phone to speaker, pulling on fresh panties, fresh gym socks, same bra. "Where are the twins now?" she gruffed, cramming herself back into her oldest pair of ripped jeans. While she'd love to give those Summerhold biddies a visit from Mrs. Claus, she'd left the outfit at Lillie's.

"They are presently detained in the library. If you'd be so kind as to retrieve them in haste, we at Summerhold Academy shall be forever grateful."

"*Detained.*" Tennessee released a snide little laugh, muttering through the sweatshirt she was yanking over her head. "You must be new. The twins are delinquents...criminal masterminds in the making. I would have thought the nuns gave fair warning to newbies."

There was steely silence before the sweetest voice in all the world soured a bit. "Yes, well, it's my first day."

"Yeah, I gotcha, Teach. Just keep 'em away from the windows. They smash crap, especially when they're bored."

"Pertinent information indeed, Miss England, albeit untimely."

"Alrighty then, just keep 'em away from any *more* windows. Hang tight, I'm on my way." Tennessee ended the call with another unspoken curse.

This fired-nanny business wasn't new. How it became Tennessee's business, though, was. She did bribes, not the dailies. It almost concerned her enough to call Lillie, or, by god, Phillip. Instead, she called Buster the butler.

Unfortunately, he didn't know much, only that Master Willie left with Master Phillip following a rather loud spat with Madame Lillie.

Regarding the firing of Miss Grimmie, Buster was certain she had quit. "Family business, Miss Tennessee, is no business of ours."

"I'm more than good with that, Buster B. Thing is, it only took five minutes for the twins to destroy Summerhold. By now, they've taken hostages. Where's Lillie?"

"She requested two Valium with her afternoon hot toddy. She's not fit for driving, and I cannot leave my post."

"*Please* tell me there's someone...you know, *capable* left in the house to get the twins..."

Buster's sigh was enough to let Tennessee know that she'd be *really*, *really* late for Christmas.

"Okay, okay...thank you, Buster B. *I'll* get the twins." Tennessee tried to put a smile in her sigh, but she could still hear grump when she ended the call.

Sensing his master's turmoil, Polar padded over, pawing Tennessee's leg. She was busy pulling her damp, frizzled hair into a tight knot on the top of her head; busy scrounging in the fridge for a fresh pack of cigs; busy tearing open the pack; but he kept pawing until she finally caved.

"Seeing as how I'm all out of kiddie tranqs," she groaned to her lion, "*you're* my backup. Let's get on with this, partner! Stinky, rotten, entitled demon brats on the menu tonight!"

It wasn't just the pawing that swayed Tennessee; she needed a beast on her side to properly wrangle those demon brats. And make no mistake, those children were demons.

The twins weren't afraid of much: not the dark, their mother, not closets or spankings; heights only stoked their crazy, and bumps in the night were prizes worth collecting. Tennessee hoped that maybe, just maybe, Polar's size and unique ability to play mean would make her job collecting the twins easier. Or at the

very least prevent her from adding a third *really* to her already late status.

Polar bounded outside, racing around the silo while Tennessee revved up the engine. On his second go-round, she pushed open the passenger door. Polar leapt in, landing a wet lick on Tennessee's cheek as she reached around him to slam the door.

Polar grumbled a growl.

"Yes, boy, I'll roll it down." Tennessee twirled the window crank until Polar could shove his massive mane out the window. Riggy was old; no power windows, no power steering, just a bunch of *noes*.

Driving past the main house should have been easy, but this day was anything but. The Jims were tending to an old oak tree; they fussed over the centenarian as if it would wither and die without their incessant fondling. Tennessee often thought their obsessive attention to nature might have the opposite effect, smothering the revered life they sought to preserve. She was thinking along these lines when Jim the Engineer waved her down.

Dammit.

"Good evening, Tennessee."

Tennessee only smiled; a little fearful this out-of-character stop signaled a hike in rent. She barely scraped by as it stood, even with the holiday suicides.

Polar gruffed his head out Tennessee's window, sniffed Jim the Engineer, then gruffed his head back out his own window.

Jim waited for Polar's approval before proceeding. He'd learned early on that Polar took his sentry duties seriously, and as a man of duty himself, he respected the job.

"Her eminence Lillie Saint James messengered over a check to cover your rent through the summer solstice. She's a keeper." Jim offered up an uncharacteristic wink. The sly quickness of that wink was uncomfortably suggestive, crossed the landlord-tenant line, and was just straight-up creepy.

Rather than peel out, Tennessee nodded her goodbye as she

eased down the gas pedal, clenching her teeth until her jaw popped. That happened sometimes, usually when Lillie overstepped. Lillie was up to something, and her pretty schemes always flipped ugly.

Tennessee played Lillie's game, negotiated fees for contracted services, but she wasn't Lillie's bought-and-paid-for bitch. The deal was *two* months' rent, not *four*! It felt awfully like a barter in the making, and Tennessee hated barters. Somehow, she always got screwed.

Tennessee didn't bother watching her speed. There were two cops in Saint James: Honey and Herd. Godzilla made a third when they needed an extra man; a quick swear-in and it was done. Downtown wasn't where she wanted to be this close to the end of a workday. Traffic would suck, and Riggy was on the verge of overheating. She meant to fill up his radiator before heading back to the Illie Estate, but Lillie pissed off Miss Grimmie and god only knows where the men ended up!

Stopping *anywhere* with those twins was never, *ever* a good plan. She'd tend to Riggy once she got the demon brats home.

Through the stop-and-go traffic, Tennessee eyed a weathered copper spire soaring heavenward atop a slate-shingled steeple that housed the town's oldest bell tower in the town's oldest cathedral. The image incited a mini revolt in the pit of her gut.

Summerhold Academy.

She had been there once. Vowed to never make it *twice*.

A sick uneasiness closed off her throat, right at the base of her neck; the same damn spot. She must have cricked something during her fall. Polar nosed her shoulder.

"I'm fine." She rolled her shoulders and stretched her neck, but the throbbing twinge intensified the closer Riggy got to Summerhold.

Now *this* building was *old*, a genuine historic landmark; steeped in history and story, even the site itself, the actual land, was drenched in legend and lore. The bloody kind. But that wasn't why Tennessee kept her distance. Hill's warnings filled her head

now as a screeching hawk turned circles around the spire. "The taint on their kind don't rinse clean. Touch one penny of theirs and be damned," Hill concluded sagaciously years ago, after Tennessee's first visit to Summerhold for a wedding that never was.

The one-time cathedral was built more as an architectural wonder than a place of worship. The Founders quickly realized the appeal of such exquisiteness. The bell's distinctive toll drew curious folk to town, and upon seeing the regal cathedral, many stayed. Soon the stone edifice was the pivot of Saint James; so much so that the entire town was built around the towering structure, encircling it like a mandala of worshippers. Or soldiers.

When the troops began encroaching on the primly planted gardens and pungent flora, the Founders erected an eight-foot stone wall, a moat, and a drawbridge over the moat. No, they didn't call it a moat—they were too savvy for that. They called it a pond, threw in some fish and posted signs welcoming locals to toss in their lines.

The Founders lived by their signs.

For generations, locals crossed the moat to attend Sunday service. If the drawbridge was down, all were welcome; if it was raised, well, worship elsewhere. All that came to a halt when a single candle left aflame on the altar spread to the pews, where Bibles and loose choral music fueled the blaze. Although money poured in to rebuild the church, the bishop was set on renovating the property into a hospital for the indigent. A lovely thought, and bishops ought to have lovely thoughts; unfortunately, this one left Saint James without a church.

Swerving past a broken-down bus, Tennessee slid into a curbside spot just as the bell tolled. It wasn't the delightful chiming she was expecting. It was a shudder, shatter, clatter, batter sort of racket.

Still clutching the steering wheel, Tennessee peered up at the bell tower. A shrill of laughter preceded a clattering of chaotic chimes.

Polar howled.

"*Demons*," Tennessee cursed, exiting Riggy with a reluctance Polar disagreed with. *This* was way more fun than sleeping all day. He nudged her rump as he made his way around her. "I'm going, geez. Can't a girl get a minute to mope?" But she knew there wasn't time. The twins might jump from the tower, just to prove they could. "Sic 'em, Polar!" Tennessee trudged as Polar raced on. "Man, how do I keep getting duped into fixing Lillie's broken life? I could be watching *Murder, She Wrote*!"

Polar raced past irate onlookers and stopped cars, unintentionally terrifying teachers, photobombing selfies, and nearly knocking a ballsy pug into the pond. Polar growled at the hairball, beating Tennessee over the drawbridge. He was just too fast, and Tennessee was just too winded.

She set a steady pace. *What have I done today? Nothing but chase Illies! At least Polar's having fun*, she thought, splitting her time watching her step on the rickety drawbridge and eyeing the tiny white-haired heads now bobbing up and down over the precarious railing that boxed in the town's treasured bell.

As suddenly as it had begun, the clattering stopped.

Tennessee stopped.

She had to take a deep breath before raising her hands to block the sun for a better view of the bell. Polar was out of sight, but from the random scream or yelp she knew exactly where he was. She stared up at the tower, straining to properly decipher the scene.

"Yep, that's about right." She ground her teeth, sighing as she reached for a cig. She lit up in full view of another damn sign the Founders erected all over town:

*No Smoking*

After a long, calming drag, Tennessee watched Millie (or Billie) climb on Billie's (or Millie's) shoulders and straddle the tip-top of the massive bell. Whichever little snit *wasn't* clinging for dear life proceeded to shove the bell with impressive muscle for such a tiny brat. Both roared with laughter because neither grasped that the

bell tower and its bell were old, rusted, left *historic* and untouched during all renovations. That meant Billie (or Millie) swinging on that bell could, at any moment, crack the joist supporting the bell and inadvertently slingshot to a nasty death; or, if they were lucky, just a bone-busting fall.

The ominous moan of wood crackling was terrifyingly audible from where Tennessee stood.

"I don't need *more* work today." She flicked the cig into the moat, cupped her hands around her mouth, and hollered like the mother of all demons, "Get your rotten asses off that bell this instant!"

Yeah, everything stopped: cars, pedestrians, that annoying barking pug, and the Illie twins' laughter. Their tiny heads looked right at Tennessee, at first with expressions of shock, not fear; more of a *how dare she!* stare. This unified snoot swiftly shifted to smug smiles and screeches.

"You said *asses*! You said *asses*! We're telling Mommy you said *asses*!"

This was why she brought Polar. The bell tower amplified his beastly growls and resounding barks, showering the town in mastiff mania. The smug chanting stopped instantly, and the bell-riding twin lost her grip, dropping like a brick on her bell-pushing twin.

Tennessee chuckled. "Good job, partner." But her hands were shaking, and it took a bit of fiddling to light another cig. After the third drag her hands shook less, and by the time Polar herded the demons over the drawbridge, her hands were stone cold.

The twins were short for their age, more like kindergartners; like pocket children or bad luck charms. Antics aside, the elfin, blue-eyed sisters were cute; trouble was, they knew it, and they used it. Just as they'd been taught. Miss Grimmie must have done that to their hair; bleached white locks parted squarely down the middle, neatly pulled into pigtails pinned in place with bright pink bows; no way Lillie approved *that*. She'd once told Tennessee, "Anything with a *pig* in the name isn't *elegant* enough

for an Illie." In keeping with her elegant extremes, she banned pork from *ever* being served at The Mirror.

Everyone wore boring, battleship grey uniforms at Summerhold; heavily woven pleated skirts and crisp white collared shirts with the Summerhold crest stitched over each child's heart. Most children added a little bow or charm or something to express their identity. Not the twins; they were *exactly* alike in *every* way. This maddening identical-ness was their superpower.

Before either one could spit insults, or literally *spit* on her, Tennessee snuffed out her cig on the sole of her boot, rubbed the ashes on her index finger, and pulled the closest twin toward her.

Polar guarded Tennessee now, which kept the twins stiff and compliant.

With her ash covered finger, Tennessee drew a large cross on the child's forehead, right between the eyes,

"You're *Millie*," she christened the demon. "Wipe that off and I let my lion eat you." That was particularly heinous because Tennessee knew the twins were nearly viciously attacked by a dog the year before; but you parent in the moment, and this was *that* moment. "Now get your *asses* in the hearse."

Tennessee cussing? Tennessee siccing her mean old dog-lion on them? Had she finally gone insane, like everyone said she might one day? This Tennessee was definitely acting weird, and a tiny bit scary. The twins gave one another a look, silently agreed, and dutifully got their asses in the hearse.

Polar squeezed in beside the twins. Tennessee slammed the door shut, took a deep breath, before swiveling around for one last look at Summerhold. Scattered amongst the colorful murals depicting Biblical expectations, originally painted for illiterate townsfolk, were faces: nuns, teachers, spectators.

"Cowards," she muttered as the faces sluggishly slinked out of view.

Except one.

She couldn't see the face, but she instantly recognized him—the man in the hoodie.

# 4.

# Open Season

In fiendish fashion, a dense plume of milky white smoke suffocated poor Riggy and his occupants. Tennessee just sat there, head slumped over the wheel; from exhaustion, pain, and a realization that her life sucked.

Polar's barks reached eardrum-bursting decibels. They needed to get out.

Millie, still marked by ash, jumped out first. Billie followed, and Polar had no choice but to leave his master. He wrangled the twins toward the mountain guardrail and waited.

Tennessee barely lifted her head from the wheel. "Come on, Riggy, don't you die on me now!" She popped the hood and a gust of wind yanked it upright. "Son-of-a-motherless-pig-goat!"

A billowy plume of smoke lifted the aroma of sweetly singed antifreeze into the air. Tennessee touched the tiny cross pendant dangling from her chain. Polar's barking had her turning toward him; she could barely see him; her eyes were watering, and she was hacking up the same smoke now spoiling the picturesque view of The Mirror. It was so close, glistening on Scraggle Bluff, within sight, only miles of winding mountain between her and freedom from these brats.

Polar barked wildly from the guardrail; his master was taking far too long to exit the smoky beast. He was lunging into each bark,

growing more crazed. The twins eyed each other, concocting a plan. Tennessee looked over just as Millie turned to run one way, and Billie, the other.

Tennessee jumped from the driver's seat, roaring like a mamma lioness for the second time today. "Stop or I'll shoot! Lord help me, I'll shoot you both!"

A teensy-weensy part of her meant it, like with a BB gun; only one pump.

Maybe the ashen cross on Millie's forehead was starting to work, because she froze.

Polar had already stormed after Billie, overshot her, and had the kid sniveling against the rail; muzzle to nose.

Tennessee pretended to tuck a gun into the back waistband of her jeans, just like her favorite detectives did, only their weapons were real; well, real enough for eighties television. It got the twins' attention. They slunk back in line, walking when Polar walked, stopping when Polar stopped.

Millie looked at Billie, who looked at Polar, then back at Millie; together they looked at Tennessee, sassing her in unison.

"You can't hold us hostage!"

"Oh, yes I can!"

The words were out before Tennessee grasped what she had inadvertently insinuated. She was tired, hungry, sweaty, smoky, and a little nauseated, from *what* she didn't know.

Hands on hips, the towheaded twins exclaimed, a little too excitedly, "So this *is* a hostage situation!"

"It's whatever I say and, right now, if it shuts you two up, then *yes*, you're my hostages!"

"Mommy doesn't pay you enough, huh?" said Billie, somehow managing to look *down* on Tennessee from her measly three feet.

"She *smokes*, Billie," said Millie, her sainthood showing. "She probably has a lot of bad habits that cost more money than she earns."

"*She* is the cat's mother! *I* am *Ms. England*...for the gazillionth time!"

Polar used his size to back up his master's words, especially since he heard something about *cats*. He didn't like those, or these kids.

Millie turned to Billie. "*She* needs cash. Bad habits take cash."

Billie agreed, adding, all smart-ass and unabashed, "Mommy won't pay, but Daddy might."

Millie giggled. "She likes Daddy. Mommy says they both like meatloaf, but eating too much meatloaf clogs your hearteries. Maybe *she* needs cash to buy more meatloaf. Look at her butt, Billie, that's from meatloaf." Millie whispered the last part, which somehow strengthened the insult, and had Tennessee wishing she was dealing with Lillie herself rather than the shrunken versions. At least she could smack Lillie! Tennessee never had, but just knowing the option was available gave her joy.

"Another damn word and I bust out the gags." Tennessee snapped her fingers. "Polar!"

The loyal mastiff growled and shook his bushy coat so violently a slobbery wad of matted hair hit Billie's cheek, bounced off, and smacked Millie right on her lips.

"Gross!" the twins hollered.

Another growl from Polar and the twins shut up, but they weren't happy about it; in fact, they were plotting their revenge. Polar sensed as much, flashed his fangs just enough to have those scrawny things taking a step back.

"You girls have cell phones?"

Polar barked and the twins replied together, "No!"

Tennessee approached Riggy with a heavy heart; she hated leaving an injured friend behind. "I'll get help." She patted his roof. "There's an emergency callbox not far along this stretch." She grabbed her backpack and walking staff, then checked her phone one last time: dead. No choice but to walk.

It might have been easier to walk down the mountain, back toward town, but her job was to get the demons *home*, and she could see the goddamn Mirror from where she stood.

So, up they went.

~

Watching the twins labor up the mountainside, Tennessee discerned the slightest difference between the sisters. It was fleeting, like hearing the rumble-zip of a hummingbird just before catching a glimpse of it flitting off. One of them—Saint Millie—walked with just a bit more swagger. Do kids have swagger? *These* did.

Over a mile into their hike, Tennessee pulled three water bottles from her backpack. She always carried water. Because when she dealt with Lillie, shit like this was bound to happen. Tennessee dumped out a plastic bag of cheese crackers into the twins' hands, flipped it inside out and filled it with water for Polar. He lapped it up greedily, thanking Tennessee with an extra wet kiss.

"Gross!" the twins squawked again.

Tennessee smirked. "If you don't like something, close your eyes."

"I bet you close your eyes every time you see a mirror," Billie snickered.

Okay, the kid was quick, but Tennessee could do first grade. She mocked Billie's words in a screeching falsetto that shut the kid down.

Billie pouted; no one talked to them the way Tennessee did. And Billie hated her for it. "I bet you don't even have a real goddamn gun!"

"Language!" Tennessee stood up. "So help me, I *will* gag you girls!"

"She doesn't have a gun." Millie stood up, so Billie stood up, causing Polar to snarl and prep for battle. "We're not going anywhere with you until we see a goddamn gun!"

"Yeah," Billie one-upped her sister, "what kind of a shitty kidnapper takes hostages straight *home*!"

"If I had a bar of soap, so help me...I'd wash out your filthy mouths! For the love of all that is holy, get a thesaurus!"

Polar's guard went up, and soon after, a revving rumble rose up the mountain.

Tennessee cleaned up in a hurry. "Someone's coming...stay close, girls. It's getting dark. We need to hitch a ride."

It wasn't Polar's growl that got everyone's attention, it was that he stopped as quickly as he started.

"Scratch that!" Tennessee corralled the twins behind some underbrush. "Stay hidden no matter what...I'm not playing around anymore...promise me." She locked eyes with each girl.

Billie almost got lippy, but Millie answered by tugging her sister deeper into the prickly brush.

Tennessee ordered Polar to follow; this went against his overriding instinct to guard his master, but she seemed to care for those difficult creatures, so he obeyed.

There were three problems with Scraggle Bluff: The Mirror, a robust wildlife that often got too close to town, and poachers. The offensive, out-of-town poachers were the worst, and with Hill's auction earlier in the day there were plenty of out-of-towners looking to nab large game for trophies, meat, or just because.

Adrienne dealt with that sort all year long, but she was prepared for it with rifles and Rocky. All Tennessee had was an imaginary gun tucked in her waistband, a wooden walking staff, and a backpack full of snacks. But it was getting late and it would get too cold for the twins, so she had to try something.

A jacked-up truck sped into view, brights on. It zoomed right past Tennessee, screeched to a halt, then reversed. The cab was full of the same sort Tennessee tended at the mortuary: accidental shooting, reckless rollover, drunken hunting, drunken driving, drunken fighting, basic bad-boy jackass stuff.

There were six of them.

After the *hey pretty lady* comments, and *it's your lucky day* comments, and *wanna hop on my lap for the ride of your life* comments, one comment actually made sense. It came from the youngest of the bunch; probably someone's baby brother along

for the ride, who wasn't as drunk or as stupid as he would be in a year.

"Excuse me, ma'am, but is that your broke-down hearse back there?"

Tennessee nodded, clutching her staff the way Godzilla taught her.

"Is there somewhere we can take you?" The clear-eyed boy pushed over his buffoon brethren. "I'll sit in the back with you. It'll be fine, ma'am, my brothers are drunk and dumb, but we've got sisters, and our momma taught us right."

She eyed the boy. Maybe that was true, but she'd never risk the twins. "I'll pass."

Now the brothers hooted and hollered and yipped like coyotes high on moonbeams. The driver howled like an alpha, peeling out, pelting Tennessee with gravel and grit before skittering back onto the highway.

"Morons," Tennessee huffed as Polar bounded out from the underbrush. She should have known he was so close, ready, probably even a little upset he didn't get to bite the howler.

Polar growled just before the jacked-up truck backfired down the mountain. This time the loyal guardian stood his ground, openly defying his master's commands to hide.

But one of the drunken dipshits pointed a rifle out the cab window and fired. The bullet ripped into Tennessee's left thigh, gouging flesh from bone. Brutal pain tumbled her to the gravel as another shot punched a hole in the guardrail. She screamed, but not in agony.

"Girls! Run!" Tennessee ordered through gritted teeth. "Go! Now!"

A clamoring of curses and threats and smashing of beer bottles preceded the truck veering out of control, pitching on its side, screeching right past Tennessee in a spark storm of sizzling, shredded iron. Even as the truck jumped the guardrail, Tennessee couldn't turn away. The squealing crunch of twisted metal vibrated her bones as the truck smashed into a redwood. She

winced with each scream until the moment all sound merged into one meek whine of a horn choking. When she finally took a breath, her lungs filled with the rich high of gasoline.

Tennessee hacked, barely managing the quivering hot pain thriving deep inside her head. As for her thigh, numb to the nicked bone. She was certain a body was thrown from the bed of the truck. She was certain it was the clear-eyed baby brother. She was certain he was dead.

She could hear the groans, the snap of branches, thuds, a whirring shrill, something ticking, crackling, and crying. But it was the potent scent of burning flesh that brought tears to her eyes.

The drunken fools took one look at Polar, an albino, and wanted him. Simple as that. Poachers stupidly assume they're doing the animal a favor; white in the wild screams target. Maybe they thought he was an albino baby bear or baby moose. It didn't matter. Those who survived would sober up and realize they'd killed their baby brother, not a baby bear or baby moose. *Their baby brother*.

From where Tennessee lay, she could tell she'd have a ton of work tomorrow morning, *if* they were local. Out-of-towners got shipped home, and that was fine by her. Except for the boy, the poor boy trying to help her; he'd obviously convinced his brothers to turn back, but then one of them saw Polar and...stupid boys.

While Tennessee was willing to put a band-aid on her wound, Polar had other ideas. The bloody men wriggling out of the crushed cab were damn near attacked by one outraged mastiff. They were so disoriented, Polar's insane barking didn't faze them. One drunk actually tried to explain himself.

"She moved, man...she jumped in my shot. You saw the boar, right...there was a f—in' white boar!"

*This* was precisely why Tennessee wanted a man who didn't drink. Nothing was as deadly as mixing alcohol, testosterone, and stupid. William drank occasionally; Phillip, never; Godzilla, *who*...her thoughts tumbled overcast, but she couldn't imagine

why. It was just a scratch. There was a lot of blood, but it couldn't *all* be coming from her; it was just a scratch. No reason to panic; she was just tired.

The twins crawled out of their hiding place, running straight to Tennessee.

"Girls, please, stay behind the guardrail...this is grownup stuff."

Millie, with the ashen cross almost washed off by sweat and grime, was in tears. Billie never once took her eyes off Tennessee, not once.

Tennessee was trying to scold them for breaking their promise to stay hidden, but her voice crackled in her ears as if she'd tuned AM instead of FM. And Polar must be running, chasing those drunken idiots because his barks were so loud one second and far away the next. Loud, soft, loud, soft, soft, softer, just a purr now...do dogs purr?

She couldn't remember.

The twins must have snuck back into the underbrush because they were gone.

"Good girls," she slurred, "let the grownups fix this..." There was just enough daylight to toss shadows over Tennessee's face. The finger-like pine branches moved in perfect time, so precise she was transfixed by them. She'd close her eyes when the shadows cooled her face, open her eyes when the setting sun warmed it. She played this game as Polar purred and only stopped when a large shadow blocked any warmth the sun had left.

She opened her eyes. "*You*. How do you keep finding me?"

The man in the hoodie said nothing as he kneeled beside Tennessee.

"I have a band-aid in my backpack," Tennessee grumbled. "It's here, somewhere..." She wasn't afraid of this hooded man. She wasn't *anything*. Not even numb. Just...Tennessee.

With a guarded yet hasty tenderness, the man cradled Tennessee in his arms.

Tennessee reached up to the man's face, and with both hands, lowered that damned hood. The face was familiar and comforting

and somehow, she knew instinctually that she didn't *want* to see this man.

He wore the scars of a long, hard life along his rigid cheekbones, yet those eyes hadn't lost their spark. They were the eyes of a warrior, no, an emperor; black onyx pearls set in regal frames, accentuated by the richness of his skin. Tennessee fell into the warmth of those eyes, but it wasn't right. Not yet. She ran her palm over his thick black beard, strands of silver shining through; it was much softer than it looked, and cold. Or was *she* cold? It was getting hard to tell where or *what* she was. The gravel that had been so uncomfortable under her turned spongy, the brisk sea air stifled to stale, and the man cradling her was speaking too fast; his words were strange, and she didn't like them at all.

"Death came early, Ten." The man's rumbly accent crossed cultures; Asian roots textured with experience, mindfulness, and peril. "I tried to prevent this...the others, they had me...*detained*."

Tennessee could no longer hear Polar's barks or see anything beyond the outline of this man. "You're...*Death*."

The man looked as though that would be a great honor, then replied humbly, "A servant."

"Do servants have names?"

The man went to speak, and Tennessee noticed that his bottom teeth were slightly crooked, and his lips were chapped, and there was a scabbed-over cut on his lower lip. He was unlike any man she knew; not a Suit, not a Cowboy. And those emperor eyes.

"I am Sho." The man bowed his head, compassion in his rasp, and wisdom in his gaze.

Tennessee rubbed his beard one more time. "The beard is new, huh?"

Sho's forehead wrinkled, and a deep crevice formed between his eyebrows. "Forgive my delay. Many fought my return to you."

"But I saw you this morning," she sang her suspicions, head cocked to one side. "No beard."

Sho placed his palm behind Tennessee's neck, right on the spot

that ached all damn day. "Time is not ours, Ten. You have a choice to make, but please, choose quickly."

Her eyes widened. "Dead people have choices?"

Sho nearly smiled. "You would not be dead. That is the choice. Mortal or immortal?"

If Sho hadn't been so damned serious, Tennessee would have laughed; as it was, she relaxed her head into his palm as if she'd done so a million times.

Tennessee gazed skyward, only mist and nothing. She wasn't in any pain; quite the opposite, she was weightless, as if she might float away if Sho released her. It was tempting, this business of immortality. She was completely at peace; well, *almost*.

It was just that the twins were still hiding in the underbrush somewhere, and a boy just died trying to be kind; she could tend to his body, make him look nice for his family; then there were her parents and Polar, Lin, Godzilla. Phillip. Hill, Adrienne. *Phillip*. Maybe *this* was her Christmas miracle...

"You have chosen bravely," Sho declared in his rumbly accent, as if he'd heard every one of Tennessee's thoughts. He went on to chant and assert and threaten as it became clear to Tennessee that they were not alone.

Sho challenged the invisible stranger, "Your efforts are wasted. She has chosen. We claim her of her own free will!"

Tennessee couldn't see this opponent, but she could hear him, a little, and he was pissed.

"You think *we* cannot see?! You marked her without consent," the unseen raged. "*Both* shall be punished for crossing into the forbidden!"

And with those words, Tennessee and Sho cried out in utter agony.

~

Tennessee hated hospitals. Most of her childhood was whitewashed by sterile walls, stiff sheets, lying doctors, and nurses too busy to smile. There was one nurse, though, whom she loved

instantly; who smelled of cherry, smoke, and ash. That familiar voice thundered now, coarse with frustration, fear maybe.

"Step aside or I'll tattoo your face with this here pipe!"

Then Godzilla's rich tone splintered, which only happened when he was confronted by short, loud things, like Lin.

Whatever Lin said, it was in whispers because all Tennessee could make out was her own name. Then Hill burst through the door first. Which, apparently, was the crux of the battle.

"Halleluiah!" Hill boomed. "Look who joined the living! Took you long enough. Thought you were going to wait until your birthday...it's just around the corner, Nessie."

Tennessee smiled at the three most important people in her life, then reprimanded each accordingly.

"No smoking, Hill. Be kind to your elders, Lin. And Godzilla, don't let a scrappy Asian scare you...no matter how scary she is."

The three exhaled their relief as Tennessee shimmied herself up and almost out of bed.

"Ness!" all three hollered, but it was Godzilla who got to her side first. He didn't look it, but he was fast.

Tennessee snarled up her face as Godzilla lifted her legs back onto the bed. The big guy was still fumbling with the tangled sheets when Phillip entered the room.

He always wore his white coat buttoned to just under the knot of his tie. Today he had on his blue striped tie, which Tennessee now focused on. All she could see was that blue striped tie, his words garbled French, Portuguese, was that Russian? Nothing he said made sense. And that tie. That blue striped tie.

"She was herself a moment ago," Lin said, and Tennessee vaguely understood. "Now she's gone. Do something, Phillip! It's getting worse."

Tennessee understood now, and found the words to convey exactly what the hell was wrong.

"Shit! Lillie didn't get her Santa!"

"You see," Lin whispered angrily. "*Shit*? She never says *shit*!"

Phillip typed a quick note in his tablet before handing it off to

Hill, who glanced at the note before handing it to Lin. As Phillip approached the bed he removed his penlight from his coat pocket, looking both distracted and somewhat hostile.

"Look at me," he ordered, as he shined Tennessee's eyes; left, right, right, left. "What day is it, kid?"

"I'm not a kid."

"You've sure been acting like one. Day?"

"It's blue striped tie day." Tennessee yanked Phillip's tie out from under his buttoned-up white coat. He knew everyone's bad habits, except his own. Every day was black tie day except mauve Monday, and blue striped *Tuesday*.

Phillip's brow creased so Tennessee stated matter-of-fact, "It's *Tuesday*, old geezer...blue striped Tuesday...which means I've been unconscious for almost a full day because it's dusk. Exactly when..." She kept the part about hallucinating Sho to herself. Why confuse matters?

Godzilla started to say something, coughed it back. Lin pretended to read the tablet, and Hill just kept on clenching her snuffed-out pipe wedged in the corner of her mouth.

Keenly observing Tennessee, Phillip announced dismissively, "You're correct, it's Tuesday."

Tennessee read much more in Phillip's laidback tone. "*But*..."

Phillip paused as if that was all he had to say.

"There's more." Tennessee crossed her arms. "You have your *but*-face on."

Godzilla chuckled and his belly shook, then his white teeth gleamed as brightly as the sterile white walls. "Good one, Ness."

Tennessee laughed. "Goddamn right!" Then, as if suddenly realizing those words were hers, she eyed Hill and Lin; both of whom were *trying* to hide their aghast. *That* curse was a bad one, *real* bad.

Phillip leaned against the hospital bed like a tired parent at story time struggling to come up with something new.

"You're right, Tenny, it's Tuesday, but it's been a *few* Tuesdays since your damsel-in-distress bit on Scraggle Bluff. The bullet

nicked an artery. The twins called Sheriff Honey, who dispatched an ambulance. We got to you just in time."

There was a long enough pause for Tennessee to panic. "The twins." She held her breath, gutted by thoughts of failing them.

"Ornery as ever, Nessie, never you mind. I whopped 'em for lying about their cell phones." Hill stared down Phillip.

But Phillip's thoughts must have turned dark as well, because he was scowling when he continued. "Going for the callbox was risky; you should have stayed put. Especially with the girls. What does it take for a grown woman to charge her cell phone?! When will you get it into that thick skull of yours? You're lucky, Tenny...but luck runs out."

This was angry Phillip. The one who preferred life bubble-wrapped. The one who was always there for her, even after *he* broke her heart. His bedside manner, though, could use some work.

"What can I say, Phillip? When my cell dies, the wild woman in me roars!" Tennessee made a crazy face. "I gotta roam, gotta *risk*, gotta grab life by the balls! Oh, that's right, you gave those to Lillie." Now she was just trying to hurt him, and she wasn't sure *why*.

Phillip rose, collecting himself with one languishing inhale. "This is a wake-up call, Tenny. You got lucky with the poachers; your injuries could have been much worse. And the rest...your seizure...what the twins saw..." He held his breath, swallowed hard. "It was a dangerous situation for everyone involved."

This was the controlling Phillip. The one who scheduled life, everything from Sunday sex to ten-minute movement walks. *This* guy was the reason they were through even though she hadn't been ready for everything to end. But he did end it and she never quite forgave him for breaking her heart. Tennessee gave Lin a look that had the brainy beautician shoving the tablet into Phillip's gut.

"Your scans are back to normal, Ness. Something got

scrambled, but that beautiful brain of yours checks out now. Isn't that right, doc!" Lin flashed Phillip her finest angry-Asian eyes.

Phillip clutched the tablet, un-hunching his tall frame. Tennessee could see he was overworked and pale, more than his normal overworked and pale. Phillip reviewed Tennessee's scans *again* before concurring with Lin.

"Stanford would be proud," he offered something of a compliment, which his deadpan delivery rescinded immediately.

Tennessee intervened before Lin could retaliate. "Lin can read anything...pie charts, bar graphs, CTs, MRIs, x-rays...gamma rays..."

Hill coughed a laugh as she took hold of the tablet to peruse Tennessee's test results. "More like hard-boiled," she mused aloud, her troubled tone pinning an ache to Tennessee's chest.

It was back.

Phillip whispered with Hill about a CT schedule for monitoring the growing cerebral aneurysm in Tennessee's brain; it was just a matter of time, maybe six months, before those weakened vessels burst, causing her death, or worse, life in a vegetative state.

Godzilla had been looking out the window. Tennessee followed his gaze to the peekaboo view of a seahorse mural painted on the massive seawall protecting half of their tight-knit town. She could feel his grief, but it had the opposite effect; it pissed her off.

"Snap out of it, Godzilla! It was just a sentinel," she blasted. "I got those warning headaches all the time with the other bleed. This is old news. Schedule the surgery, doc, cut the bastard out."

Hill looked up from the tablet, with eyes that lost their sorrow long ago. She was hard, exactly what Tennessee needed.

"We're beyond that, Nessie."

Tennessee took a breath; she knew the drill. "Right...hello migraines and nausea and hallucinations galore."

It was Hill who answered with a pointed, "Suffer well, Nessie, and all will right itself."

"Not this time, Hill," she griped, then to Phillip, "My parents?"

Phillip nodded, his tone morose, "I've been in touch daily. They've booked a flight."

That told her more than any scan would.

Tennessee lowered her eyes, tracing the lines on her left palm. Her grandmother had told her she'd have a long life. She was a good liar.

Tennessee lost the ability to smell death her second year working as a mortician, but that arid scent of absence was fresh in her nostrils now, singeing her lungs as she recalled all the bodies she'd prepped for the afterlife.

Dying wasn't the problem, everyone dies. Tennessee believed in heaven. Problem was, she also believed in hell. Come on, it can't all be waterfalls, sweet cakes, and corny walks with loved ones. She thought more of hell, what horrors might be lurking there; how she might have meticulously prepped bodies whose departed souls were being boiled in the putrid stomach acids of a satanic glutton. Would *her* soul end up on hell's beastly menu? Maybe even worse, who would meet her at hell's fiery gates? Before she could shake loose the thought, the sweet tang of salted chocolate moistened her tongue.

"Sho," she trembled an exhale; scanning the room in discreet terror. Everyone was doing something small, unimportant, something other than gawking at the dying girl.

This was her only chance.

Tennessee had been working on loosening the tape covering her IV since finding herself stuck in another hospital bed. She'd worked it all the way off and only had to tug out the plastic tubing. When she was a kid she wouldn't move her *needle hand* for fear of bleeding to death. *This* Tennessee yanked that sucker out, slipped out of bed, and headed *out*.

But she didn't account for weakness in her shot leg; it buckled beneath her weight, and she went careening into Phillip's arms.

"Not smart, Tenny." Phillip prudently escorted her back to bed. "You need more tests."

As his firm hands lifted her legs on to the bed, she focused on

his clothes rather than the electric tingles moving up her thighs; Phillip's white coat wasn't pressed as usual, and neither were his slacks; his scowl seemed eternally etched, and he had a bit of scruff on his overly tensed jawline. Maybe he needed a break too.

"I promise I'll come in, Phillip, but I really need to see Polar." Her tone was sweet and confrontational and manipulative. "*Please...*" She held his gaze longer than was safe. He was a good man and she could see the goodness in his gaze, but she had to look away the moment his scowl just barely softened.

"At least use the wheelchair."

"Thank you." Tennessee secured the back of her gown before slipping into the wheelchair Lin rolled over.

Lin was less civilized; she targeted Phillip, running over his foot as she wheeled Tennessee out. Godzilla grabbed the rest of Tennessee's belongings and followed, and although his eyes were cast down, he grunted a genuine, "Thanks, doc."

Phillip nodded, approaching Hill just as she puffed her pipe ablaze. She handed him the tablet, and he began methodically reviewing Tennessee's records for something, *anything*.

As Tennessee made her four-wheeled escape down the hall, a tug at her throat took her breath; it was uncomfortable enough that she made Lin stop. The tug loosened, and Tennessee went on with her escape, but not before overhearing Phillip's desperation,

"There's got to be something. I can't lose her..."

Tennessee inhaled the sweet scent of sun-ripened cherries on a hot summer day as Hill's words hit her,

"She's dying, Phillip. Be strong for our Nessie as she makes her goodbyes."

# 5.

# Delirium

"I know you're on vacation, Tennessee, but you gotta come get this body...er, the pieces anyway."

Tennessee was sitting in bed, her leg propped up on a stack of pillows. She had the television on mute. The movie was almost over; Doc dangled from the clock tower, McFly was out of time, lightning was about to strike, but her cell phone wouldn't stop ringing and now she was stuck in an annoying conversation with Mike, the morgue guy.

"Has there been a rash of deaths I'm unaware of, Mike?"

This guy, Mike, was new. Tennessee wasn't sure if he hated *all* women or just *her*. She hoped it was just her, because guys who hated *all* women put a panic in her gut.

"Lookie here, *Missy Small Town Mortician*," Mike got all formal and unprofessional, "pick up the body or I'm calling *Our Lady of Peace*. Guy Sutton's been asking me to send more work his way anyhow."

Tennessee clicked off the television, chucking the remote on the bed. "That's one helluva way to honor the family's wishes, Mike! Where's Marta? You remember Marta, your *boss*! And the *only* person with actual *authority* to transfer a body *without* the family's consent."

Mike got to backtracking, Tennessee not only met his bluff, she raised him fifty. She talked right over Mike's empty apologies.

He was stupid. She hated stupid.

"Just a little FYI, Mike...death professional to death professional. The Cains have long been at odds with the Suttons. You send Johnny Cain's pieces to Guy Sutton and you're done. Pack your shit and hitch your trailer because nobody in town will *ever* trust you with their dead...*never ever*, Mike...*forever never ever*, Mike!"

Mike muttered an ungracious apology as Tennessee checked a text that had her cell phone trembling. She let out a hard humph. "Open the door, Mike."

"What?"

"Open the damn door! Give the Johnny bits to the big guy. Death gets us all, Mike, some of us just end up in more pieces than others. Extend a little courtesy and maybe I'll keep all *your* pieces in one place."

A fluster of sounds preceded a terse, "Thank you."

"You're welcome." Tennessee's sweet tone rubbed sinister. "Yeah, I'll box you up real nice when you show up on my slab." She didn't wait for a goodbye, didn't offer one. Chucking the phone next to the remote, she sighed. "Newbies suck."

Tennessee used both hands to lift her bandaged thigh off the pillow stack. The bright swirling sunlit shapes splashing across her bedroom told her it was noon. She already knew what time it was, but it was always reassuring when nature confirmed technology. Staying plugged in was just another burden, another place to fail. What was it Phillip had said...

"*What does it take for a grown woman to charge her cell phone?!*"

That still irked her. He didn't *get* her, didn't even try.

Maybe she liked being unavailable, maybe being lost to the world is good for a girl.

Scooting to the edge of the queen bed took some doing.

Downstairs, Polar's ears perked up to his master's pain-induced grunts; he raced up the stairs in a flurry of dog hair and spit.

"Good boy." Tennessee watched as Polar stood sentry at the landing. "Getting used to the new staircase, huh? Yeah, it was nice of the Jims to do that, but I'll miss the wall climb."

Polar grunted, sitting a bit taller.

Tennessee met Polar's gaze; his eyes were timid, and he just sat there. It took a minute before she appreciated the significance of the moment; he was entering *her* den for the first time. Polar hadn't been able to get to the second floor before, and he wasn't certain how to navigate the newness, or even if he was allowed.

"Come here, boy." She tapped her thighs, instantly regretting hitting her left one; drunk bastards were the worst *and* best shots. It wasn't a graze; it was a gouge, and gouges hurt.

Polar bounded forward, head bobbling in joy; he couldn't skid upstairs like he could downstairs. All the shag carpet slowed him down and caught in his nails. The mountain of a dog yelped as a strip of yarn split one nail. He limped the rest of the way, lifting his injured right paw into Tennessee's waiting hands.

"Aw, you too? You gotta be careful, boy, carpet is dangerous." She hid a smirk as she doctored Polar's wound. Just a sliver of his nail lost the yarn battle. "I think you'll live, but you and me...man, we need better luck. Everybody says *be careful*, as if we're living a high-stakes life. Bungee jumping, rock climbing, skydiving, white water rafting..." Tennessee grew pensive. "Man, I haven't done *anything*...not *one* thing. I just box people who *have*."

Instead of getting out of bed, Tennessee lifted her leg back onto the pillow stack. She thumped the white comforter beside her and made a clicking sound with her tongue until Polar jumped up to claim the spot.

"Let's watch McFly save *his* future, Polar." Tennessee clicked the television on, curled up with her white lion, and tried her darndest to forget the life she failed to lead—and the little time she had left to do anything about it.

~

Beneath Earth's crust a gazillion grasshoppers rattled, a continent of crickets vibrated, and an old, odd frog croaked out

the theme song to *Knight Rider*; Tennessee would have slept the entire night if the surprisingly gentle seismic stream hadn't been broken by the *snap-snarl-growl* of her trusty lion.

"What is it boy?!" Tennessee jumped out of bed, only to let out a growl of her own as she tumbled to the ground. "Damn poachers." She gritted her teeth, watching her white gauze soak up red ooze. Instead of focusing on the throbbing result of a popped stitch, she focused on breathing, and whatever Polar was doing downstairs. His sturdy nails *tick-tapped* the floorboards, then scrawled screeching wiggles as he skidded from one side of the silo to the other.

"Polar! What's going on? Who's there?!"

The ruckus only intensified as Polar's guttural barks echoed in the sparsely furnished house. Tennessee grabbed her walking staff; without drawing attention to it, Godzilla put it beside her bed when he first brought her home. She was glad for it. It helped. She limped over to her dresser, tugged open the top drawer and pulled out her taser. *That* was a gift from Adrienne.

"All my friends think I'm a weakling," Tennessee scoffed as she hobbled to the stairs. Shuffling her way down, she was grateful for the Jims' gift. There was no way she could have climbed down the wall, especially now that blood streamed down her leg, leaving a broken red trail behind her.

"Polar." Her voice caught in her lungs.

Polar skidded over to her, still barking ferociously at *nothing* near the kitchen nook.

Tennessee stopped on the bottom step, holding her taser way out in front of her as she surveyed the kitchen: two unmatched wooden chairs, square dining table with a faded chessboard painted on top, and the stove. Nothing was on fire.

"Who's there?" She harnessed her angriest tone.

No one answered.

Polar kept a steady growl toward the kitchen as Tennessee scanned the living room. The space was cleaner than she'd left it. She'd scold Lin for picking up later, but right now there was an

intruder in her home. She went to take the final step down when her left foot slipped on a pool of blood; she was falling backwards, again.

Her staff thunked to the floor and the taser slid across the room, skidding under the couch.

Polar went hysterical, turning his madness from the kitchen to right beside Tennessee. Just before smashing her head on the brand-new cedar steps, cool hands cradled her; gently steering her to a comfortable seat on the stairs; way better than the concussion-inducing thud that would have had Phillip admitting her for good.

Polar pawed his master, wedging his body between her and nothing. Those cold hands released her.

"Uh, who's there?" She barely heard her own words. Could she be hallucinating again? But Polar never engaged in her hallucinations; he always played a passive role: slobbering, snoozing, snoring.

Fangs exposed, Polar's attention moved from the stairs to the living room. Tennessee tracked with him, but all she saw was her ratted tan sofa and flea market coffee table. The fireplace was empty and, again, nothing was ablaze. She gripped the railing to pull herself up.

Polar growled his disapproval.

"It's all right, boy, there's no one there." Wow, what a horrible liar she was. Just recalling those hands on her flesh crept crushed ice up her spine. Soon, those spiky shivers had her slinking back down on the steps.

A key jingle-jangling in the front door deadlock sent Polar back into hysterics. He lunged into the living room, knocked over a clunky bookshelf, and rammed head-first into the stone hearth. He only acted like this when he found small game to play hunt: a mole, jack rabbit, fox. Had an animal snuck in a window?

Polar slowed his movements, creeping up on his prey, trapping the unseen thing against the back door. That sharp tug at her throat returned right before a swift jerking motion toppled her

over. Hunched on her forearms and knees, she labored for one good breath.

Polar abandoned his invisible prey, skidding back to his master.

Tennessee gulped in a ragged breath; exhaled a croaky, damp groan.

Polar refused to move, lashing out in long barks as the front door crashed open.

"Ness!" Lin's panic brought her urban out. "Holy mother of shit, what happened?" The petite woman raced to her friend, while managing to group text Phillip, Godzilla, and Hill an *all hell's broke loose* message. *She* was techy.

"Ah, you know, just getting some stretches in...chillin' and stuff." Tennessee wheezed into sitting as Polar made chase, once again skidding into the kitchen. His snarls, growls, and grunts now shoved shivers down Lin's spine.

Lin hunched over Tennessee. "What are you doing out of bed? You're bleeding everywhere! Dammit, Ness, I thought you were marathoning *Back to the Future* today?"

Lin meticulously calculated her life, and according to those calculations, padding in time for potty breaks and the occasional nap, Tennessee's movie trilogy marathon had thirty minutes left.

"I *was*," Tennessee complained.

Lin cupped Tennessee's cheeks as she might a rebellious five-year old. "Then why are you on your ass bleeding like a stuck pig?"

Tennessee scowled. "*Stuck pig*, huh? You could be Phillip's nurse with that bedside manner."

"Ha!" Lin's surliness enhanced her sneer. "I'd rather enter into holy hell with Mr. Won."

"Ouch," Tennessee laughed, and Lin helped her friend limp to the couch. Together, they propped the wounded leg under a mountain of pillows. "Thank you, Lin, but I'm not an invalid. I would have made it back upstairs soon enough."

"Yes, my little island friend, you're a real badass." Lin hurried to the kitchen, hurried back to apply pressure with a handful of bright white dishtowels. When the bleeding finally stopped, Lin

retrieved dinner from her car, then settled herself in the kitchen. While reheating this and chopping that, Lin joked in her number one every-Asian accent. "Why house pig sty? You pig? You no care? Only good is red...red good luck. You keep red, maybe change luck."

"Mamma Min's back in town, huh?"

"The woman never left! She's worried about you. Be warned, she's threatening a visit."

"Bring her over next time. I'd love to see her!"

"You strange girl with strange luck. Poachers *never* shoot Lin! Mamma Min in town, get shot *lucky*!"

Tennessee was laughing pretty hard when Phillip walked in. Well, he wasn't exactly *walking*. His quick footfalls traversed the gravel pathway, pummeled the porch, soared over the threshold, and conquered the wooden floors to stop directly in front of her. She studied the man. Good thing he wasn't on the road that night; he might have massacred every last hunter in Saint James.

"I was perfecting my triple flip." Tennessee winked, but Phillip was already cutting the soiled bandage from her leg.

"Nothing would surprise me at this point. I swear, you won't be happy until you bleed to death."

"Yes, Phillip, it's the dream that keeps me going."

Phillip stayed hyper-focused on the new damage to Tennessee's thigh. "Well, you've ensured yourself a nasty scar."

"No, doc, *please*!" Tennessee threw the back of her hand on her forehead, feigning horror. "Not a scar! Not so close to my death..."

Phillip was so livid he stopped cleaning her wound, and walked out.

Lin was busy boiling and stirring when Phillip stormed by her. He paced on the porch, both hands wringing tension from his neck. He looked a man damn near broken.

"Lin." Tennessee's remorse had Polar padding over to her.

"What you need, hon?" she called back from the kitchen, keeping her eyes on the breaking man.

"How's the weather?"

"Could be rain...bouts of thunder."

They communicated the way best friends do, nuanced tones delivering unspoken truths.

Tennessee sat up, resting her stretched leg on the distressed coffee table. She hoped Phillip wouldn't leave, but she *was* pushing him; and for no good reason, but to lighten the burden of her death on *herself*. What a selfish thing to do. She ought to know he didn't have a sense of humor about death, especially *hers*.

"I'm sorry, Phillip," Tennessee shouted, sarcasm washed out. She meant this one.

Soon, those quick footfalls triggered a slackening in her shoulders; she held her breath, sinking into the couch to let the man be of use. If fixing her leg made him feel like he had a tiny bit of control over her destiny, and perhaps his own, then she ought to give him that much. For old times.

The pain shot Phillip gave her *was* a relief, so she thanked him for it, even though she didn't mind the pain. It made her feel alive, and she needed to hold onto that sensation for as long as she could.

He stitched her back up, securing a fresh bandage while offering a stern order, "You're sleeping down here tonight."

"Roger that." She flashed a thumbs-up, settling into the couch with a look that proved she *was* tired after such an eventful evening.

"What happened to your bookshelf?" Phillip finally inspected the room now that Tennessee was settled.

Lin sashayed in from the kitchen carrying a bamboo tray cluttered with a stack of bowls, a colossal bowl of rice noodles, a plate of garnishes, and a gigantic stock pot of steamy soup. "Who wants Mamma Min's cure-all pho?"

Phillip surveyed both women, back and forth. "What happened here?"

"How I know? I make pho!" Lin sassed fast.

Tennessee chuckled, shifting more upright as the rich aroma of savory broth tempted her stomach; she was starving. "It's nothing,

Phillip. Polar freaked out earlier and knocked it over. I came down to check it out and that's when I fell."

"You fell?" he snapped, a man on edge.

"Uh, yeah. The bloody footprints weren't obvious enough for you?"

Phillip craned his neck to see past Lin's pot of pho. Nothing. The place was spotless.

Lin flipped her hair. "I clean up! Mamma Min no like mess!"

"Ugh, could you stop cleaning," Tennessee moped. "I like my ugly, but I *love* my messy."

"Whatever, just eat! I had three permas today, *six* kiddie cuts. I'm in no mood."

Tennessee spooned broth into her mouth, missing twice; damn meds. "Thanks for dinner, though. I'll take food anytime."

The ladies shared a laugh, and while they ate, Phillip found Tennessee's toolbox and securely fashioned the bookshelf to the wall. Next, he set about alphabetizing the books; first the nonfiction, of which there were few; then the fiction, of which there were many.

He shared a snide, "A bit more nonfiction wouldn't hurt, Tenny."

Lin sneered, twirling noodles around chopsticks. "Says the man who needs *more* fiction." She mumbled more, but her mouth was full.

Tennessee tossed more Thai basil and beansprouts into her bowl just as Godzilla strutted through the door.

Polar grunted to his beastly friend; Godzilla grunted back. A shrewd glance assessing Tennessee's state, and the man grabbed an enormous mixing bowl from the kitchen before announcing,

"I smell chow!"

"Come eat!" Tennessee slurped up her rice noodles and, out of the corner of her eye, she watched Phillip's gaze relax and his lips lift affectionately. Dead people don't eat, so her slurping must be a good sign. Phillip shelved the last dime store romance, helped himself to a bowl of pho, and settled in beside her.

Godzilla dragged in a chair from the kitchen nook; it was made of sturdy wood and was pretty much the only chair in the house that could support him.

"Is that Mamma Min's famous pho?" He hurried to the pot, lifted the lid, and inhaled the comforting aromas of hearty beef broth and ginger.

Lin slammed her chopsticks against her bowl. "It's pronounced *fuh!* How many times do I have to explain this?"

Godzilla was still basking in the herb-spiced steam.

"Fff...uhh..." Lin asserted, grabbing the lid from Godzilla's hand. She slammed the lid back on the pot. "Say it *correctly* or you don't get any!"

"Ah come on, Lin." Godzilla had a big boy pout on. "I skipped lunch."

Tennessee kept her head down, shooting a quick glance at Phillip. He smirked, that damn smirk that crinkled his eyes and sent her stomach flipping.

"You say it!" Lin sounded just like Mamma Min, and the resemblance startled her. She locked eyes with Tennessee, who gave a little reassuring nod. Lin was so disgusted with herself she filled Godzilla's bowl with rice noodles, ladled in steaming broth, and when she added juicy slices of beef, Godzilla was all *thanks for the pho*; only this time he pronounced it perfectly,

*"Fuh."*

The contrite woman gave a quick nod, then piled on jalapenos, beansprouts, sprigs of basil and cilantro. The big man beamed as Lin squeezed fresh lime over his soup with her left hand while drizzling on hot chili oil with her right.

Tennessee let her gaze wander from friend to friend, absently stirring her soup with chopsticks. It had been more than a year since they'd all shared a meal like this; late night feasts were once a weekly occurrence, before Phillip broke off their romance and ruined it all.

After several minutes of pure enjoyment devouring his seventh

meal of the day, Godzilla asked plainly, “You guys know Maria Garcia?”

Tennessee shook her head *no*, splashing broth on her t-shirt and shorts. Phillip handed her a napkin, which she refused. He set it on her lap anyway before helping Lin clear the dishes.

Lin grabbed Godzilla’s chopsticks right out of his mouth. “Great hair. Nice woman. Cut and color every six weeks. Tips well. Why?”

“She died.” Godzilla eyed a strip of beef soaking in rich broth at the bottom of Tennessee’s bowl. “You gonna eat that?”

Tennessee handed over her bowl. “How’d she die?”

Godzilla brought the bowl to his lips and poured. Phillip was busy checking his cell phone when Godzilla, still chewing, replied, “Only know she died because they wheeled her in when I collected Johnny. Her lawn was an easy forty every two weeks.”

Tennessee shot him a horrified look.

“Relax, Ness.” Godzilla placed a meaty hand on her shoulder. “I only meant she overpaid me all the time because she had a big heart, so I did extra work around her yard when she wasn’t home. She was a really cool lady, made the best empanadas in town.”

“I’m sorry she died,” Tennessee offered, only half wondering if Maria would be boxed or burned. Nobody wanted natural burials anymore. Maybe she’d change that; make it *cool* to rot in an eco-friendly way. Nothing composts better than dead bodies...

Phillip stacked the dishes in the sink, spraying water on them as he announced, “I’m needed at the hospital.” He approached Godzilla, and with a firm handshake, “Hill said you’re taking first watch.”

Tennessee snarled, “Whoa, whoa, whoa! Hold up, Jack! Nobody’s watching anybody. I’ve got my remote control and Polar. All I need. Busy day tomorrow with Johnny’s wake, so thanks for the stitches and the soup but you can *all* leave now. Except Lin... *You* can stay if you promise to stop cleaning.”

Nobody was listening. Lin was busy washing dishes, Godzilla stretched out on his chair, and Phillip had packed his bag and

was halfway out the door when Tennessee's cell phone rang. The echoey rumble muffled down the stairs.

Phillip was the closest. Maybe he was in a hurry, maybe he'd just...

"I'll get that."

Tennessee cringed. He hadn't been in her bedroom since the breakup, and she hadn't removed *all* evidence of him yet. She meant to, but life got busy and, well, she just didn't. She tossed her head back onto the couch, in actual pain at the thought of him seeing the framed memory still sitting on her dresser; Lin snapped the photo, a rare, candid moment of a smiling Phillip kissing a smitten Tennessee, a light brush of a kiss. It was just a backyard barbeque, no fantastic location, no waterfalls and cabanas; just a real day, a real moment.

If he paused to *really* look, he'd see a handful of his t-shirts folded neatly in her dresser drawer—the one she left open retrieving her taser—ties and his favorite button-down; dammit, the phone was on her bed which still had *their* comforter set, and *his* favorite plush blanket, which was now *her* favorite blanket. Dammit. Why hadn't she obeyed all the break-up rules and burned everything? Lin told her to. Now Phillip would act all puffed up and powerful, and nothing would convince him that she'd moved on.

Did that matter? Hell, yes, it mattered!

*He* did the breaking.

And she *had* moved on. She'd been on dates. One went well.

Dammit, why didn't she burn the evidence?

"Here's your phone, Tenny. It was your mom."

"Yeah, okay!" she blasted. "I'll call her back later. She's been calling nonstop. Won't believe I'm fine until she sees me *not* dead, I guess."

Phillip placed the phone on the couch right next to her bandaged thigh. She kept her eyes closed until he said, "I'll drop by the shop tomorrow to check the leg."

"Please don't." And Tennessee saw, just for a split second,

profound emotion in his eyes; it wasn't disappointment or condescension or anything she expected; it looked a lot like misery.

Dammit, that was probably his guilt. She was a pathetic puppy, and he had kicked that pathetic puppy.

He added nonchalantly, "I found your charger in the usual place...under the bed. It's on your dresser next to..." Phillip stopped but Tennessee finished the sentence in her head "*the picture that you kept of us because that's what pathetic puppies do.*"

"Goodbye, Phillip!" She gripped a pillow. Death by smothering was still an option.

Phillip was on the porch when he thanked Lin for a delightful meal; Polar ran to him, and Tennessee swore she heard Phillip say, "Look after our girl."

That couldn't be right. She wasn't his girl. Not anymore. Was she ever?

Lin watched Tennessee, easily deciphering the woman's descent into self-annihilation.

With Phillip gone, and Godzilla snoring in the chair, Lin simply said,

"Fire *good*. Ex thinking you carry torch, *bad*."

With a long groan, Tennessee scrunched her face ugly. Polar was at her feet, cautiously nudging his huge head onto her good leg.

Lin brewed a pot of jasmine tea, and the women got to mending their broken hearts. Because Lin had a broken heart too; her best friend was dying.

There's no tea for that.

~

The only room at the Englands' Mortuary *not* decorated like some destination vacation was the body prep room. Mister was a man of efficiency: sinks, shelving, six body coolers, two hydraulic embalming tables, and a body hoist. Things of utility were silver or white; clean and cold. Non-essentials were stored out of sight.

Clutter was confusing and there was nothing confusing about death.

Tennessee opened a cooler, and there was Johnny.

Johnny Cain was a good kid, not too smart, but handsome and kind, and athletic; an all-American stud. Unfortunately for Johnny, and the wall, he was a lousy driver. It was a clear night, full moon, no traffic, otherwise perfect driving conditions, except Johnny was drunk. Doesn't matter what kind of driver you are; add alcohol, and you end up with...pieces.

It might have been different if Johnny wore a seatbelt; but, according to everyone who knew him, Johnny never buckled up. So, when a very drunk Johnny hit a very brick wall his head stayed on, his arms did not, and his torso split in two. It was worse than Tennessee imagined. Johnny wasn't just in pieces, he was mashed.

Fortunately for the unfortunate, transforming a mashed-up body into someone recognizable *and* viewable was Tennessee's specialty. Truly, it was her *art*. Eager to fix something seemingly unfixable, she slipped on her slick black apron, blasted Meat Loaf's "Bat Out of Hell" as Johnny's father requested, and got to work.

Whether from the music or the smells, Polar wasn't himself. He paced and grunted and barked at air.

"Calm down, boy. Johnny's father expects a viewing tonight. He's waited long enough to bury his son." It was stupid, getting shot and hospitalized before she had the chance to tend to Johnny's body. She didn't expect his father to wait, but he did, and she was determined to bring life back to Johnny's features no matter how much putty and paint it took.

As Tennessee cleaned the parts of Johnny that were cleanable, a tingle encircled her neck, as if her necklace snagged on something. She reached for it; the tiny cross was still there, and nothing seemed caught on the chain, not frizz or thread or anything.

Polar snapped beside Tennessee, then raced across the room, barking at the back wall.

"What in the world now?" She rubbed the pendant, and a second quick tug had her spinning to look behind her. "Who's there?"

Polar's barking grew frantic as a third tug had Tennessee grabbing a scalpel. Polar positioned his body protectively in front of his master. Her cell phone was charging on the counter across the room, still blasting Meat Loaf. She rolled her eyes. Of course, the *one* time it wasn't in her back pocket when she was working!

Polar lunged toward Johnny's prep table, and that's when she saw it too.

"Careful, boy!" She tugged Polar's collar, kneeling to hold him close. "I don't know what *that* is either, boy." Armed with a scalpel, she waved her weapon at the bizarre mist coagulating before them.

Polar snapped and growled, saliva dripping from his muzzle.

The white mist congealed, absorbing mass and bulk right before their eyes, and from the ether there soon appeared a man; the same man that haunted Tennessee's most recent hallucinations, and many of her childhood.

"Sho?!" she shot to standing, confronting her hallucination with a bit of menace. "You scared me! I thought you were...I don't know...a goddamn ghost. A *hallucination* I can handle."

Sho bowed his head, and Tennessee met those emperor eyes. She couldn't move at first; those eyes filled her with unsure memories, things forgotten and things unknown. Unnerved, she inhaled deeply. Sho did the same. Not just at the same time, but *exactly the same.*

She kept watch. This was new level weird.

Polar approached Sho, sniffing this man with more intrigue than desire to kill. Sho acknowledged Polar before addressing Tennessee.

"Hello, Ten." His weighty rasp rumbled an arctic jolt down Tennessee's spine. "You look better."

"Yeah, whatever," she shushed her hallucination. "Take a good look at Johnny."

Sho turned to view Johnny; pieces and mash. "Unfortunate soul."

"Yes, and *I'm* the unfortunate soul who needs to make him pretty for his family, so if you don't mind." Tennessee shooed Sho with a snap of her wrist. "Poof away, please."

Sho stepped aside, a plain expression carving calm over his hardened features. "I shall observe."

"Uh, no," she snapped a sharp look at Sho, "that's not how it works. *Hallucinations* wait up front."

"You are not hallucinating, Ten. *We* have a purpose."

"Up front, Sho!"

"I don't think..."

"No, you *don't think* because hallucinations *don't think*. Now get! Shoo!"

Sho didn't exactly shoo. He took slow, methodical steps away from Tennessee, but with each step the crease between his brows deepened with tension. When Sho reached the office, Polar began barking and didn't stop.

Tennessee picked up a curved needle and began threading it when a crackling snap rattled her head and a hasty tug suppressed her breath. She turned to see if her hallucination was still there. He *was*. Sho stood at the far end of the long hallway with a strange look on his face; almost apologetic.

Sho placed his palms together at his chest. "Please, do not ask...."

Tennessee flicked her wrist. "All the way to the waiting room, *please*."

Reluctantly, Sho took one more step back; out of sight.

The moment his foot hit the floor, a shattering spasm had Tennessee cowering in a hunch as she clutched her neck. Polar raced to his master's side, pawing at her legs. Tennessee gasped for breath as a sick presence choked life from her body. On the cusp of losing consciousness, she collapsed to her knees.

Maybe Sho was screaming, maybe it was just Polar's booming

barks. On her last stifled breath, Sho's rasp scratched the sane side of her mind's eye.

"Ten. Say my name. Say it now!"

Tennessee's eyelids quivered and through bluing lips, she mouthed a voiceless, "*Sho*."

Whatever had a stranglehold on her neck released; she thumped to her side, drawing in wheezing inhales between bouts of panicked coughs.

Polar growled, snapping as Sho ran into the room.

"Please, I can help her."

With a frightened whimper, Polar poked his wet nose on Tennessee's cheek. The white lion slumped in next to his master, letting Sho near enough; not a centimeter more.

Sho kneeled beside the beast. "Ten, you must never ask me to leave you," he begged, trapping her gaze with his. "It brings you great pain, and me great sorrow."

Now able to breathe with more ease, Tennessee wriggled and crept to sitting. She still couldn't scream at him; she could only mutter angrily, "Since when do hallucinations choke people? What the hell's going on?" It must have happened; her brain had burst.

Sho hung his head. "We are bound to one another. But there are rules. I must obey you. Even if your commands are...misguided."

Polar pawed Tennessee; she gave him the biggest lion hug she could manage before she scowled up at Sho. "Fat chance getting *me* to obey *you!* And what do you mean *bound*...we talkin' wedding vows? I'm *not* the marrying type! And this is one hell of a hallucination. Dammit, I should probably tell somebody about this."

"No!" Sho's rasp rounded in fury, or was that fear? "You must never speak of our bond. Their punishment for such crimes is...*unpleasant*."

"*That* was unpleasant."

"*That* was a warning. Something I cannot control."

Polar whined, curling into his master's lap.

"Careful boy, my leg."

Still lightheaded from whatever that crackling had done to her, Tennessee cuddled Polar until she felt strong again; then she got up with all the grace of a common drunk. Polar stayed close, keeping his body between Tennessee and this stranger, who may or may not have harmed his master.

"Your aneurysm exploded, Tennessee." She convinced herself as she walked to the back room. "Lucky, lucky you!"

Sho was emphatic that she was alive and quite well.

She plonked herself down on a rattan loveseat. "Then what's with all the spooky cameos and *now*?" Her leg hurt, dammit!

"Bonds work differently. For now, it appears I must be in proximity to death or impending death."

"You're serious?" She let her jaw drop; it leveled the panic-induced pressure in her ears. "You're totally creeping me out, Sho."

"I apologize."

She glared at him. "You're telling me I broke some goddamn rule I know nothing about, so you choked me?"

"I would never harm you." He grew forceful. "*They* would harm us both."

After a long, scrutinizing pause, Tennessee crooned, "*They* sound like assholes."

"Yes, they do enjoy layering in difficulties." Sho's gravelly tone armored his smirk. He kept his distance, kneeling to meet Polar's confrontational stare-down.

"What game are you playing?" Tennessee reached for Polar, but the dog was sniffing her hallucination. "And who's *they*?"

Sho lowered his gaze, resting his hand, palm up, on the floor between Polar's forepaws.

"At the accident," Tennessee pieced together her memories and her hallucination's bizarre remarks, "three poachers died."

As Polar sniffed, discerning the man's true intent, Sho offered

a low bow to honor these deaths. "Their sacrifice allowed us to repair our bond."

"I don't get it." She squeezed her head; maybe if she applied enough pressure, she'd escape this baffling mess before a paranormal quicksand swallowed her whole.

"You will. In time. For now, it is enough to know that we are reunited. The tether was unexpected, but now that I am tied to a soul, I grow more mortal with each death we encounter."

"Wait, you're *not* mortal?" Tennessee laughed at her own stupidity. "Of course you're not, I wouldn't hallucinate a hot mortal...that's too boring! I get the hot, attracted-to-death dude!" Polar growled at Sho, flashing uneasy eyes on Tennessee. "Well then," she went on, "you did a bang-up job picking a mortician."

"Ah, but Ten, *you* picked *me*."

She let that digest before tracking back. "Did you say *tether*? Like *tethered?*" Tennessee gave Sho a sideways glance. "Like *leashed?* Like dogs?"

Polar snapped a snarky bark. He hated leashes too.

Sho nodded.

"This hallucination sucks!" Tennessee scrunched a pout. "*Tethered*...I don't like it."

Sho chuckled. "No, you don't. Nor do I...I prefer the more accurate, *bonded*." Sho held his hand out for Tennessee. "There's something you need to see." His eyes were so soft and reassuring that Tennessee placed her hand in his.

Polar growled his displeasure, staying close to his master.

Sho led Tennessee to a full-length gilded mirror hanging on the wall. He stood behind her, guiding her hips against his.

Polar's growl moistened with savage resolve.

Sho stopped, kneeled before the loyal mastiff. He offered a deep bow; one mighty warrior to another, "You are a fine guardian."

Polar snorted. He already knew *that*.

"I mean your master no harm. She is also *my* master."

"I'm your *what?*" Tennessee balked.

"May I?" Sho rose, lips pressing thin as he reached his hands toward either side of her neck.

She flinched under his touch. "As long as you don't choke me to death."

"I'll refrain for as long as humanly possible." He lightened his heavy gaze.

"But you're not human." She raised a skeptical brow.

Sho chuckled, proving he had a sense of humor as he gently brushed Tennessee's crimped curls away from her neck; he reached around to unbutton her flannel; then he ran his fingers down the sides of her neck, pushing her shirt collar down around her shoulders.

His smooth touch left Tennessee woozy, the good kind.

Sho stepped back, pulling off his hooded sweatshirt. He was fit, there was no question, but what Tennessee noticed were his scars.

"Are those..." she faced her hallucination, crushing sorrow welling tears behind her eyes, "from being *detained*?" She reached for him, running her fingers down a gnarly crosshatched scar covering his abdomen.

Sho let his eyelids close on a blink, and Tennessee could tell he was more accustomed to torture than gentle. She was beginning to feel intensely protective of her imagined man; in fact, she was awfully close to doing *anything* for him.

Polar's wary growl rumbled the room.

"Who did this to you?" Tennessee demanded.

Sho tensed his jaw, deepening his gaze. "I did. You will understand everything in time. There is something you must see now." Sho's steady hands were heavy on Tennessee's hips, gently guiding her to face their reflections in the mirror. Slowly, he drew her toward him; until the hard line of his body held her upright, and the warmth of his arms surrounded her in a velvety embrace. Entangled as one, something truly heinous appeared before them.

*On* them.

# 6.

# Fifty Feet

Tennessee never mentioned the darkness. It was her secret, her burden. She wasn't angry that her glimpse of the afterlife held nothing, not a single clue of heaven or hell; she was relieved; obviously, she didn't have all the facts. Philosophizing about life-after-death wasn't actually helpful for a mortician; it was safer to stick to the facts. But Tennessee *had* died on that operating table all those years ago, and all she could recall from crossing over was a heavy, crushing *nothing*. No bright light, no warm, fuzzy euphoria, no grandmother waiting with a plate of banana donuts.

Just nothing.

At least that's what she thought until Sho's familiar heat seeped into her flesh, melting her muscles to untroubled mush; she recalled the same sensation from somewhere in that brutal blackness. *This* was not the first time he'd held her. She didn't know much more than that, but she was certain he'd been watching her all along, from the bleak hell she had fallen into when she died to her brisk morning walks on the beach outside the shop.

The realization didn't scare her, nor did it relieve her panic; it was simply comforting to know, a constant like moonrises and sunsets.

~

Tennessee had experienced many unsettling events in her almost-thirty years, but nothing as devastating as this. She wasn't sure where to put such an occurrence, where in her mind to meld this newness. She recalled Polar stuck on their new stairway landing, frozen, impatiently waiting to be told what to do. Was that what she was? Someone's pet?

That's when she heard Sho's voice, though he may have been talking all along; his words were mid-sentence words, but that didn't matter. His words told her what to do next.

"...stay within fifty feet of me and no harm will come to you...if you send me away I cannot come near you until you call my name. *Fifty feet*, Ten. The tug you've been feeling is the first warning that we are drifting too far apart. Just stop, I will come to you. I will *always* come to you. This is my promise."

His words were not comforting, but his promise was. Still, he wasn't sharing *everything*. She couldn't meet his eyes just yet; she was still focused on their reflections in the gilded mirror.

Sho still stood behind her, his arms mercifully shielding her from the ominous storm. It was soothing at first; she sensed his loyalty, his strength. Certain he wasn't there to harm her, she placed her hands over his arms, letting his calm be her calm. Her eyes fell closed, but when she opened them again, nothing had changed.

*Why* hadn't it changed?

The image was criminal; the kind of evil she ran from in her nightmares.

"Take it off!" Tennessee screamed, clutching the rusted iron collar encircling her neck. Panicked, she fumbled over the iron, searching for a latch, anything to get the damn thing off. "Sho! Take it off!"

Polar growled, snapping at Sho's leg.

Sho hung his head. "I cannot."

"I don't believe you!"

"I cannot lie to you just as I cannot disobey."

Tennessee screamed, trying to pry open the collar, turning sideways to inspect the device in the mirror, she found where the maker had welded a linked chain to the collar. She held the chain in her hands; it was heavy, a burden for any animal. Was that what she was? Or was she someone's slave? She followed the chain with a hard gaze, running both hands along every link until she found the weld attached to the back of an identical collar around Sho's neck.

Shocked, Tennessee crunched her face in disgust. It took time to absorb the horrific image; it was all wrong, like a play-mirror reflecting your worst fears. And it *was* her worst fear; being controlled, restricted, *forced* to obey.

A past horror penetrated her weakened mind. She was eight, the same age as the poor dead boy her parents had embalmed that day. Barefoot, she stood at the ocean's edge just waiting for the waves to wash over her feet, sand swallowing her toes as the ocean called back its treasures. Dickey Morgan came up from behind, shoving her face-first into the dark, wet sand. He pinned her, his knee lodged between her shoulder blades as he yanked her arms behind her back. Too weak to win, she struggled for breath as Dickey bound her wrists with kite string. She watched the waves surging in to suck her under, absolutely certain she was going to die.

Dickey leapt off Tennessee's back, hootin' and hollerin' about capturing the corpse. Tennessee was pulled underwater for so long, Dickey ran off. This wasn't the first time Dickey or his friends played *capture the corpse*. Tennessee learned to hold her breath. Eventually she washed ashore, crawling to a flop on her back; and there above her, blocking the sun from scorching her salt-burned eyes, flew Dickey's kite; an indigo octopus, its eight arms flapping triumphantly in the wind.

"What *is* this?" Tennessee gripped Sho's collar until her fingers turned white; she was trying to snap the iron, but only managed to cut her finger; blood dripped onto Sho's collar; and to Tennessee's horror the collar drank it up.

She jumped back.

Polar whimpered at her side.

"It's okay, boy, I'm hallucinating." Tennessee closed her eyes, her breath short and spotty. "When I open my eyes, I won't have a demonic madman's collar around my neck. I won't be chained to a creepy, scarred man who also has a demonic madman's collar around his neck. When I open my eyes, I won't be crazy anymore."

"Ten, this is not the way it was to be."

"You got that right." She kept her eyes closed. "I'm just supposed to die. Just die. I'm not supposed to have nightmare hallucinations! I'm not supposed to be chained to *you*!" Sho took Tennessee's hands into his. She forced an inhale. "You're *not* real. You're *not* human, you're *not* chained to me...you *can't* be..."

"Shh." Sho gathered Tennessee into his arms, gently rocking her as she muttered her mantra of everything that wasn't.

For all the disbelief, confusion, and anger, Sho's presence reassured her; more than that, she felt safe.

"How was it to be, then?" Tennessee opened her eyes, gazing up at Sho; she avoided their entwined image in the mirror; she couldn't bear to see that rusty chain and those vile collars again.

Sho contemplated where to start when Polar's barking broke the silence; only this time, it was his happy bark.

Tennessee stayed wrapped in Sho's arms, still gazing into those stark black eyes when a familiar voice interrupted her beautiful madness.

"Tenny?"

That was *not* Phillip's happy voice.

Tennessee jumped out of Sho's arms, awkwardly placing her hands on her hips; she must have looked ridiculous hugging the air; he'd think she was crazy for sure. As she scrambled for a reasonable explanation—new ballet class, yoga, qigong—Phillip astounded her by addressing Sho directly.

"We haven't met." Phillip approached, composed, hand extended.

Sho split the difference, walking toward the man. "I am Sho."

"Phillip. Tennessee's doctor, and *friend*." His words were polite, but it was apparent by his deadened delivery that the gesture stretched the limits of his good nature.

Maybe she was hallucinating Phillip too, maybe she'd finally snapped. She pinched her bad leg and nearly passed out; and when Phillip linked hands with Sho, certainty spun her senseless. She wasn't hallucinating, and like a brick falling from the sky the reality of being collared and chained to this man smacked her thick skull thin.

"Holy shit! This is real! This is really happening!"

Phillip patted Polar on the head, studying the glisten in Tennessee's gaze. "You've been crying." He shot Sho an accusatory glare.

"No! No. No...I haven't," Tennessee stammered, trying to keep from slurring her words. "I'm fine. Totally! It's all rad. Maybe a little tired, but...cool...*you're* the one being weird!"

"Is that right?" Phillip wasn't fooled.

Tennessee damn near fainted when Phillip stopped directly in front of the gilded mirror. She focused her anxious gaze to her reflection, paused, looked to Sho, and huffed, "Okay, now I don't get it!" She stared at her completely normal reflection; no rusty collar, no dirty chain. Confused, she turned her examination to Sho's shirtless physique; he was perfect; not a single scar.

Phillip cleared his throat, gently clasping Tennessee's wrist. "I'm here to check your leg. Perhaps I should have called?" he kept his eyes on his watch, tracking her pulse.

Tennessee was so flustered, she looked to Sho and simply agreed, "Perhaps."

Phillip eyed Tennessee, then Sho. "I'll make a note of it."

Thoroughly muddled, she gazed up at Phillip with a thousand things to say.

He must have seen something in that look, because he momentarily forgot his anger and gently rubbed the back of her hand the way he used to when she'd get anxious or scared. "Why don't you have a seat, so I can check that leg of yours. All right?"

Phillip led Tennessee to a chair in the room. *That* was too close to the gilded mirror. She wiggled out of his grip and headed across the shop to the Acapulco Room. She never wanted to look in that mirror again. In fact, she'd toss it out right after Phillip left. She concluded that the mirror was possessed; she watched a show on that; the narrator said *anything* can get possessed.

Sho trailed right behind, coolly putting on his sweatshirt.

Tennessee never smoked inside the mortuary; it was dangerous with all the death chemicals sitting around, but it was also disrespectful. But she'd never been enslaved before either, so she risked it.

Phillip tried to snatch the lighter from Tennessee, but she was quicker this time; she got the cig lit and took a long, deep drag; so deep, Phillip yanked the cigarette from her lips and killed it. Tennessee held the smoke in for a good minute before slowly blowing it all out in Phillip's face.

Coughing from her little stunt, she plunked herself down dead center on the loveseat; it was old and splintered and too squishy for her current weight; she sunk and sunk and sunk. She was five again, and the domineering way the men stood over her activated her bossy tendencies.

"You owe me a cigarette." She crossed her arms over her chest. "Those ain't cheap."

The men held opposing expressions; one bewildered, incensed; the other, serene, and Polar lay at her feet, eyes shifting from man to man.

Phillip tended to Tennessee's leg, head down most of the time. When there was conversation, it was bad: uncomfortable, bizarre. Tennessee was too shaken to say much at all. Sho didn't have that problem; in a curious twist, *he* did most of the talking; or at least the answering of Phillip's interrogation.

Tennessee listened intently, and Phillip more so, as Sho detailed their *relationship*; from their first blind date (burgers on the beach) to their mutual love of everything eighties (Meat Loaf,

Madonna, Marty McFly) to their joint excitement about cohabitating.

"Co...hab...huh?" Tennessee was in a daze; she'd never met anyone as smooth as Sho. He was philosophical, rugged, and tortured, but she had no idea he was such a good liar; easy manners, honest laugh, and that one dimple sealed the deal. Sure, she'd move in with him. It seemed the *only* thing to do. "My place, right?" Almost believing the lies, she needed to clarify her preference.

"Yes, love, as we agreed."

That *love* bit may have been too much. Phillip snapped off his gloves with a sharp scowl, devoid of *love*.

"Well then, Tenny, I see I'm leaving you in the right hands." Phillip glared at Sho, patted Polar on the head, and walked out.

Tennessee waited for the front door to jangle shut before she smacked Sho in the arm. "What the hell was that? We may be bound but that doesn't mean we're *bound*. Phillip is...was...ugh, we have a messy past, so...just go easy. He doesn't act it, but he's breakable."

Sho knelt before Tennessee, ran a rough hand down her cheek, and smiled. "That man needs a push, Ten, so I pushed."

"Hmmm," Tennessee re-crossed her arms in a heavy sulk, "you lie too good to be *good*."

Sho only grinned.

"Did you have to say we'll be living together?"

"It's true." Sho rose, surveying the room as if he'd lost something.

"And you're all about the truth, right?"

Sho bent down to pick up a chewed-on tennis ball. His gravity returned as he declared, "*You* are my truth, Ten. You carry our goodness. I will protect that in you...for *us*..." He tossed the ball at Polar. The happy dog caught it, rushing back to Sho.

Tennessee couldn't dispute or condemn Sho's words. And the way Polar accosted Sho with wet kisses only made Tennessee more certain.

Sho was telling the truth.

~

Gossip catches fire; *good* gossip explodes. While Tennessee prepped Johnny's pieces and mash, Phillip made a single call that set the bomb ticking.

Phillip called William.

It was innocent enough; they had plans for lunch, but doctors get busy and he was running late after his little run-in with Sho at the mortuary. It was a momentary slip, he let his emotion get the better of him when William asked,

"How's our lovely Tennessee doing? Her barista is back...perhaps I should bring her a proper mindbender. That'll make her happy."

"Call first," Phillip warned sharply, "she might have company."

The men settled on a new lunch time and went about their day. This change freed up William to run Lillie's errand. She had a craving for champagne, but he couldn't recall the vineyard and year.

William called Lillie.

*KaBoom!*

~

For pieces and mash, Johnny looked pretty damn good. Sho helped Tennessee puzzle-fit Johnny into a basic cremation casket. She didn't need to dowel his arms back on or stitch him back together again. His father wanted as little done to Johnny as possible. It was a departure from what she was usually asked to do, and it was refreshing. The more Tennessee worked with the dead, the more she became a purist.

Die and decompose. Simple.

After Phillip left, Tennessee decided Sho was a cousin, distant, maybe twice removed, but *family*; and in her traditional Island culture, you welcome family. She wasn't in any rush to figure anything out. Denial felt right.

"The Cains don't want embalming, so I'm just going to pretty him up the best I can. Hand me the eye caps...uh, those spikey,

tan, circle things." Sho did as he was told, and dutifully watched Tennessee lift Johnny's eyelids up, one at a time, and gently place the spikey caps over the dead boy's sunken eyes. "We won't be showing his left side, but...can you hand me the needle injector...uh, the metal thing that looks like an oversized pen with mouse ears...yeah, that one."

Tennessee inserted the pointed end of the injector into Johnny's mouth and shot in a needle and wire. She massaged Johnny's lips, threading the needle through his upper and lower gums until his mouth sealed with the exact expression she wanted.

Next, she brought out a briefcase full of makeup, putty, wax, and other beautification essentials. She rebuilt Johnny's trademark cheekbones with an entire jar of face putty before applying a layer of Johnny-colored foundation. She dabbed and swabbed and blotted the makeup sponge until his coloring was just right. Because he wasn't embalmed, she needed to do a little more shading than usual to fill him out a bit.

Putting the finishing touches on Johnny's *good* side, Tennessee remarked gravely,

"This is how we fool the living. You see, Sho, it's all about proper goodbyes." Work kept her sane, now more than ever.

Focus and function. That's something her father repeated; often and *loud*.

Tennessee's light hand and impassioned concentration moved Sho. "A proper goodbye is a lucky gift. You have brought great honor to the Cain family. Well done, Ten."

"Hey, you did great for a first timer...most people puke." Tennessee met his eye, tumbling out a sheepish, "Thank you, Sho."

"Please," Sho lifted his palms humbly, "I only obeyed your instruction."

"Oh, knock off that idiotic *obey* business." Tennessee covered half of Johnny's face and a quarter of his body with his favorite afghan; Johnny's grandmother crocheted his school colors,

apparently at his request. "If we're, like you say...*tethered*...and our goal is to get *untethered,* then we need to be a team. No master and slave crap, hell to the no!" Tennessee snapped her gloves off into a trashcan. "I want this collar off. I want our free will back, and dammit, I'm gonna get it done."

Sho reached into the casket, smoothing the afghan. "Only souls have free will, Ten. Without a soul, I am nothing but a beggar. I survive off the goodwill of others. I must earn my freedom first if I ever hope to know free will as you do. I must serve you, and perhaps many others like you, before I earn that privilege."

Now that just pissed her off; she went on a scattered tirade about freedom and slavery, abolition and human rights.

Sho chuckled. "Agreed, but I am not human. *Close*, perhaps another generation."

Tennessee didn't usually blurt, but around Sho she found herself blurting her first thoughts, completely uncensored. "You have to have a soul!" She closed the casket, reached down to unlock the chapel gurney wheels, and together they rolled Johnny into the Acapulco Chapel. "I mean, you're *alive*, and alive things have souls. That's how the world works. Right?"

Amused, Sho took over steering Johnny, positioning his box at the altar, dead center.

"Let's back up then. Where are you from?" Tennessee sensed Sho's reluctance to explain, but she also felt something else; an unyielding drive to obey. If she asked him a pointed question, he was compelled to answer. This discovery made her feel even safer with him.

Beside Johnny sat a stool used for flower arrangements; Sho sat on the edge of this stool, his feet fixed on the ground; he seemed relaxed yet troubled. When Polar pawed Sho's leg, the man nuzzled the dog's mane and began his story.

"One of my earliest memories was dying in battle, a samurai's honor, during Japan's Heiji Rebellion in the year 1160. I had been in service to many masters by the time I entered that life. I was

far *older*. Perhaps that is why the memory holds fast or...perhaps I cherished that life far above the others."

That Sho was a warrior came as no surprise. He carried himself like a soldier; rigid but graceful; Sho could handle himself well in a fight, and from his scars, Tennessee knew his battles were many. He touched a bit on those days, but a long life does not mean a long memory, and much of his youth had fallen to the hazards of time. Tennessee drew closer to Sho as she realized he no longer knew *where* he came from. After learning her grim prognosis—six months tops—she reflected more about *home* and legacy and the lost connection to her ancestry.

At that moment, she understood Sho completely. They were not so different after all.

The steeled man continued, "I was a child when the rebellion ravaged sacred lands, punishing treasured souls." Sho shared delicately, as if he called upon those lost souls for consent to speak these words. After a two-breath pause, he went on, "A generous empress tethered me to a great warrior who I shall not name. He rests now, and though I still mourn his destruction, I dare not disturb him. I hold his memory...he stands nobly among the warriors, declaring his lineage amidst a petal storm of cherry blossoms. These were glorious days. Honorable days. Deadly." His gaze locked on Tennessee; in her he saw hope, and an unfathomable innocence he'd die to preserve. "The battle drew us to the fabled bamboo forests. All were touched by immeasurable loss. Blood flowed hot as souls claimed what they must to survive. This day alone taught me the art of suffering. I learned to bear witness, to honor the divinity in spilling blood...to protect life and death..."

Enthralled by Sho's ability to weave a story, Tennessee released her worries. He truly had a gift; his raspy tenor beat a hypnotic rhythm that anchored listeners *inside* his memory. Sho's words spun vibrant scenes around Tennessee. It was a bizarre blur between dream walker and time traveler.

She was standing in the middle of a bamboo forest, poison-

tipped arrows zipping past her head. A bloody battle raged around her; regally dressed men slaughtered one another with mighty swords. But she didn't see death; she saw one glorious dance after another. Each warrior moved elegantly, deep in a richness of knowing the limitless nature of the human form. One warrior caught her eye, something about his ethereally seamless strikes. He bested his opponent, turning in time to catch her gaze. He was just a boy, his long, braided hair draped down his chest. She reached out to him, but horror ruined his peaceful eyes; he ran toward her, his gaze locked on something behind her; he raised his sword overhead when the quick clank of high heels prattled into the forest...

"Well, if it isn't Tennessee England, slacking as the day is long!"

Lillie Saint James? In Sho's forest?

Polar's ears perked up and he grunted; he knew the scent of Lillie, but he rarely barked at her; what *real* damage could she do?

Tennessee twisted around and the sea of striking green bamboo melted away, even the scent of cherry-blossomed death dissipated, replaced by plain old death. She caught sight of Lillie, dressed in a silver evening gown, hair twirled into a loose bun at the nape of her neck, pearls everywhere.

"You still owe me Santa! If you have time for Johnny, you have time for Christmas. I'm *paying* people to water your tree, Tennessee! And who is *this*?"

Sho was already on his feet, taking Tennessee's hands into his as he led her toward Lillie.

"Hello, Lillie," Tennessee sighed. "This is Sho, my..." She almost said cousin but then recalled all the lies Phillip now had as truths.

Sho turned on his charisma, introducing himself as Tennessee's *lover*. Yes, he said *lover,* and the jolt to Lillie's Botoxed face was worth the awkward choice of words. The corner of Sho's mouth lifted just a teensy bit; this man knew exactly what he was doing, and it was downright fun to watch.

"I can't do Christmas tonight, Lillie." Tennessee stood between

Sho and Lillie; she didn't like the way Lillie couldn't stop eyeballing Sho. "I've got Johnny's wake and cremation tonight. And Phillip doesn't want me on my leg all that much. So, maybe you should take it up with your baby brother."

Lillie flashed a flawless smile of ultra-white. "Yes, I'm not at all pleased with how you handled pickup. It takes precisely twenty minutes from Summerhold to the Illie Estate. It took *you* four hours and a bullet."

"Gosh, how annoying for you...Look, I can swing day after tomorrow," Tennessee conceded for the sake of getting the bitch out. "So, unless you want to say a few words about Johnny..."

"Oh, *please*." Lillie eyeballed Sho one last time before spinning on her heels and *clink-clanking* her way out. She may not have been the first person to meet Tennessee's new lover, but she sure as hell was going to be the second.

Polar padded after Lillie, from a safe distance with a grunt and snort. It was cute. Nobody scared Polar, but Lillie definitely unnerved him; left him trying to figure out what made her so darned grumpy.

"Let's get something to eat before the wake." Tennessee headed to the back room, grabbed her backpack and cell phone. She was in full blown denial until Sho whispered from thirty-three feet behind her,

"I'll be there in spirit, Ten."

Tennessee ran her hand over her neck. "Will people see?"

"Mirrors unveil our curse, if we are close enough to one another."

"So, it's a curse?" Rage crept in, crackling her tone tense. She wasn't about to spend her last days enslaved. A fuzzy memory surfaced, adding to her muddle. "Someone else was there...at the accident...I thought it was a nightmare, but now it makes sense. I remember he was furious. He said we'd be punished... Is *this* what he meant?"

Sho held Tennessee's shaking hands. "We can earn our freedom, Ten. I'm not certain who we were sold to. When they

decide our use, we will receive instruction. I promise you, I will see to your freedom...I'll remove the collar myself if it comes to that."

"How?" A hot tear slipped down her cheek.

"There are many ways to break a curse. Now go eat, get some fresh air." Sho wiped Tennessee's cheek with his finger. "*Fifty feet*, Ten, please remember...just stop when you feel the tug. I will come to you, whether I'm visible or not."

Tennessee nodded, and another tear fell.

~

Counting steps seemed an appropriate thing to do. The day was blustery, just how Tennessee preferred it. She was driving the Englands' shiny hearse while Riggy got a new radiator; he'd be shiny too, on the *inside*. No one would know his secret; they'd only see rust and ruin. She thought of Sho, drifting in the ether somewhere; fifty feet somewhere. Why fifty feet? Why the disappearing act? Why the curse? With this many *whys*, only a mindbender would do.

This barista didn't even charge Tennessee. The power of a hearse; death and grief spook people. The fearful do one of two things: ignore you or give you free stuff. Either way, Tennessee won.

Skidding the new guy into her favorite beachside spot was trickier than it was with Riggy. This guy didn't like skidding.

A mile beyond the bustling promenade of carnival rides, curio shops, kite vendors, and that one vegan cupcake shop sat a stretch of beach free of bikini-clad coeds and their shirtless suitors. Burrowed in a valley of sand dunes, the spot was typically empty, except for the lonely beachcomber, random artist sketching, or mortician lunching.

When she wasn't canvassing the town on Lillie's command, or getting shot, Tennessee ate lunch in this spot, like a proper loner. Something Sho said to Phillip made her grab a bag of burgers and drive here. Polar leapt out behind Tennessee, sprinting over the dunes, sliding down the dunes, all the while barking seagulls

into shrieking flight. Tennessee limped over to the hood, scooted herself into a comfortable enough position, balanced her mindbender beside her, and opened the greasy paper bag on her lap.

"They always forget the ketchup." A tear blurred the perfect view. "Great! Now I'm crying over ketchup!" Tennessee unwrapped her double cheeseburger, double *the works*, and took a mean bite. Screw depression, screw denial; hand over the burgers and fries.

She watched Polar run up and slide down, over and over. It was obvious why painters came here; sunlight played mysterious games on this stretch of sand and sea, and salted breezes sent blue seagrass into tittering fits; white butterflies nested nearby, finding sweet nectar in the thimbleberry, white clover, and wild fields of purple water mint. If you weren't paying attention, the spot was just sand and grass and waves, but if you looked a bit deeper, you'd see how a simple breeze shaped the landscape into something otherworldly.

Polar slid down a dune, sprinting back to Tennessee.

"Hungry, boy?" She dug into the bag and tossed Polar a burger. He caught the kiddie burger, no pickles, and scarfed it down. He took off again, saving his second burger for later.

Tennessee plunked a double cheeseburger down beside her. "One day, you'll eat that burger, Sho. You're not the only one who can make promises."

Tennessee tasted a hint of salted chocolate between bites of her burger. *Now* she knew what that meant; Sho was near, so near she didn't have to worry about those cursed fifty feet.

"I guess I'm glad I can't see you, because that means no one died, but death happens so I'll see you soon enough...oh, that reminds me. Remember Godzilla's Maria Garcia? I'm assuming you do, since you were busy freaking me and Polar out last night...well, I got a text from Mike, the morgue guy. Just so you know, he's a total jerk, a real imbecile, but anyway...Maria's family wants me to box her up. Seems she had a heart condition no one

knew about. Got me thinking, Sho...what's worse, knowing you're going to die? Or not knowing?" Tennessee took a modest bite, considering these choices. "Right now, *not knowing* would suck worse. Like you said, proper goodbyes are lucky...Lin says I have strange luck...maybe that's what she means...unlucky to be dying but lucky enough to kiss this gorgeous world goodbye!"

Tennessee shoved the rest of her burger into her mouth; she was still chewing when she declared war. "That's what we'll do, Sho, we'll kick this curse's ass! They've picked the wrong Island girl to enslave! Us Island girls don't do *obey*! And you're a samurai! They take names! Like write those suckers down and cross those suckers off! Bam! You're a *samurai*! God damn! I can't believe I know a samurai!" Tennessee monologued all this; cheek rounded with burger, eyes a foot past crazy.

Maybe she was imagining it, but she swore Sho's cold hand warmed the nape of her neck. "Insanity feels nice." She laughed and imagined he was laughing too.

~

"Fifty feet, Sho." Tennessee strolled through her bedroom, into the bathroom. "I'm sure you're not a creep, but, you know..." That unmistakable tug chaffed her neck. "Uh, make it forty-five feet...yeah, that's better. That's where you need to be, Sho, anytime I'm, well, indisposed!" She was shouting. Forty-five feet wasn't *that* far away, but the shower was going and she had Cyndi Lauper's "True Colors" blasting. The tug was bearable, enough to be certain she was alone.

Tennessee disrobed meditatively in front of the medicine cabinet mirror; she got real close, straining to see the collar and chain, but there was no trace; she wrapped her hands around her neck, squeezed until she coughed.

"Poor pathetic puppy." She squeezed again, released, squeezed, released.

Maybe she *was* crazy.

She hoped it was that simple.

After a quick shower, Tennessee rewrapped her leg and tried

her best to de-frizz her hair. It was no use. Only Lin could manage it. She'd see her at Johnny's wake, so until then, Tennessee yanked the crimped curls into a bushy bun on the top of her head; stubborn tendrils fell out. She let them be free. Something ought to be.

Wake attire consisted of a classic black dress, mid-calf, cinched at the waist. Her voluptuous figure made the outfit a little too risqué, so she covered up the whole thing with a baggy, gunmetal grey cashmere cardigan; paired with ballet flats made cuter by ribbon crossover ankle straps. She preferred boots, but this was a purchase she made while shopping with Lin, and she actually felt pretty in them, maybe even a little sexy. Not that she was going for sexy.

Tennessee was still debating the shoes when Polar started barking, and the doorbell rang.

"Just a minute! Man!" She limped out of the bathroom. "I'm forty-feet away!" she hollered, tasting salted chocolate as she exhaled her relief. The tug was gone, and now that she was fully clothed she knew Sho would stay close.

Polar was growling at the front door, so it wasn't Godzilla. He'd be late, as usual.

Tennessee opened the door.

There stood her landlords, the Jims. And Millie and Billie, smiling, in perfectly matched pink taffeta tutus.

The sight was confusing; she hadn't seen the twins since the accident, and they'd never been to her silo before. By the looks on the Jims faces, they were now permanently banned.

"I'm so sorry, Jim...and Jim. I'll pay for damages."

Jim the Conductor waved her off. "A few stomped-on zucchinis we've already moved to the compost bin, however, these young ladies need a shorter leash, Tennessee."

Tennessee flinched at the image his words conjured. That expression was used far too liberally! She thanked the Jims for returning the runaway twins and promised they'd bake zucchini bread to make amends.

The Jims nearly tossed the twins into the silo. "We do hope you're feeling better, Tennessee." Then Jim the Engineer's gaze traveled the length of Tennessee's body, fixing on her feet. "Oh, honey, keep the shoes, but lose the ugly sweater. Christmas is over."

Tennessee fastened a closed-lipped grin before offering a gentle rebuke, "It's a wake."

"All the more reason. Death is ugly, honey, bring the beauty."

She could respect that, and they shared an easy chuckle. The Jims didn't spend half the day, every day, beautifying their estate for nothing. "Thanks for the stairs!" she offered a little late; the Jims were already crossing over her rented lawn to their owned one.

Polar had kept the twins quiet during this exchange, but when Tennessee shut the door, they started in,

"The Jims are creep! Eeee!"

"The Jims are nice people!" Tennessee snatched a pack of cigarettes from the fridge. "Does your mother know you're out killing innocent zucchini?"

Millie (or Billie) started explaining how their parents were invited to a party; and Uncle Phillip was working; and seeing as how everyone else had somewhere to be, they decided to be somewhere too.

Tapping the cigarette pack on her thumb bone, Tennessee sighed. "Well that makes loads of sense." She limped out onto the porch and lit up.

Billie (or Millie) trailed after, followed by Millie (or Billie). They just stood there, watching Tennessee smoke; whispering to one another about bad habits and throat cancer and lung cancer and brain cancer and eyeball cancer.

Way past the agreed-upon time, Godzilla pulled up in his RV. Polar raced out just in time to leap into the open passenger door. Godzilla hollered from the driver's seat, "Hurry up, we're late!"

"Girls," Tennessee lit a cig, eyeing the twins, pink tutus and all, "wanna see a dead body?"

# 7.

# Johnny

No matter how many times Tennessee stepped into it, the Englands' Acapulco Chapel reminded her of *Fantasy Island.* If only Mr. Roarke was there to offer grieving families an escape from their reality. Of course, Roarke twisted those fantasies; still, she wondered what fantasy Johnny's father would conjure up; or Johnny himself.

Tennessee knew the exact fantasy she'd pick, and it was nowhere near Saint James.

She imagined Tattoo running up the bell tower, throwing all his tininess into ringing that bell, his loud, husky tone defying the hushed island.

"The plane, the plane," Tennessee sang to herself, watching the twins sit eerily still on the exact loveseat she had sunk into earlier in the day; only they didn't sink; they were twigs of children, scrawny and short. Seeing them there, sitting like that—at Johnny's wake of all places—softened her toward the brats; and when the sisters clasped hands as mourners filled the room, a dull ache left a bruise behind her breastbone.

Lillie and William were too busy socializing to notice what Tennessee had, clear as she'd seen that collar encircling her neck, those girls were desperately sad.

Misery didn't excuse destroying Saint James during their

demonic fits, but she was beginning to understand what made them tick. Tennessee made two plates of food and brought them to the twins,

"It's past your dinner. Eat."

The twins dug in before Tennessee could manage a contented chuckle.

"I'm sorry you have to be here." She sat beside the twins, sinking one of them along with her. All three girls giggled. "You know, my first wake wasn't nearly as nice as this one. There definitely wasn't cake."

The twins shared a look before turning their wide eyes on Tennessee.

"Yes, you can have cake. *After* you finish your dinner." She grew quiet then began sincerely, "If you girls have any questions about tonight, just ask. I'm never too busy, got it? Sometimes these things can be scary and weird. But really, it's just a nice way to say goodbye to someone you love."

"We're not scared!" The twins raised their little pug noses in the air, proving they were, in fact, terrified.

Tennessee watched the girls scarf down one egg salad sandwich each before giving them an out. "Well, my brave girls, Godzilla's outside in the RV, so if it gets too boring in here, just go and bother him. He's got a deck of cards and some pretty bad tells, so give 'em go-fish hell."

The twins grinned, already scheming to make some easy cash.

~

All the Cains were present, and Johnny's teammates, girlfriends, and buddies. Tennessee greeted each one with heartfelt condolences. Between arrivals, she checked on Johnny. Sometimes guests touched the body, so a little primping was necessary. Tennessee reached for Johnny's afghan as a tall, thin woman, modestly dressed, approached the casket.

Tennessee's hands grew ice cold; she blew warmth onto them before fixing Johnny's afghan.

"Shameful," the woman dabbed her eyes with a mass of bunched up tissues, "and stubborn."

Tennessee moved aside as the woman bent over Johnny, but when the woman started whispering, Tennessee gave her privacy. She made the rounds, comforting, directing, chatting.

Phillip spotted Tennessee from across the room. She wore the same thing for cremations; he was quite familiar with that cardigan. He should have been; it was *his*. Following a bizarrely brutal wake that ended with several arrests, two ambulances, and hundreds in damage to the Englands' Mother Mary Chapel, Phillip had found Tennessee sitting on the beach. He went to her, wrapped his cardigan around her; and never got it back.

"Tenny." Phillip's eyes were still on his cardigan.

"Welcome to my little shop of horrors." Tennessee's gaze twisted sublime; she got that way during wakes that ended with cremations. It was her zone. Burning a body took a *long* time. Lots of raking the body into the flame, out of the flame. But her favorite part was collecting the bones, because the flame never got all the bone. Families didn't like bone in their ash, and there were laws prohibiting bones in ash, but she'd been known to honor other cultures by letting them pick through the bones before she ground them up in her heavy-duty bone blender: The Cremulator.

Phillip was too busy scanning the room, looking for *what* she couldn't tell. Then he walked on by; he didn't even ask about her leg. That stung. Seeing him so often after not seeing him so often was doing bad things to her heart; cremulating that muscle to mush. She needed distance; it only worked when there was distance.

Suddenly sullen, Tennessee went to sit by the twins as a line formed to view Johnny's body; she turned toward the loveseat, but the girls were gone.

"I guess I'm not the only one hiding from Uncle Phillip," Tennessee muttered, just as Phillip approached with one plastic cup of red punch in each hand.

"Here," he handed her one of his cups, "and sit down. You've been on that leg all day."

Tennessee was so flustered she took the cup and sat down; she stopped short of drinking it, though. She hated punch; that much sugar should only be in coffee. And she didn't bother looking for the twins; they were stealth little imps. She had no doubt they were watching; the ritual of partying around a dead body captivated them. Lillie wouldn't like it, but Tennessee didn't give a damn.

Phillip stood next to the loveseat, a good distance from Tennessee, much farther than he had the previous night. It was the *lover* thing; the whole damn town had probably heard. As controlling as he was, he probably wanted to pick her next boyfriend for her.

Phillip grew pensive. "I don't see your *boyfriend*." He finally looked at her, his head dipping as her body lowered into the seat.

She was sinking. Dammit, she drank the punch.

"He's been leaving you alone a lot. You were shot. Where was he? His name never showed up on the visitor's log...or anywhere else for that matter..."

"I...he..." Tennessee couldn't believe this line of questioning, let alone respond to it; unlike Sho, she wasn't a skilled liar; she fidgeted too much or stuttered too much. Wait a minute, did he just say...she squirmed to standing. "Phillip, please tell me you didn't call your guy and run a background check on my boyfriend! Because *that* would be really stalker of you!"

"Your friends care about you, Tenny. No one's heard you talk about this guy...not Godzilla or Hill. Come on, you tell Lin *everything*...as I recall. What am I supposed to think? You're vulnerable right now. I'm...*we're* not going to let some guy come in and sweet talk you into making imprudent decisions...not in your condition!"

Tennessee was about to give Phillip a verbal wallop for being so stupid when Johnny's father approached, gushing about how well his son looked and the encouraging turnout.

"My condolences, John." Phillip shook hands with the grieving father.

"Yes, thank you. I could only trust your girl here to take care my Johnny. He looked up to you, Tennessee. Maybe you don't remember, but he spent one summer working for your father. He thought you were very brave to spend so much time with...err..." John's eyes glazed over as he mumbled darkly, "the departed..."

Tennessee placed a tender hand on John's forearm. "Of course I remember. We ate popsicles on the beach. We'd flip for the pineapple ones."

John's eyes welled over, and Tennessee hugged the man. "I'm forever grateful, Tennessee." John nodded to Phillip, then slipped out of the room as more tears fell.

Watching John leave, Tennessee got to processing the best course of action. "He needs to feed Audrey II."

Phillip flipped his palms up in a questioning manner, and Tennessee laughed.

"You've forgotten *Audrey II*...the giant oven in back. John needs to start the machine. It'll help him grieve. Take back some control."

"You sure about that?" Philip asked, just as some kid slammed the restroom door.

Startled, Tennessee bumped into Phillip. His hand found her waist, and there it stayed.

"Uh, *yes*, I'm sure. This isn't my first burn." She thought about scooting away; didn't. He wasn't in a rush to move, so it wasn't until Lin scurried into the chapel that Phillip let his hand fall.

Lin took one look at Tennessee's shoes, "Loafers? What happened to the cute ballet flats with the cute black ribbon straps? They were so cute!"

"Way too sexy for a wake, Lin. I'm cremating a body, not clubbing."

Lin's laugh almost erupted. "Mamma Min knows more about clubbing than *you*, Ness!"

"I'll change that." Sho's richly round, rumbly rasp turned heads

as he stepped from the shadows, eyes only for Tennessee. He wasn't wearing his hoodie anymore: fitted, charcoal suit, royal purple tie, shined shoes to match.

"Good evening, my love." He kissed Tennessee on the lips, a soft kiss appropriate for the venue. Still, her knees wobbled a bit; it had been a long time since a man treated her like that. His hand found the small of her back, and there it stayed.

Lin's beautiful face bent mamma-beast-mode. "Sidebar!" She seized Tennessee by the elbow, whisking her out of the room.

Lin was scrappy, might have taken Tennessee in a catfight; luckily, they weren't that sort. Lin dragged Tennessee into the prep room; she started in, angry and giggly,

"How am I only *now* seeing this guy? *Where* did you meet him? *When*? And you're already sleeping with him! That can't be right, Ness...I mean, seriously, that gorgeous man is calling you *love* and I'm clueless?" Lin jumped up and down, her little happy dance for her pathetic puppy of a best friend. "And in front of Phillip! This is too good. Dammit." She plunged her hand into her purse, digging out her cell phone. "I should have recorded it! I'm totally getting pictures of you two...this is gonna blow up the internet!"

"Yeah, headline reads: *Tennessee gets laid, no flowers involved.*" Tennessee grimaced, both from her raunchy words and from a tug at her throat. She took four steps back, but the tug was still there, so she took four steps to the right, three to the left, six back. The tug loosened, and she breathed.

Lin gawked; leaning back on her right leg, crossing her arms at her chest in Mamma Min's classic Stance of Disparagement. Lin's expression fell; she gripped Tennessee by the hand, practically tossing her best friend in a chair.

"You don't have a fever." Lin smacked her palm on Tennessee's forehead.

After huffing and gruffing and rolling her eyes, Tennessee asked sharply, "Can I go back to work now? They don't pay me unless I actually cremate the body."

"You spill your guts after the burn, got it?"

"Geez, I got it. You really are one pushy Asian."

"And you're one promiscuous Islander!"

The ladies laughed; mocking cultural stereotypes was endlessly entertaining. But the banter was *theirs* and theirs alone. If Lillie called Lin a pushy Asian she'd get two black eyes, one from Lin and the other from Tennessee.

After entering the crowded chapel, the ladies couldn't see where the men had gone, so Lin got to teasing Tennessee, "He's a good height for you...when the man is too tall and the woman too short the sex isn't so good. Not if you like to kiss when you're in the throes, which I think you like to do." Lin sedated her laugh; this was a wake, after all.

A fiery flush had Tennessee shaking off Lin's imagery; she liked to keep her bedroom escapades in the bedroom, and Lin knew that. So, when Tennessee looked up to see Phillip within earshot, she knew exactly what her pushy friend was doing. She gave Lin a quick swat before rushing off to move this damn wake along.

Sho met Tennessee in the middle of the room, and together they headed to the altar.

Tennessee recited her Chapel Director speech, tailoring it to reflect the Cains' wishes and Johnny's preferences. As she spoke, the crowd drew in, as if physical nearness to other people brought them comfort. She saw that a lot. People who hardly knew each other standing arm to arm, shoulder to shoulder, especially when the dead was a child.

She didn't look it, especially in that frumpy outfit, but Tennessee was an elegant speaker; just the right amount of delicate projection, a genuinely compassionate tone, and she always displayed a posture of strength, shoulders back and down, head level, feet firmly planted. She looked strong, as if nothing could shake her foundation. Mourners borrowed her strength, leaving her drained days after.

Reciting the last lines of Johnny's eulogy, Tennessee locked eyes with Sho; his onyx eyes gleamed proud. He bowed his head to her and the supportive gesture warmed her chilled hands; she'd

never had someone truly understand what it took to honor the dead. Sho's immediate acknowledgement of her work loosened her shoulders and filled her with renewed strength. Out of the corner of her eye, she watched Phillip watching Sho with an intensity that worried her.

If only Phillip wasn't so *Phillip*, she might consider telling him how good Sho was, how she was cursed and how she needed to keep Sho close. But he wouldn't understand. Phillip didn't love her anymore. He'd tossed her aside, just when she'd finally given him all her heart. He broke it. And now, in this moment, she knew Sho would fix it.

~

Mister and Missus encouraged families to witness their loved ones' cremations, but rarely did anyone take them up on the kind offer. They usually left after the casket was closed, and only returned to claim the ashes; a day later, maybe two, depending on Audrey II's workload.

John Cain was the first of Tennessee's clients to accept her offer to bear witness, and he felt good about his decision, until the time came to start the oven.

The crowd cleared out, the casket was closed, and John helped Tennessee wheel the chapel gurney carrying his son down the long hall, through the prep room, past the crematory's swinging double doors; John got tangled up in the heavy plastic curtains barricading the threshold. The curtains served two purposes; they helped dampen the noisy machine, and, more importantly, they kept people dust in.

Audrey II was old. Mister spent a good penny upgrading to meet new emissions standards, but she still took a while to heat up to the minimum 1400 degrees needed to properly bring a body to dust. At the low end, it would take longer to get the job done, two, maybe three, hours; if she managed anywhere near 1800 degrees, one, maybe two, hours.

"Do we take him out?" John asked tentatively.

Tennessee maneuvered the gurney directly in front of Audrey

II's mouth. "No, not at all. You chose the cremation casket. We can start whenever you feel ready. Take your time."

"I don't have to push him in, do I?"

Tennessee walked over to the button labeled *START*; Mister had stenciled that on after an inept intern left a body in the oven all night thinking Audrey II just needed more time to warm up.

"It's just here." She repressed a desire to mimic Vanna White on *Wheel of Fortune*. "I'll take care of Johnny and when you're ready, just press this button. After that you can stay or go home and get some rest."

"Who stays with Johnny?"

"I do. All night. I can even play music if you like."

John agreed with a flimsy head wobble. "He liked the same music you liked, so that should be fine...that'll be nice for him."

Tennessee slid the oven door up; it screeched a little resistance, and she instantly regretted not oiling that earlier; John flinched, and she was certain he would vomit. That screech would haunt him, dammit. She hurried up; burning dead bodies was honorable; cleaning puke was disgusting. Tennessee let the worn conveyor belt pull Johnny's casket halfway into the oven; using her father's push bar, she coaxed Johnny all the way in.

She left the door open.

"Rest in peace, Johnny." Tennessee lowered her head, gently rubbing her cross pendant. She refrained from crossing her body because that wasn't Johnny's preference.

"Now?" John's voice quivered, but he did not cry.

Tennessee backed away from the oven, softened her professional exterior, and nodded.

John took a deep breath and pushed the button.

That's when his hands shook uncontrollably.

Instantly, Audrey II engulfed Johnny with long, spirited flames. But she was only warming up, so she would get much hotter as the night went on. John was still breathing, and he wasn't vomiting, so Tennessee let him watch a little longer as she put on her slick

black apron and retrieved a pair of leather gloves and a clear faceguard.

John stood a good distance from the inferno, and Tennessee could see he was taking back control, even if it was just a momentary mask. Tennessee knew the more he wore that mask, the more it'd stick.

"Goodbye, son," John said in the most stoic tone she'd heard from him yet. He nodded once to the emptiness in front of him then walked out.

Tennessee exhaled her support, inhaled the job. As John rustled past the plastic curtains, she blasted Aerosmith's "Angel." She tucked her phone into her cardigan pocket, slipped on the leather gloves, and closed Audrey II's mouth; shaking off the gloves, she started dancing. Her bum leg restrained her moves, but she wasn't bad; a mix of geeky head banging, arm swinging, the random twirl.

And for five minutes, Tennessee danced for Johnny.

When she unwound her last whirl, she looked up to see Phillip. He was just watching her, tranquility in those emeralds. Why did he always show up when she was a mess? Sweat glistened her cheeks cognac amber, and frizzles of hair clung to her neck. She knew what *she* was doing in the crematory, so she shut up and waited for Phillip to explain his presence in a clearly marked restricted area.

"You shouldn't be dancing on that leg," he advised, not even a smirk.

Going from the high of dancing to the low of Phillip chastising her was too much; she couldn't scream, not in front of Johnny; all she could do was tear up. A quiet anger, something Phillip probably didn't notice. She turned her back to him, documenting Audrey II's temperature on a clipboard.

Tennessee resisted a flinch as Phillip's warm hand captured her waist. He was always warm; like her personal sun. She went to shove his hand off, but his fingers trapped her fingers, and Annie Lennox started singing from her cardigan pocket.

It was Tennessee's go-to heartbreak anthem, "Why."

But it only made her tears fall more, and Johnny...Phillip shouldn't be in here with Johnny.

Phillip respected her rules and quickly shared, "John asked me to be with you. He couldn't stay himself, but he didn't want you to bear the burden alone...Johnny would've liked some company."

She relaxed. Johnny deserved an untainted moment.

Although Audrey II was loud, Annie's heart-wrenching lyrics filled the space between Phillip and Tennessee.

"Dance with me." He stepped in front of her, snatching the clipboard from her hand.

"I shouldn't be dancing on my leg," she sassed as another tear fell. It was a long day and she needed sleep, not a Suit messing with her mind. And where was Sho? The twins? Her mind churned and mulled, and that was never a good thing.

Phillip tucked his right foot under Tennessee's left foot. "This is what I meant." He caught her runaway tear with the back of his pinky, and his eyes fell with remorse. "Did I do that?"

Tennessee narrowed her eyes. "You always do that."

Phillip wrapped one arm around Tennessee's waist, gently lifting her weight onto his feet. He took her hand into his. "I'm sorry, Tenny. Seeing you again after all this time, under the circumstances...well, I haven't been myself lately."

She leaned into him. "Maybe you *have* been yourself."

"I suppose I deserve that," Phillip conceded. Tennessee pressed her ear against his chest, remembering that rumble. And why did he have to smell so good?

"What are you doing?" Phillip went to stroke her back, stopped.

She caught the strained levity lurking in his rumble; avoiding his gaze was paramount. She managed a blasé, "Remembering."

"Why?"

"So I don't forget when it's time to say goodbye."

"Tenny...I...maybe I don't want to say goodbye."

She pulled away a little, unable to resist a glance. "Goodbyes are a lucky gift...Sho told me that just this morning."

All the sweetness drained from Phillip's face. "*Sho*. Well then, it must be true. Come on, Tenny, are you really with him? Honestly, I just can't see it. He's not your type..."

"No, he's sweet. And wise. And supportive of me just the way I am." She watched her words sink into Phillip like a hot blade. "He cares about me, that's why he's waiting outside. I know you saw him."

Okay, that was cheating; she knew he was less than fifty feet away.

All those sorrowful *whys* kept time with the couple as they stopped talking because it was getting them nowhere. And when the *whys* stopped, Tennessee figured Phillip was done, but the man held her tight. Johnny's long playlist continued to serenade the couple, and Johnny, just as John wanted. They danced for so long Tennessee's leg throbbed, but neither could stop.

Even when the music stopped, it took Tennessee time to say she needed to check on Johnny. Phillip released her but never took his eyes off her.

Prepped for battle with some serious heat, Tennessee slipped on the leather oven mitts and pulled down her faceguard. She tossed Phillip a mask before sliding open the oven. Audrey II was burning at 1750 degrees, effectively reducing Johnny to a blaze of brittle bones. Tennessee unhooked a rake from the side of Audrey II; she churned Johnny's remains, stoking the fire and crumbling bone. A quick twist of the rake head and Tennessee thunked Johnny's still-intact glowingly hot skull; the scarlet skull burst into white crumbs and dust. One more pass with the rake and she closed up Audrey II.

"Another hour." She set the rake aside; flipped up her faceguard.

Phillip pulled out the desk chair. "Rest."

"Doctor's orders?" She shook off her mitts.

Now Phillip was in the smirking mood. Her flesh rose to ready ripples. Damn that man. She pulled out her phone and texted Godzilla. Making sure he fed Polar was a decent distraction. She

reminded him to be on the lookout for the twins, to keep them away from the water. The last thing she needed was a pair of hypothermic demon brats.

When she finally sat down, Phillip asked, "What now?"

"We wait."

"Do you always wait?"

"If the family asks me to stay the entire time, I stay. If they don't, I might have a snack."

Phillip laughed.

Tennessee tossed her hair back. "I'm serious."

"I know, Tenny, that's why I love you."

"Ha!" She laughed. "Yeah, '*like a sister*', I recall that conversation vividly. Thanks so much, *bro*." She cringed at the break-up memory; just thinking of being related to Lillie creeped her out. "Go ahead and think of me as a sister, Phillip, but never mention it again. It's really gross."

Severity stole Phillip's smile as he processed the charge. "Tenny, I *never* said I thought of you as my sister. That's unsettling to say the least. Is that why you've been so distant? Tenny?"

Tennessee was hardly listening; Godzilla was texting about the twins. He found them on the beach; well, Polar did, and now they were all in his RV eating microwaved burritos. Relieved, she looked up at Phillip.

"We need to talk, Tenny..."

"No, we don't." She got up, shuffled paperwork on the desk. "I gotta check Johnny...just play on the internet or something..."

"About this foolish *sister* thing..."

"I'm over it." Tennessee geared-up once again and headed over to Johnny; she switched the oven off and slipped open the door. "Good job, Audrey II." She raked Johnny one last time, smashing charred chunks into dust. "All right, Johnny, cool off a bit and I'll get you out of there."

Phillip kept silent, observing Tennessee as she cared for Johnny; he'd never seen her working this closely with the dead; she wasn't

just respectful, she was nurturing. Her kindness for the dead truly inspired him, and he did something he never did: he gushed.

"You astound me, Tenny. You approach life and death with such grace. It's beautiful...*you're* beautiful."

"Wow," Tennessee gawked at Phillip from under her faceguard, "did somebody spike the punch?"

"I'm being serious."

"Oh, there you are. I was thinking body snatchers or aliens," she sneered, retrieving a cardboard box from a cabinet. She placed it under the oven door just as her cell phone rang.

"Hi Mom!" She screamed to get through the static. "Yes, I'm back at work...I'm fine, Mom! I wouldn't be at work if I died..." She laughed. "Well, maybe I would be...but I wouldn't be talking...yes, Mom, that's not funny...hey, don't worry about canceling your flight...I'm totally fine...well, *yes* actually, my warden is right here, please tell him all about it..." Tennessee handed the phone to Phillip with a spiteful glare.

Phillip took the call, speaking at length to Missus about Tennessee. From what she heard of his side of the conversation, they still spoke often; hell, he was probably more informed on her parents' comings and goings than she was, and he probably told them *everything* about her. He wasn't just her warden, he was a spy.

When he ended the call, Tennessee leered up at him. "Traitor."

He shook off a sigh. "If by traitor you mean *friend*, then yes. Guilty as charged."

That's when Phillip's phone vibrated in his jacket. He reached into his breast pocket and answered the call. "Stop screaming, Lillie. I can't understand you...slow down...no, I haven't seen the twins...yes, she's right here, *why*? Hold on, I'm putting you on speaker..."

Tennessee was shaking her head *NO*, but Lillie's voice was already booming in the crematory. "That bitch has my children! I want my children back! Tennessee! *Now*!"

Tennessee sighed. "What makes you think *I* have them?"

"This letter in my hand! Shall I read it to you?"

"No."

Lillie read it anyway. "*If you ever want to see your precious little girls alive again, give Tennessee England five thousand dollars. Bad habits are expensive. Signed, Tennessee England.*"

Phillip's befuddled expression made Tennessee chuckle.

"Clearly that's a mistake," Tennessee grumbled. "I always start at *ten* thousand."

"I'm not laughing, Tennessee!"

"Neither am I! I'm working, Lillie! Phillip's leaving *right now*...he'll bring your precious little girls home for *free*. You might want to do something about your nanny problem. Bye, bye!" Tennessee motioned for Phillip to hang up.

He didn't.

Tennessee balled her hands into fists. These people were crossing sacred lines!

Phillip finally took Lillie off speaker. Damn straight!

Tennessee unhooked a push broom, lifting it squarely into Audrey II's mouth. With meticulous movements, she swept Johnny, ash and bone, toward her and into the cardboard box she had placed on the floor. Then she rehung the broom to be cleaned later.

While Phillip calmed Lillie, Tennessee retrieved the box of Johnny.

When Phillip tucked his phone back in his jacket, Tennessee remarked casually, "Godzilla's parked out front...the twins already ate, and, apparently, they took Godzilla for a dollar at poker...that's a *hundred* in case you're still unconvinced just how good those girls hustle." She smiled up at him; it felt good; like old times.

But Phillip wasn't smiling anymore. "You should have said something earlier, Tenny. Lil's been worried all night. I know she's a pain, but she's a *mother*. She loves those girls. It was cruel not to tell her sooner."

Breath hardened behind Tennessee's breastbone. "Cruel? What happened to *grace* and *beautiful*?" She set the box of Johnny

on the worktable, yanking off her gear to get to her cell phone. She pulled up the text she sent to William right after the Jims' zucchini slaughter. "Exhibit One. William knew." She slid her phone across the worktable. "Goodbye, Phillip."

"I'm sorry." Phillip didn't even look at the text. "Dammit, I let her do it to me again. "*Please*, Tenny. I'm worried about you."

"Don't waste your worry on me. Save it for your other sister...she's the lunatic." Tennessee slammed a sheet pan on the worktable and began pouring Johnny out. She waved a heavy-duty magnet over Johnny's ash and bone. Metal debris just jammed the blender; she needed a fine ash for spreading and tossing.

When life tripped her up, Tennessee worked. There was no talking to her now. On his way out, Phillip stopped; he watched her, his evocative gaze bordering on haunting. She felt him there, thought he said something, but by the time she turned around he was gone.

*Clink!*

Something hit the magnet.

Tennessee had to pry the object off with a scalpel. It popped free, clattering on the table. Tennessee picked up the antique coin, the size of a quarter, but it wasn't a quarter at all. She turned it over and over; it didn't look like any of the foreign coins her parents collected on their travels and kept in a mason jar. The markings were a mix of strange symbols, shapes, and the hint of a spooky face. She opened a second drawer, fumbled around until she clasped a magnifying glass.

Holding the mysterious coin under a lamp, Tennessee inspected the bizarre markings. She was flipping the coin from front to back when a hand pressed down on her shoulder.

She jumped, jarring her leg. "Ow! You scared me!"

Sho's expression hardened as his gaze settled on the coin. "Where did you find that?" Sho's voice was different, a tone she hadn't heard from him yet. He'd lived too long and seen too much to be frightened for himself, so she knew it must be for her.

"Johnny." Tennessee put the coin down, decisively stepping away from it as she watched Sho's lips snarl up a little. "All right, so this is bad news for us...but, like, *how* bad?" Sho swallowed hard, and Tennessee sighed. "Man, if the samurai is freaked out, I'm in some serious shit." She noticed Sho start. "What?"

"You've been cursing more." Sho skimmed his fingers along the nape of her neck. "It's the collar. It changes you, if you are not vigilant."

Tennessee's gaze fell to the floor; she had been feeling more negative than usual, but she'd tackle that later; a few expletives wasn't her biggest problem; right now, the *coin* had her worried.

She pointed to the coin. "Bad?"

"That depends." Sho cautiously picked up the coin. "It tells me who has tethered us, and what she desires. She always sends a coin before the first job, then after...often in the most inconvenient places." Tennessee's eyes pleaded with him to hurry up. He turned his gaze on her, "You've been called by Empress Zaada, she who oversees demons *and* their wranglers. It is among the highest of honors, but the privilege to serve Zaada comes at a cost. No human wrangler..." His words drifted off with his gaze as he tucked the coin into his front pocket.

Tennessee pushed Sho's shoulder. "No human wrangler *what?*"

His eyes met hers, his rasp a vibrating whisper, "No human has survived the collar."

Tennessee put her hands on her hips. "Let me get this straight. I should be *honored* to receive a death sentence? My *third* death sentence, in case anyone's keeping count!" she screamed at the ceiling as if this Zaada, this *Empress*, was lurking about.

Although his eyes were serious, his lips curved up as he tried to quell Tennessee's panic. Soon, Sho shared a history Tennessee wished she'd never heard.

"Only humans have the power to wrangle demons who have entered Earth's realm. It continues to fascinate me how you all forsake your natural gifts. Demons fear humans. Mostly they fear the primal strength of the human soul and its ability to harness

the combined strength of multiple souls. But humans are flawed, Ten, and demons thrive on flawed souls. They exploit these imperfections to gain advantage over wranglers. Even the most experienced wranglers...after ridding the Earth of thousands of demons...fell to their own imperfections."

"Well that's not good." Tennessee slouched. This wasn't real! It couldn't be real! "I'm nothing but imperfections!"

Sho took Tennessee's hand into his. "Zaada does not call the weak, Ten. But you must never forget that, if given a chance...any opening at all, a demon *will* hijack a soul."

"Even a wrangler's soul?"

"*Especially* a wrangler's soul. A demon wielding a wrangler's gifts...the destruction on humanity pales to what ruin awaits that wrangler. It's always too much to bear. Even if the wrangler manages to exorcise the demon, the collar waits to seize control. It too craves power, Ten...never forget."

Face fallen, Tennessee grumbled, "I *can't* forget, Sho. I don't think I'll ever sleep again."

"You will sleep." Sho squeezed her hand, watching her a little too reverently. She turned her gaze as he declared, "*You* will be the first to survive the collar."

"And if I die before we get these damn collars off?"

"If a wrangler dies while collared," Sho clarified poignantly, "she becomes the very beast she sought to destroy."

"Well that doesn't sound promising given this ticking time-bomb in my brain," Tennessee stammered-slurred; she was overly tired, and her mannerisms showed it. Rooting in her cardigan for her pack of cigs, she smacked her lips, reenergizing her speech muscles. "No wrangler has *ever* survived...I'm not liking them odds, Sho..."

"They were alone." Sho gathered her icy hands into his. "This may be why Zaada chose a tether. I'm here to assist."

"For *now* you are, but," she was beginning to unravel this *collar* business; it was even more vile than she first thought, "when are you gonna, you know, *poof*?"

"It changes. How long has Johnny been dead?"

"Almost three weeks."

Sho pressed Tennessee's hands against his chest. "Still solid," he offered, hopeful levity in his gaze.

"That's good, I guess. So what? The coin's a message?"

"No," Sho exhaled, eyes hard on the crematory exit. "It's payment."

The scratchy rustle of those plastic curtains snagged their attention.

"For what?"

Sho positioned himself between Tennessee and the rustling. He slid into a fighting stance, his rasp chiseling ice as he declared, "For demon *one*."

# 8.

# Sugar & Smokes & Everything Broke

In the movies, demons are always hideous, hunched beasts with red eyes, razor-sharp claws, and a thirst for blood or souls or bloody souls. Tennessee held these images in her mind, so when a demure looking woman, thirties, tall, thin, wandered into the crematory, Tennessee relaxed.

"Oh, it's all right, Sho. She was at the wake. I saw her paying respects to Johnny." Tennessee released her cold grip on Sho's arm and casually stepped toward the woman. "You must be lost."

"No!" Sho grabbed Tennessee, whipping her behind him; but he used a little too much force, and Tennessee's injured leg buckled beneath her.

As Tennessee went careening toward the floor, the tall, thin woman lunged toward them. Sho flipped his body into the air, throwing a kick that smashed the heel of his shiny shoe smack dab on the demon's nose; blood squirted, and Sho's crisp white shirt soaked it up.

The screeching woman staggered back. "Are you crazy? John sent me to check on Johnny!"

"Stay back, demon!" Sho commanded, readying for round two.

From an undignified sprawl, Tennessee scrambled to a crawl

while Sho administered a mighty snap kick that sent the tall woman crashing against Audrey II. She bled, releasing an animalistic wail; the chilling sound had Tennessee's heart thudding from her ears to beneath her nailbeds.

"Others will come," the demonic woman growled, her words stirring an eerie echo in the sterile space. As her nose spewed blood, ragged claws grew from her boney fingers, and she used those claws to gouge at her face. She gripped her bloody nose with one claw and her mouth with her other claw; crying out in rage, she mercilessly wrenched her face apart. But she didn't stop there, she ripped and yanked and tore and splayed her torso wide open.

It took a lot to make Tennessee gag, even more to make her puke. But it was the smell, a rank mix of garbage, sulfur, and shit. Tennessee gagged, and that just pissed her off.

What stood before them was no longer human, definitely not a woman. Well, not *fully*; its bottom half still had the thin legs of a thirty-something woman, but its torn-apart torso drooped woman on either side of a beast, a globbish, reddish block of stitched-together meat and muscle.

Tennessee stammered a lot of *whats* and *hows* as Sho helped her get to standing. They stood side by side as the demon's true face stared them down.

"Fools...*we* cannot be stopped," it cackled hysterically, its crimson slits taunting them as black goo dripped from its serrated mouth. It *was* hunched and hideous, but it was also muscular and, though not fast, it was sure of itself, certain it could slay them, *would* slay them. *Tonight*.

"You're not welcome here, demon." Sho took a sure step forward, while Tennessee took a measured step back.

"Your bitch smells nice," it salivated, eyeing Tennessee. "We'll keep her on a leash too."

Tennessee had a thing about being called a bitch. It wasn't simple dislike; it was closer to hate. Yeah, it was hate. She toughened her gaze on the demon while whispering to Sho, "Does *wrangle* mean catch or kill?"

"Right now," Sho mirrored the demon's posturing, "whatever we manage."

"Well, since I don't know what the hell I'm supposed to do, my money's on *kill*!"

The demon was swaying back and forth in front of Audrey II, oozing black goo from its demon form, red blood from its human form.

"Like I said earlier," Tennessee stood a little taller, addressing the demon as she might Lillie, "you must be lost."

The demon let out a reverberating roar that rattled the cabinets and drawers. "Shut your hole, bitch! Do not address us! You are nothing to us!"

"Well, that's not very nice." Tennessee took an unsteady step in front of Sho; now he was following her. "What bad manners you have, coming into *my* house, attacking *my* friend, calling *me* names. So much rude!"

The reverberating roar deepened, followed by the mad mantra of a demon obsessed,

"Bitchbitchbitchbitchbitchbitchbitchbitchbitchbitchbitch!"

At first it sounded like nonsense or an evil demon language, but soon Tennessee made out the insult. She caught Sho's gaze and their plan was made.

The demon's mantra shook open the cabinets, spilling chemicals, scalpels, and supplies. The deafening chaos disoriented the pair. Tennessee's temples throbbed, she gripped her ears and that's when she noticed Sho was suffering too.

"Now!" Tennessee ordered, and Sho obeyed.

They rushed the demon.

Sho spun into a flying back kick, pummeling the demon into Audrey II's mouth. The demon scurried to the edge, readying to hurl itself at Sho. Tennessee snatched the rake from its hook, choked up on the handle like a baseball bat, and whacked the demon into Audrey II; it tumbled and screeched and tried to scurry out. Tennessee whacked it back, this time lodging the iron rake tines into its chest. The demon howled in pain, its flesh

bubbling to boils where pierced by the iron. It tried to thrash, but iron seemed to contain it, restricting its movements.

Tennessee released the rake with a fast shiver; she raced to her father's neat lettering: START. She slammed that button so hard her shoulder popped.

Flames shot up and down, engulfing the rake-impaled demon. It wailed and roared in a language Tennessee was glad she didn't understand.

She stood in front of Audrey II as she had done hundreds of times before, only this time was different; this time she shelved her compassion; this time, she *wanted* to watch the body burn. Tennessee stepped back, eyeing the melting demon,

"Nice matters, Blockhead."

She kicked the oven door shut. Just in case.

~

It didn't take long for the adrenaline to wear off. Tennessee's energy thinned and she couldn't feel her feet. She rushed to a chair. Her leg hurt, her shoulder hurt, her back hurt, and the blood in her head was beating faster than her racing heart. If the two didn't sync up soon, she'd pass out.

Disbelief was to be expected, but what she hadn't anticipated was the concentrated awareness of being completely out of shape. Sho was right there, kneeling beside her. She looked at him, barely managing a crooked snarl.

"Well, if *that's* what we have to do, I'm totally gonna need a fitness regimen. I'm no samurai."

Sho rested his head on her good thigh, a heavy sigh streaming from the stoic man.

"Are you hurt?" Tennessee pushed back Sho's jet-black hair.

Sho met her gaze, pride and honor in those emperor eyes. "You have a true wrangler's soul. You did not succumb to fear...as many have."

"Trust me, I'm *still* afraid!" She swallowed bitter bile creeping up her throat. "Why me?"

"Zaada chose correctly. Your handling of this demon proves this. It's an honor to serve you."

"Don't start that again, Sho. If this is what we have to do to break the curse and be free, then it's what we'll do...as a team. Got it?"

Sho bowed his head.

Tennessee's hands were still shaking; she desperately needed a cigarette. She pulled out her pack, fumbling a cig into her mouth. She wouldn't light it, but it relaxed her to know that she could. "I'm gonna need another rake," she quipped. "You can be our kicker. I have short Islander legs...don't think I can get my leg up that high." Tennessee took the cig out of her mouth, fiddled with it, put it back in.

Sho held her hands, warming them with his. "We'll train when your leg is fully healed. I believe you've injured it again."

Tennessee looked down at her thigh, and sure enough, blood saturated the bandage under her dress hem. Again. Phillip would probably admit her to the hospital, with full sedation, just to keep her still.

"Let me put Johnny to bed and we can go home."

Sho agreed, assisting Tennessee by pouring Johnny into The Cremulator. Blending Johnny took time; burning a demon took much longer.

Tennessee was exhausted, but Sho wasn't slowing down at all so she directed him on how to properly complete a burn. Sho transferred Johnny into the football urn chosen by the Cain family and dropped in a circular metal identifier tag. He hung an identical tag on the outside of the urn.

Johnny was done.

Sho turned off Audrey II. Demon ashes would be better dealt with in the morning. He kissed Tennessee's forehead, then slipped into the shadows. She finally rested her head on the worktable when Polar's rabblerousing barks blasted the room.

Then, sopping wet kisses.

"Ness? You asleep? Ness? No way Johnny took that long. Polar

went berserker on me. Ness!" Godzilla pushed his head through the plastic curtains; he knew better than to just walk in.

"Godzilla," Tennessee managed to slur as the shock of the day and night slammed her flat. She thunked her head back on the worktable as her hands trembled through Polar's fur.

Godzilla hadn't heard Tennessee slur in years; he studied her unfixed eyes, then phoned Phillip.

"We'll get you better, Ness. Don't you worry."

With Polar and Godzilla by her side, Tennessee could finally pass out.

~

The aroma of coffee and bacon on a crisp February morning made the memory of slaying a demon the night before more palatable, probable even.

Tennessee sat up in bed, taking stock of her body; all parts still intact, she scooched to the edge of her bed. Polar was sleeping on the floor. She gently rubbed his fur with her cold feet, while rubbing her hands together; she couldn't seem to get warm. The winter was long, but they weren't getting much snow in the mountains.

"Coffee," she mumbled to herself, and Polar jumped to attention. Coffee meant bacon, and dogs love bacon. Tennessee chuckled, slipping into her neon pink robe. She limped to the bathroom, washed up in a daze, then nuzzled Polar a good morning kiss. "Who's downstairs, boy?" Polar led Tennessee down the stairs. "What wonderful human being is making my all-time favorite breakfast?"

She expected Lin, Godzilla, even Hill, but she wasn't expecting William.

He was wearing her cooking apron, a gag gift from Lin that read: *Don't worry, it's chicken.* She loved that apron, wore it all the time. Seeing William wearing it did weird things to her brain. He'd never been in her silo before noon. *Never.*

And he was playing Meat Loaf's greatest hits. She didn't want to hear Meat Loaf in the morning, not after jamming with Johnny

all night, not after slaying a demon. The associations were too fresh. And William was smiling at her, spatula in hand. The whole situation rang awkwardly, well, seductive.

"Um-hmm, good morning, love..."

*Ick!*

Tennessee shot up in bed, drenched in sweat.

That hurt. Body parts she didn't know *could* hurt throbbed and singed. She scanned the room in a too-quick rush, swooshing her brain blood to a tidal whirl.

"Ow! Ow. Dammit! Ow! Did my head explode?" She howled, extending *ow* for a lengthy exhale.

"The meds are wearing off." Phillip was sitting in the corner, on a kitchen chair he must have dragged up.

"Stop drugging me, Phillip," Tennessee commanded through clenched teeth. "I don't like it!"

He went on explaining: she'd had an *episode*, meds were necessary, it was for her own good.

"Sssshhhh." She clasped her ears. "Why are you screaming," she whispered as her own voice boomed inside her head.

"I'm not." Phillip pulled a syringe from his bag. "You're due for another dose."

Tennessee threw herself out of bed, but she'd been thrashing all night and Phillip's favorite blanket had tangled around her ankle. She splatted on the floor; elbows banged, leg thunked, head knocked.

Phillip was hollering now, lashing out his best bedside manners as he peeled her off the floor.

"Dammit, Tenny, stop acting like a trapped wolf."

She twisted from his grip, leaning her bruised back against her bed. Phillip did the same, only his lean had more anger in it. Tennessee avoided Phillip's pained expression and wistful eyes. He shouldn't drug her when she didn't want drugs. Maybe she did have an episode, but she wanted to have them. If the damn bleed exploded her head, at least the wait would be over.

"I said no drugs, Phillip. I'd like to be awake when I die."

Phillip took Tennessee into his arms. By his grip he was on the verge of losing it. Maybe he was crying, or maybe he was just so angry he couldn't breathe evenly. His pain ripped through her; she snuggled closer, melting into him. Feeling his thudding heart against her throbbing head made strange sense to her. In moments like these, she was certain they fit. It was a nice thought; *faulty*, but nice.

Hill hollered up from downstairs, "Bacon's ready! Come 'n git it before the dog gits it all!"

Polar barked, slid across the tiles, barked, slid.

Tennessee looked up at Phillip. His eyes were red. "You still a vegan?"

Phillip scoffed, "I was never vegan, Tenny."

"If you don't eat bacon, you're vegan." She used Phillip's shoulder to push herself to standing, though it was more of a hunch.

Phillip shadowed her movements. He resisted leading or maneuvering her; he simply let her use his arm to go where *she* wanted. She looked up at him. "I might need some help in the shower; do you think you can handle bathing your *sister?*"

The fluster of shock and disgust washed Phillip's face white.

"Man up, Phillip. You're a doctor! I just need some help getting in and out. Like I told the twins, if you don't like something you see, close your damn eyes."

Phillip opened the bathroom door, helping Tennessee to the edge of the bathtub. They'd done this before, only she was the instigator. Phillip was a bed-only sort of lover before he'd met her. She caught a glimpse of his reflection in the mirror as he heated a washcloth; the memory wasn't far from his mind either.

She recalled her terrifying nightmare about William, and that did the trick. Instant ice. Tennessee further sterilized the environment by bringing up Sho. Phillip's shoulders tensed right on cue.

"Yes, where is your *boyfriend.*" Phillip was livid, and a little cutting.

"The way you say it," Tennessee snatched the washcloth from his hands, "I know it might be shocking to you...you know, because you think of me like a *sister*, but that doesn't mean other men don't find me desirable. I'll have you know, I have options, Phillip. Lots and lots of options!" Tennessee scrubbed her face with the washcloth, leaving her ginger-spiced skin red and raw.

Phillip snatched the washcloth back, kneeling in front of Tennessee; he took over the face washing in a far gentler manner. "Let's come to a compromise, shall we? I promise to limit your *medically sanctioned* and entirely reasonable medications to emergency situations only *if* you stop all this nonsense about me thinking of you as my *sister*. I told you last night, it's unsettling, and entirely untrue."

Tennessee shoved Phillip aside, concentrating on the shower knobs, twisting hot and cold to get her perfect mix. "No drugs unless I say?" She glowered at him. He nodded. Her relief turned coy as she said, "Maybe I *like* being your sister..."

"We were *lovers*, Tenny!" Phillip was actually furious, which didn't quite make sense to her. He *had* said it, even if he refused to admit it now. "You're *not*, nor have you ever been like my sister! I think of you as the woman I'm...as the woman I loved deeply...as a dear *friend*."

"Whatever." Tennessee turned away from Phillip, because his words had her feeling more than she wanted, and his gaze was all too...*Phillip*. She stepped into the shower, slowly disrobing; in response to the apprehension in Phillip's eyes, she flipped him the bird.

This time, with *both* fingers.

He shook his head like a tired old man, then whipped the shower curtain closed and yanked up the faucet diverter, instantly dousing Tennessee with her perfect mix of hot and cold.

She screamed then laughed then screamed.

"Hurry up, Tenny, my coffee's getting cold."

Now *that* was unlike Phillip. And she loved him for it.

~

After a hot shower Tennessee called out, "Hey, some help in here! Robe, please!"

Phillip opened the bathroom door to find Tennessee's hand sticking out from behind the shower curtain; followed by her head. She made a goofy face, and Phillip smirked, placing a stack of clothes on the counter and playfully shoving a robe into her hand.

"Much better," she congratulated him.

Phillip began a witty comeback as another man's voice overpowered his.

"I didn't know doctors still make house calls." Sho's tone was free of those pesky human tells—sarcasm, jealousy, hate. "Thank you for tending to *my* Ten. I'm certain she has been a pain. I have her now." Sho's stoic countenance was exactly what Tennessee needed to see. But it was also *not* what she *wanted* to see.

The men brushed shoulders as one walked in, and the other, out.

Tennessee motioned for Sho to shut the door, then began in a panic, "Oh my god, who died? Oh my god, who's going to die? Not Phillip! Hill? Godzilla? Dammit, too much barbeque! I've told him to cut back!" Tennessee was starting to shake when Sho pushed aside the window curtain. She craned her neck to see Riggy parked outside.

Sho and Tennessee locked eyes,

"Maria Garcia."

Easing into his natural grace, Sho gathered a robed Tennessee into his arms; he didn't notice the dampening of his clothes as her wet hair pressed against his chest, but Tennessee did. She also noticed his faded jeans, and a wool pullover fit for nights on the beach.

She glanced at the black jeans and black sweatshirt she typically wore. She'd have to try harder. She had to ask. "Where does a disappearing soulless ghost samurai tethered to a demon wrangler shop these days?"

Sho only smiled.

"Hmmm, the secrets you keep."

He pulled her closer, a rumble in his rasp. "Did you sleep well? You need to keep up your strength."

"You do, too."

"*You* are the chosen, I merely assist."

"Funny, that's not how it looked last night."

"We are a team." Sho's generous assertion sent a cold ripple circling Tennessee's neck.

"Hug me again." She fixed her gaze on the mirror. Maybe the chain was gone, maybe it had never been there.

There was mindful calculation behind Sho's movements; even so, any act of resistance was wasteful. He must obey.

Once again, Sho positioned himself behind Tennessee; and, once again, when the embrace was secured, those collars returned, and that rusty old chain.

"You're ill this morning." Sho brushed a clump of soggy frizz away from Tennessee's eye.

"Not shocking, I *am* dying."

"You are not dying, your collar needs *this*." Sho held up the coin Tennessee had discovered in Johnny's dust.

As if in response to the coin, Tennessee's collar jangled around her neck; she cringed and crunched up her shoulders as the collar's gyrating amped up to thrashing. Sho restrained the collar. Only after it settled did he hold up the coin.

"Ten, I have healed your aneurysm. As long as you wrangle demons for Zaada, she will provide payment and honor the healing. These coins keep you alive."

"Great, I'm on demon payroll now. Do I have a choice?"

"You made your choice when you chose mortality."

"Well, it's not like I read the fine print."

"I am sorry."

"Forget it. It's done. What do we do now?"

Sho tightened his grip on Tennessee's collar. "A thousand more and she is absolved of her crimes. She is released from serving

Zaada as wrangler...with her healing intact," Sho demanded of the collar.

"Wait! This thing's *alive?*" She breathed deeply to stop a pukey sensation from getting its way.

"As alive as magical things can be." Sho's quick reply settled nothing in Tennessee's gut. He tempted the collar with the coin. "Have we a deal?"

The collar settled into a steady vibration like a cat's tranquil purr. Confirmation enough.

"Do not be so impatient next time. She's not to be harmed, as you have done this morning."

"My headache?"

Sho nodded. Then he fed the collar the coin. That's the only way she could explain what happened. Sho touched the coin on her collar, and her collar absorbed it; just as Sho's collar drank her blood when she pricked her finger on the rusty iron.

But something else happened, something more magical than anything she'd seen yet. A tremor, originating from within her collar, pulsed a shockwave through the iron chain to Sho's collar. He flinched as the shock zapped his body, and Tennessee watched the jagged scar crisscrossing Sho's neck completely disappear.

"Oh," she gasped as their arrangement started to make some sense.

Sho displayed a rare moment of shame as he stroked his smooth, scar-less neck. "I'd rather have kept that one."

Tennessee made a face; now that *didn't* make sense.

Sho sighed. "I considered it a lucky gift. It was entrusted to me by a samurai of great renown and compassion. He and I were tethered, as you and I are now. I carried that scar for him so that he could live...without burden."

"Was he a wrangler?"

"No, he was something else, but it will be the same with us. Your injuries become my burdens...easing your pain is my gift to you. Don't look so worried, Ten, my kind is bred for this."

Tennessee adjusted her weight from side to side; nothing hurt. "Take off your pants!"

Sho recoiled. "I'd rather not."

"Ah, come on..."

"We are a team, yes?"

"Yes."

"And you know that I *must* obey."

"Yes."

Sho stood there, eyes heavy on his feet.

"You're right, I'm sorry...I was just..." Tennessee flung open the vanity drawer, rifled until she found scissors to cut the bandage from her thigh.

"Your instinct is correct. Your scar is now my scar. I've taken the pain and its limiting aspects." He lifted his eyes, and they were dark with a lighthearted intrigue. "I didn't think you'd mind."

"Well, I do happen to mind, *a lot* actually." Tennessee ran her fingers over her perfect thigh. "Why should *you* be in constant pain?"

"It is my birthright." He was all matter-of-fact. "My kind have a unique relationship with pain. I promise, I can handle your little scar." Sho arched one brow, a buoyant bravado squaring his shoulders.

"I bet you can." Tennessee got real close, just barely touching him. "So...thank you. The leg feels great."

He touched her face; a quick, rough caress. She liked the way he did that.

As they separated, she took a good look in the mirror, remembering those heinous scars hiding beneath Sho's sweater. Tennessee got to thinking. She didn't like where her patchwork theories took her, so she kept it simple, stupid.

"So, this is what it feels like to be *owned?*"

He studied her, waiting for another wave of panic. Tennessee let it subside, moving on. "Right now, we don't have a choice. *I* don't have a choice. Promise me, the second there's another way out, you'll tell me. I'm all up for rebelling...it's in my blood," she

declared wily as memories of her family's long history protesting colonial rule on the islands scorched her mind's eye.

A shimmer of pride deepened Sho's reverential gaze. "Yes, of course."

"We kill demons. Pay the bitch. I earn my freedom and *you* earn a shot at human life. That's all I care about, Sho. That's all I want from here on out."

Sho's expression softened with playful doubt. "And coffee?"

"That's another category, but, yeah, coffee," she agreed, laughing as she shoved him out of the bathroom so she could finish getting dressed. "And sugar," she hollered, "and bacon!"

~

Godzilla waited outside in Riggy, Maria Garcia in a body bag in the back. He had the front windows down but kept the cool a/c on for Maria. He usually used his old van to pick up bodies—less conspicuous and such—but its transmission was shot, and Godzilla needed to nab a few more jobs before he could fix it.

Hill watched Godzilla devour one of the three bacon and egg sandwiches she delivered. She was puffing on her pipe when Phillip stormed onto the porch.

"How's Nessie?" Hill held up her pipe to the moping doctor. "She kick yer ass for drugging her?" Hill sniffed at Phillip's dejected shrug. "She's in the right. She'll go out Nessie-style. We owe her that."

Phillip was absorbed in pacing on the porch when Sho walked out.

"And who is this young fella?" Hill puffed her pipe, cinched brow crinkling her crinkled face.

Confusion flashed across Phillip's face; hadn't they been introduced when Sho arrived?

Sho wanted to walk over to Hill and bid her a proper hello, but he couldn't move from his spot; forty-two feet gave Tennessee leeway to move about the kitchen and get her breakfast.

"I am honored to meet you. I am Sho." He bowed deeply, eyes down, honoring the woman's wisdom and life.

Impressed, Hill bowed her head then raised her pipe to him. "Nessie's new boy. I heard it from Lin, and Phillip here. You goin' do right by our girl?"

"Yes, Obaasan." Sho bowed again, this time with his hands in prayer at his chest.

Hill raised a crinkled brow. "Oh, I like this fella. Look at that, Phillip, we're already family. That's grandmother, if memory serves."

"Ten's family is my family."

Phillip eyed Sho. "Ten?"

"Because that's what I am," Tennessee sang, doing a little hip shimmy as she strolled on to the porch. She popped two strips of bacon in her mouth while slipping one arm around Sho's waist. He brought out her easy nature, her endearing way of laughing at herself. And she laughed harder when Godzilla held a double thumbs-up out Riggy's window.

"My man! Riggy looks fantastic! Wash *and* wax! Dang, even his curtains look clean!" Tennessee bounded down the stairs, completely forgetting about those pesky fifty feet.

Sho chased after; his swift reaction had both Phillip and Hill contemplating the weirdness.

"Hill made bacon!" Tennessee ducked her head in the passenger window. "You eat yet?"

Godzilla shoved the rest of his second sandwich in his mouth. "No."

Tennessee laughed at her forever-hungry friend, then got serious. "Maria Garcia?"

"Yep, she gets the works!"

"Oh, good for her!" Tennessee patted the body bag in back. "Nails, makeup, *and* hair! Girl, it's gonna be rad!" She turned around to see Sho standing aimlessly in an empty space between the silo and the hearse; that's when she remembered the fifty feet. She wrinkled her nose up, mouthing an apology that was not lost on Phillip or Hill.

After an effortless recovery, Sho approached, greeting Godzilla

with full charisma. "Ten's guardian angel. You have my gratitude." Sho reached through the passenger window to shake Godzilla's hand.

Godzilla refused to make eye contact; he clasped hands with Sho and squeezed, *hard*. He made sure to leave a slick of bacon grease on Sho's palm, just to see how he'd handle it; he was either gonna be a man about it or a candy-ass pansy.

Tennessee squinted her eyes at Godzilla, but he wasn't about to get out to properly greet *some guy*. Then she saw the grease.

"Get in, Ness. Maria's ready."

Sho wasn't doing anything about his oil-slicked hand, so Tennessee grabbed a wad of napkins from the glove compartment box. It took a bit of searching; she had all the essentials in there: ketchup, creamer, sugar, salt, pepper, even mustard and relish.

"Polar and Sho are coming with, so scooch over, big guy. I'm driving!"

Godzilla boomed, "*He* sits in back!"

Godzilla wouldn't budge, and Sho wouldn't take the napkins, so Tennessee was battling with both men when Phillip approached.

"It's a squash, Tenny, I'll drop you at the shop..." he paused in reflection. "Or Sho, either way."

Tennessee almost flipped out over the kind, and completely *normal*, gesture. It was a broken puzzle; she couldn't separate from Sho, but she couldn't ride with Sho in Phillip's car either. What if they got too far from Maria Garcia and Sho poofed? That's all she needed; her new guy disappearing in front of her old guy. Explain that!

Phillip almost went to Tennessee, to put his arm around her waist and lead her away, but then he remembered: that pleasure belonged to Sho.

Tennessee took a breath and worked out the puzzle.

"Hill, don't you need those storage units cleared out?" Hill nodded. "Godzilla, don't you need some cash for your van?" Godzilla's eyes brightened. "Here's how it's gonna be...I'll drive

Maria, Sho, and Polar back to the shop and get started. You go with Hill, and I'll meet you at Lin's shop...she's invited us to dinner. Mamma Min leaves tomorrow." Phillip was already walking to his car. "Hey, Phillip, thanks for the offer. See you tonight? Lin expects the *entire* crew to show up, otherwise, Mamma Min will pay her too much attention."

Surprised to be included in the *crew*, Phillip smirked, that smirk she loved. "Lambs to the slaughter. An offer I can't refuse."

"See you there?" she asked again, with a little too much urgency. Where the hell was *that* coming from?

Maybe it was seeing him walk away again. Maybe it was their conversation earlier, or the dancing, or maybe it was that smirk. She shoved all that aside; it was the *drugs*. Damn him.

Godzilla exited Riggy, dropping the vehicle down with his weight, slingshotting it into a swaying motion once he was out; he tossed Tennessee the keys without a heads-up. She didn't need one; she snatched them out of the air as if by routine.

Sho opened the passenger side door, waiting for Tennessee to climb in.

Polar grunted, shot his eyes up to his master, back to Sho.

Even from afar, Tennessee saw Phillip's disparaging head shake as he got in his car. Godzilla laughed at the confused expression on Sho's face; the poor newbie didn't have a clue. And Hill strolled by, whacking the boy with her cane as she puffed cherry tobacco in his face,

"You ain't earned it, boy."

Sho took his hands off Riggy, observed the way Tennessee was holding the set of keys cradled in both palms. "Ah, I see. Go on in, Polar." As Polar jumped in, Sho bowed to Hill and Godzilla before settling himself into the passenger's seat.

Hill wedged her pipe into the corner of her mouth. "This one's smart, Nessie."

Tennessee tried her best *not* to hug Hill, but the moment got the better of her. She leaned in, embraced the old woman and thanked her for...nothing *and* everything. After her parents left,

Tennessee had turned to Hill for all the confusing life stuff; the old crow was her godmother and so much more.

Hill whopped Tennessee's back, as she might someone choking. "Go on now, git." Tennessee rounded Riggy and was opening his door when Hill muttered, "You've demons to wrangle."

Tennessee stopped, took a long breath before meeting Hill's eye. She was about ready to freak out when Hill winked. "Them twins, I mean. Bound to rot without you."

Tennessee's cold hands dropped a full degree as she watched Hill stroll up the porch stairs; and as Hill slipped into the silo, Tennessee swore she saw, just for a blink, a long, slinky, black tail waggle behind the old woman.

Then again, she could have sworn to a great many truths that had since been proven wrong. Given her diagnosis, a history of hallucinating, Phillip's druggings, and being tethered to a soulless nonhuman, Tennessee no longer had a description for *reality*.

And without reality, anything was possible.

# 9.

# Strange Luck

The death of Maria Garcia, while regrettable and awful and just plain sad, was what Lin would call *strange luck*. Tennessee had three stops to make before heading to the shop, and she wanted Sho *visible* for one of them. First, she required her daily mindbender. Easy. They drove through for that one. Second, she was out of embalming fluid. She parked in the back lot of Teller's Medical Supply; the cashier was less than fifty feet from the back entrance. Tennessee called in her order so all she had to do was jump out and pick up the box. Done.

The next one was tricky; a quick test.

"So...how far can you be from Maria Garcia before you poof?"

Polar was sitting between Sho and Tennessee. Sho had to lean way back in the seat to see her. "The distance varies. It's best to assume the more time that passes after death, the closer we must be. If death is imminent, I may bear witness to the soul's departure."

Tennessee sat with that for a bit, guzzling her mindbender. "Because you also carry emotional scars...right?"

Sho nodded.

"I don't like it."

"No." Sho's tensed jaw had Tennessee feeling he preferred physical scars to emotional ones. She had to agree with that.

Far beyond the bustle of beach tourists and locals just trying to get to work, Tennessee pulled onto a dirt road, drove another half mile before pulling into an empty gravel parking lot. It was somewhat secluded, a garden oasis once upon a time. She slid Riggy into a slot near the entrance; she still wasn't sure if Sho was going to poof.

"Stumpy's?" Sho read a busted-up metal sign hanging from a rusted post; there were three bullet holes in it, and when the wind blew the sign made a hostile metallic screech; if the wind went wild, the sign banged against the rusted post; a clattering capable of scaring off honest clientele.

"If you poof here, only Stumpy will notice, and he's..." She checked her cell phone, it was ten-thirty. "Oh yeah, he's down a twelve pack by now." Tennessee left Riggy running, flinging open the door. "Be cool, Maria. Back in five."

"Why are we here, Ten?"

"You'll see."

Polar squeezed around Tennessee; he loved Stumpy's; there were rabbits and moles and lots of cats to chase. He raced into the unkempt garden, disturbing a murder of crows. The black birds took flight, cawing at the white beast, and a crumpled fast food burger wrapper fluttered after. The murder flew back down to their feast, attacking a hunk of meat.

"Hmmm," Tennessee watched the birds devour the burger, "it's not like Stumpy to toss a perfectly good burger."

As they walked on, the rustle of discarded paper wrappers from every burger joint in town whipped in the wind, adding a dumpy charm to the place. A gust blew a sun-bleached wrapper against Tennessee's shin; she shook off the trash with a grumble of *ick*.

Sho was close behind, scanning the shadows, as they strolled into Stumpy's.

The welcoming aroma could only be described as dirt.

The nursery was once an English garden run by unmarried church ladies who had never been to England but wished they had. Miss Ellie Champagne, besides having a great name, led the

women's group to five successful *Best in Show* awards and a two-page spread in her favorite magazine, *The English View.* Establishing the garden was a ton of work, but maintaining it was worse. Weeding, watering, *bending*. As the ladies grew too old to properly tend a large garden, and the younger church ladies formed Pilates groups and booty boot camp groups and social media groups, the English Garden grew old too.

Luckily for Miss Ellie Champagne, she died before the garden fell to ruin and into the hands of one Stumpy Beetle.

Stumpy was a junker, so he ran the nursery like a U-pick junkyard. Only he didn't figure out the difference between junk and plants until it was too late. The Jims were one of the many town residents who picked Miss Ellie's garden to damn near death. Where there was once lavender, stinging nettle thrived; where there was once foxglove, blackberry brambles took root; and rude clusters of crabgrass dethroned the mighty peonies, phlox, and hollyhocks.

Hill said Stumpy's stupidity was something wonderful; by leaving the *weeds* to bloom, Stumpy had inadvertently created a wild psychic garden; she took Tennessee once to collect thistle, chicory, burdock, and dandelion for use in her medicinal teas and creams. Tennessee was impressionably young at the time, and thought Hill smoked the weeds. She told her mother about smoking weeds and Missus never let Tennessee accompany Hill to Stumpy's again.

Wild grasses hid the cobblestone path, but Tennessee remembered the way. Sho trailed behind, eyeing the drooping willows and forlorn birch. Tufts of Polar's thick, white fur caught on dead thorn apple and dormant brambles. Plucking the clumps of fur off a spike, Tennessee glanced back at Sho,

"How many feet from Maria?"

"One-hundred twenty-three. Why are we here?"

"I need a new rake. Some demon took mine...and..." Tennessee stopped, waited for Sho to catch up. "I was curious." She caught

his gaze and squinted, pressing her hand against his chest. "Yep, still solid."

Sho took her icy hand into his; a flash of panic overtook his calm. "It's not safe. We need to find Polar!"

Tennessee's ramble turned into a race; Sho was chasing Polar, and she wasn't sure why.

"I'm sure he's fine. Polar used to run out here all the time, but ever since a branch from that oak tree over there fell on Stumpy's head he's been...*off*. We stopped coming by so much. He's got a memory like a sieve."

"I think this Stumpy is dangerous."

"He wishes. Relax, Stumpy doesn't own a gun...uh, well, he's not *allowed* to..."

"I am certain this Stumpy owns a gun."

"And what makes you so sure?"

"The trees."

Tennessee strained to focus on a tree, but Sho was dragging her through the weed garden and she was trying to stay on her feet. It wasn't until they ducked under a lopsided cedar arbor that Tennessee saw it: the maples, birch, willows, decomposing benches, and yard art, *all* riddled with bullet holes.

Tennessee's hands were freezing; Sho gave her a sharp glance, and then they were running. She yelled for Polar, but he didn't bark or growl or anything. Now Sho was keeping pace with her.

"Tell me what you know!" Tennessee wheezed, breaking into a sprint.

Sho was a lot taller than Tennessee, and fit; it took little effort to talk and run. "There's a demon out there."

"You can sense it? Because that skill would've been good to know earlier!"

"No, *you* can sense it. Your body temperature falls when a demon is near."

Tennessee let that sink in, balling up her freezing hands into tight fists. They *were* cold, and getting colder. She stopped talking. Ran faster.

They were exiting the main flower garden when someone hollered at them, "I'm closed!"

They tracked the holler to a field of unharvested, rotten wheat.

"We're closed! Git on!" A stodgy man, not much taller than Tennessee, guzzled a beer, crunched the can, chucked it into the wheat.

Tennessee locked eyes with Stumpy. "I'm Hill's friend, remember? Name's Tennessee." As she stepped forward, Sho grabbed her arm just above the elbow. "We've met...quite often, actually. My dog ran out this way. Have you seen him? He's big and white."

"Hill!" Stumpy scuttled the four yards across rock, weed, and dirt to get to Tennessee. "She have her auction yet?"

"Weeks ago."

Stumpy swore, stomped, and sucked his chew tobacco into a wad under his bottom lip. "I was lookin' forward to it! Always git my X-mas presents from those units, blasted Hill! Er, I ain't seen no dog. I've been out here all morning tendin' the yard. Ain't seen no dog."

Tennessee searched left and right, but she couldn't see Polar, and since the yard looked like crap, she wondered *what* Stumpy could possibly be tending. She was just about to threaten the forgetful man when Polar came running up behind Stumpy. He wasn't barking or growling or whimpering; he was excited, wagging his tail and panting like he always did after a good rabbit chase.

"Guess you found yer dog." Stumpy pulled at his oily overalls; he wasn't even wearing a shirt. "Right ugly dog...it looks like an electrified cat."

Polar barked. He didn't see any cats, but he was ready.

"Thank you, sir, we'll be on our way now." Sho shot Stumpy a swift head bow, pulling Tennessee back the way they had come. She resisted, she really didn't like Stumpy's *ugly* comment.

"There's a faster way out." The greasy man burped, scuttling toward a ramshackle shack to their right. Stumpy led his visitors

on a gravel path, somewhat clear of weeds, thanks to the gallons of empty, toppled over pesticide barrels strewn about the yard.

"Mind the junk. I'm fixin' a yard sale come spring."

Everywhere she looked there were old toilets, rusted cars, engines, refrigerators, bumpers, even a six-foot tall granite statue: an exact replica of Founder Saint James. She recognized it. Besides being Phillip's (and Lillie's) ancestor, the statue was a fixture in town before it was stolen.

"How'd you end up with Stoner James?"

Stumpy got a kick out of the name. That's what true townies called it.

Tennessee's hands were cold, but not as frozen as before. She didn't relax, but she was certain Stumpy wasn't their demon.

Stumpy cracked a toothless grin. "I tell ya, I hafta kill ya." He slapped his thigh and kicked his boot in dirt. "I've always wanted to say that..." When the greasy man stopped his hyena laughter, he lambasted, "All this stuff come from Hill's auctions. Modern day treasure huntin'...this is why I'm real POed she ain't called me. We have an arrangement, see. She's just hot cuz I shut up the u-pick. She liked the u-pick for the herbs. I grow the best herbs in the state."

Sho looked back at the brittle garden as Tennessee reminisced out loud.

"I used to come here with Hill...helped her gather."

Stumpy cocked his head askew, eyeing Tennessee's frizzy mane; then, to her horror, he reached out and touched her hair.

Polar growled, and Sho nearly punched the guy. But Tennessee was used to people doing that. She *hated* it, but she was used to it.

"You remember the hair, huh." Tennessee made nice because she spotted a heap of old garden tools piled up like a bonfire, and two faded red gas containers tucked under a tree.

She was already down one rake.

Stumpy patted Tennessee's hair again, and leered creepily. "You come a few times, I remember now. Hill's godbaby, yeah?"

"Yeah."

"Well den, git on and tell your godmommy what I said here today."

Tennessee assured him she would before negotiating a little something for her trouble. "Hey, Stumpy, about that pile of busted-up tools...got a number in mind for the useless heap?"

Stumpy got to squinting and pulling at his overalls again; his junk was only useless if nobody wanted it, and it seemed to him that Tennessee wanted it.

The man twitched; she had him on the hook, started reeling him in. "We clear a spot for your yard sale, and you skip the bonfire. Spend your cash on the drinking kind of accelerant."

Polar grunted and Sho put his arm around Tennessee. She loosened his hold a tad; she was haggling here, she needed space to work a deal.

"I'd do a nickel." Stumpy sucked in hard, then spat black snuff spit inches from Tennessee's boot. A wry expression from Tennessee had Stumpy amending his absurd offer. "Cuz you're Hill's godbaby and all, I'd take a hit and do...er..." Stumpy couldn't read Tennessee; her stone-cold expression had him shouting out random amounts for the junk he meant to burn after another six pack.

Sho watched her; the way she haggled by *not* haggling showed real skill, and patience.

After letting the haggle go to ice, Tennessee countered with, "I could do a *dollar* for the pile, top to dirt." She held up a hundred.

Stumpy snatched the bill. "Help yourself, Hill's godbaby! I've got a beer run to git done. Bye now!" The pudgy man scuttled off behind the shack, and soon after a motor scooter puttered off down the road.

Sho clutched Tennessee's hand.

"It wasn't him," she declared, bending down to nuzzle Polar and scold him for running off too far. "Come on, Sho, help me load this junk into Riggy. Maria won't mind. It's for her protection too."

"What is this *junk*?" Sho led the way, still on edge.

"Demons don't like iron, right?" Tennessee was still guessing, but she was the proactive type. "So, we need all the iron we can get..." Tennessee scrambled up the pile, tugged an iron rake from the heap. "And *this* is to replace the one that Blockhead wouldn't give back."

Tennessee stood victorious on that burn pile, holding her new rake overhead, her divinely wild mane whipping as cool wind swept in. She started quoting famous lines from famous movies; silly got her through life's rough patches, why stop now?

Sho watched Tennessee, captivated by her innate ability to find playfulness when others couldn't. She tossed him a shovel, her light gaze meeting his intensity; *that* look wouldn't do either of them any good.

"Don't fall in love with me, Sho," Tennessee ordered, dead serious. She thought maybe a splat of rouge marked Sho's cheekbones just before he bowed his head.

Sho gripped the shovel. "Indeed, that would be unwise."

Tennessee climbed down her mountain. "I won't fall in love with you either, okay." She was still serious, but there was worry in her eyes.

Now there was worry in Sho's eyes.

Tennessee spat in her palm then held her hand out for Sho to shake on it. He didn't understand.

"You spit, then we shake," she explained. "It seals the promise."

Sho still didn't understand, his eyes hardened on her outstretched hand. "Do I spit in *your* hand or my own?"

It was a good question. Tennessee didn't know the history of the mainland tradition, and she never participated in it; she didn't know why she started now.

"I've only seen people spit in their own hand."

"I see." Sho turned his back to Tennessee, brought his hand over his mouth and spit. It was impolite to spit where he came from, but he was under orders.

The pair shook on it, both a little grossed-out by the sticky squish.

Climbing back up the mound, Tennessee tossed Sho another shovel before spotting an iron manhole cover teetering atop more iron.

"Score!"

"Why would this man collect this much iron?"

"He's a junker. People come here, make piles, but if they can't agree on a price, the pile stays. I doubt Stumpy even knows all the stuff that's under here."

It took nearly an hour to unearth their iron treasures and load up Riggy. They scavenged dozens of gardening tools, eighteen iron fence posts, two windmill blades, an actual antique iron, four cast iron frying pans, and a box of horseshoes.

Not bad for a dollar.

~

Maria Garcia died alone. She was the youngest, the only daughter in a family with seven sons. Adora Garcia had died three minutes after birthing her precious baby girl. By the fourth minute, Maria's father vowed to forsake Maria for killing his one true love. Maria's brothers conformed to the patriarch's wishes, denying their sister. The family mourned Maria's birth as if it was her death.

The feeble little girl walked through life witnessing love all around her, none of which was bestowed on her. She had a chance to find love, *once*. When Mr. Garcia fell ill shortly after Maria's fourteenth birthday, Maria never left his side. In a household of obey, the little girl accepted her calling. She was to serve. Maria nursed her father into remission, and, in a moment of gratitude, Mr. Garcia released her from the family. "Go far," he ordered. "Do not look back."

It was the only order Maria ever disobeyed.

Maria declared she'd never marry, never have children, and never leave her father's home. She fulfilled her oath, and on her twenty-eighth birthday, she died. Her brothers claimed it was her curse on them; to die on the anniversary of their mother's death was cruel and vengeful. The eldest brother claimed to see his

mother descend from heaven to collect Maria from her personal hell. Fearing retaliation from the dead women, the Garcia family vowed to make Maria's death the best time of her life.

After tucking Maria's body-bagged body in a cooler in the prep room, Tennessee washed up, twirled her tangled locks into a messy bun; then she applied dark coal eyeliner, a brush of powder, and pink lip gloss. She inspected the drab suit hanging behind the bathroom door. Lin wouldn't approve of the pantsuit, but Lin didn't have a meeting with a grieving father and his seven grieving sons in exactly three minutes.

"May I help?" Sho carried in the last batch of garden tools.

"Just the tools, Sho. Leave the rest in Riggy...if you can make a pot of coffee that'd be great!" She raced out of the bathroom, eyeing the wall clock. "Two minutes!"

Sho rushed into the waiting room, but Tennessee beat him there. She sped behind the refreshment counter, tore open a package of day-old Danish pastries, set them out on a tray, then popped a pan of premade chocolate chip cookies into a compact toaster oven tucked behind the counter. That was a trick Missus taught her; the aroma of home baked cookies countered the high stress situation of *making arrangements*.

Tennessee didn't believe any of it, but she too did as she was told.

"How's that coffee coming?" Tennessee glanced at Sho. He was standing over the coffee pot, flustered.

"Water, filter, but how much coffee?"

"A tablespoon for each cup of water...here, I'll show you." She knocked him aside with her hip, and he happily knocked her back. The two were laughing, playfully pushing one another like teenagers when the Garcia family walked in.

Mr. Garcia cleared his throat like a bear might scatter a pack of wolves. "We have an appointment with *Miss* England."

Tennessee turned with poise, invoking her Funeral Director charm. "Hello, welcome. Mr. Garcia, we spoke on the phone. Please, call me Tennessee. This is my assistant, Sho." With a

dusting of makeup, heels, and the fitted suit, she looked professional, likeable, and, most importantly, capable. "We are deeply sorry for your loss."

Mr. Garcia removed his hat, brandishing a clean cut of silver. The Garcia sons eyed Sho, who started the coffee before taking his place beside Tennessee. Mr. Garcia shook hands with both Tennessee and Sho; his seven sons did not. They were respectful, good-looking men, all Suits, but it was clear who was in charge. Tennessee led the patriarch to her desk where she walked him through the paperwork required to give Maria all she deserved. Godzilla was good friends with one of the seven sons, so he'd heard the family's wishes before Tennessee had. She was expecting an embalming with the works, and a full funeral plan; so, when Mr. Garcia asked for Maria's wake to be held the following day, without embalming, without the works, Tennessee nodded compassionately until she could answer in her nicest tone.

"Certainly, Mr. Garcia." She pulled out a binder with wake themes and celebration of life ideas.

With an irritated glare, Mr. Garcia slammed the binder shut. Sho, who had been standing behind the refreshment counter, moved closer to the office. The seven sons stood all at once, staring at Sho.

"I pray you find peace," Sho professed, but he didn't bow, and he didn't take his eyes off the seven sons.

This wasn't Tennessee's *first* encounter with an angry mourner, but it *was* the first time she feared the angry mourner might reach across the desk and strangle her. It was the strangest flash in her mind's eye. Mr. Garcia *was* capable of hurting her. Tennessee got to thinking: was he also capable of hurting Maria?

"I was informed you handle everything." He stood, a strategic, shoulder-width stance.

Tennessee stood up too; this was *her* house, dammit. "Once I know your preferences, I plan accordingly."

"Modest. That is all I ask. Maria was barren. Her burial should be as well."

All appropriate responses would get her fired, so she swapped the binder for a stack of forms. "I'll need your consent to care for Maria." She grabbed a neon yellow highlighter, swiping brutally. "Sign *here* and *here* and *here*."

The not-so-grief-stricken father signed everything without reading anything. "Tomorrow night at six. Be done by seven." With that, he eyed Tennessee disapprovingly—storm-touched curls to blocky heels—reset his hat, then left.

One by one, his seven sons followed.

Tennessee watched the Garcia men slide into their fancy cars and drive off before she dared comment.

"That was weird." She glared out the window when...

*Bam!*

Godzilla slammed himself against the front window, laughing hysterically as Tennessee jumped, screamed, and nearly fell to the ground. Sho held her up, and Tennessee was sure he was laughing too.

"Boys!" She smoothed her blazer then poured herself a giant mug of hot coffee, spiked with a cup of sugar. "Polar, you can come out now."

Polar had been sleeping in the back room, the one with the gilded mirror; but she saw him sneak a peek into her office when Mr. Garcia was getting irate. He knew the rules of the mortuary: *no dogs*. But he had his own rules: no threats to his master.

The white beast ran into the waiting room, pawing Tennessee. She knelt to hug her lion when she noticed a blotch of red on Polar's fur. As Tennessee searched for a cause, Godzilla came in, helped himself to half the pastries, and when Sho took out the cookies, Godzilla ate those too.

"What'd you get into, boy?" She examined Polar's skin, pulling aside the fur all along his back until she came upon a nick. It wasn't scabbed over yet and it didn't look too bad, but when she brushed too near the nick, Polar whimpered.

Tennessee called Sho over. "What do you make of this?" she whispered. "Just brambles or should I be worried?" The nick was just a bramble wound, nothing more. She repeated this mantra to the silent collapse of her heart.

Sho stroked Polar's head as he inspected the nick. "Perhaps something tried for your guardian. Keep an eye on him. If something's amiss, it'll show soon."

"Don't run off like that again, boy...especially now."

"He'll be fine, Ten. He's strong and a good protector," Sho added to abate Tennessee's fears.

"He's more than that." She nuzzled her nose to Polar's, and then came his wet kisses. "He's family."

"I understand. How may I help?"

"Get the first aid kit under the refreshment counter, please."

Sho did as he was told.

When Sho moved aside, Godzilla lobbed Polar a dry Danish; he chomped it midair. Tennessee shot Godzilla a look of warning; too many pastries weren't good for either of them. Godzilla held the last Danish out for her, but she scrunched up her face, so he ate that one too.

"Hey, Ness, we got 335 at auction. Lemme know when you're ready to open her up."

"Score one for the Islanders!" Tennessee was applying antiseptic to Polar's wound, finishing it off with a dab of ointment. "Riggy's full up right now...if my plans fall through, we can shove the load in 335."

Godzilla made a face. "You two went *shopping* with Maria?"

"How could I embalm her if I'm out of embalming fluid?"

Conceding with a grunt, Godzilla asked, "When's the wake?"

"Tomorrow and there's no frills. It's a no-fuss rush." Tennessee saw Godzilla's disappointment, added kindly, "Sometimes it's easier for the family to say goodbye quickly. Embalming's not necessary. I'll make it nice for Maria. You know I prefer natural burials anyway...let's go eco!"

"This guy a death nerd like you?"

She mumbled incoherently, unable to commit to one lie.

Sho handed Tennessee her pink bunny coffee mug; she noticed he had a mug too. She almost blurted her shock that he *could* drink; but there he was sipping coffee, and he seemed to be enjoying it. Potential problem averted; if he hated coffee, they just couldn't be friends.

Godzilla stared at them; he didn't get the *lover* vibe. He'd seen Tennessee in love; she got clumsy, giddy, and silly. She wasn't any of those things around Sho; she was more somber than he'd ever seen her, especially in the shop; working always cheered her up. Whether Sho was in love with her, he couldn't tell; it looked more like he was working for her; baking cookies, getting the first aid kit, getting her coffee. Phillip never did that, and he was certain Phillip was in love with Tennessee.

Tennessee glanced up at Godzilla, noticed he had his *figuring-shit-out* face on. "What?!"

He shrugged. "Nothin'."

"Whatever." Tennessee checked her messages. One text from Lin: *Help!* She smirked, then walked outside for a smoke.

Sho followed right behind, and that's when Godzilla stepped in front of him. Tennessee was already outside, lighting a cigarette.

"I'm not buying it." Godzilla shut the door, blocked the exit. "You and Ness. Did Lin hire you to make Phillip jealous? I can see *that*."

Sho met the monster's gaze, revealing nothing. He trusted Godzilla, knew he'd do anything for Tennessee, but he was bound by the curse, so he simply said, "We're dating. Perhaps *I* care for her far more than she cares for me, but I do care for her."

"She's like my little sister. You hurt her, you gotta die, man. No offense."

Godzilla didn't know just *how* accurate he was. Sho bowed his head, then motioned toward the door.

"May I?"

An open challenge tacked to his glare, Godzilla stepped aside.

"I'm watchin' you, man." He crammed the last chocolate chip cookie into his mouth, chewing menacingly.

~

There was more traffic than usual, so Tennessee shouted at Lin, and Lin shouted back. When Sho walked out, Lin waved her little broom overhead, shouted her goodbyes, and sauntered into her shop.

"Godzilla set you straight?" Tennessee took a long drag, her brow creased.

Sho mimicked her tight brow, taking the cigarette from her hand; she defended her actions: she was quitting, it was her first cigarette of the day, leave her the hell alone. Amused, Sho cocked his head, then took a long drag. It definitely wasn't his first cigarette. She watched his shoulders relax, flashing a curt frown,

"Coffee...cigarettes...watch out, Sho, next thing it's bad words and breaking curfew!"

With a steamy gaze, Sho puffed smoke in Tennessee's face. "Horrible role models."

Tennessee took back the cig, leaning into Sho's good mood. They talked, laughed, and smoked until Lillie roared her little red Corvette into the lot.

Tennessee clumsily reached for the cig, clasping Sho's fingers with her newly cold hands. Her gaze snapped up to meet his; and they both exhaled,

"Shit."

# 10.

# Devil Doll

Tennessee whisked Sho inside, bolting the door behind them.

"It's all right, Ten."

Polar's ears perked up, and his alarmed barks swelled to frenzied. Godzilla stopped drilling holes in the wall to gruff,

"We being robbed?"

"Just closing early..." Tennessee stuttered some nonsense as Sho led her past her office toward the prep room. Godzilla knew she was lying. She could tell by his gloominess. He wasn't a gloomy guy, he was Godzilla!

Polar raced up the hall, barking; skidded down the hall, growling; howling in between.

Godzilla shouted down the hall, "I guess I'll lock up when I finish hanging your shelf?"

"Thanks, Godzilla!" Tennessee hollered from the prep room before Sho locked that door.

"It's not what you think, so just breathe," Sho assured her, his gaze deciphering her comprehension. "She was..." he searched for a modern phrase, "*demon-free* when I met her yesterday. Something has changed. Tell me about this woman."

"Total bitch." Tennessee's stomach snarled a fit; she was thinking about the twins and William and... "Phillip. I can't kill

Phillip's sister! How the hell am I going to explain that?! He'll hate me..."

"Your hands." Sho rubbed Tennessee's fingers. "They're cold..."

"But not *that* cold," Tennessee sighed. "I mean, I've dreamt of killing Lillie, but...so what does this mean?"

Lillie was banging on the front door, and continued banging on the front door. Soon, it got quiet and Tennessee's cell phone clanked out "Bitch" by Meredith Brooks.

"That's her."

"Answer it."

"Nu-uh."

"She's *not* a demon, Ten...not yet. She is a favorite."

After a snarky laugh, Tennessee quipped, "Yeah, the devil's favorite!" And the look in those emperor eyes sent a hard, icy spike into her spine. Then Lillie was on speaker,

"I saw you and your boyfriend smoking, Tennessee. Your Santa's sucking down a bag of coronary crisps and your goddamn dog won't shut the hell up!"

"I'm swamped, Lillie! Dead bodies everywhere! *Piles*! *Heaps*! It's horrifying!"

"I can handle whatever *you* can handle, Tennessee!" Lillie cursed and hollered and demanded to be let in.

"Or you'll huff and you'll puff..."

The scream that woman let out had Polar baring his teeth with a sinister growl.

Tennessee hung up, her tone ripe with filth. "A favorite? She's their goddamn queen!"

Before letting the screaming woman in, Tennessee asked for the *must-knows*.

In a measured tone, Sho got to it. "The demons influencing favorites are *allowed* to be here. In this case, it's likely an assessment. When you're called to serve, Zaada will assess your allies."

"Like a test?"

"Yes." Sho bowed his head. "Demons thrive in the negative sphere around humans. The ripe fester feeds them. Demons are drawn to human negativity. They didn't create it, but they can manipulate it once they've penetrated the sphere. Sometimes they share the space with other demons, but they develop favorites. *Those* they don't share. Only stronger demons can hold a favorite."

"Like spirit leeches?" Tennessee experienced a full-body quake, ending with cold quivers down her jawbone and bottom lip.

"Hmmm," Sho shared a discerning scowl, "*yes*!"

"So, I *don't* have to kill Lillie." Tennessee moped a little, momentarily conflicted.

"Not unless the demon gains complete control of the favorite. That would be a breach of their contract. We would be called to wrangle the demon out of the favorite...or..."

A quiver gnarled a triple knot in her gut. Had the Blockhead demon been controlling a favorite? Had she let a woman die? Had she *killed* that woman the night of Johnny's wake?

Sho recognized the fallen features of guilt, but Lillie was raging, so he kept it short. "We do what we *must*. Many die if we fail." He led Tennessee to the waiting room and, because she wouldn't, he unlocked the front door.

Lillie stomped over, her hands flying to her hips, and began a ten-minute tirade.

Tennessee kept wringing her hands, waiting for the cold to freeze. She worried she'd have to slay Lillie in front of Godzilla. She couldn't ask him to lie for her; she *wouldn't*. Then everybody would know. There might be a trial. She might go to jail; and how many demons would she meet *there*? How would she handle Sho? He'd poof in and out. There'd be riots.

"...so...imagine my surprise, Tennessee, when Phillip informs me of his previous engagement tonight...with *you people*!"

Tennessee caught half of Lillie's outburst, and as the woman went on with the other half, Tennessee studied Lillie's outfit: skinny jeans, red high heels, and a white lacey crop top. She didn't like Lillie, but that woman had style and always *looked* the part

of a classy lady. This outfit was a definite *don't*; something Lillie wouldn't be caught dead in.

Godzilla was on his second bag of chips, enjoying the show; his heavy gaze on Lillie's stripper heels. Tennessee met his eye and they both snickered.

"...and what's so funny, Tennessee?! You haven't heard a word I've said!" Lillie shimmied over to Godzilla, snatched the potato chip right out of his hand. Sensually sliding the salted crisp on her tongue, she closed her eyes in mini-rapture.

Godzilla's jaw dropped, Sho squinted, and Tennessee wringed warmth into her freezing hands.

Lillie was an all-organic, low-fat, gluten-free, non-GMO vegan. In no world did Godzilla's chips meet Lillie's gold-star standard.

Lillie went on complaining about Tennessee one second, seductively stealing Godzilla's chips the next. It was like watching madman Jack, the town loon who lived on the corner of Crescent and Bloom, battle his crazy as tourists snapped selfies from a safe distance. It was disconcerting. Spooky. Some freaky shit.

Even Polar was confused; he kept watch beside Tennessee, whimpering every time Lillie got too close to Godzilla. But what could he do? This was Lillie. Her behavior always baffled him. Was she his master's friend, or not? He still wasn't sure, but he kept his guard. Just in case.

After the initial shock wore off and Lillie finished Godzilla's entire bag of chips, Tennessee's hands settled on cool. Then Lillie was shouting,

"Get that repulsive junk food away from me! Why is this beast-man feeding me car lubricant!" She gawked at Tennessee, reeling back looking for something to wipe clean the grease slick from her fingers. That's when she caught sight of her red stilettoes. "What is *this*? Why am I wearing yard sale hooker heels?"

It was like watching bubblegum pop. You're smiling, enjoying the sweet sugar expanding, then *pop!* you're covered in sticky goo wondering what went wrong.

"I think you look great," Tennessee offered in a teensy-tiny tone.

Lillie's eyes shot daggers at her, which had Tennessee wondering if Lillie's demon could shoot *literal* daggers because, while that would be rad, it'd be a pain in the ass to battle.

"I want my Santa." Lillie's tone resonated a little too deeply.

Tennessee's hands grew colder; Sho must have seen the worry on her face because his hands were now fists. Polar maneuvered his mountainous body between Lillie and his master with a growl that matched any lion king.

"Well, I never." Lillie was her fake self again, stylishly shaken.

Sho clasped Tennessee's hand. Scarcely cool.

Tennessee had seen enough. "Lillie, where are the twins?" Millie and Billie were all she could think about. Kids, even the demon brats, shouldn't be around *real* demons. Lillie would break if she hurt the twins. And Tennessee really didn't want to be the one doing the breaking if that woman damaged those girls.

"Summerhold," Lillie whispered.

"I'll do pick-up." Tennessee knelt to calm Polar. "I apologize for having to reschedule, again. Mamma Min leaves tonight and I have a wake tomorrow night. Nothing should stop Christmas after that."

Sho shot Tennessee a tight glare. He was right. She really shouldn't have said that.

Lillie was rubbing her temples, mumbled something about not feeling well; agreed to reschedule Christmas. There was a little tremble in her tone as she offered Mamma Min a safe trip home. Lillie didn't shimmy out the door; she shuffled, a little hunched, her hands still circling her temples.

When Lillie was standing outside, Tennessee whispered to Sho, "Should we take her home?"

"No, but we must act quickly..." He stopped.

They were not alone.

Godzilla stood up. "Ness, what's wrong with Madam Illie? And

what's up with you two? You're acting weird. Locking Lillie out...*shushing* and *whispering*..."

Tennessee didn't have a good answer, and she hated lying to Godzilla, so she kept quiet. Godzilla knew what that meant.

"You should call Phillip. Madame Illie ain't right."

"*You* call Phillip," Tennessee snapped, then sulked under the weight of Godzilla's dreaded Headshake of Disappointment; that was worse than Lin's inherited Stance of Disparagement. "Fine, I'll call Phillip! But I do have Maria to box and I still need to buy Mamma Min's present. It's barely lunch and I'm already behind!"

Godzilla was still shaking his head. "Maybe if you trusted your *real* friends a little more you wouldn't be so...*behind*."

It was the dig she'd been waiting for. He didn't approve. Not of Sho, not of her handling of Phillip, not of anything. He was on her side before her latest diagnosis. Now, he was like everybody else who decided they knew what was best for their dying friend.

But Sho said she *wasn't* dying anymore; at least, not from an aneurysm. Nobody would believe that. Hell, *she* didn't believe that.

Tennessee walked over to Godzilla. He had fixed her shelf. She only had to ask once and it was done. He was right, she needed to trust her friends. She punched his bicep, tweaking her wrist in the process.

"No fair tensing up!" She shook out her wrist. "Man, that hurt!"

"Teach you to punch a monster." Godzilla looked down at her and beamed with all his teeth.

She smiled back, just enough to flaunt her snaggletooth.

Godzilla turned his attention on leveling the shelf. Sho went to follow Tennessee, but she waved him back, mouthing, "Help him!" She knew Godzilla just needed some time to get to know Sho. She needed them both. Hell, she needed *all* her friends. Now more than ever.

~

Back in the prep room, Tennessee took off her blazer, slipped

her slick black apron over her silky camisole. She went to call Phillip; cell phone in hand, she practiced out loud,

"I'm sorry, Phillip, but your sister's a favorite among demons. One is sharing her rank sphere right now, swimming in it, licking its pruney fingers...I'm sorry, Phillip, but your sister's not an ordinary bitch, she's a demon bitch, the Queen of demon bitches...Phillip, your sister's a demon's bitch..."

Tennessee sighed, sending a quick text instead: *call me.*

She snapped on surgical gloves and slid open Maria's cold cooler.

Finally, she could relax.

~

Maria was a looker: thick, black, *manageable* hair, wide-set eyes that gave her an allure even in death, and perfect teeth. Tennessee envied teeth as perfect as Maria's. Hers weren't perfect; hell, very little about Tennessee was perfect. She laughed at the idea of perfection.

"I'd probably trip and knock 'em all out," she confessed to Maria as she wiped a warm, wet towel over the corpse's long arms. For a short woman, Maria had exceptionally long arms, or maybe they just looked longer now that she was dead. "Death by natural causes," Tennessee whispered; she often kept up a conversation while washing the dead. It was a lengthy process; there are lots of crevices on the human body, and Tennessee paid extra attention to the details; between the toes and fingers, under the chin, crook of the elbow.

Every corpse got a thorough washing before burial or cremation; most people don't spruce up before dying. Death comes whether you have filth under your fingernails, wax in your ears, or prickly hairs on your unshaved legs.

Death is dirty like that.

Tennessee finished wiping down Maria with a clean, dry cloth. She draped a towel over Maria's body, then filled a pitcher with warm water. She didn't need to use warm water, but she always did. She covered Maria's face with a washcloth as she poured

water over Maria's hair. "You seem like a peppermint sort of gal." Tennessee worked the tingly shampoo into a lather, gently rinsing Maria's scalp clean; she repeated with a heap of conditioner. Maria had a ton of hair. No wonder she visited Lin so often. It must have been the one thing she did for herself.

The sudsy water flowed down the channeled sides of the metal prep table, draining into a deep sink. When the water ran clear, she squeezed out Maria's thick hair, toweled it to damp before hitting it with the hair dryer.

While Tennessee worked, the collar twitched and tugged. Nothing painful, nothing Sho didn't compensate for immediately. When one conspicuously biting tug didn't let up, Tennessee left Maria's side to get a cup of coffee.

Sho's agitation faded when Tennessee entered the room; he negotiated his footing around the writing desks, holding one end of a couch nearly overhead. Godzilla needed a new couch and the shop had way too many. They shared a sweet smile, and Tennessee noticed Godzilla watching. Well, that was good. Now maybe he'd think she truly had a thing for Sho. One less lie to stumble about *proving*.

When the boys were done rearranging the waiting room, Tennessee took her sugary coffee back to the prep room.

One of Maria's seven brothers left her outfit wrapped in a dry-cleaning bag. Tennessee took a pair of scissors to the clear plastic, unveiling a plain brown housedress. Not just any plain housedress; a shapeless, dingy, downright *ugly* housedress.

Sho walked into the prep room just in time to hear Tennessee say, "Maria Garcia will be buried in a brown sack." She looked up at Sho. "Why did they choose *this*? I've seen those guys around town, they've always seemed...decent enough and well-dressed to boot. I think the eldest is a teacher at Summerhold, and Godzilla played ball with one of the middle ones. Why would they bury their only sister in this ugly dress? Um...sorry, Maria." She studied Maria's face, riveted by the woman's poise in death. "Everyone

deserves a good death. No, she doesn't want this dress. It's an insult." Tennessee slapped the garment against Sho's chest.

"It's itchy..." Sho scratched his arms, "and *hot*!"

Tennessee spun around. "What's the matter with you?"

Sho tossed the dress from hand to hand until he couldn't handle it anymore. He chucked the dress into the utility sink, and there it burst into flames.

They stared at the sink, then each other.

"Sho, I need you, man," Godzilla called out from the waiting room.

By his expression, Sho was glad to be called. As he damn near sprinted out of the room, Tennessee found *one* thing reassuring; Godzilla was warming to Sho. She approached the sink; there was nothing left of the dress, only a bit of ash in the drain.

Demon one turned to ash, and now that dress turned to ash, but only *after* Sho touched it. Her mind zipped to horrible places, her collar yanked a fit, and her cell phone blasted Phillip's new ringtone: "Why."

Dammit.

~

Godzilla opened the tailgate of his borrowed truck, leaving Sho practically carrying the couch all by himself. Tennessee went ahead and laughed even though she knew Godzilla was being a little mean to Sho. Unlike the possible *assessment* Sho mentioned earlier, this was absolutely a test. Godzilla needed to know Sho was *all in*. It wasn't quite hazing, but close enough. Men have an annoying alpha thing, just like dogs.

Polar usually chased seagulls, but today he crumpled into a pile by her feet. When she cupped his muzzle to check his eyes, his wet tongue doused her with spit, and his heavy paws whapped her leg.

"All right, boy. I'll stop babying you."

Tennessee lit another cig. Annie Lennox started all those *whys* again. This time she answered. "England."

"Tenny, I got your text." Phillip had his doctor voice on. He was probably in the hall, signing nurses' clipboards; if nurses still used

clipboards. She pictured the old movies where doctors smoked in the halls like rock stars, autographing prescription slips thrust their way. "Tenny, I'm in a bit of a rush."

She wanted to scream, "I'm trying *not* to kill your sister!" Instead she bluntly voiced her concern. "Lillie's on a bender. Probably been abusing those prescription privileges again."

Phillip didn't answer.

"I'm worried about the twins. Maybe they should visit that aunt of theirs...the one in Vermont...just until Lillie gets clean or William hires another nanny. *I'm* doing pickup." Tennessee overheard bits of the other conversation Phillip was having with a nurse; apparently, someone got into the opiates again.

"I appreciate your concern, Tenny, but I'm certain William knows what's best for his own children. It's not our place to..."

"Lillie was just here, Phillip," Tennessee cut him off with a terse tone, "dolled-up in skinny jeans and a crop top...*and* she ate Godzilla's chips!"

"I'm working, Tenny, Lil breaking her diet isn't an emergency."

"Did I mention the hooker heels?"

Phillip must have been under a ton of stress because he cracked his neck, *twice*. "I'll make a few calls."

A rustle, then a beep. He hung up on her!

"Jerk," Tennessee snapped back, but when she went to put her phone away Phillip's voice hummed over the line.

"Tenny. Tenny?"

She wasn't good at awkward, so she just hung up.

Only half of the couch fit inside the bed of Godzilla's truck. After strapping that side down, he revved the engine and waved. "See you at Lin's."

Tennessee waved back; she hadn't thought though what she'd do if Godzilla asked Sho to go with him. Luckily that didn't happen, because in the state she was in, she'd probably have said *sure*.

It was time for one of those in-depth talks she'd been avoiding.

"Come on, Polar."

The lazy dog barely made it into the shop before plonking down in a snore.

Tennessee walked to the back side of the mortuary; there was an iron table and set of patio chairs. It was private, with a perfect view of the sea. She set her lighter and pack of cigarettes on the table, lit another cig, took a puff.

Sho sat across from Tennessee, took her cig.

They didn't stop talking until they'd finished the pack.

~

Turns out the demon world is just as twisted and crazy as the human world. They have rulers and wars, just like us; likes and dislikes, just like us; and wants and needs, just like us. Who's to say they're *right* and we're *wrong*, or the reverse? Well, apparently, some demon chick named Zaada and her ex-lover-turned-nemesis, Ibrahim.

Their love-hate relationship played out across the demonverse and humanverse. Seemed Zaada kicked Ibrahim's ass to the curb, only he didn't stop there; he jumped the curb and headed straight to Earth. He cozied up with some deeply dark humans and set down some rotten roots. But Ibrahim was a creeper, a real stalker type; he couldn't let Zaada go. So, when he heard she'd moved on with some other demon dude, he opened a door linking the demonverse and humanverse just to get her undivided attention.

That door was still open.

Of course, these dimensional creatures who fed off negativity and violence loved humans. There's so much *hate* to love! Earth was a holiday, a place to get fat on gloom and relax in the balminess of misery and woe; most rode the vortex back home and dreamed of visiting again. For some demons, the vacation was just too good; they never wanted to leave. So, they didn't. They hitched a ride on a particularly negative human and lazed about. Most did no more harm than send their human into irrational states of moodiness and ick. But some demons were stronger than their human; now, *they* could sway a human over a line or push them off the edge; from road rage to mass murder. The demon

wasn't making the final choice, just funneling the human's own anger on itself.

Negativity was malleable for demons; they played it like a finely tuned instrument; and the results were grisly. Favorites were seen as welcoming the demon, because they, too, thrived in the negative.

"Zaada frowns upon possession." Sho smashed another cig into a clam shell ashtray. "Wranglers can only intervene when the demon oversteps and begins *making* choices."

Tennessee remained unconvinced. "Her generosity astounds." She lit another cig.

"Better we serve Zaada than Ibrahim. She rids Earth of demons; he infests it. Their feud is endless. Yes, we're pawns in their disaster of a relationship, but *our* mission remains the same. Slay a thousand more demons and break the curse."

Tennessee smirked. "I'd better keep track, then...can't expect the evil guys to play fair."

Sho stole the cig from her lips, pushing away from the table, his chair screeching a shrill protest against concrete. He faced the sea, flicking ash to sand; Tennessee watched the black dust surf the beige sand, scattering white, drifting to nothing.

"You're keeping something from me, but I won't force you to tell me."

Sho grew more pensive, bringing the cig to his lips. He held in the smoke for an eternity before breathing out a billowing plume rivaling any dragon. "You have a bounty on your head."

A hot swell rushed over Tennessee, and her heart missed a thud.

Sho dropped his arms by his sides, watching the sea. But she wasn't fooled; his shoulders tensed and the veins scaling the backs of his hands and forearms swelled as his fists balled up reflexively.

He had her back.

She went to him, smoothly slipping her fingers into his palm; he watched her intently; she was steel, not a tremor or shake, and when she slid her fingers from his, she had the cig.

"That's old news." She took a drag.

His cynical smirk had her playfully glaring back at him,

"A burning dress is too obvious, Sho. *Please*! Had *bounty on Tennessee's head* written all over it. Cheeky demon bastards." She placed the cig in her mouth, and before he could respond she bent down in the sand. "I'm like this guy." She stood up, shoved her open palms at Sho. A teeny hermit crab tucked its body into its shell. She rolled it onto one palm, retrieving the cig from her mouth. "Poor guy's minding his own business when some stupid, smoky giant plucks him from his nice, boring life. He hides, of course, because he *should*, he's not stupid. But after a while..." Tennessee and Sho watched the crab gradually, ever so carefully, peek its head out and bravely attempt escape. "I'm sure I'll tuck my big butt into my shell again, but I'm counting on you to stay put. I promise I'll come out, if you promise to wait."

Sho bowed deeply. "Without end."

"And I'm guessing demons aren't the only creepy critters out there."

"Not nearly the creepiest."

"Wonderful."

Tennessee put the cig back in her mouth before setting the hermit crab free. Soon, it was crawling back to its nice, boring life. Sho's gravity lightened as he snatched the cig from her mouth. He snuffed it out with his thumb and index finger. Damn that was sexy. Then he drew her into a skintight embrace. It was the most emotion she'd seen from him yet. It told her more than his warning had. It told her they were underdogs. The bounty hunters were sick bastards. She'd never be safe. But right now, she had a hard time believing that. Right now, wrapped up in Sho, she was invincible.

Her life was going to be short. She had always known that. Until meeting Sho, she figured her legacy would be boxing dead people. That was a decent legacy; actually, it was a damn fine legacy, but it was an inherited legacy; it belonged to her parents.

In less than forty-eight hours, she'd discovered a path to raze on her own.

She was a good mortician.

Maybe, just maybe, she'd be a *great* wrangler.

For however long she could manage it, she'd slay, learn the trade, slay.

~

Mamma Min was screaming, a unique, full-bodied shriek that had you at the throat; you either ran toward that screech, or away.

Sho ran toward such commotions. "What can I do?"

"She crazy! My daughter thinks worship devil brings good life. Shut devil off!"

Lin dashed about the kitchen, clanging pots on the stove, pans in the oven. She usually listened to Norah Jones, soft jazz all day and night, so why she'd be listening to Devil Doll was just too obvious.

*Tennessee* loved Devil Doll, especially the man-done-me-wrong song, "King of Brooklyn." But Lin blasting that angsty song while Mamma Min was sipping hot tea in the living room was just too good a story not to pursue.

"I'll straighten her out." Tennessee patted Mamma Min's hand after giving the woman a loving hug and a re-gifted, shoddily-wrapped bar of fancy soap she'd received from a client. "Crazy girl! Close your ears, Mamma Min. There might be bad words in that song."

Mamma Min put her hands over her ears while Sho stayed behind to pour the frazzled old woman another cup of jasmine tea. Tennessee counted her steps, and at fifteen she turned back to see Mamma Min swatting Sho's hand away from the teapot.

"No, you do it wrong! Like *this*! Not like *this*! Now, show me..."

Sho did it Mamma Min's way; he glanced up at Tennessee, eyes wide.

Tennessee gave a double thumbs-up, then counted three more steps and stayed put.

Lin's kitchen was not made for two people. Tennessee kept to

the threshold separating the kitchen from the living room. By the deep lines etched across Lin's forehead and her pursed lips, she wasn't ready to vent. Tennessee turned off the stereo, but the silence was chilling, so she switched the stream to classical.

Mamma Min exclaimed her ears' relief and praised Sho's rapid mind; he was well on his way to learning the secrets of developing the best flavor out of the least amount of tea.

Hosting didn't play to Lin's strengths; in fact, she hated it. And that was the crux of tonight's trouble. Lin wanted to go out to a restaurant for Mamma Min's goodbye. But a *good* daughter wouldn't dare let a *stranger* cook her mother's goodbye meal. Lin's place was too cramped to host a proper party, but Mamma Min didn't care. She grew up poor, a roof overhead is rich; no matter if Lin's roof was a teensy apartment over a teensy beauty shop.

Mamma Min was on her third week cramped in Lin's bedroom; and Lin was on the couch. The two couldn't stand each other when they were living in the Mins' mansion just outside Stanford. *This* was hell.

Tennessee felt bad for Lin, but Mamma Min's stubbornness was Tennessee's good fortune. Sho was within range of Maria Garcia. He could play the part of her boyfriend and set her friends' minds at ease. She did feel a teensy bit guilty for not chasing Lillie down and ripping the demon from her sphere—if *that's* how it worked—but she had Phillip working the kid angle, and that was her top priority.

The doorbell rang.

Sho opened the door just as Tennessee got to his side; so, it was surprise on Godzilla's face and a crushing confusion on Phillip's to be greeted by the new couple.

Tennessee waved them in, sneaking out as Mamma Min took over. Lin was still banging pots for no good reason. This time, Tennessee got in there.

"We're only waiting on Hill."

"Where's Polar?" Lin whacked a pan. "I saved him a rib."

"Sleeping. Too much adventuring, I guess." She hoped it was just that. He seemed fine otherwise.

"Better wrap it for him or else Godzilla will eat it."

Tennessee got to wrapping while Lin *kabamed* and *whammed.*

"Where?"

"Where what?" Tennessee pinched foil into a perfect square.

"*Adventuring*?"

"Um...just...Stumpy's..."

Lin banged a pot. "That place is gross. Don't go there! Go to Freida's Farm. Where do you think I got all these veggies?"

"Will do, Mamma *Lin.*" Tennessee stole a carrot and Lin threw a spoon. "Tomorrow morning Mamma will catch the train. Life will snap back. It'll be wine and foot soaks. Maybe I'll even let you dye a huge white skunk stripe down my head."

Lin smirked. "What would Sho think?"

"Ah, he loves my ugly." Tennessee's peppy tone had Lin believing her words.

"Strange luck." Lin dredged chicken in flour.

"How's that..."

Phillip tapped Tennessee's shoulder. "Tenny..."

Lin's simmering laugh boiled over, and the moody woman flung chicken into crackling oil. There, she felt better already.

Tennessee closed her eyes, taking a deep breath, before turning to face Phillip. "The twins?" She laid on the pep.

Urgency replaced Phillip's usual displeasure. "We need to talk. Can we step outside for a minute?"

Tennessee estimated the number of steps to *outside*. "I think so."

"You *think* so?" Phillip's eyes constricted with chagrin.

"God, Phillip!" Tennessee dragged Phillip outside like a mother might a tantrummy brat.

Sho stood up, he was counting steps too.

She nodded, and he sat back down. But she did leave the door ajar to make it easier to keep within those infuriating fifty feet.

"Bro," Godzilla whacked Sho's shoulder, "be cool. He's her

*doctor*...plus Ness doesn't like clingy guys. Be like me...just chill and let the honeys flock..."

"Big guy right!" Mamma Min shouted. She was much tinier than Lin, louder; and minus a dozen wrinkles and eyes like wells of wisdom, she looked exactly like her daughter. And when she smiled, it was Lin's smile lined with a bit more menace. "Woman want strong man. Man who stands by decisions. Man who comes home, drinks little, makes us laugh. Lin could marry Mr. Won, but no! She stays here with no man and all bad luck everywhere she go...all bad luck!"

Godzilla muttered something about Lin's business doing well, but Mamma Min was already on to her daughter's next set of flaws.

Phillip pulled Tennessee away from the door. A snippy tug grabbed her attention, but she took one more step anyway. When he released her hand, she took a step back, counteracting the collar's combative control.

"I see Mamma Min's still trying to marry Lin off." Phillip's resigned tone indicated far more was on his mind.

He was making small talk? It made no sense.

"Where are the twins? I called Summerhold after Lillie left, but they said the twins weren't at school today and that nobody called."

"They're with William. He doesn't agree with your assessment."

That word—*assessment*—creeped her out. If only he knew what that meant in the demon world.

"He thinks Lillie's of sound mind?" Tennessee huffed, "*Really*? Mrs. Crop Top and *red* hooker heels?" Phillip's deeply creased brow told Tennessee that he agreed with her, so she softened her approach. "What should we do? The last intervention nearly got us maimed."

When the twins were babies, life's crummy disturbances, mainly excess baby weight, exacerbated Lillie's reliance on prescription meds. She opted for an out-patient detox, but only

after going after Phillip with a silver steak knife. Tennessee knocked the woman out because the brother couldn't. After that episode, Phillip confided in Tennessee; told her all about Lillie's lifelong battle with manic depression. Lillie's monthly therapy bills and happy pill allowance could pay for the master's degree Tennessee kept putting off.

"Right now, I think we trust William to care for his own children. I'll check on Lillie after dinner. *I'd* take the twins, but my hours are so..."

"Yeah." Tennessee recollected the late-night calls summoning Phillip to the hospital. A memory pushed forward; if a call interrupted her sleep, he'd have breakfast delivered to her silo at precisely eight in the morning—four buttermilk pancakes, crispy bacon, and a mindbender. A sly look accompanied a shoulder shrug. "I didn't mind the bribes so much."

Phillip wasn't smiling; he looked more pained by the memory than anything.

Screw it, she moved on. "Text me tonight when you see the twins, all right?"

"I'd rather call."

Tennessee turned away. "Whatever."

"You sure Sho won't mind?" His tone was respectful, a tad hesitant.

Tennessee looked over her shoulder, spice on her lips. "Absolutely not, he's a deep sleeper."

There was a slight crack in Phillip's steadfast gaze; he really didn't need the reminder that she was no longer his.

Dammit, she didn't want that look to affect her, but it did. Beyond that, she was disappointed in herself for *wanting* to hurt him. Then she remembered something Sho said about the collar. She stopped, turning toward Phillip with remorseful eyes,

"That wasn't nice." She clutched his ring finger and pinky, the way she always used to. "I'm sorry, 'kay?"

A sort of relief mellowed Phillip's stern countenance. "I want to

be friends, Tenny. If he makes you happy...I can only be happy for you."

Tennessee was on the verge of saying something too honest when Phillip took her whole hand into his. "Tenny? Are you feeling all right? Your hands are freezing."

Across the street, every light in the England's Mortuary flashed on at once; the neighborhood dogs went wild, and a familiar yowl wrenched through Tennessee's chest, then a shrilling whine buzzed her eardrums useless.

Silence.

"Polar!"

Tennessee raced down the stairs, jumping two at a time. She was so focused on getting to Polar she didn't feel the tug. She leapt over the last step, and was midair when the crackling shriek of the collar snapped her body back; she released a single, bone-chilling scream before her legs whipped out from under her, thwacking the back of her head on the hard cedar steps.

*Wa-bam!*

# 11.

# Man of the Hour

When Sho sensed the first tug, he made his way to the front door and did his best *not* to listen to Tennessee's private conversation with Phillip. He was prepared to move a few feet here and there, but he never expected Tennessee to bolt.

He might have made it, if Phillip hadn't inadvertently blocked the stairway at exactly the wrong time.

Sho was forced to improvise.

Hearing Tennessee's tortured scream, Sho hurled himself over the balcony with such power he almost overshot his target: a flagpole, flying beachy windcatchers, adjacent to the stairway. Sho only just seized the pole with both hands. He whipped around once before spiraling down with unreal speed.

Tennessee lay on her side, curled up, scarcely conscious. Sho lifted her into his arms as one might a shattered treasure.

"Don't move her!" Phillip hollered, and didn't stop. "She might have a neck injury or spinal bruise or...Godzilla! Call an ambulance!"

"She'll be fine," Sho declared, caressing the scrapes on Tennessee's temple, elbows, and hands. "I'll take care of her."

"I'm a doctor, Sho!" Phillip knelt to examine Tennessee's eyes. He flashed his penlight into her left eye, then right.

"Ow, cut it out!" Tennessee groaned. In a fiery flash, she

recalled why she'd bolted in the first place. "Polar! Someone's in the shop!" Her words came out slurred and saggy.

Phillip instructed Tennessee to lay still while Sho checked the shop.

"No!" The couple vetoed Phillip's plan.

"I'm fine." Tennessee let Sho lift her to standing. She watched Phillip's jaw clench and the vein running across his temple throb an uprising; he stood up, arms by his side in loathsome defeat. "Come on, Phillip, you can finish your examination at the shop. I'm pretty sure I banged my head..."

"*That's why...*" Phillip began a firm reprimand only to stop himself. "Will you at least let Sho carry you? He jumped off a building for you, I'm sure he won't mind." He managed a smirk that crinkled his eyes. She could tell he was impressed by Sho's actions, and a little humiliated that he hadn't done it himself. Of course, Phillip didn't know her demonic collar was going to keep shocking her until Sho got within fifty feet.

"I've got it, man," Godzilla boomed onto the scene. He was a lot bigger than Sho: taller, wider, and he knew how to handle Tennessee. He *needed* to do it. There wasn't much he could do to help his best bud. But he could do this. And he could do it well.

Tennessee shooed Phillip and Sho. "Go on, guys, check Polar!" She leaned on Godzilla, and while she wouldn't dare let anyone *carry* her, Godzilla held her at the waist, taking the weight she couldn't yet manage alone.

Sho jogged ahead, keeping close; Phillip ran for *fun*, so he was fast, and Tennessee supposed the good doctor might make it a race. But then she remembered this was Phillip. He wasn't about to lower himself to a footrace with a rival. Then again, he sprinted at the end and made it to the shop first.

Tennessee watched Phillip walk right in. She always locked the shop. All the lights were on. Those two things didn't worry her as much as the white smoke billowing from the crematory's old, red brick chimney. The snowy puffs stood out against the black

starless night. A frantic shiver had Tennessee holding her breath. And then she ran.

She ran past Godzilla. She ran past Sho. She ran past Phillip. She didn't stop running until she threw open Audrey II's mouth. The men caught up just as Tennessee released one tortured scream.

Sho held her up, but her knees buckled to grief and she crumpled to the crematory floor. Tennessee's torment brought tears to everyone's eyes as her trembling hands covered her tear-streaked face.

The men gathered around Audrey II, grief-stricken, as they watched the blazing remains of a canine blacken to ash. They were whispering to one another. Tennessee couldn't see them, couldn't hear them. The horrific image of Polar burning was all she could see; the singed crackling was all she could hear.

And the smell.

Nothing would ever be the same.

Nothing.

~

When Tennessee could move, she ran to the bathroom and puked. She puked until all she had left was air. Then she scrubbed off her smeared coal eyeliner, swished with water, and dug out her keys from her jeans pocket. She exited the bathroom to a team of worried eyes; as she walked to the waiting room, she tossed her keyring in her hand until she found the safe key.

Tennessee opened her desk drawer, clunked a fireproof safe on the desk, unlocked it, lifted the lid, and retrieved a 9mm handgun.

The men made a bunch of noise, but she still didn't hear them; it was all shocked eyes and palms flying up in protest. Sho was calmer than the other two. Still, he didn't approach her. And she didn't want him to.

Tennessee slapped in a clip.

"Get out." She gave her friends ample warning, then eyed Sho. "It's here." And through clenched teeth she hissed, "I can *feel* it."

A demon killed Polar.

She would kill that demon.

Sho was speaking with the other men when Lin ran in. She started yelling at the sight of Tennessee holding a gun. Godzilla dragged her out. Phillip followed, cell phone drawn. There were lights flashing in the parking lot.

Tennessee raced past the chapels, but Sho easily overtook her.

"You have to stop, Ten. Don't let the collar lead. *You* are in charge. Ten!" Sho didn't touch Tennessee; in fact, he kept a good distance from her. She wasn't acting like herself; she hardly looked like herself.

Her light was gone.

"It killed..." She couldn't say his name. "I *need* to kill it."

Sho took a long breath. "You *need* to grieve."

"Not while that bastard is in *my* house! Move! I swear to god, Sho, I'll shoot you..."

Standing tall and calm, Sho narrowed his gaze to a hard stare. "You do *this* and you become the collar's slave. Forever."

"Leave her be," Tennessee growled in another's voice, crushing Sho against the Mother Mary Chapel door. His limp body dripped to the floor. Tennessee stepped over him, strolling back down the hall to the waiting room, well past fifty feet, into the crematory.

At sixty-one feet, the foul-sweetened aroma of burnt fur buckled Tennessee's knees. She gagged as hot tears blurred her clouded vision.

Polar.

She watched her right arm rise from her side, stretching straight out in front of her; she stared at the gun in her hand. It didn't feel like her arm, and that gun, what was her *father's* gun doing in *her* hand?

"Sho? Sho..." Tennessee labored for breath, squeezing her eyes shut as she fought the collar's hold. "Get out of my head, you sick shit! Get out!" A sharp tug made her cough; a second one had heat behind it, but she didn't know which way to go. Was Sho behind her or in front?

"Ten." Sho's weakened rasp rumbled in from the hall.

When the sizzling crackle started, Tennessee crawled until she gained enough strength to stand. "I'm here." She staggered toward his voice, slipping to her knees as the crackling threatened a bone-hollowing zap. When she rounded the corner, Sho was on his hands and knees, trying to get to her.

Tennessee practically dove into him.

"Sho!" She crushed him in her arms, and the wounded man didn't wince once. But when she brought her hands to his face, she still held the gun. "My god, what happened?" She dropped the gun beside her, clasping Sho's face as if she only now noticed his labored breaths. "Did I do this?" Tennessee hid her remorseful eyes beneath a clump of squiggly curls. "I'm so sorry I hurt you."

Sho never took his eyes off her, a note of awe in his rugged rasp as he declared, "You broke the collar's hold...Ten, that effort takes unfathomable strength..."

"Was that Zaada? Is she testing me?"

"No, the collar, too, is cursed. It wants freedom. Collars have been known to take control and seek their own vengeance rather than wait for the host to complete Zaada's assignment."

"Goddammit! I have to worry about being possessed by the collar, too?"

"It should not attempt control again." There was Sho's pride again, precious gems chiseled from his gritty tone. "You have done a great service to many humans. The collars prefer efficiency. They don't wrangle demons *out* of humans, they slaughter souls...entire towns if it means they gain freedom faster."

"How can you be sure it won't rip into my head again?" She dropped her hands to her side, tears threatening a flood.

Polar was dead.

Nothing mattered.

Sho moved guardedly, without a grumble or groan, as he positioned his bruised and battered back against the wall; his head lifted in a strained stretch, and he held Tennessee's gaze with lifetimes behind those silky black eyes.

"Because you are Tennessee England." He opened his arms for

her. "Only one with more love than hate in her heart can break the collar's hold."

Sinking into sorrow, Tennessee curled herself against Sho's ribs, buried her face in his chest, and cried.

~

It was nearing midnight by the time the town's lone deputy completed his shoddy investigation. A robbery gone bad. Nothing stolen. Case closed. As for the cremated dog? Deputy Herd left that for the morning shift. One Sheriff Honey.

Tennessee suffered a mild concussion, facial abrasions, and substantial bruising all along her left side. Unlike Sho, she'd need follow-up care and rest. Sho's four broken ribs had healed before the paramedics were done with her.

They all told Tennessee to go home. But Polar wasn't at home. Polar was *here*. Polar was in Audrey II. And that was no place to leave a friend.

"Not without my dog," she rebuffed when directed to go home by yet another medic.

While Tennessee was a pain in the ass, Sho was a wonder. He won everyone over with his selfless behavior toward Tennessee. Phillip even shook his hand. Still, no one would leave Tennessee alone to tend to Polar. They all filed into the crematory hoping to be of use. Mamma Min was there too, with her tablecloth and candles and incense. She made Lin find a photo of Polar and bring bowls of rice, meat, fruit, and cake. Only Lin didn't have cake, so Mamma Min grabbed a handful of Oreos. The little woman shuffled about preparing Polar's altar, all while clutching those Oreos. It wasn't until Lin gently placed her hand on her mother's boney shoulder that the old woman released the cookies.

Mamma Min didn't like dogs. But Mamma Min loved Tennessee.

Audrey II was silent. And cold.

Polar was ready.

Phillip was holding Tennessee's gear. She went to him, but refused to look him in the eye. Polar was as much his dog as he

was hers. And while *she* hadn't seen Phillip in months, he'd often seen Polar; he'd pick up Polar from the silo every Monday while Tennessee was working and have the dog safely back before she got home. This was the only reason Phillip still had a key to the silo. It was part of their break-up settlement. They shared the dog. They couldn't agree on much, but they both loved Polar.

Tennessee knew Phillip had been crying. His handkerchief was partially sticking out of his jacket pocket. Phillip slipped the slick black apron over Tennessee's head, drawing the ties around her back, securing a tight knot right above her navel. She pulled on her faceguard and glanced at Godzilla; he was leaning against the far back wall; *he* was the one she truly worried about.

Godzilla knew a ton of people, and a ton of people knew Godzilla. But the big guy had just a few good friends, and most of them were in that room, and one of them was now dead.

Tennessee swiped through her cell phone, clicked on the perfect song. She tugged on surgical gloves, unhooked the push broom; and as Norah Jones sang "Man of the Hour," Tennessee collected her beloved white lion.

# 12.

# Neon Haze

Mamma Min's incense spiced the stale air. Polar would have liked that; he never liked the smell of death.

A tear dripped onto Tennessee's faceguard as she poured Polar's ashes on the sheet pan.

*Clink!*

Her gut flipped.

"What was that?" Phillip moved closer.

Sho approached unhurried as Tennessee picked up the piece of metal; it was shaped like a heart. She pulled out a magnifying glass to read the engraved lettering.

"It's...it's..." Tennessee tore off her faceguard. "It's not Polar! It's not Polar." She threw herself into Phillip's arms, and kissed him square on the lips.

And he kissed her back.

~

Sho had his bare hand in canine dust, sifting around for another clue. If this *wasn't* Polar, they had an even bigger problem. This was a message, and Polar was bait.

Lin was momentarily too distracted by the exes kissing to celebrate. Godzilla hoped Tennessee was right about Polar, and the kissing wasn't a surprise; he secretly rooted for the couple to get back together.

Mamma Min clapped loudly; she always did like Phillip—he was a *doctor*, and that was a *very* lucky match.

Sho washed his hands in the sink, glancing over his shoulder at Tennessee and Phillip; peaceably lost in their moment, he patiently waited for their celebration to end. His calm confused Lin especially. If that was *her* boyfriend kissing his ex, there would be blood.

Tennessee ended the kiss in a fluster, apologized a dozen times; half to Phillip, even though he didn't have to kiss her back—what was *he* thinking—and the other half to Sho. Then Phillip apologized to Sho, but it came out a little terse, and he still had his arm around Tennessee. Phillip might not have removed his hand from Tennessee's hip if Lin hadn't demanded Tennessee's attention,

"You sure, Ness? I mean, it's not like you had *two* dogs in here."

"This isn't Polar's tag. This dog's name is Dave. Does anybody know why a dog named Dave would be in Audrey II? Better yet...*who* would put a dog named Dave in Audrey II?"

"Dave?" Godzilla peeled himself off the back wall. "Maria had a dog named Dave. A black and white lab. Is that..."

"I think so...it's late, but maybe you could call..."

Godzilla was already on the phone.

Phillip took the tag from Tennessee to investigate. They shared a strange look, maybe a little embarrassed, maybe a little nostalgic. Tennessee went to Sho, whispered yet another apology.

With an indulgent smile, he gathered her into his arms. "Your joy brings me great joy."

The way he said it, Tennessee was certain Sho could sense her emotions. She began to think he wasn't tethered to her just to take her physical pain; he was there to *feel* what it was to be human.

She tiptoed to kiss him; when her lips touched his cheek, he leaned into her, his grip growing hungrier on her hip.

"There's a phone number on here." Phillip had the tag under a lamp, under Tennessee's magnifying glass. He met Sho's gaze.

Tennessee perceived a little heat between the men, but she was still half out of her mind from the night's events. Her head ached from the fall *and* the collar *and* the pain of thinking she'd lost Polar.

She *needed* to believe Polar was still alive. Phillip read out the numbers. Tennessee jotted them down, but Lin punched the numbers directly into her cell phone. She was pissed, and she was going to let Dave's owner know just how pissed a scrappy Asian could get.

Mamma Min lit more incense; this time she prayed to bring Polar to his earthly home instead of his spiritual one.

Godzilla walked over to Lin, put his huge hand over her phone and said, "It's Maria's dog. Cruz said the lame dog never left her side. They haven't seen Dave since he chased after the ambulance. They figured he'd give up and come back, but...I told him Dave is dead, but not *how*. Cruz asked if we'd take care of Dave...put his ashes in with Maria."

Lin made the number a contact anyway, under *Dave's Daddy*. Just in case.

Still holding Tennessee close by his side, Sho reasoned, "Whoever took Polar wanted Ten to believe he died."

Tennessee stared at Godzilla, sluggish to catch up; it hurt to think. "He said *ashes*?"

Godzilla scowled a squint. "Yeah, I caught that too."

"It's late." Lin eyed her mother. Mamma Min was on her knees, praying in front of Polar's altar. "Should we meet here tomorrow to figure things out? Do some recon..."

Godzilla met Lin's eye, which might have been easier had he taken a knee. "You do a lot of recon at the beauty shop?" Godzilla wasn't meaning to be chastising, but Lin decoded intonations like bookies calculate odds.

"And you?! Mr. Inconspicuous! Everybody in town knows you...you're no private eye!"

Now Godzilla was hurt. "Oh yeah, what can you see from three-foot-two? You'll get nothin' but pictures of knees..."

Lin blew up, rampaging in her native tongue.

Aghast by her daughter's speech, Mamma Min went on her own mini rampage. Their soprano duet left a ringing in everyone's ears. Tennessee wished she understood; watching the mother-daughter fight made her miss her own mother. She promised herself she'd call Missus once Polar was safely home.

"Lin's right." Tennessee refocused. "We'll tackle this after sunrise. We're staying here tonight...just in case Polar comes back. If anybody hears or sees anything, *please* call us."

Maybe it was the way she said *us*, but Phillip slammed the metal tag on the desk beside poor Dave's ashes. "I'll check out the silo before heading home. I have the morning shift, but please..."

"I'll call you." Tennessee eased his mind with a reassuring nod. "Of course, I will. Thank you..." she broke from his heavy gaze, "uh, guys...I don't know what I'd do if you guys weren't here." Tennessee teared up, and Sho held her closer as they escorted their friends out.

It was too late for Mamma Min; she grabbed hold of Godzilla's arm to steady her tired feet. She liked the man; he ate everything she cooked, even her duckbill soup. As he escorted the Mins home, Mamma Min exclaimed loudly, "I stay in town for you and dog. Better I pray *here*. Better luck for dog. Sleep! You tired!" She patted Tennessee's arm, gave the girl a hug, before shuffling across the street with Godzilla on one arm and her daughter on the other.

Phillip might have given Tennessee another hug, but Sho was glued to her side, his hand entwined with hers. The good doctor walked across the street, got in his car, and drove off.

Tennessee stood outside a while longer calling for Polar. Sho walked the perimeter one last time. After locking up the shop, Tennessee gazed up at Sho.

"I'm going to catch that demon, Sho. I'm going to catch it and kill it. And that's all *me* talking."

Sho's sympathetic gaze lightened with pride. "I believe you."

~

There wasn't much left in the Englands' apartment above the mortuary. Tennessee had shipped most of her parents' belongings home upon their request. They expected her to live there, because living where you worked was convenient. Tennessee looked at it differently. She'd spent her entire life living over dead people. A girl needs a break.

But she couldn't go home. Not without Polar. He was her home. No, until she found him, she'd stay at the shop.

The back room, the one with the gilded mirror, had a stairway tucked in the corner, leading up to the Englands' apartment. It was way bigger than Lin's. The entire upstairs was living space: open floor plan family room and kitchen, two full baths, master bedroom, and Tennessee's old room.

She hadn't been up there in months; entering it now, and with Sho, gave her a queasy, time-traveling sickness. Her room was exactly how she left it years ago: not quite a child's room, but close enough. Painted neon green, neon yellow, and neon pink, it screamed eighties, or LSD. Framed posters of classic eighties hits hung on the wall: *The Breakfast Club*, *The Goonies*, *Pretty in Pink*. She had others, all framed, all stored in her closet to be changed out with the seasons. Her room overlooked the ocean; seeing the view again almost made her want to move back. Twin bed, desk, the basics.

She walked through the apartment, throwing open windows. She couldn't breathe. She wrung her hands; the night was cold. If Polar was out there, he'd be freezing.

Sho took an unguided tour while Tennessee made a pot of coffee in the kitchen. That space was efficient and simple; only what a family of three would need, nothing more. Before Tennessee got sick, they had enough china and cutlery to host a fiesta in honor of Santa Marian Kamalen. After the Founders blocked the sale of the mortuary, England-hosted fiestas were a thing of the past.

Mister and Missus settled for *enough*, and the entire space screamed it.

Sho walked through the barren living room. "I could move up some furniture...if you wish."

She knew what he was saying; he wouldn't poof as much here as at the silo, since there was usually a dead body at the shop. And with a demon tailing Lillie, and another one cremating poor Dave—not to mention the bounty on her head—the less he poofed, the better.

Tennessee managed a vague roll of her shoulders; she couldn't commit, not yet. She'd have to ask Polar what he thought. He loved the silo, the gardens, the lack of death smells.

She started with the sugar, poured in powdered cream, and waited for the coffee, tapping a teaspoon in time with the thud in her temples. She'd had worse concussions, but this one was probably made worse by the collar digging around her brain, mining her memories. Her teaspoon tapping wound up her wild worst-case scenarios.

"Ten," Sho slid his hand over hers, "we'll find him."

Tennessee snapped her head up with a jolt of insight. "Stumpy's got him!"

"The drunken man with no shirt?" Sho poured her coffee, then his. "Why would he take Polar? This is not typical behavior for demons and Stumpy's not a demon..."

"But a demon was there and Stumpy lied about seeing Polar. Someone or *something* kept Polar away from my calls. He always comes back when I call." She thunked the teaspoon again, trying to connect invisible dots. "Don't ask me *why*, Sho. Nothing about all this makes much sense to me." But another dot coalesced into a clue. "Except maybe the burger. Someone, or something, left awfully quick when we showed up. And all those fast food wrappers blowing around...it's no wonder Stumpy's been shooting up the place..."

Sho recalled the crows eating a burger and all the trees spattered with bullet holes. "You think Stumpy's been trigger-happy because..."

"Yep," she tossed the teaspoon in the sink, "he's got a demon problem."

After a moment of contemplation, Sho rasped an impressed, "Fine detective work for a mortician."

"Other girls wanted to be Miss America. I wanted to be Jessica Fletcher." Tennessee laughed at Sho's expressionless face. "Famous sleuth on *Murder, She Wrote*? Man, after we get Polar back I'm totally introducing you to TV...you'll *love* it!"

"As you wish."

Tennessee exhaled a patchy breath, reeling from Sho's simple words. He wasn't well-versed in popular culture and what not, so he didn't know the significance of such a common phrase, and she didn't tell him. She'd save that movie for much, much later in their burgeoning fairy tale.

~

Tennessee prepared to sleep despite knowing she wouldn't; she showered, brushed her teeth, slipped into her favorite Blondie t-shirt; it was a tad short, but no one was looking. She sat on her twin bed, waiting for the sun to rise. A few hours inhaling sea breezes cleared her mind enough to rest her eyes.

When she opened them, the sunlight hurt, and her brain pounded against her skull. It took effort to sit up; her ribs ached, and a pukey sensation whooshed her back onto the pillow. She tracked the textured neon ceiling, down the neon wall, stopping on the fuzzy pink blanket covering her that hadn't been on the bed before she accidently fell asleep. Sho must have done that. The night's events lazily leaked into non-swollen crevices of her brain, between throbs of raw, numbing pain, but the memories were sketchy with huge chunks blotted out.

"Sho!" She got a yell out, couldn't imagine mustering another. They said *mild* concussion, but she would have placed it closer to the *severe* end of things. She wasn't a wuss, but, damn, this hurt.

Maybe it was the collar getting even for her pushing the bastard out of her head. Her brain was mush. She tried to recall an early memory, something below double digits; nothing. Her clearest

memories were of Polar and Sho. In fact, all she could think of was Polar and Sho.

The aroma of fresh coffee had her struggling to get up, but she didn't get very far when Sho strolled in with a tray of coffee and cake.

"Mamma Min came by precisely at sunrise to give you this mung bean cake..." Sho's smile sunk with displeasure. "You don't look rested. In fact..." He put the tray on the desk, examining her as he approached. He took her hands into his, felt her normal coolness. "I'll phone Phillip."

"Who?"

Sho's brow bunched a deep crease down his forehead, his rich tone doused with concern. "What do you remember about last night?" He stroked her face; she was clammy, a little hotter than usual, but her hands were still cool.

"We found Maria's dog...Dave. We still need to find Polar. Lillie's a favorite and Stumpy's got a demon problem. But..." She rubbed her temple with one hand, waved her other toward the coffee. Sho brought her mug over. She took a big gulp. It was exactly right. The boy paid attention. She wondered if he slept, where he slept, if he ate...

"Ten." Sho recognized that look. When Tennessee's eyes spaced out, her mind raced.

"There are more blanks. I..." she stammered, trying *not* to freak out, "I can't remember much...or anything really, but you and Polar. And that song "Why." You know it?" She could tell he didn't. "Anyway, everything...people are fuzzy...like I watched them on TV once...I kind of remember them...but..."

"Where's your cell phone? Phillip should know."

Tennessee waved to the bedside table. "Who's Phillip?"

Sho stopped mid-movement, replying with ease, "He's your doctor, Ten. A close friend."

"That doesn't sound right." She shook her head, but that hurt so she stopped. "I hate doctors."

While Sho figured out Tennessee's phone, she finished her

coffee and managed to get up and retrieve Mamma Min's mung bean cake. It tasted way better than it sounded. She finished the entire plate, drank Sho's coffee, stretched a teensy bit. Then she stopped because it hurt to move.

"Tenny! How are you feeling?" Phillip was on speaker. "Thank you for calling, I've been worried..."

Sho stopped him, explained the situation and promised to bring Tennessee in immediately for some tests.

"What *does* she remember?"

"Polar and...me..."

"I see."

"It's the concussion?" Sho was watching Tennessee pretend to stretch as if she were in perfect health. He might have called out her ruse if he wasn't so worried.

"Tell that doctor guy, I'm fine. I'll be in after I find my dog. I don't know why, but I hate hospitals." Tennessee raised her voice, "Hey, doctor guy, it's just a headache! I remember my boyfriend and my dog...that's all I need!"

Phillip's deep sigh filled the room. "I'll be right over. I'm just a few blocks away. Sho, keep her there. I need to examine her. If she has a...just keep her still, would you."

"I understand. I'll leave the shop unlocked, just take the stairs at..."

"I know the way." Phillip's flat, doctorly tone turned dark. He hung up.

Sho let out a huff of air. "That man is lost without..."

"I said I don't like doctors..." Tennessee slid her feet onto the freezing floor; that actually *helped* her head. She gripped the windowsill, pulling herself upright, then jimmied the screen out. The wind went wild on her curls, tying knots over knots as she shoved her head out the window.

"Hey, Sho, after we get Polar and I kill that demon, let's put up a porch. I've always wanted a porch. We can have our coffee right here. *Every* morning. It could be our ritual, our *thing*." Tennessee leaned way out the window.

Sho went to her, amusement relaxing the severe crease of his brow as he wrapped his arms around her waist to keep her from falling out; she was wobbly, a little irrational. "You deserve a porch, and we deserve a ritual of our own."

"After we find Polar." She clasped his hands at her navel, trying not to cry.

Sho kissed the back of her frizzed mane. "I anticipate finding him today."

"I need him, Sho."

"I know you do." Sho's hands found Tennessee's shoulders. He maneuvered her back to bed, where he tended to her sore neck. Tennessee stopped thinking; she was useless under his caress. Before long she was lying on her stomach, cushioned by downy pillows; Sho's expert hands undoing life's mark on her muscles. "May I?" He held the bottom of her t-shirt; he was after those bruised ribs.

Tennessee rolled onto her back, murmuring a sleepily seductive *please*, so he proceeded to lift her shirt just enough to examine her ribs while maintaining her modesty. She was glad she'd chosen her pretty pink panties with the lace trim, rather than the granny panties she usually wore to bed. But Sho wasn't looking at her lacy panties; the swirling ribbons of purple-black bruises marring her left ribs and abdomen had all his attention.

"I neglected to apply ice last night," Sho chastised himself, but Tennessee was dazed; his expertly delicate touch had her more relaxed than she deemed acceptable. She had crap to do, Polar to find, and a demon to slay, but this was therapeutic, and she *had* hit her head.

Sho ran his hand over Tennessee's ribs, his thumb disappearing in the heated crevice under her braless bra line. Guilt crept in as Sho's healing touch left her craving *more*. Why guilt? He was her boyfriend.

"How long before that doctor gets here?" She purred a sultry invitation.

Sho either missed the innuendo or he was ignoring her. "I'll get some ice."

"Oh, ice is fun." Her tone casual and racy.

Sho frowned, but his eyes were glistening with delight. "You'll need your memory back before I indulge such requests, my dear."

"*Indulge.*" She tapered her eyes seductively. "I like the sound of that."

Sho slipped out of the room, concealing his amusement; but his gravelly chuckle rumbled in from the hall. Followed by an incessant knock.

The doctor.

Damn.

Tennessee yanked a pink neon pillow out from under her head and plopped it on her face. Doctors ruin everything. Her t-shirt was still hiked up over her ribs; her lacey pink panties in plain view. She didn't care. He was a doctor.

She overheard Sho direct this *Phillip* to her room; he was still getting ice. She listened to the doctor's steps; they were quick. She wondered what the rush was. It's not like she was dying. Except for a sadistic migraine, a desperate need to find Polar, and the whole memory loss thing, she was peachy.

The doctor stopped at the threshold, just stopped.

Maybe he'd overshot her room. It was too quiet.

"I'm in here." She removed the pillow to see the concerned, sullen doctor studying her bruised ribs, bare legs. He looked all depressed, like he'd lost something. Maybe his patient died or took a turn. "The ribs look bad but they're fine, doc. I told Sho not to call you, but he's the classic worried boyfriend. Sorry you came all this way for nothing. So, I hit my head...big whoop...I'm alive, right?"

"It would seem." Phillip approached Tennessee, took another glance at her ribs, and her perfect legs. "I'm Dr. Saint James. *Phillip.*" Tennessee shook his hand like she would any stranger. He cleared his throat, sitting on the edge of her bed while discreetly pulling her shirt down. "Are you able to sit up without pain?"

Tennessee said nothing as she pushed herself up to sitting with a petulant grumble.

"That looked painful," Phillip observed crossly as he shined his penlight in her eyes. "I see your leg has healed remarkably well." He went to touch her leg, stopped. "If I hadn't stitched you up myself, I wouldn't believe you were shot in that leg." There was something unsure in his gaze.

"No scars are *good*, right doc?" Now Tennessee's gaze was uncertain.

"I'd like to run some scans."

"Nah."

"With head injuries such as yours, judgement is often impaired. You signed over power of attorney for that very reason. I could get approval."

"Dammit, Sho would probably want scans." Tennessee rolled her eyes, gaze glued on the ceiling.

"Sho doesn't hold your power of attorney, Tenny."

Tennessee pushed herself up a little more, sloppily this time; she used Phillip to brace herself as she worked her legs over the side of the bed. "Oh yeah, doctor guy, then who is?" She scooted herself beside the good doctor, resting her hand next to his.

Phillip took a focused breath, before cautiously placing his hand over Tennessee's; he met her questioning gaze with steadfast strength. "I am."

Tennessee grew quiet, blood sloshed her mind clean and a dash of a memory throbbed her brain. With it came a surge of heat and excruciating pain; she bowled over, teeth gnashed, hands gripping the bed.

Sho walked in; he dropped the ice and ran to Tennessee.

"You should go now." He glared at Phillip.

Phillip stood tall. "What happened to her leg?"

Sho's confused expression had Phillip explaining the gunshot wound Tennessee had suffered; a serious injury that brought all her friends to the hospital, except her *boyfriend*. Yeah, he slung that.

"She should have a scar on her left leg. Scars don't just disappear."

Sho lifted Tennessee onto the bed, attentively draping the fuzzy pink blanket over her. "She is healed of that debilitating injury. Beyond *that*, what does it matter?"

Sho faced Phillip; he was taller than the doctor, sturdier, but Phillip possessed a chilling severity that Sho didn't wear. Both men had saved lives, *taken* lives. On *that* ground, they were equals.

"She needs to be admitted," Phillip demanded, his eyes on Tennessee. "Perhaps you're not aware of her condition..."

"I am intimately aware, Phillip."

"Then you know," Phillip seethed, "as the bleed worsens, she may experience personality changes, engage in risky behavior, say and do things the Tennessee *I* know wouldn't...." Phillip strained to say the words. "Her condition is *terminal*. Your Eastern remedies cannot change that."

"Her *condition* will improve with rest and when she is reunited with her guardian. The stress of being without Polar is causing her great pain. Please, leave us now..."

Phillip remained tied to that damn spot. Sho asked him again, but the good doctor didn't budge.

Understanding far too well, Sho placed a firm hand on Phillip's shoulder. "Some coffee, then?"

~

For three hours, the men sat vigil in Tennessee's neon room, drinking coffee and, occasionally, talking. Sho's easy charisma eventually worked Phillip into an acceptable mood. No one was more surprised by that than Phillip.

Others dropped by, but Tennessee had the pillow over her head because one of them was way too loud. She liked it when it was just Sho and Phillip. Even though they were talking, their tones soothed. Tennessee was mostly sleeping, but she caught good bits and bad bits. She liked what she heard about Sho; he was her boyfriend after all, and the more she learned about him the faster her heart beat.

But this doctor, this Phillip guy, he was interesting. There was something about the way he talked, the cadence of his speech, that relaxed her. She almost said something about it, but she didn't want to interrupt his melody. It was painful to think, so she didn't; she just listened to Phillip's voice, and soon she was sleeping again. It went on like this until an intense chill had her thrashing in bed.

She sprang up in a damp haze, screaming, "Demons!"

Sho rushed over, ignoring Phillip's hard glares. "Ten...I'm here...you are safe."

Phillip sat back, listening, curious to observe Sho's handling of demonic hallucinations.

Sho had Tennessee's hand in his; she was warm. His whisperings in her ear had her laying back down. Tennessee gazed over at the doctor. "*Phillip*, right?" She wondered why a flash of hurt darkened his earnest green eyes. "I like it when you talk."

Phillip leaned forward in his seat, thinking of something to say.

Tennessee closed her eyes, waiting.

"Read to her," Sho said it like an invitation. "Anything. Your voice heals her."

"Healing doesn't work like that," Phillip shot back. "My voice can't cure her."

"Then you must leave. Only those who believe she can be cured may stay." Sho's gruff tone grew sympathetic as Phillip glanced around the room. "I recall a small library in the living room. Read or go, it is your choice." Sho walked out to replenish Tennessee's ice bag. When he returned, Phillip hardly noticed. He was reading Judy Blume's *Superfudge*.

It was an odd story for a grown man to read aloud to a grown woman.

But Phillip knew it was one of Tennessee's all-time faves. She loved Judy Blume and anything with the word *fudge* in it. Put the two together and it's an all-night party. She told him that once, so he bought her the copy he now read. He was surprised she

kept it, even if it was stashed in her parents' home, and downright astonished she hadn't ripped out the inscription:

*For my girl,*

*I love your quirk.*

*Saint James*

They had stayed up all night, eating chocolate truffles, sharing childhood memories, and reading *Superfudge*. He knew she wouldn't remember that night, but he was determined to remember for them both. She had been slipping away before this; her sudden memory loss put miles more between them. Maybe all he had were the memories. Maybe he was out of hope.

Phillip kept reading as Sho tended to Tennessee's bruises. He looked up just as Sho was pulling down Tennessee's shirt.

"Wait..." Phillip approached the bed. "How did you...she had bruises!"

Sho kept Phillip from lifting Tennessee's shirt. "She is healing. As I said, only those with hope may stay. Keep reading, Phillip. Ten will be well by sundown. Then we'll find Polar."

~

While Phillip helped heal Tennessee's mind, it took Sho a full day to heal Tennessee's physical injuries. The brunt of the problem was the collar. If it was only the concussion, a few hours would have done it. While Tennessee had squashed the collar's bid for control, it rattled her already-rattled brain, magnifying the damage.

Hours later, Tennessee awoke to Phillip reading *Otherwise Known as Sheila the Great*.

"Why are you reading Judy Blume? It might be sexy if it wasn't so weird." She labored to sit up, testing her head. No throbbing. "Halleluiah, I'm healed!" she teased, but there was something of hope in her eyes.

Sho looked certain. Phillip knew better. Her prognosis had always been grim. He approached with his trusty penlight.

Tennessee growled, "*What* do you keep looking at with that damn penlight?"

"Your pupils."

"Well, doc," Tennessee threw her legs over the side of the bed, pointed her toes, crossed her thighs, arched her back, "how do my pupils look?"

Phillip actually chuckled.

*That* laugh was too familiar; it tickled her teeth.

The men noticed her change in demeanor.

"You remembered something?" Sho kneeled in front of Tennessee, hands on her bare thighs.

That move almost turned the good doctor bad. He got up, stopped short of leaving the room.

"Just that doctor-man Phillip doesn't laugh very much, so when he *does* it comes as a shock," Tennessee rationalized her sudden emotion toward the doctor. Then she got out of bed and wiggled into a pair of jeans as the men turned away. That made her laugh. "You've got to be kidding! I'm sleeping with *you*, and *you're* my doctor. A little leg makes you two blush? Well, you've earned your gentleman badges, now let's find Polar. First stop, Stumpy's." She threw a flannel button-up over her Blondie t-shirt.

"Take it easy, Tenny, you're still recovering." Phillip turned to Sho. "You have my cell number. Use it."

"You have my gratitude." Sho shook Phillip's hand. "I'll call you when her memory fills in."

"Yes, you will." Phillip's penetrating gaze brought a wily smirk out of Sho.

Tennessee clamped her arms around both men. "A good memory is bad for relationships. I like starting over. Clean slate. I've got a sexy boyfriend and," she paused, suddenly flushed by Phillip's emerald gaze, "a capable doctor. Now all I need is my dog." Tennessee nearly skipped out of the room.

She glanced over her shoulder. That Phillip guy was still sulky. She wondered if he found what he'd lost.

~

Tennessee skipped down the stairs, into the shop. She took one look at the Mother Mary Chapel, the wall clock, then freaked out,

"I'm supposed to be doing something tonight! A wake, I think?" Tennessee wiggled her cell phone from her back pocket, but as she swiped through her contacts for a caterer, Sho slipped the phone from her hand.

"It's been taken care of. You have more friends than you think."

"I do?"

"Lin and Mamma Min prepared food and drink. Godzilla prepared the chapel and delivered proper invitations to the family. Hill provided flower arrangements. She said Maria kept the tidiest storage unit, next to yours, of course."

"I need to dress and prepare a speech."

Sho took Tennessee by the waist, leading her outside. "Respectfully, the family requested a private ceremony. No eulogy. Godzilla and Lin volunteered to oversee the shop while we search for Polar."

"Dammit, you'll poof out here. Let me grab my father's handgun."

"No guns, Ten."

"No guns?"

"No."

"Why the hell not? There be demons..." She was pretty sure she'd always wanted to say that.

"Because they don't work. Otherwise Stumpy wouldn't have a demon problem."

Tennessee complained *a lot* until Sho opened Riggy's passenger door. On the chair sat a golden, paw-shaped urn; engraved with the name *Dave*.

Now *that* was ingenuity she could appreciate. "Dave's gonna help us catch his killer *and* find Polar. I think I love this dog."

"He is a good dog." Sho jumped in, tossing Tennessee the keys.

She caught them as she climbed behind the wheel. Sitting there, she felt one step closer to Polar. "Well, Riggy, good buddy," she patted his steering wheel, "it's time to wrangle us a demon and bring our lion home. But first, burgers and fries!"

# 13.

# Forge Ahead

Turns out demons love junk food.

Tennessee sensed at least three *favorites* in the drive-through of her go-to burger joint, Bad Moon Burgers. That would explain Lillie's sudden devouring of Godzilla's potato chips. She couldn't do anything about *favorites,* so she ordered her burger, fries, and soda; then doubled the order. Sho seemed hungry, too, and maybe a little worn down.

With a sky full of stars overhead and briny breezes giving Riggy a much-needed cleanse, Tennessee and Sho ate their burgers and fries. She finished before Sho. She'd only had coffee and mung bean cakes. A girl couldn't live on bean cakes alone. On coffee, maybe.

Stumpy's wasn't a good place to be at night. He lived mostly off grid, so no power. The lot was pitch black except for what the heavens deemed worthy of view. The moon was half, better than nothing. She could have done without the rusty squeak of a shifting weathervane; the slightest gust nudged a soaring iron owl welded atop a forged arrow spindle rotating north, south, east, west. Tennessee stared at the compass points; Stumpy got it all wrong; he had the giant *N* pointing south and the giant S pointing north. Drunken idiot.

Clasping hands, Sho led Tennessee through Stumpy's weed

garden, searching for *what* they weren't really sure. It was a beautiful night walk; the stars were out and the crisp February evening was exactly what Tennessee needed after another invalid day in bed. She hated invalid days. Lately, every day ended with injured status.

She almost wished the twins were riding the Summerhold bell again; at least Polar would be there. What a day that had been, and it all started with Lillie and her damn Santa.

"Wait!" She clutched Sho's arm. "I remember something from before I hit my head..."

"Good." Sho drew Tennessee nearer. "You've found a point of entry." He cupped her dazed face in his hands, gently pressing his forehead to hers. "Now I can heal the pathways."

It took less than a minute for Sho to untangle the collar's cobwebbed mess. Tennessee dripped into Sho's arms as the memories rushed over her mind's eye. It wasn't *all* bad. Not nearly.

"*Crap*," she muttered as the memory of her failed seduction of Sho flashed; she blushed at that brazen girl. "I suppose you *did* earn your gentleman badge today."

Sho steeled his gaze. "A very long time ago, Ten."

Tennessee stroked the stubble along his gritted jaw. "I know." She tiptoed to kiss a hint of silver. She lingered, and Sho's steady hand pressed against the small of her back. Sho nestled into her and that stubble transmitted tickly joules down her neck. Her head went heavy; her mind went dizzy.

"The healing," he breathed, "it can be...intense...intimate..."

Tennessee wasn't just leaning anymore; she was clinging to Sho. She *needed* to be close to him.

Sho pulled back, a little, slowing his breath, and soon Tennessee's breath slowed too.

"If we focus," his rasp deepened, "the *need* fades."

Tennessee clenched her fists, refocused on finding Polar. It was only difficult to begin; once she thought of something other than Sho, she was back in control. She stepped back, her gaze on his chest,

"Is it always like that?"

Sho's hard chuckle summoned her curious glare; he met it cautiously, and because he couldn't lie to her, he didn't. "Not for me. It is typically a reflexive exchange, sterile. The impassioned bond creates its own difficulties. *Ours*, it appears, is heightened."

"Heightened? Is that what the kids are calling it these days." She held his gaze. "You might want to keep a close shave from now on because that stubble isn't helping." Tennessee pushed away, faking composure, but she stepped in a rut, wobbled, comically finding her footing as Sho's rumbly chuckle accompanied his stabilizing hands on her shoulders.

"It's *dark* out here, Sho!" She slapped his chest before stomping off toward Stumpy's ramshackle shack.

"I can see just fine." Sho playfully caught her hand, but his levity was fleeting.

Tennessee's palm was stone cold.

"We need to leave." Sho's ferocity had Tennessee tripping into his arms.

"Damn ruts!" She fell behind Sho's lead. Now it wasn't just her *hands*; her entire body was freezing. Her icy fingers found her bluing lips. "Sho?" She watched her breath carry his name into a hazy mist of crystallized exhales.

"There are too many," Sho answered as bits of ice landed on his lips. He seized her hand, dragging her toward a shortcut edging the rotten wheat fields.

The weathervane's annoying screech shrilled into a maniacal shriek as the owl's frenetic spinning shot sparks over the parched fields. Sho raced Tennessee past a decayed scarecrow dressed in moldy overalls and a sun-faded flannel. Tennessee's misty exhales froze midair like stalled snowflakes seeking sanctuary as the scarecrow shook, happily at first, then violently, until it was ripped off its rusted cross.

Tennessee screamed as the thing rattled its clothes to shreds, exploding its rotten wheat guts into evil fireworks across the night sky.

"Run!" Tennessee yelled as each individual straw tumbled and rolled into a single, spitefully twisted tornado.

"Get to Riggy!" Sho hollered, positioning himself between Tennessee and the tornado.

The wicked twister gained speed and mass as it devoured huge hunks of Stumpy's rotten fields and rancid earth. The couple weaved and ran as the weathervane screeched, forecasting the crackle-crunch of an F-3 tornado. As the whirring wheat whipped up more fuel, it spat long, sinister stalks at the escaping couple; spears zipped by Tennessee's head, piercing straight through an overturned red wheelbarrow.

"Keep your head down!" Sho leapt into a forward roll, drawing fire away from Tennessee as the tornado spat shards at them; a serrated stem nailed him in the bicep.

As Tennessee turned to make sure Sho wasn't injured, the tip of her boot snagged on a surface root; she might have rolled, but her foot was wedged fast; she slammed her forearms on dirt. Then came the flying toilets and rusted rims.

Sho grabbed Tennessee, lifting her to her feet, rushing her past the English garden gates.

An eardrum-shattering wail whooshed in after them, slamming to a resounding thud at the garden gates. The tornado whirred to a spinetingling screech. Sho threw himself over Tennessee as a roaring blast burst the deadly threat into a giant mess of hay.

When the noise stopped, Sho had to dig them out of their hay burial.

Tennessee yanked a rotten kernel from her hair. "Demons are so stupid! I'll be finding straw in my hair for days."

Sho tugged Tennessee up again, practically tossing her into Riggy's passenger seat. "Stay down!"

He rushed to the driver's side as a demon-infused teen hulk lunged at him.

Sho's roundhouse to the demon teen's gut and uppercut to the jaw bought just enough time for Tennessee to grab one of the spiked fence posts they still had in the back from yesterday's

scavenge. It was difficult; with numbing hands, she fumbled to get a firm grasp on the post.

Sho turned to check Tennessee; the demon teen got a good kick in, knocking him onto Riggy's hood; a stream of blood dripped from Sho's eyebrow, oozing onto Riggy's windshield.

Tennessee sprung from her seat, post in hand as the demon rounded Riggy.

Sho back-rolled onto Riggy's roof, performed a spectacular flip dismount, landing silently next to Tennessee.

Wearing a black and red Saint James High Tritons football jersey, the demon teen only had eyes for Tennessee. "Finally, a bitch on a collar. Many are looking for you. Ha! I'll have that head long before the others arrive."

Frightened and freezing, but also furious from being called *bitch* yet again, Tennessee rounded the front bumper; if she was going to do this, she needed to channel a strong heroine; she tried to harness the badassness of She-Ra or Wonder Woman (without the corset), but her mind kept jumping back to Penny from *Inspector Gadget*, probably because Penny always had her brilliant dog, Brain, by her side. She'd have Polar by her side again, no matter what it took. Hell, Penny was the bravest ten-year-old she knew, and nice too! Tennessee went with it.

"You steal that jersey? Tritons cut you, huh. Yeah, they did, poor wannabe QB." She tightened her grip on the fence post.

"Bitch, you don't know shit! What kind of wrangler comes to a demon dance with a post?"

"A Mortician."

"A *dead*, bitch mortician."

"Name's *Tennessee England*." She twirled the post in a figure eight, exactly how Godzilla taught her. "So, what's your sorry ass nickname?" Okay, Penny wouldn't say *ass*, but She-Ra would, if she weren't a Saturday morning cartoon. "Because *I'm* nice, and *not* a mean ol' demon, I'll just call you *Benchwarmer*."

"Bitch! I'm first string!" The hulky demon teen ground his teeth

into a shriek. He squatted low, springing up onto Riggy's hood with spectacular speed.

Tennessee jabbed at the teen, just missing a solid stab to its ribs.

A squealing snicker. "*That's* starting speed! No one can outrun this body. That's why I chose it. Fast and agile. I'll take that head and hand it to Lord Ibrahim himself."

The demon-infused teen was getting ahead of itself. And Tennessee told him so. "You're outnumbered, you idiot. And get your stinky hooves off my ride!"

The snickering slowed as the demon stalked its prey, angling himself to better take that head. "We are also two. This boy's dirty soul gives me strength."

Twirling the post between herself and the demon boy, Tennessee saw an opening; she shot a quick glance at Sho. He dipped his head, and she should have lunged that post into the demon's gut. But she hesitated. The demon leapt off Riggy's hood. Sho tackled it midair; but the beast got a grip on Tennessee's ankle. She plonked to her butt.

Sho wrestled the demon, exposing its back for the taking.

Another perfect opening; Tennessee took it, whacking the iron post across its shoulder blades.

It thrashed and seized and cried out in rage.

Sho kicked the beast. It stumbled face-first to dirt.

Tennessee got to her feet, corralling the demon with a slow and steady stalk. She watched the demon maneuvering on the ground, its head slightly arched back. It was weird until Tennessee remembered poker night with the boys.

This demon had a tell.

Its odd cowering was protecting a weakness. A flaw.

"Hold it down," Tennessee ordered Sho. As he held the demon face down in dirt, Tennessee jammed her boot against the back of its head. There it was, a mark right on the base of its spine: a red, raised, rectangular scar, about an inch in size.

Sho bowed his head. "You have good instincts. You sensed where the demon has entered. Ibrahim has chosen the spine."

"This is where it got in?" Tennessee craned her head to one side. "If you squint, it kinda looks like an *enter here* latch...sick bastards."

"Use the iron," Sho instructed calmly. "Put it to the mark and extract the demon." Sho's eyes narrowed as Tennessee's breath cooled the night air, and a sheet of ice formed where her hands touched the iron post. "Ten."

"I know," she breathed and ice crackled on her lips. "Demons are *watching*..." Tennessee held the post with both hands as if readying to drive the iron straight into the ground; she paused, this wasn't like staking a GARAGE SALE sign in her front yard. Then her hands numbed, and she recalled the scourge of demons hidden in the dark, no doubt assessing her grit.

"You wanna watch, you bastards?" Tennessee raised the iron post overhead. "Watch *this*!"

One swift thrust and she pierced the demon's latch.

A surge of darkness roiled to a sulfuric boil of a hundred rotten eggs; the pungent stench drained from the latch, oozing out of the boy as if being sucked up into the iron post. The aroma of fresh decay leeched into the air around Tennessee. She almost gagged.

A whirring screech encircled Riggy, emanating from deep in the wheat and weeds; a tortured cry rumbled the earth beneath their feet, vibrating Riggy's loose hood, growing louder, more terrifying as Tennessee's weapon burned so hot it glowed white. Though her hands were shaking, she didn't let go. The heat warmed her hands like toasty wool mittens after a swift winter walk.

When the sulfuric stench subsided, Tennessee dislodged the iron from the boy's neck with a look of desperate guilt.

Sho still kneeled beside the fallen lineman, his gaze on the boy's broken latch. He ran his fingers over the wound. "You did well, Ten. The demon is safely trapped in the iron."

"I just killed a kid, Sho. Please stop talking."

Tennessee chucked her demon-infused post into Riggy, sliding

in after; she was about to start crying when the dead boy groaned. Her hands froze, and a vibrating moan shook the world.

And then Sho was yelling at *her*,

"Move! We've got to move!" He lifted the boy into his arms and practically threw him on the scavenged iron in the back of Riggy.

"I severed his spine. No way he's still alive!" Tennessee freaked for a second; *now* wasn't the time.

She revved the engine as the earth rippled and rolled beneath Riggy's wheels. They careened left, right. She gunned it, skidding burnt rubber across the parking lot, seesawing as the ground heaved to that sinister shrill; Riggy found a groove and off they went, leaving the evil flock to suck their demon-wrangling dust.

~

"Not bad, *Tennessee England*, mortician." Sho clasped Tennessee's hand. Her warm, steady pulse told him two things: she wasn't in shock and the demons weren't following them.

"No fair teasing." Tennessee eased off the gas, slowing to five miles over the limit. "Give me a minute to come up with a decent catchphrase. I had nothing but cartoons in my head. Damn."

Sho's sanguine expression proved he was proud of her, with or without a decent catchphrase.

Tennessee adjusted the rearview mirror to keep an eye on their cargo. The boy was groggy, muttering about being hazed by the football team, forced to sleep outside and eat greasy burgers.

"Hey, kid, you know Johnny Cain?" Tennessee eyed the boy.

He nodded, turning a pasty pale. When his hand flew over his mouth, Tennessee jerked the wheel, skidding onto the shoulder,

"You puke in my ride, kid, and I'll kill you *again*!" She hopped out, ran to the back, grabbed the kid by the collar, and tossed him out.

The amount that boy puked even had Sho holding his gut and turning away.

"I need a smoke." Tennessee patted her pockets. Nothing. She rummaged through Riggy, eventually finding one cig in a

crumpled pack under the passenger seat. She lit up, sat cross-legged on Riggy's hood.

The boy was still hurling, making disgusting hurling noises.

Her gaze found the little dipper. "They have stars where you're from, Sho?"

Sho leaned on Riggy, "If you count luminous souls overhead as *stars*, then yes."

"Whoa." She struggled to comprehend such a wondrous world. She handed Sho the cig, watching him take a long drag before saying, "Can I visit?"

Sho moved in real close, gently placing the cig between her lips. "Where do you think we met?"

Those emperor eyes took her breath. "Great," she puffed and coughed, cig dangling from her moist lips, "I don't even know my own backstory." Sho's rumbly laugh doused her in goose bumps, the pleasurable kind.

Sho checked on the boy; he had hurled himself into a pile on his knees. And he was crying.

"Ah, man." Tennessee hopped off the hood. "Do they *all* cry?" She snatched a water bottle from the backseat. "That's gonna suck."

"The extraction is disorienting." Sho watched the boy sob. "He *does* seem particularly disturbed."

Tennessee set the bottled water on the dirt next to the boy. She even opened it. The boy gawked up at her, a mess in a puddle. He guzzled the entire bottle as she asked, "What's your name?"

"Henry."

"Okay, Henry. You're safe now. So, you knew Johnny." Tennessee needed answers, fast.

"He was my best friend."

"I'm sorry to have to tell you this, but Johnny's dead."

The boy nodded, still pasty and pale. "Yes, ma'am. I was there when they killed him." He burst into a sniveling, snuffling story. There were too many splotches in his memory to fully grasp the *whos* and *whys*, but he adequately supplied the *when* and *how*.

It all started at a drunken tailgate party, end of January. The entire high school offensive line partied until they blacked out. That was typical for a tailgate; the weird part came when they woke up. Hung over, but sober enough, the linemen found themselves stuffed in a shack, shackled at the hands and ankles, the scent of burning garbage wafting in from holes in the cracked wood. They couldn't break the chains, so they waited. For days they waited until, one by one, they turned on each other to get whatever food and drink their captives tossed in.

"When Taylor let loose on Johnny, they came in and took Taylor."

"Who came in?"

"A man wearing a black hood and farmer overalls."

Tennessee glared at Sho. Maybe Stumpy was something after all.

"Me and Johnny were the last ones left in the shack. We didn't have much water left and...Johnny needed it, but I was so thirsty. Shit, I'm sorry Johnny. I'm sorry, man!"

Tennessee understood Henry's guilt, but refused his burden. He could see a shrink like everyone else. "You happen to see a big white dog?" She focused on Polar because poor Johnny's murder wrenched her raw.

"No ma'am," he snuffled.

She pressed on; she still had Polar to find, dammit. "So, they took you out and left Johnny. That about right?"

He was sniveling again. "I overheard them saying he wasn't gonna break. But he'd seen too much so they were gonna take care of him. Make it look like an accident."

"He drank and he was a bad driver, so no questions asked..." Tennessee took a knee, looking the boy in the eye. "Your linemen, they were with you back there?"

"I think so...and others...but I can't remember..."

"Name your master." Sho's grisly tone had Tennessee shuddering.

"My *what*? Did you say...who the hell are you people?"

"The people who just saved your sorry ass." Tennessee nudged the boy's leg with the steel tip of her boot. "Answer the nice man, before he's not so nice anymore."

"I don't know!" the boy sniveled. "My head hurts! It's like when you wake up from a shitty nightmare and you're trying to remember what got you to piss your pants but the more you try the more it doesn't make any sense..."

Tennessee recoiled. "You still wet the bed? Man, kid, that's pitiful."

Sho helped the boy up, propped him upright in Riggy's passenger seat while Tennessee laid down the law with poor, sniveling Henry,

"You piss in my ride and it's back to the shack for you."

"The longer the demon is out," Sho offered grimly, "the less the vessel recalls. We're lucky to know this much."

"So, he's worthless now?"

"For *information*, it would seem."

"Is it what I think? Because what I think is some seriously sicko evil shit, and *please* tell me they can't make dogs demons..."

Sho grew solemn.

Tennessee clenched her teeth. "Wonderful. Stumpy's torturing stupid kids so demons can jump in their sphere and possess them. That right?"

"You'll stop him." Sho roughly touched Tennessee's face. Yeah, she still liked that.

"Like I need more shit to do." She stomped toward Riggy. "If Stumpy's got Polar *and* a lineman army, we're gonna need more than a pile of posts. Good thing I know a guy. One more stop, Sho, then The Mirror. If Lillie's full demon bitch by now we gotta get the twins far away from her, and I don't give a rat's ass what William has to say about it!"

"Rat's ass?" Sho flashed a quizzical grimace.

"That's right...a *fat rat's ass*! And that's *me* talking!"

~

Inland, on the outskirts of Saint James, there lived a modern-

day renaissance man. Went by the name Jasper, but Tennessee always called him Casper, the friendly blacksmith. They had a thing, forever ago; it was good, never went bad. Those kids simply grew up. Tennessee started college locally and Jasper went far away, studying the art of metalworking on several continents; he'd always had a thing for iron.

She had heard rumors that he'd moved back to town in January after buying the Longhorn farm. She took a gamble that town gossip got it right, otherwise it was time and gas wasted. Phillip didn't know about Jasper. She pondered such secrets now, driving out to Jasper's rumored farm-turned-forge.

If Jasper was where she hoped he would be, she'd have her go-to guy for anything iron. *One* problem solved.

Henry fidgeted to find a comfortable position on top of all that iron.

"Am I in a hearse? Man, that's tight!" He was acting less like a demonic puppet, more like a meathead, which was probably closer to the real Henry.

Tennessee caught his eye in the rearview mirror, sassed back, "Yeah, totally radical, man. You can get the body...it's our next stop." Henry's shock told her he was a lightweight; she'd have to keep the demon talk on the down low. "Your parents worried about you?"

"Nah, I come and go."

"Well, think about *where* you're goin' after this, all right."

Henry was thinking real hard when Tennessee pulled down a cobbled lane lined with stately oaks. Winter thinned out the overhead canopy that would shade the lane through spring and summer. But she preferred the sparse, sickly look of the coastal oaks; they resembled wiry old sentinels, guarding Jasper's metalworking magic. Yeah, Jasper brought out the macabre poet in her.

Forging iron was his love, but he worked other metals; anything he could heat and hammer.

As Tennessee maneuvered around the circular drive dotted

with wrought-iron streetlamps and intricate sculptures, she locked eyes with a brawny, bearded man, not quite six feet, blazing autumn eyes framed in rich ebony; he wore flannel, jeans, cowboy boots, and a work-worn leather apron.

Tennessee rolled down her window, addressing her friend as if no time had passed. "I give it six months and you bolt. Town's always been too quiet for you."

"Tennessee England." Jasper leaned in the window, bursting Tennessee's personal bubble; he didn't have a *zone* with her. "Isn't it past your bedtime?" His tone was all baritone and brass, his keen eyes aflame.

"I see you're still up with the owls, sledging through the night."

Jasper tapped the tip of Tennessee's nose. "You're the only one who refers to it like that."

Sho's hand fell hard on hers now, and she watched Jasper's gaze drop precisely when Sho's grip tightened. When Jasper's gaze once again found hers, he smiled. He wasn't a big smiler, but smiles came easy tonight. Soon, he shifted his discerning gaze from Sho to Henry to the heap of iron.

"For me?" He opened Tennessee's door.

Tennessee slid out, walking into Jasper's open arms.

"I'm gritty," he said.

"I'm dusty," she said.

"Just like old times then." He picked a sliver of hay from her hair.

Tennessee nearly disappeared in Jasper's burly embrace. When he released her, she ran her fingers through his curly beard, stalling on a fresh patch of white glimmering in the lamplight.

"You got old," she teased.

Jasper chuckled, lifting her chin. "You didn't." He brushed frizz from her face. "How's that thick skull of yours?"

"Ah," she scrunched her nose, "not as thick."

He tugged her back into a long embrace, his hands caressing the nape of her neck. He whispered in her ear,

"Your boyfriend thinks I'm trying to seduce you."

"*I* think you're trying to seduce me." She pulled away to meet his eye, but leaving his embrace was way more difficult than it should have been.

"You come to me wearing this..." Jasper hooked Tennessee's cross between his beefy fingers, "you're *absolutely* trying to seduce me."

He had made the gift especially for her eighteenth birthday—just after proposing, just after she said *yes*.

Fidgeting from the heft of such memories, she quipped, "Not with an audience, I'm not."

Jasper released her with a salty grin, stepping back as Sho stepped to Tennessee's side. "Now who's *old*, Tennessee."

It had been a long time since he'd said her name in that tone. Jasper called her Tennessee *all* the time. He said there was power in a name, and he wouldn't dare tamper with hers. He was always saying things like that. Jasper the Poet.

While Tennessee's mind's eye flooded with youthful escapades, Jasper introduced himself to Sho as Tennessee's greatest regret.

Sho looked pleased by that, but offered a civil, "Sorry to hear that."

Tennessee grabbed Sho's arm, knowing full well that Jasper meant something entirely different. They were each other's *the one that got away*. And that's how they liked it. Jasper called it their poetry. He was a renaissance man, after all. Funneling that angst into his art made him a very wealthy man.

"This your dream forge?" Tennessee examined the rundown barn behind Jasper.

"Will be."

"It's..."

"A fixer-upper." He scrutinized his most recent investment. "It's got great bones, Tennessee. Come on." Jasper grabbed her free hand, coaxing her away from Sho with an easy directive for the man. "Why don't you and the boy bring in my iron...that's no job for my lady."

For a bewildering moment, Tennessee was holding hands with both men.

Although Sho released first without complaint, she saw the struggle in his set jaw, and the samurai in his patient gaze.

Tennessee glanced over her shoulder. "Thank you, Sho."

Then they started counting.

At forty-two feet, she found the aged barn door of extreme interest and got Jasper talking about restoring it until Sho and Henry muscled in the iron manhole and some posts.

"Just leave the *one*." Tennessee eyed Sho.

Sho bowed his head as he walked by her. "I set aside your favorite. It'll look great in *our* garden."

Even Henry caught the tinge of possession in Sho's casual comment.

This was exactly why she'd never mentioned Jasper to any of her boyfriends (real or pretend); Jasper had a way of instantly sending other men into a spiral of jealousy. Maybe it was all the man-ness he exuded. Tennessee watched Jasper now...*yes*, it was definitely all that man-ness...

"That corner is fine...there...yeah, that'll do." Jasper pointed out the only empty spot in the barn, then went about escorting Tennessee around the expansive, scrap-crammed space. Jasper the blacksmith had big plans for the place.

The compact brick forge was only phase one. He showed Tennessee the makings of a much larger forge for his more ambitious projects. They passed his workstation, overrun with tools of his trade: tongs, hammers, punches, chisels, and enough scrap metal for two lifetimes. Her eye caught a pile of half-done projects. It wasn't like him to leave things unfinished. She had a sense Jasper's life had become far more complicated than he let on.

He kept the tour going, and she kept her concerns holstered. The man collected anvils in every size, piled them below his elegant metalwork showcased on an entire barn wall. He forged the old way, learned the art without modernization in mind.

But the barn had electricity, and when Jasper breezed by gas tanks and torches, Tennessee teased, "*Welding* is awfully modern." When she spied the industrial belt grinder, she let loose, "Oh, the horror, you're letting a *machine* sharpen your blades? You've gone soft, my man...never thought I'd see the day...Casper the soulless blacksmith."

A sly squint tempered Jasper's defensive comeback. "All my *art* is hammer and anvil...but some commissions do require more modern techniques to make deadline." He was disappointed in himself, so Tennessee stopped after *one* "I told you so."

By the scrap piles, she knew Jasper was still collecting steel. He salvaged all sorts of metals, but mostly iron. It was comforting for her, being in the middle of all that iron. And the barn was covered in iron shavings. She almost crouched down to collect them; she might be taking this iron thing a little too far.

Jasper still had hay bales and troughs to clear out; there was even a combine to deal with. It had been a working farm up until a year ago when the owners died.

"Did you?" Jasper laid his hand right between Tennessee's shoulder blades, his gaze intent on her as she spoke. He had a way about him. *Really* paying attention.

"The Longhorns, yes...they died within hours of one another. Their only wish was to be cremated together...uh, you know, their ashes are in your back forty."

Jasper surveyed the rafters. "Would you believe me if I told you they're still here, looking after the place?"

"That's crazy." Tennessee choked on a panicky giggle. Hell yeah, she believed in a pair of octogenarian ghosts! It took everything *not* to tell Jasper she had a demon trapped in an iron post out in Riggy.

He took it the wrong way, brushed off the hauntings as a bad joke. "So, what's the deal, Tennessee? Only bad girls come bearing all this iron at this hour."

Tennessee's ability to lie was a touch better now that she *had* to, but it wasn't going to fool Jasper. "Well, Jasper, I'm..."

"You must be in deep shit if you're calling me Jasper." He lifted her chin again, forcing her wandering gaze on him. "You're scared. Does this have anything to do with your new, insecure guy over there? What happened to your doctor?"

"He's not *my* doctor." Tennessee swiveled free, shifting her attention back to Sho and Henry. Sho had Henry doing all the work now, while he stood guard by the barn door, giving her a full forty-eight feet. "I mean, technically he's my doctor, but we haven't been...I think he's...I'm..."

"You're trying *not* to lie to me, Tennessee," Jasper asserted with a shrewd grin. "You still blather when you lie."

"I just can't tell you right now, okay," she clasped Jasper's hand, "but I need your help all the same."

"If you're in trouble, I'm your guy. But how the hell can I help if I don't know squat?"

"You *can* help. I kinda need you to make me something...some iron tools...real specific to my job."

"At the shop?" A mortician needing hand-wrought iron tools perplexed the man.

"Well," she fiddled with his fingers, thinking of a good lie, "it's a sideline thing..."

Jasper gently squeezed her fingers. "I'd rather you not lie, Tennessee. It's enough to know that you *want* to tell me the truth. You have specs for these *tools*?"

"Mainly I need them to be sharp."

"Sharp?" he asked warily.

"Yeah, like real pointy." She bit her lip; great, that didn't sound psychopathic at all.

"*Sharp* and *pointy*. Easy enough."

"And light because I need to be able to...you know...uh...wield it and stuff..."

Jasper was staring at Sho now.

Tennessee spun around and confirmed that Sho was staring right back at Jasper.

"Cool it, boys." She gripped her hips. "This is a business transaction. We can all play nice-nice."

"What's he gotten you into, Tennessee?" Jasper took steps toward Sho.

Sho took steps toward Jasper.

Tennessee puffed up her cheeks. "I need a smoke."

"Whoa, I thought we quit."

Tennessee patted her pockets. "Shit, I'm out."

"Whoa, since when do you say *shit?*"

"You say *shit.*"

Jasper turned on Sho. "Hey, you need to take better care of my girl...smoking *and* cussing? She's better than all that. Always has been."

Sho chuckled, barely raised his rasp to say, "She is in much better hands *now* than she has been in the past."

"Wow," Tennessee flashed both men a disgusted scowl, "this is not misogynistic at all." She stormed out of the barn and was headed toward Riggy when she stopped cold. "Sho. Casper...guys! We've got a...*situation.*"

Sho was at Tennessee's side, gripping her chilled hand. Jasper ran out after, more perplexed than ever. He arched a mean brow,

"Why's that boy licking a post?"

Tennessee wished she could answer that excellent question. Why Henry was standing right in the open licking the demon-infested post was beyond her wildest imaginings of common demonic behavior.

Sho whispered, "It calls to him. We have to cleanse the iron."

"How the hell do we cleanse iron?" Tennessee forgot to whisper.

Jasper's confusion eased into a knowing grin. "We burn it, melt it down, make it into one of these." He ran a finger across Tennessee's silver chain until her cross slipped into the crook of his finger. "Only way to get the unholy shit out of an object." His grin slanted wicked.

The samurai nodded to the blacksmith, and the blacksmith nodded to the samurai.

A rowdy scuffle and the men extracted the iron post from Henry; it clanged to the ground in a clobbering of its own. Poor Henry was having a very bad day. He lay sprawled out on the cobblestone path, a confused heap of meathead, his two bruised and blackened eyes welling over.

Tennessee picked up the post; caught a whiff of demon stench as she twirled it like she'd been twirling demon-infused iron all her life.

"Light your forge, Casper." Tennessee sauntered into the barn. "We've got some unholy shit to burn."

# 14.

# Giant Problems

Forging the old-fashioned way takes time, the kind of time rookie wranglers don't have. As Jasper stoked the tidy fire he had blazing in his forge, Tennessee paced. The neatly constructed brick stove had a peekaboo chimney piping smoke out the side of the old barn. It was the exact forge Jasper dreamed of having. Tennessee settled down a little, thinking of the past; at least someone's dreams had come true.

Once Jasper fired up his melting furnace and set a large crucible inside the barrel, Tennessee's breathing was back to normal.

With the furnace heating up, Jasper searched the barn for a suitable mold.

"You're in luck, Tennessee." He slid a four-foot-tall cross mold next to the furnace. "The sweetest church lady commissioned a bunch of these last year."

She flashed a rueful grin; he was always all in when it came to her schemes and adventures, but this wasn't skipping class to camp on the beach. This was different; this was dangerous.

Sho was busy tying up the boy.

"Ouch!" Henry cried out, then he started sobbing. "Please, just take me home...I promise I'll be good."

"Relax, kid." Tennessee patted the boy's head. "It's just so you

don't hurt *yourself*. We're the good guys. I promise, once we're done here we'll take you home."

Sho secured a knot, then he escorted Henry to Riggy; said it was necessary until the link was broken. Jasper didn't appear to be paying too much attention to their conversation, but Tennessee knew he was. Jasper was a smart man, but beyond that he was a believer in all things unseen; part of the reason she called him Casper.

So when she met his eye to hand him the demon-infused fence post, there was a hint of an *I told you so* in there. But there was also worry, and when he took the post from her, he drew her close and kissed her tangled mane. It was everything she needed.

Jasper got to cutting down the post. It broke down just fine, but when he started feeding the pieces to the crimson crucible inside the furnace, things got weird. It started with an ominous hum deep in the pit of the blaze, then the furnace vibrated, slowly at first; rapidly shuddering to a rowdy jostle that had Jasper working pretty damn hard to steady the barrel with monster-sized metal tongs.

"Tennessee," Jasper muttered out, straining to steady the furnace, "toss in the last piece, but use the..." He was going to say leather gloves, but Tennessee already had them on. He smirked. "How's Audrey II?"

"Could use a tune-up." Tennessee held the chunk of iron over the furnace; the flames lashed out at her, and a shrieking shatter seemed to turn that chunk of iron in her hand flaming cherry-red. She should have tossed the chunk in, but she didn't.

Jasper's complete disbelief was evident by his hollers for her to drop the iron before she burned.

Sho flanked her side, in deep concentration, as the chunk blazed a snowball white, catching her glove on fire.

Tennessee shook off the glove, tossing the blistering chunk into her other leathered hand; after *that* glove caught fire, she dropped the blazing chunk into her bare hand, shaking free from her second flaming glove.

To Jasper's horrifying yells, Tennessee cupped her hands together, pooling molten iron into a bright orange puddle. Entering a trancelike state, she poured the last of the demon into the furnace, and as she spoke, her natural voice echoed unnaturally.

"In Empress Zaada's name, I banish you! Let it be known, this is *my* dominion, where *I* reign!"

A rattle, whir, and whine, and the furnace settled to still; Jasper released his death grip on his monster tong. He stared at Tennessee. Clearly, she was far more than the young lady he'd dated in high school. Pride was the overriding emotion, and respect.

Because she was freaked out by what she had said—all that dominion stuff sounded more like Zaada—Tennessee followed her demon wrangling promise with the Lord's prayer. Then she dusted dried soot from her hands, crossed herself, and meant it. The Englands were a devoutly religious family, and while Tennessee didn't practice many Catholic rituals anymore, she believed deeply in *something*. The prayers she was taught as a child seemed to be working, so she stuck with what she knew until she learned something new.

Sho took Tennessee's hands into his, methodically cleaning them with the front of his shirt; then with a deep bow, he kissed each palm; the heat of his breath warming the frozen tips of her pinkies.

Jasper watched this exchange while preparing to remove the crucible from the furnace. With a long iron bar, he lifted the crucible out and set it on a concrete slab. From there, he grabbed a rusted set of tongs and clasped the side of the crucible. He poured the molten iron into the cross mold to the gloomy sounds of Tennessee reciting the same protection prayer she learned from her grandmother; the secret one; the one forbidden from being spoken aloud or anywhere near church.

Jasper set his tools aside, shook off his gloves, and sat on a pile of wood. He didn't look concerned for himself, though there may

have been a bit of that; but Tennessee was so tiny and already in fragile health; now she was caught up in something truly dangerous, and damn spooky.

“That was some crazy shit.” Jasper ran his hand through his beard.

Tennessee whispered to Sho, “And Benchwarmer was just a rookie. Don’t ask me how I know. I just do.”

Jasper pulled a pack of reds from his back pocket, tossed the pack to Tennessee.

She snarled, turning to Sho. “He cheats at poker too.”

“Only strip poker.” Jasper was staring at Tennessee’s perfectly unscorched hands. She let him, lit up, then tossed him the pack. She handed the cig to Sho. But he waved her off, his tight gaze on the iron cooling in the cross mold.

Tennessee’s cell phone rang out “Why.” Jasper was calming down with a smoke and Sho was distracted, so she answered the call; but she walked forty-nine feet from the men before she started talking.

“What now?”

“Where are you?” Phillip’s voice sounded weird, more harassed than his usual harassed.

“Uh...you know...we’re just...blacksmithing and stuff...um, at...the Longhorns...” She was trying *not* to scream, “I just wrangled a demon! And now we’re melting the bastard into a cross to make goddamn sure *it* doesn’t possess another meathead.” She got out another string of ums and uhs.

“Now’s not the time for a date night, Tenny!”

“Uh,” she cursed *a lot* in her head, “yeah, because blacksmithing screams *date night*. Wow, Phillip.”

“Have you found Polar?”

“No.” Her breath hitched on hope. “Have you?”

“No, but I might have a lead. I need you at Lil’s! The twins...”

A crash.

“Phillip?

Silence.

Phillip!"

Sho was already by her side. "Tell me."

"The twins!" She spun toward Jasper. "I'm sorry to dump this on you, but we've gotta..."

"Go." Jasper tossed his cig in the dirt, smashed it with his boot. "I've got this." He walked toward the barn door, ducking behind a stack of hay. "Take these, I sharpened the ends to stake in the ground, but I haven't designed the tops yet...another commissioned project...ah, consider it a homecoming gift...every girl needs a set of spears, right?"

"Homecoming? I haven't had a vacation in seven years, man. I've been nowhere but *home*..."

Jasper stepped from the shadows, carrying a dozen four-foot wrought iron stakes, lighter and more user-friendly than her fence posts. "You're home *now*...ain't that right, Sho?" Jasper shoved the stakes at Sho with a quick wink at Tennessee.

Finally, he approved of her *boyfriend*.

Sho bowed graciously before heading toward Riggy.

Tennessee gave Jasper a long hug. "I'm sorry I dragged you into this."

"Nonsense." Jasper kissed her messy mane again. "Best night I've had in years."

"Promise me you'll watch your back."

He chuckled. "I got a feeling that's why *you're* here, love."

His weighty gaze had a way of whittling her away. She needed to hurry, but he needed *something*, so she divulged what she could, "They took my dog."

"Hellfire and brimstone." Jasper scowled with pride. "I pity the fool!"

Tennessee laughed. Only Jasper could pull off a solid Mr. T impersonation without sounding cheesy. She hopped in Riggy, revved the engine, and peeled out with a quick wave to Casper, the friendly blacksmith.

~

Tennessee raced back into town; something was happening at

The Mirror, and a call from Phillip was *always* a bad omen. Ditching Henry would have to wait.

Sho protested; he didn't want another witness. Involving Jasper was unfortunate, but unavoidable.

"He's asleep, Sho," Tennessee scoffed. "Untie the meathead and we'll call him a cab from The Mirror. All right? I don't want another witness, but I *really* don't want the kid hurt."

"You are right." Sho went to touch Tennessee's shoulder, changed his mind.

After everything they'd been through, why censor his emotions now? Curious, she tried to catch his eye, but the road was winding, and he kept his gaze fixed out his side window. It wasn't going to work like this. Tennessee reached over, gathering Sho's hand into hers. She didn't say anything, kept her gaze on the road.

In time, Sho returned the sentiment with an affectionate squeeze.

She worried that maybe he was different with her because of Jasper, but then he said, "You might lose someone you care for tonight."

He let that sink in.

When her breathing fell back in line with his, he continued, "Unlike possessions, wrangling favorites is *problematic*. The demon jumps in and out. If you wrangle her while the demon is *out*...Ten, I can mend a broken latch, but," his eyes fell to their clasped hands, "I cannot resurrect the dead."

Tennessee reclaimed her other hand to better handle the slick road. It was only sprinkling, but murky clouds condemned the sky; a heavy rain was coming.

"The dead stay dead," she grumbled. "I'm good with that."

A busted-up guardrail and line of headless trees marked the location where Tennessee was shot. She let up on the gas.

"That's where Zaada tethered us..."

Sho hardly glimpsed the spot as Tennessee sped on.

She crinkled her nose into a quirky smirk. "Not the sentimental type, huh?"

Sho's gaze found Tennessee, then wandered back out his window. "*Once*."

"Ooo, I had something to do with that *once* business, huh?"

Sho anxiously glanced at her, a glimmer of desperation marring his emperor eyes. "We have known one another a long time. Your knowledge of *me* broke rules. You will recollect this when the time is right. I'm sorry I could not stop Zaada from tethering you. I failed."

Tennessee grappled with a sensation she hadn't considered possible given her circumstance. The tether gave her Sho, and she already couldn't imagine being without him.

"Remind me to thank her." She damn near hydroplaned around Scraggle Bluff's most notorious death-drop curve.

Sho's softened gaze was on her now, but she left all that tethering business alone; she didn't like lingering in the past any more than Sho.

Wispy winter rain splattered water blots on Riggy's frosty windshield; his wipers slowed to a slosh of screechy streaks as Tennessee zoomed past the wide-open gates.

Phillip must have done that. She *hoped* it was Phillip.

"*That's* what you meant by The Mirror." Sho surveyed the teetering glass house; illuminated from within and made sparkly by moonlit rain, it could have been a beacon luring lost travelers home.

Tennessee grabbed a sharpened iron spear. If she *had to* kill Lillie she'd lure her out, away from her family. They were on a cliff; *anything* could happen. Tennessee jumped out into the rain, catching a fleeting sulfuric scent; she was expecting instant frostbite, but got a dousing of hot water instead.

"Damn, the rain's *hot*!"

"No, Ten." Sho grabbed a stake and was by her side. "You're *cold*."

The wind rustled trees and the ocean thrashed. "Shoot," Tennessee shouted over the thundery ruckus, "you'd better grab more iron then!"

Sho did as ordered, easily catching up to Tennessee. The front double doors were wide open, and windswept rain puddled Lillie's favorite tile. Buster the butler would not be pleased. He was nowhere in sight.

Nobody was.

Terrible, wild things churned through her mind. But she plowed forward, running straight through the foyer swamp without slipping once.

A loud, slow clapping challenged the thunderous night.

Tennessee slid to a stop, crashing into William's grand piano. Sho skated the water masterfully, gliding to a graceful stop between Tennessee and someone clapping in the living room.

Vigilantly, they entered the vaulted room.

"Phillip?" Tennessee observed the man relaxing in William's leather chair. Even though he was wearing Phillip's favorite three-piece suit, he didn't *look* like her Phillip. This man's pleasure didn't crinkle the corners of his eyes, and his smirk was cocky. The room was all wrong too; someone bunched all the furniture into a barricade, leaving two couches facing Phillip's chair.

Phillip stopped clapping as he pulled a vintage silver timepiece from his vest pocket; light caught the watch face, splashing a peculiar metallic sheen of elaborate speckles and spots across the vaulted ceiling. The swirling show reminded Tennessee of snowflakes, each unique in their gear-like shapes.

Phillip pressed the top button with his thumb. "*Twenty minutes.* If I were a betting man, I'd have lost this noteworthy wager. I had you caring far more for your dear dog, but when you didn't come I had to take *this* tragic body." Phillip stretched his arms out, delivering a crooked, cocky grin that Tennessee already hated.

Her heart thunked. Phillip was...she couldn't process it.

Sho positioned himself in front of Tennessee, holding his hand out behind him. She placed her hand in his, and only then realized that her hand was a normal temperature; not the way it had been around Lillie. Whatever *this* Phillip was, he was *not* a demon.

Tennessee and Sho shared a look; whatever had been watching them outside The Mirror was gone now.

"Takes a pair to mess with a girl's dog." Tennessee pushed past Sho, rushing toward the man who wasn't Phillip. "I never thought I could *kill* a man, but looking at you, yeah, I *can*."

Phillip didn't like that at all, but he kept his crooked grin; his ebony eyes bore through her, and a sliver of red peeked through his pupils.

"Ten." Sho flanked her left side, drawing her attention to the couches.

Tennessee kept her back away from the windows. What was it Godzilla said? *Stay nimble.*

"Please," Phillip stood up, "join *us*." Now the red stopped playing peek-a-boo and stayed put. Those eyes flamed bright when Tennessee didn't obey. "I *insist*."

Sho locked eyes on Tennessee, and that's when she saw what he'd already seen.

The four Illies were in the room, sleeping on those two couches facing Phillip. Tennessee approached, praying they were just *asleep*. The worst shuddered her heart, until Lillie's chest moved. It was a slow rise and fall, but she was alive.

Lillie lay sprawled on the sofa closest to Philip; her head resting near William's head. He was hunched on the floor, his head arched back. It didn't look right, the way his head fell on the couch. Tennessee directed Sho to sit with them. She needed to be with the twins.

The twins slouched side by side, their hands entwined, their heads bent forward in a sullen prayer. Tennessee took up the little girl's wrist closest to her, searched for a pulse. When she found it, she cursed the man who wasn't Phillip.

"If you hurt these kids, I *won't* kill you...even when you beg me to."

"Children do not amuse me." Phillip obsessively watched seconds tick away on his timepiece. "You, however, *do. Twenty minutes*," he grumbled. "You come for this man in less than half

an hour. He *must* be important to you. I've had your dog," he checked his watch again, "thirty hours, ten minutes, and sixteen seconds...seventeen...eighteen...and you did not come..."

Tennessee scowled. "Next time leave a note and I'll be there in *five*."

"Ah, but I did."

"Sorry, didn't get it."

Phillip's brow wrinkled. Tennessee had to look away. *That* was a look her Phillip did make, and she didn't want to see *her* Phillip in *this* man.

She was getting real tired of this game. "Seriously, you left me a note? Like words on paper, or is that some kind of otherworldly-demon-creepy-things code?" She glanced at Phillip, then Sho.

Braced for battle, Sho never turned his steel gaze from the madman.

"Truly, I was diligent in my penmanship. These hands lack the suppleness I am accustomed to. Despite my ransom note falling victim to treacherous hands, I can attest to Fate's benevolent charms for bringing us together in this serendipitous fashion."

"Fate?" Tennessee snapped. "You called my cell! Nothing mystical about *that*."

Phillip checked his watch again. "Time is not on our side, my plaything. You have three minutes before these souls perish."

"What have you done to them?" Tennessee stood up. "And what the hell do you want with me?"

"What have *you* done to them, *Tennessee England*, mortician is it?" Phillip's pulsing red eyes surveyed Tennessee, top to toe. It reminded her of Lillie's sanctimonious once-overs. "*Ten thousand* coin? For *that* head? I can't see it. My last ten thousand coin went for a *prince*. His sentinels alone took months to pick apart. *You* are easy prey...just a maggot."

Sho had enough. "Mind your tongue, hunter. *She* hears your insults. You are in the presence of the Empress's champion."

There was a subdued start in Phillip's demeanor, and his red eyes quickened. Hell, if she'd known calling herself the Empress's

champion would have garnered that sort of reaction, she'd have led with that.

Phillip shifted in his chair, neurotically checking his watch. "Less than *two* minutes remain." He was a cocky bastard. A Suit. She hated cocky bastard Suits. Fake Phillip was still gazing at his watch, so she slammed her iron spear on the ground, cracking Lillie's beautifully overpriced tile. Tennessee twirled the spear in her favorite figure eight; angling the weapon at Phillip, pointy end out. Striding into a fighting stance, she lifted her lip in a snarl.

"*They* die, *you* die. The end."

Phillip tried to stand, but Sho's spear was within striking distance.

"Good pooch," Phillip applauded Sho, "but times are hard...hunters must travel in packs now."

Just then, four men, all dressed like bottom-feeder bankers, all bigger than Sho, and *way* bigger than Tennessee, stepped out from the children's wing. Still, Tennessee's hands were only cool. They weren't demons, and by their red, pulsing eyes, they weren't human, either. Each man carried a weapon; two had samurai swords, one had a He-Man sword, and the runt of the bunch had a double-bladed barbarian battle-axe.

Not that Tennessee was complaining, but guns didn't seem part of this strange new world. That left the bloody stuff: gouging, slashing, dismembering. Your basic gore fest. Her stomach soured gristly-black. She handled *dead* no problem, but could she dismember someone who was *alive*? *Just imagine they're already dead*, she thought, battling her tumbling gut, *dead people don't hunt you or dismember you...think of the twins, Tennessee! They're alive. Keep them that way. And keep the dead people dead...you got this, Tennessee! You do this crap every damn day!* She took a deep breath, lowering her spear.

"You have *me*. Let this family live."

"And what of your puppy? What shall I do with him?" Phillip snapped his fingers and the He-Man of the bunch disappeared down into the hall and reappeared with Polar on the end of a

spiked leather leash; a horrific, bloodstained muzzle silencing her great white lion's roar.

"Polar," Tennessee uttered, shock shifting to fury. As Polar whined and struggled to get to her, she found herself fully capable of dismembering the living. Vengeance pumped her heart pale; she faced Phillip, the imposter. "This ends now."

"But this is rather fun." The dog-napper eyed his watch. "For *you*, my plaything, I'll gift your friends ten minutes of life." This Phillip was so busy being cocky, he didn't notice Sho's quick advance.

Sho got Phillip into a headlock, spear thrust against the chuckling man's jugular.

"You kill *me*, they die, little pooch," Phillip didn't bother defending himself. "And your lady's beloved guardian's head hangs on my wall."

Sho slit the man's throat. No hesitation, no remorse. And when Sho's spear severed spine, Phillip slumped into a heap on the tile. It was so bloody nobody noticed Sho palm the dead man's watch.

"Smaller pack, bigger cut!" the *most* giant man said. "Never liked the cocky son of a bitch."

Tennessee tried not to faint, but she wasn't breathing; she *had to* start breathing. Sho killed Phillip. Sho just *killed* Phillip!

Sho ran to her, kept her from falling.

Polar still thrashed under the giant's grip. The hunters celebrated, thanking Sho for solving that problem.

"Ten, sever the head," Sho drew her to his side. "It's effective and fast." His hand brushed her back pocket, but he was talking so fast she needed to focus on each word. "Stay on my right, no matter what. Ten!"

Sho was guiding Tennessee and the hunters *away* from the Illies. They were passing the grand piano, well into the swampy foyer, when a gust of wind blew in bitterly cold sleet.

The hunters fanned out, trying to ensnare their prey against the foyer wall. Sho wasn't having it; he backed out the front door, back into the storm.

"Outside we have a chance," Sho declared.

Tennessee stared at the bloody tile. "You killed Phillip."

"*That* was not Phillip."

"Sure as hell looked like Phillip!"

"Ten! You must focus, or the children die."

Something inside her snapped back into place. She eyed the man with the battle-axe; maybe she could take him; she wasn't confident about the giants though.

"Ten, they're *shifters*...they morph...shapeshift into whatever beings inhabit their destination. Now, focus on freeing Polar."

Sho couldn't lie. Phillip was alive, somewhere. And Polar was alive, leashed but unharmed as much as she could tell. She *had* to believe all of this, so she did.

"Fine, you get He-Man and his clones. I'll take the little one."

Tennessee quickly channeled Gadget's niece Penny and a little She-Ra, because sleet pelting her face was annoying *and* it hurt. The fake Phillip gave her ten minutes a minute ago; she needed to wrap up this hunt.

"Fantastic weather we're having!" Tennessee provoked the runt; she caught He-Man tying Polar so tightly to a tree her poor lion was wheezing for air.

The runt swung his battle-axe at the raindrops, expelling a grunting noise that sounded a lot like a hog.

"I gotcha, you're a tropical vacay guy." Tennessee kept talking as Sho kept luring. "Have you tried Fried Freddy's fish joint yet? The fish and chips are the bomb-diggity!"

The runt lifted his upper lip, exposing two enormous front teeth that tapered to a needle-tipped point; a dribble of spit accumulated at the tips, crashing to earth in a spectacular splatter that Tennessee heard despite her rapid pulse thrashing behind her temples.

"Oh, you're *vegan*!" Tennessee watched his red eye slits blink faster as he skulked closer. "Just here for our rockin' all-you-can eat salad bar?"

Sho pushed his hip against her side, keeping her slightly behind

him. "Ten, shifters aren't allied with Ibrahim or Zaada...they hunt for prized game. Many keep their kill rather than cash in the bounty."

The most giant of the shifters raised his He-Man sword overhead, swooshing it down with a gruffy laugh. "Your lapdog is right, I might keep that head. Just for the hair."

"*Really?*" Tennessee glowered at the wannabe He-Man. "A hair joke? You sure Lin didn't send you?"

"I *will* take your head in thirty seconds and this *Lin's* head by sunrise." He unleashed a reverberating growl so devastatingly deep it vibrated Tennessee's ribs, zapping her with evil shivers.

She glanced at Sho; he seemed unaffected. Any louder, and Tennessee feared her heart might burst from his sonic gnarr. She was grumbling about the shifters' obsession with time when movement near Riggy caught her eye; it was getting harder to see through the constant fluctuation of sleet and rain, but she was confident it was Henry running away from the men with swords.

Sho followed her gaze then went on the offensive. While the shifters watched Henry scamper, slip, fall, get up, fall, scamper, Sho hurled his spear at the closest samurai-sword-wielding shifter. The iron pierced the man's head; dead center.

The giant fell, his sword sloshing on the lawn. The three remaining shifters scattered back. And Polar's wheezing worsened as he squirmed to free himself; he'd risk death to save his master.

"It's okay, boy!" Tennessee hollered over the gusting chill. "I'm on my way!"

Sho leapt toward the wayward sword, curling up midair, executing a graceful forward roll. He was soundless, effortless. Sho claimed the sword, and Tennessee watched a satisfied smirk strengthen his gaze. As he swished his new toy side to side, feeling its weight, the shifters congratulated each other on a higher bounty. They split up, the runt guarding their trophy; the other two would take Sho; maybe he'd fetch them a bonus.

"Let's go, Chinaman," He-Man hollered, and that gnarr had Tennessee's heart adding beats.

She wondered if these creatures saw what she saw. The way Sho held his sword was terrifying. It seemed already a part of him, a seamless extension of his will. It was a feather in his hands—a poisoned-tipped feather. Sho raised his sword up near his right shoulder, pulling it level with the ground; his ready focus, a beautifully sinister invitation.

He-Man and the wannabe samurai attacked.

That left the runt for her.

Maybe she should throw the spear too; it *was* in her blood—her ancestors chucked spears and threw damn accurate sling stones. No, she'd have to be creative; this guy was the runt, but he still towered over her; hell, he would tower over Godzilla!

She stalked left and right; the runt stalked left and right, wielding his battle-axe more like a berserker than a barbarian. After this juvenile display, he let out a battle cry; not the painful gnarr of He-Man, more of a tantrum, a whine.

"Ah, big boys *do* cry," Tennessee tried shame; it always worked on insecure little boys.

The runt stepped up his game, trying out a big boy growl. It fell short, but Tennessee had to admit it did rumble her ribs, only the floating ones.

He was only supposed to *guard* her. One look at those blinking eye slits and Tennessee knew he had other plans. While not *smart*, this one could count. If he took her head and ran, he'd get it all.

"Out for glory, huh?" Tennessee hunted the shifter, keeping the sharp end of her spear aimed at the runt's pointy teeth. "Yeah, I could use a little glory too." She smirked. "I have this desperate little bare spot on my wall...your ugly mug will make the perfect conversation starter."

"You talk too much!" The runt swung his axe, stomped forward, swung again.

Tennessee had to duck on the last one, but when she came

up, her boot slipped in the mud; she plonked on her butt; sleet clouded her vision then something whacked her across the face.

What? Really? A slap? How insulting!

A *you're nothing* battle slap was *way* worse than being called a bitch!

Tennessee couldn't see clearly, but she could hear the runt's weak snarl at her left and farther off, Polar's choked whine. Gripping her spear, she jerked her body into a fierce twist, cracking the runt's knees. He splatted face first in a glop of mud. His howl was much better, and Tennessee told him so. She jumped to her feet, but instead of getting distance or finishing him, she couldn't resist the urge for vengeance.

Tennessee slapped him.

Then she ran.

She glanced over her shoulder; a silver studded battle-axe soared straight for her head; she weaved to one side, but not before the sharp edge clipped her head. The gash wasn't too bad, but it gushed anyway.

A sharp tug stole a breath. She snatched up the battle-axe; it was heavy—she was lucky it hadn't taken her head—but the heft felt satisfying in her hands. She hurried toward the screams, arriving in time to witness Sho masterfully playing samurai with the shifters. He was moving closer to her, but not *too* close; a graceful dance with death. He had injured both opponents, and with a push-pull of his sword he took the last wanna-be samurai's head.

Then there were two.

Polar's scratchy whimper in the distance had Tennessee fearing he'd choke himself before she got to him. "Polar! Stop! Sit still, boy. I got this jerk!" Reluctantly, Polar settled into a sitting slump by the tree, his thrashing stopped but not his monstrous growls. Next, she knew Sho was distracted keeping an eye on her. "Don't worry about me!" she hollered, gazing skyward to rinse her bloody face with slushy rain. She could see a little better now, clear enough to watch the runt lumbering toward her; he stopped in

front of his fallen comrade, flashing a cockeyed, razor-toothed grin at Tennessee as he yanked out the spear from the dead man's head.

Only thing is, the spear didn't come out clean; it took the head along for the ride.

So, Tennessee watched the runt limp toward her with a head-tipped spear.

She almost barfed.

"It's totally cool, Tennessee," she muttered aloud, "the head is dead. Totally in your job description. Pull your shit together or that'll be your head on a goddamn stick."

She dug into a fighting stance, right foot securely planted behind her, left foot in front. After a bout with bullies, Mister had Tennessee in the dojo five days a week with Sensei Chen. She earned a green belt, but never used it. Sensei Chen taught her the way of a smart mouth. That, with ample sass and good posture, usually prevented skirmishes. Right about now Tennessee wished she *had* practiced each technique ten thousand times as Sensei Chen instructed.

"Ten thousand," she griped, "wasn't that the price on my head? Damn karma."

The runt stopped just shy of striking distance. She could see it in his red slit eyes; he pegged her weak, a nothing. He slammed the speared head on the ground, jammed the heel of his shoe on the forehead and tried to pry off the dead man's skull.

Sensei Chen might have the perfect Bruce Lee quote for this moment, but Tennessee went with her own: never underestimate an Island girl with crazy hair!

Tennessee imagined the runt was already dead, so when he looked down in annoyance at the unmoving dead head, she positioned herself at the best angle. She stiffened her grip, swung the battle-axe high overhead, jumped to get a smidge more height, slammed her eyes closed, and let gravity do the rest.

The axe swooped down, slicing clean through the runt's stubby neck.

The splatter-gurgle-ooze wasn't so bad. Dead people did that sometimes. What had Tennessee jumping back with the heebie-jeebies was something dead people didn't do; the runt's eyes flickered bright orange before fading to black, and a forked tongue hissed out from behind those spiky teeth.

"Teach you to slap a girl." Tennessee reclaimed her spear and the battle-axe as a sleeted gust blew across the Illie lawn. Feeling another slight tug, she moved toward Sho; that's when she saw Riggy's already-ajar passenger door fling wide open, and a flurry of sleet dive in.

"Damn that kid! Even cowards can shut doors!"

While Tennessee mourned, an itsy-bitsy bit, over slaying a creepy creature from another dimension, the golden paw urn holding Dave's ashes shook in time with the frigid gusts whipping through Riggy. The paw urn tottered on Riggy's dash, shimmying dangerously toward the edge. It was a long drop, but with the wind lashing about as it was, Dave's ashes didn't fall when the urn toppled over and the lid fell open. Dave's ashes sailed out Riggy's open door, soaring into the woods, up to the sky, out to sea.

Dave was free.

"Sho!" Tennessee screamed as her samurai, mid strike, dissolved to nothing, his sword splatting in mud.

With Sho gone and Polar once again choking himself to get free, Tennessee nearly succumbed to the torrent of stony sleet beating her body. Blood-rich tears stained her cheeks. But she didn't have time for that. She couldn't quit now.

Tennessee stood in the center of the lawn, battle-axe in one hand, spear in the other.

She had *three* minutes to save the Illies.

And *one* to slay a giant.

# 15.

# Whiskey & Water

Sensei Chen had worshipped Bruce Lee. She quoted him daily, watched all his movies ten thousand times, read all his books, even had a tattoo of her idol on her thigh so she could see him every time she snap-kicked.

Tennessee heard Sensei Chen now, quoting the philosopher, Bruce Lee; she tried to recall his sage wisdom, something about water; it was simple and genius—anything to give her courage—but she couldn't remember one goddamn word!

With He-Man posturing toward her, Polar tied up, and the Illies slowly dying, Tennessee dropped her weapons. She crossed herself with a quick prayer. "Die later, Tennessee. Maybe tomorrow. Yeah, it's always better to die tomorrow." She clutched her tiny cross pendant and bowed her head in defeat.

It was an open invitation to take her head, collect the bounty, mount her bloody bones on his bloody wall.

He-Man started to run; he raised his sword, unleashing his blasting sonic gnarr that had Tennessee's bones vibrating so fast she flushed hot, or cold; it was impossible to tell. She pressed her hands into a prayer, squeezed her eyes shut.

As He-Man rushed on, Tennessee channeled Bruce Lee. "Water...just water...*be* water..."

He-Man cried out, "I claim this head and all the bounty!" He

swooshed his sword with such might and accuracy it should have severed Tennessee's head.

But, like water, Tennessee fell.

She dropped to her knees, but she was done praying. She snatched up the runt's battle-axe and sliced He-Man across the torso. As the top half was falling, a familiar roar thundered forth from the shadows; Polar leapt onto the tumbling torso, tackling it away from his master. The wild beast kept his paws on the enemy's chest; he sniffed the human-looking creature, tried to snap at it from behind his muzzle, and settled for growling his hate.

Tennessee kneeled beside Polar, tears cleaning her blood-drizzled face. "I'm so sorry they did this to you, boy." She could barely untie the wicked muzzle with her trembling hands. Only when she had Polar wrapped in her arms did the shaking settle. She tapped her nose to his. "I'll never let anyone hurt you again."

Polar licked his master's tears, then his ears perked up. His scratchy growls surged to hoarse barks.

"Ugh, not dead, huh?" She pushed herself up, hands rock steady; she just wanted to take Polar home, but this giant still had its head.

Polar stood guard as Tennessee retrieved He-Man's sword. That's how the old movies did it; use the villain's weapon on the villain. Sends a message. Tennessee raised the sword, imagining the giant was already dead.

"In Empress Zaada's name, I claim this head."

~

The next thing Tennessee knew she was staring into the dead black eyes of the severed head she was holding.

Polar had tried to run off with the head. She won the quick tug-of-war, but the splatter made it look like she'd lost.

"Tenny? Oh, Christ, Tenny! Are you all right?!"

Tennessee jerked her head toward that voice. "Phillip?" She dropped the He-Man sword, the giant's head. "Phillip!" She ran to him.

"Tenny!"

She was going to hug him, but he would scold her, say all sorts of horrible things; blame her for all the dead people and for bleeding and for his family knocked out cold in the living room.

He looked pale, maybe even ill. He took her into his arms, whispering, "I've been worried sick about you."

She didn't get it; where was the screaming reprimand for slaughtering all these men? Did he think she routinely slaughtered giant, sword-wielding intruders? She was a mortician, not a mass murderer.

Polar got between the two; whining, grunting, pawing.

"Tenny, are you injured?"

"No." She shook from the adrenaline, the sickness of taking life. It took a lot to slay *two* giants, even if one was just a runt. And severing heads was particularly draining. "The twins are..." The words drew Tennessee back to the task. A buzz-rumble-buzz. Another buzz-rumble-buzz. She checked her jeans, and there in her back pocket, the one Sho had brushed against earlier, was the timepiece belonging to the man who was *not* Phillip.

This Phillip was consoling her again, pressing his handkerchief to her head wound. "You're hurt, Tenny...you're bleeding."

"Sssshhhh, Phillip! I'm *thinking*." She swatted his tending hands.

Another buzz-rumble-buzz and the watch flashed a hologram countdown: 10...9...8...7...

"You've gotta be kidding. I bet you...if I just..." Tennessee pressed the silver button on the top of the watch. The hologram disappeared into the watch face and the buzz-rumble-buzz stopped. "Come on, boy!" Tennessee tapped her thigh, then took off running toward the house.

Polar barked, swiftly taking the lead.

Phillip chased them into the foyer, where he grabbed Tennessee at the elbow. "What have you done to them?"

Tennessee searched for the *other* Phillip, but he was nowhere to be seen; not his body, not his head, not the gruesome gruel of

spine and brain. She'd deal with that later. This Phillip was still trying to discern her emotional well-being. He had his hands on her shoulders.

"They should wake up…any minute now." She prayed to everything almighty as she sat on the grand piano bench; she clasped her knees to keep her trembles secret; sure, she had reason to hope, but if she was wrong…

Polar whined, pawing Tennessee's legs. And in exactly one minute…

"Tennessee England! This is all *your* fault!!"

It was the first time Tennessee was thrilled to hear that woman's whining wail. Lillie clattered over to her swamped foyer, belittling, berating, chastising, damn near *fining* Tennessee for the damages to the Illies' most humble abode.

Polar grunted, fretfully pushing himself up against Tennessee's hip. Giants he could handle, but *this* lady was, well, *Lillie.*

Phillip's hands were heavy on her shoulders. He was taking her back outside, back into the cold, the sleet, and slush; back to the headless men.

"Tend to the twins, Lillie," Phillip ordered gently. "You and William have obviously been drinking too much. And the girls got into the whiskey, *again.*"

"What," Lillie screeched. "That was *one* time, a special occasion, and I have never…get out, Tennessee! The next time one of your friends comes here looking for you, I won't let them in!" Lillie slammed the door on Tennessee's relieved face.

Tennessee shouted anyway, "Good! Don't *ever* let my friends in, Lillie…*never*!" She faced Phillip, eyes absorbed in her own shattered image reflected in his glossy pupils. "They're *not* my friends." She shoved him off her. "*You're* not my friend."

"Well, I don't know about *that,*" Phillip lifted his hand to smooth Tennessee's sopping mane, "after all we've shared tonight." His hand streamed down her cheek. "*I* consider you a friend, *Tennessee England, mortician.*" The cocky smirk returned to

Phillip's suddenly fierce features as he slipped his watch from her grip.

Polar growled and snapped.

She stumbled back, searching for a weapon. "I can't say I'm surprised," she sneered. "You don't play Phillip very well. Too campy. Total B-movie."

"In time, you'll never know the difference." The man who was not Phillip held his watch in his palm, and with an easy chuckle pressed a button. Tennessee watched his eyes change first, into those familiar red slits, then all Phillip's features morphed into a flat black canvass of nothing. His humanoid form blurred at the edges, leaving a shadowy mist of shapeable essence.

Polar was whining again, adjusting his body to keep Tennessee from *not Phillip*.

"Who are you?"

Even without features, those red eyes glowed expressive as the being's voice roamed Tennessee's mind. "Your language limits your comprehension of my designation. However, I have grown fond of the human name..."

"Listen up, Watchdog," Tennessee squeezed her temples, "I'll figure out a way to kill you if you don't get out of my head! Even then, I'll figure out a way to kill you!"

The being's eyes shone. "You see, I have learned only *friends* bestow pet names, *Tenny*. I joyfully accept your pet name for me."

"It's *nick*names, doofus! And I'm not your pet!" Tennessee thought she heard a chuckle, but it sounded more like tiny bells chiming.

"I am *Watchdog*, your friend. And as your friend, I shall visit from time to time."

"What's up with you demons? Sicko peeping Toms." Tennessee spotted a metal wind spinner staked in a ceramic pot of blooming snowdrops and witch hazel; she snatched it, aiming the pointy end at her latest stalker.

His tone was amused as he, somehow, made her makeshift weapon disappear. "I find you endlessly entertaining. While you

dispatched my pack, I went back to watch Zaada collar you to the keeper; a talent, indeed, warrior *and* mender. I knew then that the Empress has great plans for you. What an enviable prize your talents be. I must confess, *wrangler* was not what *I* would have chosen. Alas, having observed you for weeks..."

"*Stalked* is more accurate, creeper!" Tennessee stopped searching for a weapon; Polar was salivating, eagerly waiting for her to say *boo*.

"Indeed, Zaada has chosen wisely. A feminine who voices her mind as you so recklessly do is a rarity in my world...they have all been removed. Harshly. Unfortunately. You needn't fear me, Tenny. I am but a tourist, seeking knowledge of humanity."

"You muzzled my dog! You tried to *kill me*!"

"You have not discerned all angles. There are many hands in our little game. In honor of our *friendship*, I'll remove my comrades to bring ease to your evening."

"Dude, we're *not* friends!"

"Now you shall owe me a lesson in humanity."

"I don't owe you shit! If anyone can clean up dead bodies, it's me, you freakazoid!"

Watchdog was clearly laughing, a tinkling of windchimes, as he bid farewell. "Until next time, my friend, my *Tenny*."

"Don't call me that!" She winced as the being exited her mind, his form dissipating to nothing. "Just wait, you sick bastard, I'm a get-even girl."

Her headache wasn't as bad as when the collar pulled that stunt; that one left a thud, *this* one left a burn. When she could lift her head, she scanned the lawn for bodies. Nothing but perfectly cut blades of grass wilted in patches of melting hail. Overhead, a downspout busted, drizzling dirty ice water on her drenched curls. "Okay, I deserve that." She sucked in a shallow breath, steadily slinking to the flooded patio floor.

She killed people tonight. Creature-people, but still.

She hugged her soggy lion; and, if she didn't know any better, she was certain he purred.

~

With so much death, Tennessee couldn't figure out why Sho had disappeared. Then she got to thinking about those *angles* Watchdog mentioned and the crappy game she was now being forced to play. Maybe Sho had poofed because none of those deaths were humans, or dogs. She rambled on out loud. Sho could hear her, she was sure. She could *feel* him nearby, keeping within those pesky fifty feet.

All were accounted for, except *her* Phillip. A few swipes of her phone and Phillip was, once again, back on her speed dial favorites. How quickly things change when death is on the line. Phillip's phone went straight to voicemail. What did she expect? It was nearly sunrise. He'd be asleep or on his way to sleep. Tennessee listened to the soothing cadence of his voice, then hung up at the beep. She called another six times, just to listen to *her* Phillip instruct callers to leave a message or call the hospital or dial 911. When she regained a semblance of her former self, Tennessee peeled off the cold patio floor.

Watchdog had cleared out the bodies and gore, but he left the weapons. He probably expected another goddamn favor for that! Tennessee loaded the spears and swords into Riggy; as for the double-bladed barbarian battle-axe, she kept that baby up front with her and Polar. It was a nifty weapon; she'd have to keep it away from demon stench. Melting that beauty down would totally suck.

"That psycho, Watchdog, wasn't going to kill the Illies, huh? Otherwise you would have poofed in to witness. What a creep-o! Another sick test? From Ibrahim or Zaada? Yeah, you're right, who the hell knows. I bet we have to smash his watch to kill him...you think it could be *that* easy...nah, too scripted...he's like a smoke being...so we can't burn him...maybe, geez...someone's got to have a book on this crap...Oh, and thanks for releasing Polar. Don't know how a ghost samurai could do that, but it's a good trick to have...I'll never put Polar on a leash again..."

Tennessee peeled out of the Illie estate; she flipped her lights on as she passed the iron gates.

"Goddammit!" She cringed, slamming the breaks. Polar went crashing into the dash.

Millie and Billie were standing in the middle of the road. Two wet brats.

"What the hell, girls?" Tennessee leapt from Riggy. "Almost dying *once* tonight isn't enough chaos for you?"

"We knew it! Something weird's going on tonight! Mommy would *never* give the staff a night off!" The twins engaged in a full-blown *I told you so* bicker-battle.

Tennessee didn't bother taking anything back; the twins were smart, and they knew bad men when they saw bad men; even if one looked like their Uncle Phillip. She would have lit up a cig if she had one. She didn't bother reversing Riggy; she strolled across the lawn in the rain, the twins trailing her like soggy baby ducks. Polar took up the rear; if they booked it, he was ready.

William was waiting for them on the porch, a glass of brandy in one hand and a cigar in the other. "I thought the girls might want to say goodbye." His tone was shockingly metered for a man whose children were traipsing around in a freezing February storm.

Tennessee faked a smile; not a very convincing one. This was all her fault. "Sorry for the trouble, William. I'll make it up to you...a discount on a snazzy new casket maybe." She winced at her ill-timed humor. She reassessed her words; they could have been interpreted as a threat. William was a bit regal for Tennessee. And when faced with regality, she got mouthy.

But William knew all this about Tennessee, and so much more; he put on his princely grin. "I'll drop by the shop next week. Take a look."

His tone put a lump in her throat. "Lillie, too?"

William raised one brow. "Just me. Lillie's not been herself lately. Oh, I found an old mixtape from my academy days. You'll enjoy it."

A little nod was all Tennessee would risk. A reproach from Lillie was nothing, but William was her friend. They connected on stuff; if *he* was upset with her, it mattered. A lot.

"Give Lillie her Christmas tonight." William sipped his brandy, hard eyes surveying the rocky cliffs. "Bring your new fella. I'd like to meet the man who's managed the impossible. Phillip's been reduced to a shamefully pitiful state...*point* to Tennessee."

"I'm not playing a game, William. We broke up."

"We both know better. Now, Tennessee, please, invite your friends. I'd like to meet them *all*."

She had excuses aplenty, and for a moment she had the perfect one, but this was William—her island of sanity when dealing with Lillie and their bratty twins. Excuses were empty. He was *business*. All the time.

"Of course." She plastered on her Funeral Director face. "That works perfectly with my schedule. We'll see you this evening."

Millie and Billie shot Tennessee looks well beyond their age. Tennessee took a knee and Millie (or Billie) came in for a hug.

"Uncle Phillip's been here," the girl whispered, her boney hands patting Tennessee's back.

Then Billie (or Millie) came in for her hug. "*A lot*." The girl finished what her sister started.

Tennessee kept her eyes down until she could put the light back in her gaze. "I've got it covered." She detached one clingy child at a time. "I'll see you *tonight*. Have you heard? Santa's coming to town!"

The twins faked ignorant bliss that only fooled William.

"To Santa!" William raised his glass for a toast, swigged the top-shelf shot before escorting the girls inside.

On the puddled trek back to Riggy, Tennessee had a *long* conversation with herself, Sho, and Polar. Other than lots of what-ifs, whys, and what-the-hells, Tennessee had nothing. She was exhausted, starving, and pretty freaking unnerved. So, when she got close to Riggy and Polar went wild, she almost lost it.

"For the love of everything holy! What now?!"

Pitchy screams and cracking *oh my gods* echoed across the frosty ridge as Polar chased a boy from Riggy. Henry stumbled in sleet, smashing his face outside Riggy's passenger side door.

"Well if it isn't boy wonder." Tennessee crossed her arms. "What'd you do, hide all that muscle in the bushes? What a waste."

Henry blathered on about all that he'd seen; he was animated and agitated, like retelling a ghost story or summer slasher hit.

"Never happened," Tennessee scoffed, getting back in Riggy.

"It *did* happen." He climbed in the passenger seat.

She coughed an *ahem*, and Polar barked.

"Uh, right." Henry climbed into the back, once again sitting on iron, and now two samurai swords. Come on! Then what's this?" He picked up a spear.

Tennessee eyed him in the rearview mirror. "Your funeral."

"So, it..." the boy's eyes widened; his memory was so joggled he wasn't sure *what* was real.

"Never happened." She trapped Henry's gaze in hers, and that was that.

She flipped on the radio; the early-morning talk shows were on; she hated cross-talking banter. She popped in a mixtape and as she gazed at the pink sunrise haloing the rocky cliffs, Prince's "When Doves Cry" salvaged her mood.

Polar nuzzled his head on her lap as she twirled her grimy hand in his wet fur. The rain had washed the red speckles peppering his fur to a pink hue, matching the sunrise.

The drive to town was so uneventful, Tennessee found herself fighting sleep. She was in a daze and never bothered to look at herself, so when she jumped out to grab some smokes, she didn't associate the gasps and shocked glares with *her*. It wasn't until she went to pay for the pack she'd already opened that she noticed her reflection in the mirror bolted behind the register.

"Shit."

Besides being a soggy mess, a mucky mass of black goo matted her frizzled mane right over a gnarly slice on her forehead. Her

flannel button-up was torn; she didn't know when *that* happened; maybe the runt? She'd have to retire Blondie after tonight; no way that amount of blood was coming out. If she wanted to salvage the jeans from the splattering of mud-green stains, she'd have to cut them into shorts, and her black cowboy boots could use a good scrub. Tennessee touched her face; what could she do about those eyes?

Nothing, absolutely nothing.

She popped a cig in her mouth, paid for the pack, then left.

"Where's that samurai dude?" Henry hollered right when Tennessee got in.

"Maybe I killed him." She lit up, held in the drag, then slowly blew smoke on Henry's reflection in the rearview mirror.

Henry didn't say much after that. Only an address, after he found his nerve.

~

Henry's friends lived in a shady part of town, on the corner of dime bags and flop houses.

"Bye, kid, steer clear of tailgates and Tritons."

"Can I have one?" Henry pointed to her cig.

"That would be contributing to the delinquency of a minor." She was dead serious.

"*You're* practically a minor!"

"Dude, I'm, like, *thirty* years old!"

"You don't look thirty."

"Yeah," she lit another cig, "well, you don't look like a street kid but here you are."

"My folks kicked me out."

"And you're sure you want me to leave you on this corner?"

"Not really."

"Look, kid, I'm in a hurry here. Where do your folks live?"

"Other side of town."

Tennessee popped Riggy into gear. "Damn kids," she grumbled as a squad of skateboarding teens whooshed across the street, flip-flopping their tattered boards beneath their pristine Converse,

blowing dense clouds with their fruity-flavored vapes. Vanilla, strawberry, and cherry seasoned the seedy air.

"That smell!" Henry hunkered down in the back, eyes crammed shut.

"Yeah, I hate that fake crap...come on, man up and smoke a *real* cigarette." She imagined Sho chastising her, amusement in his seductively gritty accent. "When you're *eighteen*," she clarified. "Got that, kid? All the magic happens at *eighteen*."

When the skaters and the smoke cleared, Tennessee skidded out onto the street.

Henry was still sullen in back, and Polar noticed. He pawed Tennessee until she gave a damn.

"You sick? Or just cowering again?"

"I remember it..." he quivered. "Back there, the cherry smoke..."

Henry's words set the baby hairs on Tennessee's neck on end. She only knew one person who frequented Stumpy's *and* smelled of cherry smoke.

Hill.

# 16.

# Feast or Famine

The posher sort of beachcomber lived on Henry's street. Arty flags for every cause flying high above manicured lawns rife with driftwood, clattering shell windchimes, and glistening gazing globes. Tennessee wanted a gazing globe for her *un*manicured shop, but every time she looked at one, her cheeks puffed up in her reflection, and nobody wanted puffed-up cheeks at a mortuary.

Henry's house wasn't the loftiest on the block; it was the homiest. Tennessee liked the greyed cedar shakes, blue front door, and the line of seagrass framing the pebbled walk. The one-story bungalow had a peekaboo view of the sea; if they added another story, they'd have a killer view. She told him so; tried to cheer the boy up before she cut him loose.

"Mom's been sick, and Dad's a commercial fisherman so he's gone a lot."

"I'd walk you in but..." Tennessee yanked on her gristle-soaked flannel.

"Nah, I've got it."

Polar squished against Tennessee to give Henry space. The boy climbed out, bending down to say, "Mind if I come by the shop sometime?"

Tennessee didn't need or *want* another kid to babysit. She

killed her cig in the open ashtray before eyeing the boy to tell him *no*. But behind Henry, the blue door opened and a frail lady clutching a walker started to weep.

Dammit.

"Can you make coffee?" Tennessee narrowed her gaze.

When Henry experienced genuine happiness, he looked twelve. "I make kickass coffee!"

"*Strong* is fine. I'm open nine to nine most days."

"Thanks, Mrs..."

"*England*, Tennessee England." She smirked; she'd been saying that a lot lately. "Later, kid."

Riggy roared out of the cul-de-sac. Tennessee adjusted her rearview mirror to see Henry sink into his mother's embrace.

"You see that, Sho? Good deed number one."

"More like *five*, but who's counting." Sho's husky rasp and sudden appearance busted up Tennessee's solo conversation. She swerved, hopped a curb, and nearly took out a line of rickety mailboxes.

A blaring siren and Polar's howls drowned her curses as an ambulance pulled out of a neighboring street, followed by the lone sheriff in town.

Sho roughly ran his palm down Tennessee's cheek.

She couldn't help but smile. "Damn."

Resting his head against the headrest, tired eyes on Tennessee, Sho smiled back. "Damn."

~

On the drive, it became clear that Sho *had* heard everything. He was always there, regardless of the annoying poofing-from-visual-existence thing. It didn't always work that way, but Zaada had been losing a lot to Ibrahim. Keepers were her last hope. Watchdog wasn't lying when he sang Sho's praises. Tethering such a strong keeper to a new wrangler meant the Empress had to restrict his freedoms or risk Ibrahim calling a *no-fairsies*. This was a demon war, after all.

Tennessee tried to thank Sho for saving her.

"You saved yourself, Ten." He was bending forward, straining to reach something rattling under his seat. "You slayed the...*He-Man*, was it?"

"Yeah, only the real He-Man would have been on *our* side but go on...I accept all forms of accolades for my newly tapped slaughtering skills." Tennessee laughed, but a pit in her stomach hardened. At some point, when left alone, she'd puke it out.

Sho caught that look, and Tennessee caught his.

"Not this time, Sho." She skidded Riggy into the shop parking lot; now that Maria Garcia was inside, Sho wouldn't poof, so she had time to set some things straight. "I wanna keep this angst. Don't *mend* me unless I ask, okay? That's the stuff that makes me, *me*, you know. I mean, what if Lin tamed my hair too much? I'd be a freak." There was more. "I was wondering..." She considered not asking, but who was she kidding? She barely kept the blurt from blurting. "Did you take my memories of Phillip from me? You know, when you were healing my head?"

Sho dropped his head just enough for Tennessee to understand that, if he had, he didn't mean to.

"I'd like to keep those. Hey, just promise me you'll go easy on all the fixing." She touched his face, "And I'll try not to need so much fixing."

Sho promised, his gaze studying Dave's empty paw urn in his hand.

Tennessee wrinkled her nose. "Poor Dave. We still need to find *his* killer. Watchdog didn't do it."

"You certain?"

"Yeah, he had no reason to kill a random dog. *That's* about Maria Garcia, her father, or her brothers, I'm sure of it. There's something off about a family who buries their dead in an ugly brown rag and doesn't have a problem coming up with a *second* identical ugly brown rag after you tell them the first one got stained."

Sho struggled with Tennessee's logic, which hinged on an ugly brown dress. "Perhaps they killed Dave, but the dress is another

matter. Why would the family warn you if they meant to harm you? Anyone could have cursed the dress to warn you of the bounty."

"Not anyone, Sho. Only someone who knew *you'd* interpret the message correctly. Only someone who had access to the dress and who *wanted* to warn us."

"We must consider anonymous allies."

"*Exactly*. So, who's on our side, but doesn't want anyone to *know* they're on our side...answer that one." Tennessee grabbed Dave's urn on her way out. She kneeled by the walkway, scooping an urn-full of sand. "Rest in peace, Dave. You're a damn fine dog. You looked after Maria even in the end. You're a hero, buddy. You helped us slay a demon and three nasty giants and a rude little runt. I'm sorry I lost your ashes."

Sho watched Tennessee, enticed and beholden. "You are a gift to the dead."

Tennessee attached the paw top and accepted a sopping wet kiss from Polar before facing Sho with half closed eyes. "Huh?" She wiped her tired eyes with her blood-splattered flannel, leaving crusty bits on her eyelashes.

Sho went to her, wrapping her in his arms. She sunk into him as she might a down comforter. Having Polar and Sho back, Tennessee could have fallen asleep right there.

With a gratified chuckle, Sho brushed her eyelashes clean. "I thought you would have gone to the silo. You must sleep." His stormy unrest rumbled in her ear.

"You kidding?" She burrowed into his chest. "I just got you back."

Sho's rumbly sigh eased the last bit of tension seizing her temples. She knew he didn't mean to take her pain; it was simply who he was; he couldn't stop it any more than she could stop tending to the dead. She forgave him, and he chuckled some more, but as his rough hands smoothed her hair and his lips brushed against her temple, she was wide awake.

Tennessee drew back to look up at Sho; he tugged her closer.

He was right to do that. The more he healed her, the more intense the urges. It *was* intimate. His essence entered hers, purely. It surpassed physical. Soul slicing came to her mind. It felt like that; his soul split open, her soul split open, and they merged, each taking and giving as needed.

The way *they* did it, the merge flamed desire.

"Feels a lot like the crazy, kill-for kind of *love...*" Tennessee murmured into Sho's chest.

Sho didn't answer, or maybe he couldn't.

His palm pressed her hips into his and his breathing hastened hers; his hand tangled in her hair, and he gently tugged her head back; she was waiting for him to give her what she wanted when Polar's happy bark shattered the spell.

A commotion of hoorays and hoorahs flowed out of the mortuary. And then *ooohs* and *oh my gods* started. Sho handled the concerns over Tennessee's shocking appearance with his charismatic alter ego; he explained how Tennessee had fallen into a ravine searching for Polar, whacked her head on a branch and got a bloody nose.

No one questioned the fabricated tale. It was *so* Tennessee.

The whole gang was there: Lin on the ground, hugging Polar; Mamma Min, standing, scolding Lin in her brassiest tone.

"Ground not swept, Lin! Dirty dog get you filthy! Not ladylike be on dirty ground for filthy dog! I get you broom, Tennessee, you sweep morning time! Bring good luck!"

Godzilla kneeled beside Lin to join in the Polar hugs and wet kisses. The big guy's eyes welled-over as he jostled Polar's head; something only Tennessee seemed to notice. Phillip wouldn't have noticed anyway; he was staring at *her*.

She couldn't read his expression, not one bit, before he walked back into the shop. She was still clutching Sho's waist, half her body sinking into the man. The desire had subsided, but she was exhausted and needed a little stability. Even the joy was making her knees wobble; good adrenaline, bad adrenaline, didn't matter, both made her jittery.

As Sho led Tennessee into the shop, Godzilla stopped her. "You reek, Ness." He socked her arm. "Hit the shower."

"Whatever, beast," she laughed. "Santa at The Mirror. Tonight. Still on?"

"*Ho-Ho-Ho.*" Godzilla held his big belly. "Just waitin' on my reindeer." He stroked Polar's back.

But before she could relax, she needed to hear some details. "How was Maria's wake? Did Mr. Garcia approve? Please tell me he was, if not decent, at least pleased."

Godzilla rolled one huge shoulder. "You know, he wasn't kind, but he never is. He kept his cool except for Maria's hair."

Lin swooped in, talking over Godzilla. "I fixed it, didn't I?"

"You did, doll. Maria looked beautiful."

"Thank you." Lin's tone wasn't its usual commanding grate.

"You're welcome."

When a fight didn't ensue, Tennessee gushed, "Whoa, my friends are being *nice* to each other? Since when?"

Godzilla just chuckled, going right back to roughhousing with Polar. Lin grew quiet, her gaze tracking his every move. Tennessee's mouth opened a little and her astonishment stalled on Lin. When Lin's attention drifted back to Tennessee she dismissed her friend's questioning stare and resumed her scrappy tone.

"Come on, Ness, who knew she wasn't *allowed* to wear her hair down. I gave Mr. Garcia the plain-Jane bun he demanded on his daughter, but that's *so* not the hairdo Maria loved. After meeting the man, I'm shocked he didn't hack off Maria's hair himself."

Tennessee fidgeted as Lin filled her in on the night's events, bumps and all; dammit, she should have been there to handle things herself; like the hitch with the mellow music Godzilla had selected for ambiance. She'd already guessed Mr. Garcia was not the ambiance type.

Godzilla added tactfully, "Don't feel bad, Ness. They mourned Maria in complete silence for exactly twenty minutes, then left. It was all good."

"Godzilla's right. It was fine. Just the hair and the music. I heard the father say, 'ten minutes for each decade of life.'" Lin tucked away a tiny sulk. "We stayed another hour with Maria because that's what you would have done...for the life she would have lived..."

"Music blasting," Godzilla boomed with a grin.

Feeling less guilty but more lightheaded now, Tennessee socked Godzilla's arm and hugged Lin. "Thanks for taking care of Maria. I owe you guys."

They both insisted she get some rest, immediately.

"Will do," Tennessee promised, finally entering the shop.

Inside, she splotted down on the same bulky couch three of Mr. Garcia's seven sons had sat on the other day. She was thinking of Maria, her hair pulled in a tight bun for eternity when Phillip walked straight to Sho, gripped him on the arm, and dragged him into the office. Phillip could be like that; he wasn't a samurai, and Sho *let* him do it, but he'd seen his share of brutish behavior as a doctor in the Marines. He knew a thing or two; taught her a thing or two.

"Phillip, don't be a punk!" Tennessee went to stand, but Sho raised one firm hand. "Whatever, alpha dog it out! Have fun!"

~

Tennessee woke up choking. She threw herself forward, knocked a glass of water from a table, slipped on the shattered glass, then dropped to her knees, effectively shredding both kneecaps; blood oozed from the fresh cuts. She barely noticed because she still couldn't breathe. Crawling forward, her dripping wounds marred the wood floors with an eerie trail of gore.

Sho was there now, but Tennessee still couldn't breathe.

Phillip was there now; yelling, cursing.

"Hang on, Ten, it wants payment." Sho lifted Tennessee into his arms, racing toward Audrey II.

Tennessee's lips blued, her sight blurred black, and the last thing she heard was Phillip's anguished voice.

"Don't leave me. I love you."

~

Tennessee flung awake, fresh sweat swirling dried blood to fresh bleeds. The fake leather couch squeaked beneath her damp jeans, and Phillip was reprimanding Sho for, oh, lots of things, everything, whatever came to mind.

Sho wasn't defending himself; he took Phillip's wrath; he even *apologized.*

*That* was more than Tennessee could handle.

"Cool it, Phillip!" Tennessee hollered, checking her knees for slashes and shards of glass. Nothing. Just her perfectly chubby knees. "You boys are giving me nightmares!" The men lowered their argument as Tennessee counted her steps to the staff bathroom. "Damn you, collar! If I found the coin earlier, I would have paid you! Threatening me in my sleep is low, even for a demonic dog collar! It's probably at Jasper's. You'll get your goddamn coin when I *find* your goddamn coin."

An ominous tug was unclear; it could be Sho moving around, or the collar agreeing.

"Choke me and see how fast you get paid, tin can."

The tug eased to nothing, so Tennessee ran the shower, undressed, and set her cell phone to play her eighties mix. When Bon Jovi's "Wanted Dead or Alive" started, she stepped under the hot water and sang her heart out.

It seemed fitting after the day she'd had. Three songs later, Jon Bon Jovi's hit "Blaze of Glory" came on, and she laughed; she didn't know she had that one. But when her phone screeched out a jumbled shrill before blasting Bruce Springsteen's "A Night with the Jersey Devil," she knew these songs weren't random. She didn't even have *that* song in the mix.

She listened to it, and halfway through, toweled off with a, "Ha ha...of course *I* get the smart-ass collar...clever, I'll give you that." A tiny tug had Tennessee calling for Sho.

Sho flung the door open.

"Dang!" Tennessee scrambled to cover the important bits. "I was just checking!"

"Are you injured?" Sho averted his eyes; Phillip gave a doctorly once-over while Polar ran to her side.

"No." She kicked the door shut. "Why are you two standing right outside my bathroom? It's totally creepy!"

"We heard you...*singing*..." Sho answered.

Phillip chuckled. "But it didn't *sound* like singing."

"Oh, ha ha." She secured one towel around her body, twirled another one on top of her head, then opened the door. "Move, scram, get!" Tennessee glared at the men as they got out of her way. "My clothes are upstairs. I'm sure you're *both* going to follow me."

Phillip started in, "As I reminded Sho, you were due at the hospital this morning. You didn't show, then I get a strange call from Lillie about some of your friends and a crazy party at the estate."

Tennessee ignored Phillip, but Sho didn't.

"As I explained, an examination was unnecessary once Ten's memory resurfaced." Sho's sympathetic tone infuriated Phillip.

"*I'm* her doctor! *I'll* make that diagnosis!"

Tennessee let Sho open the apartment door for her, offering a curt, "Shoes off, boys! Island rules!"

The men removed their shoes. Polar ran to the kitchen, pawing at the cupboard where Mister and Missus stored doggie treats for the customers with doggies. Tennessee gave Sho a look. He bowed his head, went to the kitchen, started a pot of coffee, filled a bowl of water for Polar, and tossed him a treat.

Phillip was still in the threshold. "All that from a look?" he grumbled as Tennessee headed down the hall.

"The man *knows* me." She glanced over her shoulder.

Phillip's face fell with a bit of shame. She wasn't going for *that,* but she'd take it.

After ten minutes, Tennessee sauntered out of her bedroom dressed like a sexy Santa's helper. Everything was a little too snug; she'd put on a few pounds since wearing it last.

Before anyone said anything, she sassed, "Shut up! It's all I've got! I left Mrs. Claus at The Mirror."

Sho was puzzled. Polar wagged his tail.

And Phillip groaned, "*That's* tonight?"

"Yes, Phillip," Tennessee almost whined. "William declared it so! And he wants *all* my friends to come. So, the faster I get this night with the living over with, the faster I'm back to my quiet days with the dead."

Handing Tennessee her sugared coffee, Sho asked curiously, "*Why* do you have such an outfit?"

Phillip rolled his eyes, standing at attention before retreating to the kitchen.

Tennessee took a long sip, old memories scorching her rouge. "Halloween?" she lied.

"Ah." Sho grinned, bending to kiss her cheek. "Polar needs a wash." He glanced back at Phillip. "I'll take care of him." Sho patted his thigh, and Polar chased after, but not before he stopped at Tennessee for another round of hugs.

Polar was his old energetic self again, not tired at all, not like...

Tennessee kneeled to check the nick he got at Stumpy's. "Oh my god, they drugged you." She ran her fingers over his scab, contemplating the precise method of killing the bastards responsible. She could do that now, kill.

She *had*.

"Ten," Sho kneeled beside her, rubbing her back, "he's safe now. They can't hurt him."

Tennessee wiped a renegade tear. Sho kissed her head, then gently led Polar down the hall. She stayed on her knees, wiping away a few more tears. She almost lost him. With demons on the loose and hunters after her head, she *might* still lose him. Or someone else she loved. How could she protect everyone? Tennessee sat with the impossible until Phillip's soothing words carved out a nugget of hope,

"You can't save the world, Tennessee."

He used to say that a lot. When she'd stress about finals or

meeting deadlines during busy shop times—*you can't save the world, Tennessee.* When families demanded something she couldn't give—*you can't save the world, Tennessee.* When her parents called to say they were staying on the island—*you can't save the world, Tennessee.*

Phillip was kneeling before her now, his hands cupped around hers. "But you saved Polar. And that's a good day's work."

Tennessee met his heartening gaze, and somehow his words lightened her burdens. She sighed. "We got Polar back, Saint James."

That's what she used to call him. Her very own Saint James.

The momentary surprise and subsequent serenity that crossed his face, and the way his hands refused to release hers, told her more than she could handle. His gaze wandered to the almost-healed cut on her forehead, then his fingers were in her hair, retracing the erogenous paths they once paved.

"Why must you always be putting yourself in danger? You only have *one* of these." Phillip held the back of her head, gently leaning in to rest his forehead against hers. "I need you *here*, Tenny. Whatever you and Sho are up to, please be careful."

This was Phillip, *her* Phillip. It was easy to tell; the scolding, yelling, tending. But it was more than that. When *her* Phillip was near, that hard pit in her gut softened; maybe, just maybe, she could survive another awful day.

From wedged under her sexy Santa's helper belt, Tennessee's cell phone drummed out the chorus to George Michael's "I Want Your Sex."

She was going to strangle that goddamn collar.

~

Mamma Min didn't believe in Santa Claus. Lin didn't either, but she loved cookies and free booze.

"Champagne at The Mirror." Lin clapped her hands. "I'm so in!"

Phillip was in, of course, for the twins and to observe Lillie's behavior.

Sho didn't like it. None of it. But he had to wait for Lin to finish styling Tennessee's hair, and everyone else to leave, before voicing his concerns.

"Why tonight?" Sho finished washing their guests' cups and glasses. "Why all your friends? This William wants something."

Tennessee was sitting at the kitchen counter, stirring her fifth cup of coffee.

"Yeah, it's weird, but he's not a demon," she rationalized between bites of a peanut butter sandwich. "Maybe he's one of those shifters. The twins said something strange tonight. William *knows* Watchdog. Maybe not *what* he is, but Watchdog has been masquerading around as Phillip...doing something with William, I'm sure of it. And then Henry freaked out about cherry smoke, but I can't think about that now. Hill's my godmother, for Christ's sake! No, she can't be involved...right?"

Tennessee figured if all her friends were in one place, she'd have a better chance of keeping them safe. There was just one hiccup.

She needed a dead body.

~

Poor Maria Garcia was set to be buried the following day. It was unethical to even consider moving her body until then; most decidedly unscrupulous. Totally immoral to take her for one last drive, no matter how nice the February air was way up there at The Mirror. And it was just plain rude to use a dead body for personal gain, and at Christmas for Christ's sake!

"I mean, really, what would Santa do?"

Sho grew pensive. "I'm unfamiliar with that man's reasoning."

Tennessee tried not to laugh. "He'd put Maria on ice and save Christmas, that's what." Nearing a moral edge, she lifted her palms, and a jagged giggle escaped as her teeth gnashed into her lower lip. "I'm risking my rep on this, but we *have to*. Seriously, William didn't blink or even seem to notice all the gore I was flaunting this morning. Yeah, it was dark, but, come on!"

"Yes, I saw."

"He *knows* something. If he's not our ally, he's *something* we might need to fear."

"You are right." Sho bowed. "We should prepare as if he is our foe."

Tennessee hated thinking of William that way. No one liked Meat Loaf more than William, except maybe her. He took care of the twins when Lillie *couldn't*. He even brought her mindbenders on occasion, simply because. He was Phillip's best friend. More than that, he stayed her friend after Phillip broke her heart. In fact, he checked on her often, sat with her during a marathon of John Hughes' films. *Some Kind of Wonderful* was his favorite.

They had their own thing, and she didn't want to lose that. Sho gravitated toward her as she navigated a potential loss. The pull was mutual, and penetrating.

"I'd like to keep some disappointment, Sho." She studied her empty coffee cup. "It's what makes me human."

Sho's eyes were on his task; he dried each dish *twice* before abandoning them to fling open a window in the living room. He challenged the sea with a leaden glare, salty air drying his wet hair.

Tennessee studied Sho anew. He'd showered and dressed in a fitted suit he'd found among the clothes on hand for folks who didn't have, or couldn't afford, a decent ensemble for their dead.

"What, no magical wardrobe change this time?" she joked, but she really did wonder what had changed.

"The longer I am *here*, the less I am *there*," he replied bluntly, no further explanation.

Observing the shamed subtleties of Sho's silent, meticulous movements sparked an epiphany in Tennessee.

"So *that's* what you're not telling me." She went to him, locking her fingers around his. "You *need* my pain."

"Forgive me..." Sho's head fell, and there it stayed. Another heavy breath and he shared his dark secret, "I feed on your heart's suffering."

Tennessee cupped his scruffy chin with her heated hand. "What happens to you without it?"

He met her dread with repentant eyes. "I perish."

A sting shuddered through her; even her toes trembled from the jolt.

"My kind has only known what it is to be tethered." Sho's merciful rasp soured in torment. "If we were to exist on our own, without a soul of our own, we'd be..."

Tennessee sucked in a distressed gasp. "Demons."

Sho lowered his gaze; *this* was dishonor.

"Earlier, in the parking lot," Tennessee forced Sho to look at her; she needed to see his eyes; they weren't as black as they should be; an ashen tinge muted the emperor's glory, "you needed to feed. You still do."

Sho broke free from her grasp, cursing in a foreign tongue, which incited deep inside Tennessee the succulent anguish he hungered for. "You must know how this torments me! My life is only to protect your life, and yet..."

"My suffering *feeds* your life." Tennessee went to touch him, but he grew rigid from her attempt. "Why are you so hungry? You've healed me, you've taken my pain...isn't that how you feed?"

"Healing your physical body is my gift to you...it's my sacrifice."

"Your scars," Tennessee sighed, remembering how little of Sho's true skin was *not* hacked and marred. She put her hand on his chest. "Emotion sustains you."

"*Suffering*." He pulled away. "That is why we are sold to warriors...and those plagued by illness...the emotional struggle is taxing...we can feed without injuring our masters."

Horrified, Tennessee moved away from Sho; she crossed the room, wringing her hands as she contemplated his words, all the caverns of their curse.

Absorbing her rage, Sho begged forgiveness for dishonoring her, and vowed to break the tether.

But he had it all wrong.

It was the *sold* part that had Tennessee furious.

"This collar," she clasped the invisible iron around her neck,

storming back to Sho, "you've never been without it, have you? They probably put this on you as a baby!"

Sho's shame concealed the stoic samurai.

"Don't do that!" Tennessee grabbed Sho's face with both hands. "Don't let them shame you! You're not to blame, Sho. Some demented bastard slaps a collar on a baby and *you* feel like the bad guy? Hell no! *They're* wrong. Not you." Tennessee softened her tone, stroking her samurai's stubble with her warm fingertips. "I need you with me. I *want* you. I won't let you leave me and I won't let you starve. Nobody starves in an Islander's home."

Sho fought her grasp, but his desire, his desperate need to feed, was too great.

"It can be a delicate exchange." His reedy rasp betrayed his famine. Her mighty samurai, drained. "It requires time and practice. If I take too much, you may not *feel* as you should."

"Not feeling might be good in battle though, right?"

"No, Ten," Sho held *her* face now, "warriors must hold their humanity close. Losing that is like becoming the darkness we vowed to defeat."

Tennessee pondered the possibilities. "I think I get it." She began unbuttoning her fur-lined, red velvet jacket. She undid the neckline just a bit—no, a bit more—yes. When she properly exposed the creamy skin of her neck, she tossed her head back with a wry sneer. "Bite me."

Sho's confused expression had Tennessee giggling,

"Ah, come on, you've got to know *that* movie!"

By Sho's expression, he was about to pull a Phillip and start scolding her for making light of a heavy situation, but Tennessee shut him up with pragmatism. "Biology 101, Sho. Obviously, we have a symbiotic relationship. I need *you* and you need *me*. It's not ideal, but we'll work around all the gloom and doom until you earn your soul...and, or...I kill the bastards who enslaved you. End of story. Now...if you don't *bite* me, how do you..."

Sho's lips were already on hers.

It was a soft crush that swelled to a fever. Sho had her up against the window, icy breezes doing nothing to cool their fire. He took a little of her disappointment, a lot of fears, worry, and regret; he left her remorse untouched. It wasn't easy for Tennessee to stop kissing Sho; she could feel his restraint, heavy against her flesh, which made her want to tempt it. Any other day, his command, his control of her might have concerned her; today, she didn't want to lead, she wanted to follow. Sho may have taken what he needed, but he gave her something in return; he hushed the horror with a moment of bliss.

Then he stopped.

Then she stopped.

Tennessee laughed. Before *she* took more of him, she licked his lingering sweetness from her moist lips. "You kiss all the girls like that?"

Sho touched her face with subdued discretion. "A touch is usually sufficient, but you've proven most difficult."

"Aw, you say the nicest things." She wrinkled her nose, resting her head on Sho's chest. "So, all those little kisses you've been giving me lately..." She listened as Sho's heartbeat tumbled chaotic.

Sho apologized.

"Maybe I'm weird, but I kinda dig being snacked on." Tennessee's spunky laugh finally put Sho at ease.

"The more I'm *here*, the more I'll need to *snack*," Sho confessed lightly, but as they talked on about their new arrangement his gravity returned. "You must remain aware of how much I consume during the exchange. You may regain what I've taken, in time, but..."

Tennessee put her hands on her hips. "Then don't kiss me like that."

The line of Sho's jaw hardened, and he apologized. Again.

"We'll work on your sense of humor. I told you," Tennessee straightened out her velvet suit, "I may go in my shell, but I'll find my way out...sooner or later..."

"Allow me." He slid down the gold buckle of her black belt to just below her navel, smoothing the velvet he had crushed. "Correct me if I am wrong, but men will surely find this outfit alluring." There was a hint of possession in his dewy declaration, but she could only laugh; his emperor eyes were once again a glistening black onyx.

"Don't worry, samurai. Nobody's gonna snack on me but *you*." Tennessee rolled her hips.

Tennessee's hip rolls would have been the envy of many an Island dancer. Only a handful of people had witnessed her awesomeness when Mister and Missus required her to perform a traditional dance on her sixteenth birthday. By Sho's expression he was either enthralled or ready for another snack. Either one was good; Sho's smile was back.

"Now," she clutched his hand, "it's time I showed you what a goddamn Christmas miracle looks like."

# 17.

# Tiki Lane

Tiki torches weren't traditional Christmas lights stateside, but Lillie had a thing for them; Lille was always appropriating indigenous cultures as her own. That shit pissed Tennessee off. She charged extra to include appropriated bullshit—like, highway robbery extra! But nothing dissuaded Lillie. The socialite always got what she wanted. Tonight was no different.

Tennessee made a few calls, hired a few crews, and turned the Illies' front lawn into a grand winter fairyland. Tiki-lined meandering walkways led guests to two gleaming white party tents, fully accented with arched windows, billowing drapes, and crystal-encrusted chandeliers. Soft yellow bulbs dangling from the tents glowed like frolicking fireflies, creating an ethereal buffer to the canopy of fog rolling in from the wintry sea.

Guests were met in the first tent with expensive champagne, Beluga caviar, Wagyu beef meatballs, and an array of exotic cheeses, fruits, vegetables, and pastries galore. As mommies and daddies settled into their most comfortable roles, nannies and mannies accompanied their entitled charges to the second tent.

While equally sophisticated, the second tent offered a bit more Christmas. Tennessee had the tree brought out, along with a monster-sized wooden chair fit for a Santa king. Even Polar was

ready to play his part, decked out in his reindeer gear. He settled in on the red rug laid out next to Santa's chair; he enjoyed being a reindeer; he got lots of pats *and* peppermint sticks.

That's where Tennessee stood pretty much all night, greeting knee-high demons with stockings stuffed with sugary sweets and cold meats, because every brat came with a miniature pet of some sort nestled in its own designer handbag. Tennessee handed a stocking to one mannie who'd given up on life; the pug peeking out of a trendy sling carrier strapped to the mannie's chest was proof enough.

"Cool doggie sling bag thingy," Tennessee commented, a pinch of mean girl. She couldn't judge too much; she *was* dressed like Santa's slutty mistress, after all.

The kids gathered around Polar. Tennessee found herself gravitating toward Polar most of the night. She'd slayed a giant and a runt on that lawn mere hours earlier. The memory was more than a little disturbing. She wasn't sure she could shake loose the panic. She caught Sho's gaze flash on her, then away.

William strolled in, brandy warming his hand; he always wore a tuxedo to these events; he was a handsome man, nobility in those bones. Tennessee hadn't felt ridiculous in her outfit until now. There was never smut in his gaze, but tonight his eyes lingered on the curve of red velvet glued on a lovely hourglass figure.

"Good evening, Mrs. Claus. Walk with me." William tucked Tennessee's arm into the curve of his, locking her at his side before she could muster a reply.

Tennessee caught Phillip's gaze. She wasn't sure where William was taking her, but her face flushed as her mind went wild.

Could she kill a *man*? Could she kill a man she considered a friend? Could she kill him on his own lawn at his kids' Christmas bribe? All doubtful. Then again, if he tried to kill *her*...

William escorted Tennessee into the foyer, through the living room, stopping in the dining room. She sensed her samurai close, so she didn't run or scream. The room was dark, too dark to be any good. Tennessee kept her hand near her candy cane striped

stocking; she'd found an antique cast-iron letter opener in her mother's desk. The perfect weapon for close-quarters demon wrangling.

Rustling in the distance had her clutching the iron handle until her fingertips numbed, then...

"Surprise!"

The lights glared on, blinding Tennessee in a confused daze as the room screamed a pitchy, "Happy Birthday!"

Photo flashes accompanied a flurry of boisterous best wishes. Lin's volcanic laugh erupted behind a mountain-sized coffin cake; big black letters scrawled on top:

*So I'm 30! Eat me!*

Tennessee wasn't planning on celebrating her birthday. She'd lost track of days at this point, and with everything going on, it seemed too normal a thing to be doing anyhow.

"A party planner shouldn't organize her own event," William announced, and the fondness in his eyes meant more to Tennessee than a bunch of people screaming birthday blessings in her face.

"You had me worried for a minute." Tennessee fiddled with her stocking, shoving the letter opener back in. She let William give her a crushingly long hug. "I thought maybe you were going to fire me." She tried to lie, but her laugh was still too shaky, scaling up to a creepy shrill.

"Yeah," Phillip was there now, standing possessively close to Tennessee, "I was prepared to defend her honor against my loutish brother-in-law."

William's shock flipped injured. "Get a grip, Phillip. Tennessee's like my little sister! *I'd* defend her honor!"

Tennessee flashed a saucy wink at Phillip, mouthing, "*Like a sister*." As she slunk off to mingle, she snarled back, "*I* can defend my own honor, thank you very much!"

Buster the butler was there, and her favorite barista, Gabriel, and Marta and Mike from the morgue. Mike wasn't a friend; in fact, she hated him, but he wasn't insulting her at the moment;

he was shoving coffin cake down his stupid throat, so what the hell. Godzilla was eating cake too; Lin served him a huge piece; she only yelled a little, but mostly she was smiling. And way in the back Tennessee spied—

"Hill," she grumbled, watching a puff of smoke trail outside. Tennessee chased the cherry smoke, catching up with Hill on the terrace overlooking the thrashing sea. "I've been meaning to call you. Stumpy says *hey*." Tennessee let that information sink in before zinging, "A boy named Henry too."

Hill turned to greet Tennessee, her creased face seeming to wrinkle as she waited; she removed her pipe, affixing a wide grin. "They said you wouldn't make it to thirty. I said she will. Here we are, Nessie. Happy Birthday."

"I almost *didn't* make it." A flash of rage dirtied Hill's breezy gaze and for a scary moment Tennessee supposed maybe Hill *wanted* her dead; then she remembered this was *Hill*. "I had help, didn't I?"

"You got what you needed when it was right that you should. How you got it don't matter. Good people do all sorts of questionable acts for the right reasons, or for the wrong. We live with what we do. Unexpected folk surprise...good to remember that. Make it work, Nessie, and you'll see ninety. Fight it, and you won't make thirty-one. Keep to your heart and you can't go astray."

Tennessee had to ask about Dave and Watchdog's missing ransom letter, but Hill would only puff her pipe and nod. After a long silence, she patted the back of Tennessee's hand. "You quit the stick?"

"You quit the pipe?"

They shared a laidback laugh before Hill professed, "You'll quit as more delightful pursuits come about. You're a midnight baby, as I recall."

"Eleven-fifty-nine."

"That's about right. Till then, watch your head. The heir needs

a head..." Hill walked off the terrace, down the tiki lane; disappearing into the fog.

"Heir?" Tennessee wandered back to her birthday party, her mind foggier than the raging Pacific. Friends accosted her with hugs, presents, and a huge slice of cake ablaze with thirty dinosaur candles. And from beneath the white tablecloth, something grabbed her right ankle, then the left. She prepared to stomp whatever beast lay beneath when twin giggles preceded two towheads gazing up at her.

The twins were lying on their backs, one head beside Tennessee's shiny left boot, one beside her right; the tablecloth severing their heads from their bodies, their tongues hanging out. For a crazy second, she thought it was their sneaky way of letting her know they witnessed her decapitation shenanigans with the giant and runt. She scanned the room. Who else knew she was a killer?

Then she remembered Watchdog knocked out the Illies, and only Henry actually *saw* her slay giants on the lawn that morning, *and* she was suffering from posttraumatic stress.

All the guests were listening to Lin's stories; she was a fabulous storyteller; only problem was most of the stories were about Tennessee, and they were *embarrassing*. Tennessee growled at the twins; puffing out her thirty candles while dragging one finger in a clump of ashy grey frosting. She leaned over and drew a frosting cross on one towhead.

"You're *Billie*. Now beat it!"

The twins snickered and snarkled, stuck their tongues out at Tennessee, then slunk back under the tablecloth with such stealth she swore someone dragged them under.

Lin was in the middle of a story about a desperate Island girl who took a job jumping out of cakes. All eyes shifted to Tennessee.

"Hey, the outfit stayed *on* at all times." Tennessee set down her cake to run her fingers along the furry white faux fur of her knee-high boots. "Tips went *here*!"

The room burst into laughter.

Phillip's furrowed brow and Sho's tight gaze had Tennessee scrunching her face into a cute mess.

"Dudes, relax." Godzilla slapped both men on the back, big bear whaps. "She worked *bachelorette* parties!" Godzilla's loud laugh joyfully rolled into a *Ho-Ho-Ho* that caught the attention of several wandering trust-fund babies. The big man strolled back to his throne to grant more December wishes in the dead of February.

"Joy sucker," Tennessee pouted. "I like *my* story better."

Sho bowed his head as he crossed the room for champagne.

"I don't." Phillip downed his glass of water.

He was too tense for Christmas or birthdays or even a day off. "You on call?" She couldn't tell if he was angry at her or simply distracted. When he finally answered, she couldn't hear him over Lin's hollering,

"Ness! Open my present first! I *know* you don't have one of these!" Her history of perfectly twisted gag gifts had Tennessee protesting; it was bound to be awkward, but Lin would have her way.

A cautious look at Phillip, and Tennessee tore a tiny piece of pink wrapping from the corner; as if sedated, she peeked at the contents.

"Oh, just rip it!" Lin tore off the paper. "To replace your *old* one!" Lin directed her dark giggles at Phillip; buoyantly jogging back toward the champagne.

Phillip tugged the framed photograph from Tennessee's iron grip. He examined it for some time before replying tersely, "Very healthy, Tenny." He handed it back, swiftly walking off, presumably to check on Lillie; who had yet to make her grand entrance.

"Dammit." Tennessee stared at a smoky photograph of her and Sho; she was laughing so hard her eyes were crescent slits, Sho gazing down at her in joyful admiration, their hands entwined, holding the same cigarette. She remembered that exact moment,

and while she hated that Lin shoved that moment in Phillip's face, she was glad her best friend was the stalker type. Tennessee liked the picture, but she *loved* the moment. It was now her second favorite. She'd put it next to her first if she ever got back to the sanctuary of her silo.

"What's that?" Sho weaved out of the crowd, carrying two glasses of champagne.

Tennessee showed him Lin's gift, downing half her glass as he examined the photo. And in response to his surprised expression, "She has a telescopic lens."

"Oh." He examined the photo, pleasure emphasizing those high cheekbones. "Your laughter brings me joy."

Looking down at the photo, Tennessee scrunched a pout. "We're bad for each other?"

Sho bowed deeply, clinked his champagne glass to hers, and with a suave simplicity replied, "Onmyōdō," before gulping half his champagne.

Reaching for her cell phone, Tennessee opened a dictionary app and grimaced. "Spell it..."

Her rigid brow had Sho chuckling. He pulled her in for a quick hug. "You are the yin to my yang, Ten. The world is lucky you were born, and I am lucky to be chained to you."

She chuckled, curling against Sho. "You know, I've always wanted my own samurai." She clinked his glass, and this time, they both drank.

~

When Phillip returned to the party, Lillie was on his arm, waving like a princess addressing her royal court. She *looked* like the old Lillie; no hooker heels and crop tops. And when she talked, she was definitely the old Lillie—all bitch.

"Well, if it isn't Tennessee England, stealing my angels' spotlight. It's grotesquely obvious yet I feel utterly compelled to share that only a wretched case of self-importance would drive a grown woman to celebrate her birthday on the twins' Christmas.

Really, Tennessee, must you always be dumping your poor taste all over our impeccable home?"

"Lil!" Phillip released his sister, a bit roughly. "That's enough. This was William's idea as you very well know."

The flashy woman handed William a little blue box with a big white bow. "Willie, give it to her," she ordered her livid husband.

Tennessee wanted to refuse the gift, but William placed it in her hand with a sincere crush.

"For all the trouble you've caused me, Tennessee." Lillie snatched William's brandy, chugged it. "My decision is final, you're our new nanny. Figure out the schedule and stick to it!" She snuffed her nose up at Tennessee. "Spinsters can't be choosers."

Tennessee had the perfect cuss-free comeback, but Phillip's hands were on her waist, towing her out of clawing distance.

"Now, if you'll excuse me, *my* guests are waiting for *me*." Lillie shoved the empty glass into William's hand, then commenced parading through her loyal peasantry.

Before Tennessee could protest, William soothed the situation with a simple, "Consider it a personal favor, for *me*. I'll owe you one, Tennessee. It's only temporary. My people are looking for a good fit, but it's been slow going."

Phillip still had Tennessee in a firm hold. "Tenny's overworked as is, William. Adding nanny duties to her already-tenuous health is unconscionable. Her condition worsens every day..." The man stopped before he said what he really meant: *she's dying*.

"I would never risk her health," William challenged Phillip, but it was Tennessee who decided the matter.

"I'll do it." She peeled Phillip's fingers from her hips. "I'm not dead yet."

Tennessee had plenty of reasons to reject the horrible gig, but none came to mind. Lillie was a demon's favorite. The twins needed protecting. Simple. No one could do that job better than her. She rallied with a sultry, "I like the idea of William *owing* me."

There it was again, the flirt tacked to her words. What was it about him that brought out that girl? Maybe it was the tux.

William's lips curled into an entertained smirk; he winked at her, rambling off to refill his brandy.

"You're shameless." Phillip couldn't help but chuckle. "You've always had a crush on William."

"I do not. Have not. *Don't.*"

Phillip's critical smolder had Tennessee pouting until he reconciled the matter with wistful ease. "I've always thought it was sweet. He's a good guy, and Lil treats him...well, like her servant. I think it helps knowing someone looks up to him the way you do."

While still denying any ridiculous crush, Tennessee conceded, "Well, he was there, you know, when..."

"I know." Phillip's gaze wouldn't lock onto anything. "He told me."

Tennessee was considering how much William might have *shared* when Marta, town pathologist extraordinaire, strolled on by, admiring the couple.

"Love birds back in the same nest. I never lost hope."

"We're not..." Tennessee hesitated, looking up at Phillip with expectant eyes.

Phillip's gaze barely settled on hers before it went roaming once again. "Not compatible."

A piercing tug gripped Tennessee at her throat, only this ache had absolutely nothing to do with the demonic collar enslaving her. "Yeah, what the hell were we thinking," she grumbled, tearing open Lillie's gift.

It was another pair of socks. Expensive socks, with the original receipt attached. Lillie always gave her socks. Tennessee kept some, returned some. *These* she'd return. They were large and fuzzy and puke green, and they cost one hundred dollars. She'd buy something else, like cigarettes.

"Another pair of socks?" Phillip crinkled his gaze.

Tennessee shrugged. "Better than nothing, I guess." She was

aiming for gratitude but landed on an indictment. Phillip hadn't given her anything. She sidestepped the awkward conversation by bringing up Sho. Yeah, *so* less awkward.

Phillip retaliated with, "And what was Mr. Wonderful's gift to you?"

Tennessee almost choked on her response, she needed to edit, omit, and lie. "Uh, well, it was...a...sort of like...you know...how it is when...there's...uhmmm..."

"Here." He shoved a slim black cylinder into her palm, barely bigger than a stick of gum.

She flipped the device over in her hands. "Uh..."

"It's an emergency charger for your cell phone. I also put one in Riggy's glove compartment." He grinned, like all his problems were solved by this single technological wonder. "You're welcome."

Sho joined them now, carrying a slice of coffin cake.

"Look, Sho," Tennessee held up her shiny new charger, sarcasm radiating, "Phillip got me a battery!"

Instead of eating the hunk of cake on his fork, Sho fed the piece to Tennessee, leaving the fork in her mouth; he took the charger, so she took his plate.

"A prudent item." Sho inspected the device. "Thank you, Phillip." He faced Tennessee. "We should get another one, leave it in Riggy for emergencies."

Sho's eagerness, and Phillip's gratified grin, had Tennessee storming off to tell Lin just how horrible her boyfriend and ex-boyfriend were treating her on her goddamn birthday!

~

After a little more mingling, Tennessee thanked William for the surprise party. She also introduced Sho, which played out like any other routine introduction; not at all the penance she imagined. She could tell William approved. Sho's emotions were less readable.

Before the mini-socialites got restless, Tennessee headed back with Sho to the Christmas tent. Once there, Sho restocked the

organic, non-GMO, BPA-free, compostable juice boxes as Tennessee opened another bag of chocolate kisses. Godzilla had things under control and Polar kept the trust fund babies corralled in the tent, so Tennessee grabbed Sho's hand, juice box and all, and dragged him from the tent, down the Tiki torch path, toward a private nook on the windswept ridge. No one went there but her and Phillip, and that was a long time ago.

"Hill's responsible for Dave." Tennessee focused on a far-off illumination cutting through the nubilous night; it came from the town's sole lighthouse, still a guiding force for seafarers and drifters alike.

"She confessed?"

"No, but she said something that got me thinking...this connection we have, it's addictive, isn't it?" Tennessee kept her distance, unsure if she even wanted him to answer that.

Sho could taste the spice of her anxiety on his tongue. "If you lack balance, yes. As with anything. However, I believe your heart will ground you."

"And where does my heart lie?" Tennessee sat on a rock, searching her skimpy outfit for a smoke. "Shoot, I left my pack in Riggy."

"I'll get it." Sho was trying to leave quickly, but he was also having a hard time leaving quickly. Riggy was well over fifty feet away.

Fog horns groaned, not far offshore. They reminded Tennessee of the giant she slayed that morning, of his drumming gnarr that almost shattered her heart. She struggled to take a full breath, reliving the moment she sliced off his head. It was *not* a moment she wished to remember. Ever. When she finally managed a full inhale, she exhaled a cloud of frozen breath.

"Ten," Sho took her hands, "we're not alone..."

"We never are." Tennessee stood up. "I'm starting to think they like watching us. Plus, do you know how much money and power is in that tent? Demons like that, right? The *Founders* are hobnobbing with the Illies in that tent...and judges, lawyers,

finance dudes, kingpins, moguls, you name it...souls were sold! And it's not just *here*...they're everywhere, all the time...favorites, drop-ins...the town is either infested by demons or I'm just getting used to feeling them."

"Probably a little of both."

"We have nine hundred and ninety-nine demons left before we're free." Tennessee mourned the inevitable loss. "But, Sho...who will I be after taking all those lives?"

"You need not take lives, Ten."

"I already have!"

"In self-defense. The first demon killed that woman. It is unfortunate, but you had no hand it that. We had to destroy that demon, it left us no choice. Look at Henry. He is alive because of you."

"A fluke."

"No," he snapped. "*Skill*. In this war, you can only hope to minimize the number of deaths. You may choose to extract, *wrangle*, demons from the host. You've already found a way. Iron traps the demon, detains it until Zaada claims it. *You* are not killing...not the human or the demon. Other wranglers may have chosen to destroy demon and host. Zaada need not claim the demon in that eventuality, it goes to her upon destruction in this realm. They sought efficiency. You seek something more...humane."

"*Humane* usually means there's a catch..." She squinted, it couldn't be good.

He sighed, confessing delicately, "You must watch over those you detain. Others will come for them, perhaps Ibrahim himself one day. Demons are a commodity, Ten, as are other creatures...you and I included. Wrangling is the riskier path, but one that may save lives."

"Shoot, now I'm a warden too? That's totally Phillip's gig."

"Caretaker then." He smirked.

"But even if I take *one* human life. Who will I be?"

"You will be Tennessee England: daughter, mortician,

wrangler, master, and friend. You will be all that you ever were, and *more*." Sho moved closer, and before either of them was fully aware, his hands were guiding her lips toward his. He was on the verge of taking a bit of Tennessee's despair, when an annoying little voice had her turning away.

"I told you I saw her walk over here with her boyfriend!" Billie, the one with the frosting cross on her forehead, was dragging Phillip around the rocky outcropping. "Why wouldn't you believe me? *She wouldn't do that*, you said. *Not there*, you said. But look, she's here...right where I said she'd be. I was right!" The little girl put her hands on her little hips.

Then Millie walked up, mirroring her twin. "That's the guy from the accident, Uncle Phillip. Remember, how we were telling you. He saved Tennessee from the creepizoids wearing cloaks. He's like magic."

"Okay, girls, that's enough make-believe!" Tennessee grabbed one twin in each hand, dragging them back to Christmas. "Time for presents!"

She couldn't look Phillip in the eye, not after her betrayal. She shouldn't have taken Sho to *their* place; she should have been stronger, resisted the addictive urge to have Sho fix her. She just wanted him to take the edge off. Sho was better for her lungs than smoking, and he smelled way better than tobacco. She swam in his scent; a welcome distraction until the twins started to complain.

"Your hands are freezing!" Millie wailed.

"Ouch! You're giving us frostbite!" Billie exaggerated.

Tennessee rushed the girls down tiki lane toward Riggy. She needed a spear or her battle-axe, anything iron. The collar tugged and crackled. Stopped.

Sho was coming.

The girls were shrilling "Frosty the Snowman."

"Sshh, quiet girls. You'll wake the dead."

Tennessee flung open Riggy's trunk, and out jumped Maria.

# 18.

# LARPing 101

"Zombie!"

A mortician's worst nightmare. The girls screamed. Tennessee stumbled back, tripped over tiny feet, splatting on her ass; she never let go of the twins, so they piled on top.

Maria was dead, and she looked it. Despite Tennessee's makeup magic, there was a sallowness to Maria's soggy skin, a depleted cakiness, as if she had been sweating in her casket, or maybe crying. Her eyes were glued closed, her nostrils stuffed with cotton, and her mouth lightly sewn shut, but she seemed aware of Tennessee's movements, and she seemed to have something to say.

Tennessee yanked the curious twins behind her, their perfectly curled heads peeking out from either side. Maria sniffed, shuffling toward Tennessee. The dead Maria held her rickety body slumped and loose, arms dangling at her sides, knees clunking together, and feet wobbling past her hips. But her hair, ah, that hair was full of life and spring and bounce. Gone was the bun Lin had pinned in place.

"Whatcha doin', Maria?" Tennessee sang sweetly. Because this wasn't happening. No way in hell this was real.

Maria cocked her head at a painful angle; she hissed once, scurrying off through the wet grass toward the tents. The music,

bustle, and laughter from partygoers spooked the dead woman; she veered off into the misty forest.

The twins froze, then burst into snarkle-cackle-giggles.

"Awesome jump scare!"

"Best Christmas prank ever!"

Tennessee pulled her battle-axe from Riggy, followed by a spear and a samurai sword. "Yeah, totally rad. Merry Christmas...*again*! Now go back to the party, girls. I'll let my old pal Maria here know what a fantastic job she did. Head's up, big knife!" Tennessee tossed a sword over the twins' heads. They ducked and didn't come up until they heard another voice.

"Come on, Ten, she went this way." Sho was running, sword in hand.

Then Tennessee was running. "Girls! Find your uncle. Stay in the light!"

Giggling a little less, the twins ran down tiki lane, but when Tennessee turned to make sure they made it to the tents, two men sprang from the shadows, grabbed the twins, and attempted to drag them into the fog.

But these were no ordinary seven-year old girls; they kicked and bit, screamed and cussed. Oh, the swears those girls shrieked.

Billie's dried frosting cross smeared as she went limp, slipping herself under her attacker's armpit; the gutsy twin even pirouetted in front of her would-be attacker right before snap-kicking his knee. The man's leg buckled, exactly as she'd intended.

Millie bit her attacker's forearm, fraying his suit jacket and losing her last front baby tooth.

"Give it back!" she howled, blood dripping from her mouth, as the man gawked in horror at his tooth-stabbed arm.

Tennessee raced toward the girls, forcing Sho to turn back.

Polar leapt from the second tent, followed by a very pissed-off Santabeast.

Having been thwarted by children, *girls*, the men scrambled off.

Polar kept after them. She wasn't going to lose him a second time, but the twins...

"Girls," she kneeled by them, "you all right?"

The twins were so angry they started to cry.

"Stay with them," Godzilla demanded. "Sho, let's go!"

Sho didn't budge.

"Dude, you can't be chicken-shit! Not with *that*...wait, why the hell do you have a sword?" Polar barked and howled. "Whatever, man!" One last disgusted glance at Sho and Godzilla ran after Polar. "Candyass!"

"Girls! I need you to pull it together." Tennessee didn't want to yell at them, but they needed it. "You were right about Sho. He's magic. Let him avenge you now."

"You'll tell us all about it?" It was Billie, smeared coffin-colored frosting adorning her forehead.

"Yes, anything!"

"Deal!"

Then pride seeped through. "Way to kick ass, girls." Tennessee raised her battle-axe.

"Indeed," Sho bowed his respect, "you bear the warrior's heart."

The girls' smiles widened as they ran toward the tents.

It didn't take long for Sho to catch up with Godzilla; it took Tennessee approximately fifty feet longer. She was slowing Sho down, which she would address once she had a goddamn chance to get fit; if people would just stop trying to kill her for a few days she'd get in some cardio.

"He's not chicken-shit." Tennessee's blistered rebuff had Godzilla cocking back a punch.

"What the hell are *you* doing here, Ness? You're in no condition to kick some ass."

"Humph." She smirked, waving her battle-axe and spear in his face. "Says the guy *not* holding these wicked-awesome weapons."

Godzilla stopped, took a close look at his friends. "Santa's slutty helper wielding medieval weapons? A man in black with a samurai sword..."

"*Katana*, big guy." Sho swung the blade with awe in his gaze. "Or as Ten says, *big knife*."

Godzilla's glare held *many* other names for Sho's goddamn katana; he almost growled at Tennessee. "A samurai? Two kiddie-nappers? When did I miss casting calls for *The Twilight Zone?*"

"And *one* zombie!" Tennessee pushed past Godzilla, nailing Maria in the gut with the blunt end of the axe head. It stunned the dead woman, changed her direction, but didn't stop her scurrying.

"What the f—..." Godzilla stumbled back, doubling over to level his jagged breath.

"The *head*, Ten," Sho instructed patiently. "It is always your first strike."

Tennessee huffed a sigh. "I know, but I worked so hard getting her head just right."

Both men stared at her.

"Fine!" She picked up the iron spear she had dropped, then gave the battle-axe to Godzilla. "You can *borrow* this one, but I want it back. It has sentimental value. I got it from a giant..." Tennessee smirked, excited to *finally* tell someone something. "A giant I *slayed*!" She wiggled her hips.

Godzilla's mouth gaped in disbelief, but his eyes were on her spear. "*That* gonna slay a zombie?"

Tennessee wrenched her shoulders up. "Damned if I know. Maria's my first zombie."

"*That's* Maria Garcia?!"

Tennessee nodded. "Just stay alive, okay. I'm new at this too."

Godzilla raised the axe over his shoulder. "Stay behind me, Ness. I won't let nothin' touch you. Damn, I knew you were hiding something, but I figured you were playing around with both dudes...but *this* actually makes more sense."

Tennessee was so insulted that Godzilla would think her a two-timing cheat, she was actually ready to take someone's head. When Maria leapt from the fog, Tennessee swung for Maria's neck, but the dead woman performed a remarkable double flip over Tennessee's head.

"Is it just me, or is Maria Garcia getting way more agile?" She swung again, only to miss because Maria leapt into a tree. "*I* can't do that."

Maria mumbled behind sewn lips. She worked on untying the stitches as the three backed up to get a better view of the situation.

Polar's hysterical barking grew louder; he was headed back their way, which meant others were, too.

Eight men stepped out of the fog, uniformly surrounding the tree Maria perched on.

"Cruz?" Godzilla recognized his college buddy. Cruz said nothing, kept his eyes at his feet.

Polar skidded out from the fog, panting his way to Tennessee's side, eyeing Mr. Garcia and his seven sons just like everyone else.

Godzilla, Sho, and Tennessee boxed in the men.

"*This* is why we requested a quick burial." Mr. Garcia stepped forward, his chiding tone gutting Tennessee.

She wanted to apologize for disgracing his daughter's death, because this was *her* fault, she was sure. She must have done something to make Maria turn into, well, whatever she was turning into. Then she remembered the fear in the twins' eyes.

"Your boys tried to take *my* girls!" Tennessee aimed her spear at Mr. Garcia's throat. "Why?"

"You took *our* girl."

Dammit, that was true.

"*Borrowed* her...I was going to bring her back," Tennessee challenged the man who would bury his daughter in a rag. "Difference is, your girl is *dead*."

"That's a matter of opinion."

"Well, in my professional opinion, Maria *is* dead. If you jerks did something to make her *not* dead, then that's on *you*!" She wasn't ready to confess just yet. Even morticians make mistakes. Maybe Maria *wasn't* dead.

"You are as brazen as your grandmother. She was also a Tennessee." The words pulled a perverse glare from Mr. Garcia.

"You want my head, is that it? Well, get in line!"

The seven sons began to chant in a language Tennessee was convinced she should understand, but didn't. Sho moved closer to her, Polar howled, and Godzilla got the creeps. Mr. Garcia wasn't about to explain anything.

Someone was about to die. As Tennessee's hands chilled to icy blocks, she knew *they* came to watch.

"Now, now, Santo," a new voice drummed out of the fog.

"Hill?" Tennessee turned as the old woman strolled into the clearing, carrying her crooked cane and cherry-spiced pipe.

Hill continued, "You've crossed a line trying to snatch them girls."

Mr. Garcia's macho demeanor betrayed a modicum of fear. He cleared his throat before accusing anew, "*Your* charge crossed a line. She killed Dave. Without Dave, Maria rose. That is a problem we have come to remedy."

"Nessie," Hill kept her gaze on Mr. Garcia, "you kill this man's dog?"

"Of course not! I thought someone killed *my* dog!"

"Ask her about Maria's dress," Mr. Garcia commanded.

"Nessie?"

"It got...stained?" Tennessee stuttered, and everybody knew she was lying. "Fine, it burst into flames! Not my fault!"

The seven sons stopped chanting. There was quiet until they announced in a single booming voice, "The competition has begun. The legion of Ibrahim hunts. The Empress has chosen her champion. The tethered feeds."

Mr. Garcia backed away from Tennessee, disgust in his gaze. The seven sons abandoned their stations beneath the cedar, and Hill settled the commotion with the same stringency she used to run her auctions.

"Silence!" She slammed her cane on the grass, and somehow it rumbled the ground with little shuddering earthquakes. "Nessie, you have fed your keeper?"

"Uh, I don't kiss and tell, Hill."

The Garcia men increased their distance from Tennessee and

Sho. Mr. Garcia's revulsion put a little quake in the tremor of his speech. "You may hold power, Hill, but we are the guardians of this realm. What is done cannot be undone. The wrangler and keeper are lost to us."

Hill wedged her pipe in the crick of her mouth. "You'd do well not to judge, Santo. Tethers make do, as Maria made do. You claim to be guardians of Saint James, yet you've sacrificed your kin. And for what? Maria suffers still. The guardians were once impartial noblemen; watchers and archivists for all happenings. They had no hand in matters of fate."

"We still are!" Mr. Garcia blasted. "What this girl has done violates the sanctity of the tether. You failed her. She should have secured her keeper's healing gifts without accepting the tether. He was to rot off. Now, if *he* rots, *she* rots."

That pit in Tennessee's stomach burned. "Rot? I'm not letting Sho rot!" She looked to Sho, then to Hill.

"By feeding this demon your suffering, you've accepted Zaada's deal and thus Ibrahim's challenge," Hill explained. "He's opened a new portal, right here in Saint James."

"Sho's not a demon!" Tennessee shoved her iron spear into his hands. "See! Iron does nothing to him! He's helping me *fight* demons! He won't hurt me, Hill. He has to obey me; he has to tell me the truth!"

Hill puffed her pipe. "Your soul protects him from himself. If you had not fed him, he would have perished, and the tether, broken. He does not lie to you because he *is* you. He obeys you because he *is* you."

"You're talking in circles. If he's a demon, then I'm a demon. Sho is a good man. I don't give a god damn what any of you say!"

"Ten," Sho placed the spear at Tennessee's feet, "please forgive me. Had I known any of this...I'd have..."

"Don't! Everyone just shut up and let me think! You're all trying to confuse me...you're trying to twist what I know is true into something evil..." Tennessee backed up a little too close to Maria's tree. The *not* dead woman leapt down beside her. Maria

had successfully removed the stitching inside her mouth and was about to speak when a shifting of movement from the Garcia camp caught the gang's attention.

Cruz aimed a 9mm at his sister, and fired.

Godzilla hollered. Sho ran toward Tennessee, but she shoved Maria out of the way; the undead woman scampered on her hands and knees back into the fog. Polar didn't move; he just laid there, curled up beside his master, as Tennessee bled from a gunshot wound to her gut.

There was chaos.

Sho rushed to Tennessee's side, falling to his knees, head bowed. He failed his master, but he would not let her die.

Hill lashed out at the Garcia men, unleashing a ghoulish roar so chilling the men scattered off in all directions. Except for Mr. Garcia.

"Leave her, keeper! Your gift taints her soul. You will drain her until nothing remains."

Sho met the man's furious glare with a defiance that made the patriarch flinch; he never once took his hands off Tennessee's wound. The bleeding slowed.

Hill laid her hand on Sho's shoulder. "Do stop. Santo is correct. Your gift takes her goodness. Each time you heal her, she changes. One day, she will come back all wrong. Perhaps, a demon or, worse, a favorite."

"Sho," Tennessee whispered, feebly gripping his bloody hand, "please stop. I've said my goodbyes."

The keeper warred against his inborn need to save his wrangler, and to obey.

Polar whined, looking from Sho to Tennessee and back again.

"A wrangler deserves a dignified life and honorable death." Sho's tortured words echoed the agony behind his dulling eyes. He held both her hands. "*Tennessee England* deserves better...better than this demon can give. *This* wasn't the deal. We shall perish together. I promise you no pain."

Already serenity laced her veins, leaving a hint of salt

languishing on her tongue. Her lashes weighed down her eyelids, stalling blinks to long lulls of near slumber.

Satisfied, Mr. Garcia left.

"Ness! No!" Godzilla ripped off his shirt, wadded the cloth over the once again gushing wound.

Phillip was there now, and Godzilla expressed his relief, but even Tennessee, in her flummoxed state, knew that was too fast.

"Keeping tabs on me?" she muttered, burgundy streams of blood trickling past her paling lips.

"Yes, actually." He flashed a cocky smirk.

"Dammit, Watchdog." Tennessee's head flopped to one side. She closed her eyes, feeling lethargic but no pain.

Watchdog grabbed Sho. "Now would be the time, keeper!"

Godzilla's shirt couldn't soak up any more blood. He boomed, "I don't know what the hell's going on, but whatever you're gonna do, do it now, people! Hang in there, Ness. I got you..."

Tennessee gurgled her gratitude. "I owe you a great big steak, big guy...you've always got my back...watch out for this shifty bastard, he likes to wear Phillip's meatsuit, but he ain't my Phillip...tell my Phillip I died au-la naturel...no drugs required..."

Now Godzilla *and* Watchdog were demanding Sho *do something*!

Sho met their tormented looks with a samurai's resolve. "If she stays tethered to me, she'll fall. You don't want her in the demon realm, trust me." Sho's eyes found Tennessee's and he whispered a lover's protective rasp, "I won't condemn you. Ten, I...I..." She waited for the words that would match his ardent gaze. Then, with the passion of a loyal servant, his sight plagued by suffering, "I know what they do to wranglers in hell."

Before Tennessee could uncurl her smile, Hill smacked Sho's head with her crooked cane. "Don't be a dolt! Even the damn dog knew I was lying through my dentures." Polar barked, licking Tennessee's face as Hill explained further, "Your healings only weaken Nessie if she no longer loves. You must feed prudently to ensure she retains her humanity. Many tethers fail because

one takes too much from the other. Act as equals and Nessie shall retain her soul, and you might earn yours. Santo and the guardians must prove they can once again be trusted. We must keep them guessing. *You* have almost as much to prove, young samurai. Get to it, keeper. Save my girl. Quickly!"

Watchdog and Godzilla backed away, giving Sho space.

"Do you agree, keeper?" Hill's roar brought Sho hope.

"I do." Sho stroked Tennessee's cheek. "Ten must agree as well."

"I do," Tennessee slurred, laughed, and said it again. "I do."

Even before Sho laid his hands back on Tennessee, her coloring improved, and the bleeding had stopped. Sho forced a frail grin, his black eyes once again muted.

Tennessee's forehead wrinkled with worry. "You're hungry."

"Not at all." Sho bowed his head in deep meditation. "I'm merely welcoming your wound as my own."

She swatted his hands away. "Kiss me."

"I am *trying* to save you, Ten." He resisted his overriding need to obey.

"Kiss me," she tried pushing his hands away, "then save me."

"Absolutely not." The urge was almost too great.

"You've forgotten that I'm the boss of you."

"I have not forgotten." Sho raised a staunch brow, yet he was leaning closer to her. "I thought we had a deal about such orders."

"Jesus, Mary, and Joseph!" Hill roared. "Kiss the woman!"

The sparring couple laughed at the reprimand. Then Sho's hands were on Tennessee's cheeks, and his lips were on hers.

Hill and Godzilla looked away; Watchdog and Polar did not.

Watchdog clocked the healing at exactly two minutes and seven seconds. A record for such a wound.

For Tennessee and Sho, it was a lifetime.

~

As everyone, minus Watchdog, walked back to the Christmas tent, the real Phillip met the crew. He stood in the center of tiki lane, arms outstretched.

"Someone want to explain why the twins are claiming to have seen a zombie, been briefly abducted by sexy Spaniards, and then rescued by a magic man and his hot, axe-wielding sidekick?"

It was Sho who responded with a brilliant, ready-made lie. "Did Ten never mention my LARPing hobby?"

"*Larping?*" Phillip practically spat the ridiculous word.

"Yes," Sho still clutched his sword, which he now used to slice and skewer the air, "Live Action Role Playing. It's a great adventure of the imagination. You may join. If you dare."

"Seriously?" Phillip was aghast as Hill walked ahead, along with Sho followed by Godzilla.

"Yes, Phillip. And I take offense to being Sho's sidekick!" Tennessee sauntered over, entwining her arm around his. "*I'm* the hot superhero, you see. And Sho's *my* magic-man sidekick. Now, Godzilla there is the battle-axe-wielding Santabeast, but he's only borrowing the axe from me; he needs to get his own gear. He's new to the crew, just joined up tonight."

When lying was Tennessee's kryptonite, the truth was her only option.

"Really? And Hill's into this play-acting?" Phillip doubted.

"Nah, she was just calling us to eat."

Phillip laughed. "That sounds like Hill." Mildly amused and completely taken in by her playfulness, he pulled her closer, securing her arm with his hand. "And the zombie?"

"Gone. She took off. *You* can fill in if you're game."

"No, thank you." Phillip examined her head-to-toe; he tugged the damp, blood-splattered hole in her velvet coat. "Let me guess...method acting."

"Caught a bullet in the gut," she pouted, inspecting the hole. "It's too bad, I really liked this one..."

Phillip's redolent smile crinkled the corners of his eyes as he murmured, "I did too."

Tennessee watched Phillip's emerald gaze brighten before resting her head against his shoulder. It was part exhaustion, part joy in being alive. "Lunch tomorrow?"

That was unexpected. *This* was his old Tennessee, not the one who avoided him, resented him, and flipped him the bird every chance she got. Reason told him to admit her, run more scans, but his heart told him to shut up.

"How about pizza," Tennessee suggested. "I'm tired of burgers."

"You sure you're all right?" He checked her forehead for a fever. "You love burgers."

She met his gaze with a surly smile. "Things change."

The fresh hope on Phillip's face was the perfect *normal* ending to a wildly abnormal evening. She had some answers, and Phillip. For now, it was enough.

# 19.

# Fighting Chance

When Sho poofed, Tennessee knew Maria had roamed too far from The Mirror. She'd deal with the zombie in the a.m. It was pretty traumatic driving Riggy home without Sho riding shotgun, but at least she had Polar; and, really, Sho *was* right there.

Mike and Marta had a body for Tennessee anyway. Godzilla was set to pick him up in the morning. So, Tennessee drove home to her silo; showered in her shower, ate in her kitchen, sat in her living room, and fell asleep in her own bed. She approached her last night in her silo with a somber deliberation.

She loved her silo, but she loved Sho more.

When the morning sun played a spectacle on her ceiling, Tennessee cried.

She wasn't made for letting go.

Polar scooted closer to her on the bed, whining just enough to let her know he understood. He was sad too; he loved their life before all this weird stuff.

Tennessee snoozed her alarm six times before peeling off the sheets and dressing for the day. She opted for ripped jeans and a soft, fitted tee; messy pony and no makeup. She was in moving mode; she grabbed a suitcase, flung open her dresser, and started

tossing in clothes. She clutched one of Phillip's old t-shirts until her fist turned white.

"*Not compatible.*" She let another tear fall; better *here* than out there.

She rummaged through her closet, looking for...there it was: Phillip's old gym bag, the one she'd kept for no good reason. Lin was right, it was time to toss and burn. After packing up all of Phillip's clothes, she stared at her favorite photo sitting on her dresser. Tears were tumbling by the time her cell phone moaned out "Why."

"What." Tennessee shoved the frame into Phillip's gym bag.

Phillip didn't say anything.

"What do you *need*, Phillip?" She wiped her nose with the back of her hand.

"Tenny," he knew she was crying, "are you alone?"

"Polar's here." She sniffled, struggling for control of her voice. "I'm meeting Sho at the shop. Why?"

Polar raced downstairs, his tail wagging him sideways.

"Open up, I'm on your porch."

"Oh, that's...actually convenient." She tossed in one final shirt, her favorite. "Be right down." She grabbed a tissue, another, taking her damn time descending the stairs. She wasn't in the mood for company, so she walked outside instead of inviting Phillip in.

Polar rushed Phillip; the man took a knee to hug his dog.

"Godzilla's got a body on ice, so...um, here..." Tennessee tossed Phillip his old gym bag. "I'm moving to the shop...with Sho..."

He stood up pensively. It wasn't the welcome he was expecting. She had been *different* last night. Phillip unzipped the bag, pushing clothes aside in search of something. He must have found it because the hardness of his gaze, and grind of his clenched jaw, had Tennessee changing the subject.

"Since I'm on nanny duty now, the twins will be at the shop...like, with *dead people*. I hope William understands that. I have obligations and..."

Phillip wasn't listening, he was staring at the framed photo of *them*. "We were happy, weren't we?" His gaze, trapped in their past, had Tennessee fighting tears of her own.

She backed up against the front door, hand on the doorknob, gaze on Phillip's shoes because those emerald eyes were killing her. *This* was her Phillip, the man who made her hands clammy just by laying those eyes on her. She couldn't trust herself. He'd hurt her. Left her. Without a damn good reason.

"Probably not," she managed, but it was a lie. And he knew it. She caught a glimpse, and it hurt. "We're not compatible, remember..."

"Maybe *I* was lying."

"You'd do that?" Tennessee gazed up at him, astonished. "On my birthday?"

"No, not when it might be..." He stopped. He couldn't.

"What? My last?" She could.

"I'm sorry, Tenny." His gaze wandered, sticking on their photo, then he was muttering, mostly to himself, "*I* ruined us. I held you so tightly, I nearly broke you. I could see what I was doing to you...preventing you from experiencing life the way you wanted, the way you deserved. I was holding you back, Tenny, so I let you go. I realize now how wrong I was...how much time we've lost..."

She wanted to forget, to tell him it was a long time ago, but she only got out a timid, "I'm *different* now...we both are."

Phillip placed the photo in the bag, eyes on her. "Seeing you with Sho...you laugh, Tenny. You're happy. I don't think I ever made you laugh the way he does. *That's* what I wanted for you. That's what I couldn't give you...I wish to hell I could because I still lov..."

Tennessee couldn't hear this; she opened the front door and slipped in.

Phillip might have completed his sentiment, said the words she knew he was about to say, but she didn't hear any of it. She ran upstairs and puked.

It wasn't nerves or posttraumatic stress or even fear; it was the

collar. It wanted its coin, and it was going to make her deathly ill until it got paid. She freshened up, grabbed her suitcase on her way back downstairs. She expected Phillip to be gone, not waiting for her exactly where she'd left him.

Phillip stood on the porch, more reserved than before; Polar at his side.

"Sorry about that...I suddenly felt sick." Tennessee went with the truth, even if it sounded like Phillip was at fault.

"I shouldn't have..."

She waved him off. "We still on for lunch?"

He rocked back. "I'm confused. You just ran from me, but you still want to have lunch?"

"I just got sick, Phillip...no big deal..."

Phillip's gaze soured to shock as he took in her pale skin and tired eyes. "Are you...as your doctor, I need to ask..." The emblazed words speared his heart, ripping fresh wounds over old, threatening a permanent sever of their shared artery. "Are you pregnant?"

Tennessee had to think about that one. She didn't remember having any fun that might end up with the *pitter-patter* of tiny feet. Her delay, though, only heightened Phillip's mania.

"Oh my god, you *are* pregnant! All the signs were there. I can't believe I missed them..."

Tennessee laughed with a snort then spurted out, "Man, I'm glad *you're* not the father because that reaction could wreck a girl."

Now Phillip looked like *he* might be sick.

She shoved him. "I'm not pregnant, you idiot! God! You're a freak!"

"Please tell me you're being careful!"

"Ah, god! Stop! You're gonna make me hurl again!"

"I'm your doctor, Tenny."

"Nu-uh! Gross! You handle my *brain*, not my other bits! I'm *never* going to discuss my sex life with you. Ugh, god. This is *not* happening..."

Phillip apologized, but Tennessee couldn't let the double standard go.

"You know, I don't ask you about your *string* of girlfriends after me...I hope *you're* being careful! Damn."

Phillip inhaled a deep breath, nearly over the shock. "If you asked, I would tell you the truth. We're adults."

"All I have to say to that is *eeww*! No."

Relieved, Phillip confessed, "Yeah, I'd rather not know what you've been up to, either."

After a bit of quiet, Tennessee quipped, "*Friend zone?*"

Phillip hesitated. Soon, his eyes found hers. "For now."

"Whatever, Phillip, you've lost your mind...I know you've got a string of women at your beck and call, you don't need to press rewind." He was a catch; she saw how the ladies looked at him. He told her she was being ridiculous; he scarcely had time for himself, let alone a *string* of women. "A handful then," she scoffed, checking her phone for Godzilla's text. She was getting anxious to see Sho.

Phillip could tell. She didn't know it, but her lips bunched to one side in an endearing little scrunch when she talked about Sho; anytime she made that face Phillip knew where her mind had drifted. One day, soon, she might be fine hearing about his love life after her. Then, she'd be lost to him forever. Of course, if he told her the truth, that he'd been miserable without her, lost, *faithful*, taking double shifts to avoid entanglements, she'd probably laugh at him. It sounded like a lie to him too.

Tennessee shot off a quick text to Godzilla. She looked up in time to catch Phillip's studied gaze on her. "What?"

"Nothing."

But in Phillip's gaze, Tennessee recognized an ache; it was the same ache she'd caught in her own eyes after seeing Phillip in town with women—maybe friends, maybe lovers. She didn't know, was afraid to ask. *She'd* been the one pining; she never imagined *he'd* pined for her; not for a second.

"Lillie said you're back with Catherine." Tennessee played with her phone, scrubbed an invisible smudge from the screen.

Phillip's shoulders sank as he leaned against the porch railing; no wonder she hated him. It was a lie, of course, and Catherine was a lot like Lillie, always demeaning Tennessee. There's no coming back from *that* kind of betrayal. "Lil is wrong. I wouldn't do that, Tenny. Not to *you* or *myself*."

"Hey, you can play half the coast if you want, no concern of mine." That damn smudge wasn't coming off the damn screen.

"*Play*," Phillip balked, "not my style as you very well know."

"Ha!" Tennessee plunked to a slouchy seat on the steps. "What the hell do *I* know? All I've been doing lately is finding out how much I *don't* know...every damn thing, it's all upside down." She reached for a pack of cigs she had stashed in a flower pot. "I mean, I *knew* we were happy, but apparently, I was delusional...I think it runs in my family..." She almost chuckled. "Don't worry, I won't smoke until you're gone. Don't want the good doctor smelling like the crazy mortician's dirty ashtray..."

Tennessee fiddled with her cig until Phillip's shoes were right beside her; she put the cig in her mouth, cupping the end to light up.

"I'm not gone yet, Tenny."

"Sure, you are." She flicked her lighter again and again, humor in her gaze.

"And I'm *not* going anywhere." Phillip dropped his gym bag in Tennessee's lap. "In fact, I'm tossing my hat back in. Whatever time we have left together, I'm taking it. See you at noon. Be ready."

Tennessee was so stunned she didn't throw the bag at Phillip's head as he walked away, didn't sling curses, or even flip him the bird. And when Phillip shot her a fiery glance over his shoulder, she had yet to catch her breath.

# 20.

# You Can't Save the World, Tennessee

Polar leapt out of Riggy, growling at the burly, bearded guy leaning against a badass, jacked-up black dually. Jasper took a knee, hand open and low; Polar sniffed the man, grunted, then wedged between his master and this man who smelled of metal and ash.

"I see you got your dog back." Jasper flashed an assured grin, flipping a coin with his thumb, catching it in his palm.

"Straight up." Tennessee crooned though her gaze was on that coin. She recognized it right away, but waited for Jasper to haul the wrought iron cross out of the bed of his truck first.

"Where do you want it? It's heavier than it looks."

She opened the dead end of Riggy. "This will do."

"It's not staying *here* at the shop?" Jasper laid the cross next to iron spears, swords, and a sweet battle-axe. A note of concern in his tone, he chuckled, "Tough night?"

"Ah, average as nights go these days." She sipped her mindbender.

Polar still blocked Tennessee, so when Jasper reached over to hand her the coin, he had to stretch over the dog. Polar grunted as Jasper dropped the coin into Tennessee's palm.

"*That* was sitting on the cross when I opened the mold. I guess anything's possible, right?"

"I hope to hell not." Tennessee shoved the coin in her pocket; the collar was getting testy, tugging and twitching. "Thanks again, Casper. So...you'll probably be seeing more of me now that...um..."

Jasper lowered his gaze, running his hand over his beard. "I'd like that, Tennessee. I'll have those *tools* completed by week's end. That gonna work for your...sideline?"

"Should do." She nuzzled Polar with her free hand while sipping her mindbender. "Bill me, 'kay?"

"With you, it's barter or nothing." Jasper strolled back to his truck, Polar's deep growl flipping Tennessee's gut.

"Ah, actually..." She *hated* owing people.

Jasper knew her too well. "It's not like that, my love. It's simple...I won't take money from the girl whose heart beats in rhythm with mine."

Tennessee dropped her gaze to take a sip, trying not to giggle hot coffee straight up her nose; Jasper's heaviness was seductive when they were young, but now it seemed a little cheesy. Even so, that man was *so*...Jasper.

"You've got the hard job, Tennessee. All I do is melt shit." Jasper winked, then drove off as Godzilla pulled in with the dead body she'd been waiting for.

~

Apparently, a Mr. Gloor slipped in his bathtub and drowned. Tragically common. Tennessee had seen too many slips in the bath, one of the reasons she preferred showers.

Godzilla just got Mr. Gloor wheeled into the prep room when Lin's every-Asian accent screeched in from the front.

"How you not call? I worry! You no call!"

"Hey, chick, it's a little early for angry Asian. Oh, and thanks *a lot* for that photo stunt with Phillip. *Nice*."

"Some of my best work." Lin plonked herself on a comfy chaise lounge as Godzilla positioned himself behind the refreshment

counter; he tore open six pastries, shoving an entire blueberry muffin in his mouth. Lin went on and on about the trials of getting Mamma Min's ass on a train bound for *somewhere*. Lin wove a wonderfully hilarious story that had Godzilla spewing stale pastry crumbs between guffaws and stuffing his face.

Tennessee was waiting for Lin's abrasive sanctions on cholesterol and inflammatory commentary on trans fats, but the sanctimonious lectures never came; only giggles. The woman was *not* a giggler. And if *that* wasn't bizarre enough, Lin wasn't wearing the disgusted face she usually sported when looking at Godzilla; her natural beauty shimmered lovelier than ever.

"Oh my god! When? How?" Tennessee dropped her mindbender.

Poofing in from nowhere, Sho caught the sloshing coffee cup midair. "Careful, Ten," he warned sensually, presenting the cup as gallantly as he might breakfast in bed.

She clutched the cup, shaken by Sho's chivalrous entrance. Her mind was still buzzing with the most shocking news of her life—her girl best friend was totally crushing on her boy best friend!

Lin yelled, "Wow, that was fast! When did you get here?" She inspected the man before turning on Godzilla. "Can *you* do that?" Lin's tone was too sweet, and Godzilla was grinning way too much.

Tennessee dropped the mindbender again; this time splashing sugary, milky goodness all over Sho's jeans. His attention was divided, his primary focus on a military hummer pulling in out front.

"Dude," Godzilla chucked Sho a roll of paper towels, "Ness ain't *really* awake before noon."

"My apologies, I should have caught that...again." Sho held the roll as Tennessee pulled an endless stream of paper towels straight to the floor. He knelt to help, gripping her fingers as she sloppily smeared wet sugar everywhere. She gripped back, examining his eyes. Still shiny black. She relaxed, made a scrunchy face as they

both sopped up her mess. They were just about done when the front door jangled.

Adrienne walked in decked out in full camo, sidearm slung, a bright red bandanna knotted on her head to keep her bangs back for better aim.

At first Tennessee couldn't figure why Adrienne would be in her shop. She rarely came into town at all. Then she remembered her promise made weeks ago.

"Addy! Perfect timing. Godzilla just agreed to pick up the seedlings and plant them on Mount Orion!"

Godzilla stopped chewing, his eyes huge with excitement *and* fear. He'd never been truly alone with Adrienne.

As Tennessee gawked at Lin gawking at Godzilla gawking at Adrienne, a little red corvette skittered tiny pebbles on the shop window. The passenger door swung open and out hopped Millie and Billie in their pajamas and matted pigtails. Tennessee got a good look at Lillie's crop top and burger; she couldn't see the hooker heels, but she knew they were there.

Lillie tossed her greasy fast food wrapper out the window, peeled out, pelting another batch of pebbles at the shop.

"At some point we'll have to address that," Tennessee whispered to Sho.

"At some point." Sho rasped with a sly smile as he pulled her closer.

The twins blew past Adrienne, playing kill-the-zombie with their matching pink teddy bears. Adrienne didn't believe in kids; she kept her hand on her sidearm, making a beeline for Tennessee as Polar corralled the noisy things in the office.

"This your man?" The redhead sized up Sho, thumbs defiantly tucked in her handmade leather belt.

Sho's bow was shallower than usual. Tennessee expected him to lay on his charisma, but he didn't. He was the most reserved she had ever seen him.

"You're far from home, Addy. What brings you in?" Tennessee chucked her soiled mindbender in the trash.

"A mutt told me you were out of the hospital and back to work. A bit soon if you ask me."

The only mutt ballsy enough to call Adrienne on her satellite phone was Phillip.

Adrienne hugged Tennessee, eyeing Sho the entire time. "You hurt my girl, I'll make a stew of your gristle, feed it to my wolves."

Now Tennessee watched a frisky smirk thicken Sho's lips.

He replied in kind, "My sentiments exactly."

Adrienne's frown flickered her inner menace, but Lin was shouting from Tennessee's office.

"How these girls have hair like *this* with a mamma like *that*?"

"Madame Illie isn't well." Godzilla brushed crumbs from his shirt.

Lin gruffed her aghast; did he just defend that hateful woman? Tennessee prepared for a full-volume shout fest, but when Godzilla caught Lin's scalding gaze he grinned, pulling his 'fro into a tight manbun.

"No disrespect, doll."

Without even addressing the misogynistic undertones of the infantilizing term *doll*, Lin replied to Godzilla in a *sweet* tone, "None taken." As Tennessee's jaw flopped open, Lin's mannerisms normalized. "Hey, Ness, there's goop I can't identify in these tails. They're in dire need of a wash and comb out. Mind if I take this mess to my shop?" Lin bent to ask the girls their names.

They were quiet, identical snarls on their faces.

Tennessee walked over to the twins, leaving Adrienne in Sho's suddenly indifferent care.

"Well, Millie lost her front tooth last night so..." Tennessee squeezed both twins' cheeks until their lips pursed open. She compared their bites; they were identical. "Man, I'd admire your dedication if it wasn't so freakishly gruesome. How did you do it? Doorknob? Pliers?"

"They're nuts!" Lin gushed when they confessed to borrowing the gardener's pliers. "Godzilla, look at this..."

But Godzilla was leaning against the open front door, stuttering out something about being ready and *available*.

Tennessee watched her little friend's smile drip away as Adrienne met Godzilla at the door.

"Catch you later, Ness!" Adrienne shot Sho a hateful scowl. "I don't like you."

Sho placed his palms together at his chest, barely bowing; his slick grin steeling his rasp. "I shall withhold judgment until next we meet."

Tennessee was too busy wrangling the demon twins with Lin to fully take in this exchange, but she saw something in Adrienne that she hadn't before. The woman was intrigued by Sho; it only took a glance to see the warrior in him. A flush of pride warmed through her, and she finally understood why Adrienne only dated soldiers. Their sacrifice was *your* sacrifice; their victories, *your* victories. That kind of partnership transcends the ordinary.

Tennessee watched Lin escort the twins across the street to the House of Beauty. She sent Polar with; Lin would need the help. Adrienne offered to drive Godzilla to the nursery, to Mount Orion, and back again. It was odd for her to make that many trips; the girl must be lonely.

That left Sho and Tennessee exactly one hour before her *noon* date with Phillip.

"You heard our talk this morning," she inquired even though she knew he had; she dug out the demon coin from her pocket, placed it in Sho's palm. "For our rookie Benchwarmer."

"I was wondering where this ended up." Sho turned the coin over. "And, *yes*, I heard Phillip declare his intentions." Sho lifted Tennessee's chin, his rasp gritty with promises. "I, too, am going nowhere." Then he kissed her. He took a heap of worry and a smidge of resentment. Tennessee caved to the need, losing herself in him. When she stopped, Sho wasn't quite done; which made her swoon.

After having his fill, Sho's lips brushed her ear. "I'm willing to *share*. Is he?"

She trembled from those salacious words delivered with a sensual intensity that'd definitely keep her up at night.

Phillip was too square to share; and she'd never even *dated* two guys at once. It was an intriguing solution, though, one she didn't immediately reject.

Eyes satisfied, gilded with persuasion, Sho grasped her hand, leading her to the back room, the one with the gilded mirror.

~

Sho faced Tennessee, seized her collar, and spoke to the thing in a language she finally recognized; it was the same language the seven sons were chanting around Maria. Sho wasn't pleased with the collar; this was the first time he'd spoken to it since it tried to possess Tennessee. They must have reached an understanding, because Sho fed the collar the Benchwarmer's coin.

As the collar washed the back room in a radiant burst of gold, Tennessee's cell phone thumped out Donna Summer's "She Works Hard for the Money."

Sho's head tilted with a question.

"Uh, yeah," Tennessee twisted her lips askew, "about that..."

~

Tennessee sent Phillip a text:

*A Cup of Madness. Noon.*

With Mr. Gloor in the cooler, she couldn't figure a way to make Sho poof discreetly. This way, he'd poof long before she pulled into the parking lot.

Tennessee was sitting on Riggy's bumper, downing another mindbender when Phillip pulled into the lot.

He parked beside Riggy. "Hop in."

"I'm driving."

"*Of course.*" Phillip got out. "Where's your magic man this afternoon?"

"Ah, you know, not far...he's probably stalking us right now...hanging back fifty feet, listening to our every word."

Phillip scanned the sand, shop, and sea. "I highly doubt it, Tenny. But I'm glad he's comfortable with our lunch dates."

"*Dates*? With an *s*...that's plural, you know...more than *one*."

"Yes, Tenny, A-plus."

Tennessee flipped him the bird.

Instead of reprimanding her, Phillip stood in front of her, grabbed her finger and kissed it.

She laughed, but she blushed all the same. "You're so dumb."

Phillip sighed. "I *have* been."

Tennessee wasn't about to touch Phillip's suddenly self-aware confession; she rounded Riggy. Phillip seized the door handle,

"My lady..." He bowed.

"Who says?" She decked his arm.

Playfulness looked good on him. She actually stared. He chuckled, rounding to the passenger side.

"All right, doctor, I have a confession to make."

Phillip leaned in, trying not to hope.

"I've been thinking about grad school again...stupid, huh?"

Phillip tucked a clump of frizz behind Tennessee's ear; after she flinched and fussed his hand away he responded assuredly, "I think it's about damn time you did something for yourself."

Eyes focused ahead, Tennessee revved Riggy, rolled down her window, and tore out of the parking lot.

"Why must you skid everywhere? Just pull out into traffic, nice and controlled."

"Relax, Phillip," she scoffed. "*I'm* the demon-wrangling superhero, remember?"

"I'm not seven, Tenny. You needn't play imaginary games with me."

"What do you know? *You're* just a zombie."

"Please slow down. I can't be a zombie if I'm dead."

"Actually..."

"Yeah, I heard it when I said it. You rattle me, Tennessee England, like no one else."

"You're welcome." She stopped at a red light. "Oh look, a flyer for a lost kitty...another one...what? Wow...what's going on?"

"You can't save the world, Tennessee."

"Sure, I can."

"Oh yeah, *how?*"

"One demon at a time, Saint James, one demon at a time!"

The light turned green. Tennessee whammed the gas, burning rubber all down Main Street.

# Tennessee's Mixtape #1

"Bitch" by Meredith Brooks
"Bat Out Of Hell" by Meat Loaf
"Two Out Of Three Ain't Bad" by Meat Loaf
"I'll Do Anything For Love (but I won't do that)" by Meat Loaf
"I'd Lie For You (and that's the Truth)" by Meat Loaf
"J'ai Deux Amours" by Madeleine Peyroux
"True Colors" by Cyndi Lauper
"Angel" by Aerosmith
"Why" by Annie Lennox
"King of Brooklyn" by Devil Doll
"Man of the Hour" by Norah Jones
"When Doves Cry" by Prince
"Wanted Dead or Alive" by Bon Jovi
"Blaze of Glory" by Jon Bon Jovi
"A Night with the Jersey Devil" by Bruce Springsteen
"I Want Your Sex" by George Michael
"She Works Hard for the Money" by Donna Summer

Mixtape available on Spotify

# The Tennessee England Series

For more information visit www.disadawn.com

# BOOKS BY DISA DAWN

THE SEEKIN TRILOGY

*Of Water and Sky (Book 1)*

*Of Ash and Snow (Book 2)*

*Of Souls and Stone (Book 3)*

THE TENNESSEE ENGLAND SERIES

*Stone Cold Mortal (Book 1)*

*999 Lives (Book 2)*

*Iron Crossed (Book 3)*

*Fruit Bats in the Belfry (Book 4)*

*Love Thy Demon (Book 5)*

*Jailbirds Don't Sing (Book 6)*

*More to come...*

HANA BLOOM BREAKS THE UNIVERSE

*Volumes 1-5*

Subscribe at disadawn.com for updates on new releases!

# Acknowledgements

This series is dedicated to my superheroes:

My kindred spirit Jane Beaston, for sharing her wisdom, joys, sorrows, and heartfelt stories garnered during her fourteen-year career in the death care industry. Jane's gift for mending the souls left behind truly inspired me (and Tennessee). Jane's firsthand knowledge of trocars, retorts, chapel gurneys, and church keys brought life to Englands' Mortuary. Thank you, Jane!

My kickass crew: editor Tara Blaine (www.krop.com/profile/tarablaine), cover artist J Caleb Clark (www.jcalebdesign.com), and invaluable editorial support from Sunwalker Press (www.sunwalkerpress.com).

My loving tribe, for being true in a world of false.

My mother, for teaching me how to slay my demons. My father, for chopping down a *Taotaomo'na* tree and unleashing ancestral spirits into our home. My sister, for knowing how to sling a swear. My brother, for killing that snake that one time with a machete. Sunshine, Darkbringer, and Johnny Toast, for their belief in all things possible. The Marxs, for spiritual grounding. The Quintanillas and Garridos, for holding down our island fort.

My husband, for all the chocolate. And Redshadow, for reminding me that even mommies can play make believe.

# About the Author

Disa Dawn writes cozy supernatural adventures, urban fantasy, and paranormal romance. Her stories feature bold heroines who also happen to be nice. Disa graduated from Naropa University with an MFA in Creative Writing. She lives in the Pacific Northwest with her family and a skeleton named Charlie.

# Stay in Touch

Visit disadawn.com to subscribe for updates on new releases and exclusive content.

Follow Disa on Facebook or on Instagram, or send her an email: disadawn@disadawn.com

If you enjoyed this book, be rad and totally leave a review online. Just a line or two helps indie authors *tremendously*! You rock!

21917126R00202

Made in the USA
San Bernardino, CA
13 January 2019